cf 4/20

D0587701

BIS

Please renew or return items by the date shown on your receipt

www.hertsdirect.org/libraries

enewals and
quiries:

0300 123 4049

phone for hearing
ech impaired

0300 123 4041

By Larissa Ione

Lords of Deliverance series:
Eternal Rider
Immortal Rider
Lethal Rider
Rogue Rider

Demonica series:
Pleasure Unbound
Desire Unchained
Passion Unleashed
Ecstasy Unveiled
Sin Undone

LETHAL RIDER

LARISSA IONE

piatkus

PIATKUS

First published in the US in 2012 by Grand Central Publishing,
A division of Hachette Book Group, Inc.
First published in Great Britain as a paperback original in 2012 by Piatkus
Reprinted 2013

A CIP catalogue record for this book
is available from the British Library.

ISBN 978-0-7499-5552-6

Printed and bound in Great Britain by
Clays Ltd, St Ives plc

Papers used by Piatkus are from well-managed forests
and other responsible sources.

MIX
Paper from
responsible sources
FSC
www.fsc.org   FSC® C104740

Piatkus
An imprint of
Little, Brown Book Group
100 Victoria Embankment
London EC4Y 0DY

An Hachette UK Company
www.hachette.co.uk

www.piatkus.co.uk

For the Sisterhood of the Traveling Werefly: Penny, Bells, Dren, Tigris, Larissa B, Jen, Danielle, Marq, and Lara Adrian. Do you remember the Big Spoiler, or is my Jedi Mind Wipe still working? Love you guys!

Acknowledgments

Thank you so very, very much to all of my fabulous readers. Whether you e-mail me, chat with me on Twitter or Facebook, or simply buy my books, you need to know that you keep me sane, laughing, and writing. Your enthusiasm and energy is precious to me, and I am incredibly lucky to have you.

Special thanks to everyone involved in the publishing community who helps make my books available to readers, especially my publishers both overseas and in the United States. And huge, mushy thanks to everyone at Grand Central Publishing—you make me feel special. Thank you!

Big shout-outs to Judie Bouldry and Syd Gill for being awesome, to Cyndi, Joan Swan, and Suzi Tunning for your medical expertise (and for your name, Suzi!) and to Erika Fotis, Cid Tyer, Amber Hansford, and Elena Bradley for lending me some guys to um, eliminate, in the last couple of books. I hope I did them justice!

Glossary

The Aegis—Society of human warriors dedicated to protecting the world from evil. See: Guardians, Regent, Sigil.

Agimortus—A trigger for the breaking of a Horseman's Seal. An agimortus can be identified as a symbol engraved or branded upon the host person or object. Three kinds of agimorti have been identified, and may take the form of a person, an object, or an event.

Camborian—The human offpring of a parent under the possession of a demon at the time of conception. Camborians may or may not possess supernatural powers that vary in type and strength, depending on the species of demon inhabiting the body of the parent at the time of conception.

Daemonica—The demon bible and basis for dozens of demon religions. Its prophesies regarding the Apocalypse, should they come to pass, will ensure that the Four Horsemen fight on the side of evil.

Fallen Angel—Believed to be evil by most humans, fallen angels can be grouped into two categories: True Fallen and Unfallen. Unfallen angels have been cast from Heaven and are earthbound, living a life in which they are neither truly good nor truly evil. In this state, they can, rarely, earn their way back into Heaven. Or they can choose to enter Sheoul, the demon realm, in order to complete their fall and become True Fallens, taking their places as demons at Satan's side.

Guardians—Warriors for The Aegis, trained in combat techniques, weapons, and magic. Upon induction into The Aegis, all Guardians are presented with an enchanted piece of jewelry bearing the Aegis shield, which, among other things, allows for night vision and the ability to see through demon invisibility enchantments.

Harrowgate—Vertical portals, invisible to humans, which demons use to travel between locations on Earth and Sheoul. A very few beings can summon their own personal Harrowgates.

Khote—An invisibility spell that allows the caster to move among humans without being seen or, usually, heard.

Marked Sentinel—A human charmed by angels and tasked with protecting a vital artifact. Sentinels are immortal and immune to harm. Only angels (fallen included) can injure or kill a Sentinel. Their existence is a closely guarded secret.

Quantamun—A state of superaccelerated existence on a plane that allows some supernatural beings to travel among humans. Humans, unaware of what moves within their world, appear frozen in time to those inside the quantamun. This differs from the *khote* in that the *khote* operates in real time and is a spell rather than a plane of existence.

Regent—Head(s) of local Aegis cells.

Sheoul—Demon realm. Located deep in the bowels of the Earth, accessible only by Harrowgates and hellmouths.

Sheoul-gra—A holding tank for demon souls. The place where demon souls go until they can be reborn or kept in torturous limbo.

Sheoulic—Universal demon language spoken by all, although many species also speak their own language.

Sigil—Board of twelve humans known as Elders, who serve as the supreme leaders of The Aegis. Based in Berlin, they oversee all Aegis cells worldwide.

Ter'taceo—Demons who can pass as human, either because their species is naturally human in appearance, or because they can shapeshift into human form.

Watchers—Individuals assigned to keep an eye on the Four Horsemen. As part of the agreement forged during the original negotiations between angels and demons that led to Ares, Reseph, Limos, and Thanatos being cursed to spearhead the Apocalypse, one Watcher is an angel, the other is a fallen angel. Neither Watcher may directly assist any Horseman's efforts to either start or stop Armageddon, but they can lend a hand behind the scenes. Doing so, however, may have them walking a fine line, that, to cross, could prove worse than fatal.

LETHAL RIDER

LETHAL RIDER

One

Regan Matthews was going to die.

She knew it as sure as she knew the sky was blue. Knew it as sure as she knew the baby inside her was a boy.

Knew it as sure as she knew the baby's father would be the one to end her life.

Screaming, she bolted upright in bed, her eyes focusing on the glow of the nightlight in the bathroom. It took a second to realize she was awake, safe and secure inside The Aegis's Berlin headquarters.

The dream had come to her again, the one where she saw herself lying on a floor and covered in her own blood, too much blood. Thanatos, known to much of the human population as Death, fourth Horseman of the Apocalypse, knelt next to her, blood coating his hands, dripping from his pale hair, and splashed across his bone armor.

She took a deep, calming breath, forcing herself to relax. Thanatos couldn't touch her. Not here, in the apartment complex deep below the headquarters building that housed the twelve Elders who ran the ancient demon-hunting organization. Most of the Elders used their apartments only when they came to Germany for Aegis business, but Regan had called this spartan apartment home for years, and despite the fact that she was due to give birth in less than a month, she hadn't done a single thing to prepare for the baby. There would be no decorating, no toys, no cribs.

She'd always hated pastels anyway.

Her hand, so pregnancy-swollen that she no longer wore her Sigil ring, trembled as she rubbed her belly through the cotton fabric of the maternity nightgown, hoping the baby would stay asleep. He was one hell of a kicker, and her organs were still recovering from his last round of hacky sack.

Regan fumbled in the darkness for the bedside table lamp. Her hand fell first to the hellhound-spit coated Aegis dagger all twelve Elders were required to carry as defense against evil Horsemen, and then to the bit of parchment next to the lamp. She allowed herself a moment to smooth her fingers over the inked lettering. The Latin words were a prayer of sorts, but that wasn't where Regan found comfort.

No, as a psychometric empath, she could divine information with a touch or, more specifically, feel the emotions of the person who put ink to skin. This particular bit of writing had been penned while the author was feeling serene. Regan had kept the page with her for years, borrowing the emotions of the author like some sort of psychic vampire, and she'd needed it more than ever over these last few months.

With one Horseman turned evil, his Seal broken

according to the prophecy in the *Daemonica*, the demon bible, Earth was falling into chaos. No Apocalypse promised a party, but Regan often wondered why they couldn't be dealing with the Bible's prophecy instead. At least in the biblical version, the Horsemen would be fighting on the side of good instead of evil.

But that was only part of why she'd needed the parchment. Her regret over what she'd done to Thanatos ate at her, and while she didn't deserve anything less, for the baby's sake she had to find peace where she could.

She allowed the parchment to soothe her for another thirty seconds, thankful to have it. The final page from a tiny book penned by an angel who had given her life to save a Guardian, it was beyond priceless. Regan's fellow Elders had been after Regan to give it up for years, but they'd have to wait. She wasn't giving it up until she was dead.

Which might be sooner than she'd like, if Thanatos got hold of her.

She lifted her fingers from the parchment, but before she found the lamp switch, a noise froze her. It wasn't a loud sound, and in fact she thought the echo of footsteps might be in her head. But what she couldn't dismiss was the trickle of awareness that filtered through her system, an internal alarm that made no sense.

No place on Earth was safer than where she was right now.

Still, she found herself fisting her dagger and easing out of bed. Heart pounding, she crept across the room and put her ear to the door. Nothing. So why was her entire body quivering with static undercurrents that warned of danger?

You're just being paranoid. The nightmare about Thanatos must have freaked her out more than usual.

But it couldn't hurt to check things out. Her Guardian instincts had never failed her, and she'd known more than one Guardian who had paid the price of ignoring that deep-down sense that something was amiss.

As quickly and silently as possible, she tugged on a maternity blouse and a pair of khaki pants, and at her hip she secured her pregnancy-modified weapon belt and cell phone clip. She didn't go anywhere without being armed. She traded out the dagger with a stang, preferring the double-ended, S-shaped blade in battle.

Clutching the stang in a white-knuckled grip, she opened the door and slipped out into the hallway. The darkness, usually her friend, now became a liability without her Aegis ring, which would have lent a measure of night vision.

Regan put her back to the wall and moved toward the light switch outlined in a faint green glow. But when she flipped it, nothing happened.

"Just a burned-out bulb," she whispered to herself. She even said it again, but a niggling sense of doubt joined the feelings of danger.

She glanced back toward her room, wondering if her smartest option was to go back inside and lock the door, but duh... anything that was a threat to her inside Aegis Headquarters wasn't going to be stopped by even a thick slab of wood and a deadbolt.

Besides, she had a secret weapon, one she'd been forbidden to use—unless the baby's life was in danger.

She crept forward, the hairs on the back of her neck prickling with every step.

"Who's there?" There was no answer, but then, no demon would happily offer up his name.

The baby had clearly turned her brain to mush, and she'd become a classic horror movie dipshit who got killed in the first five minutes of the film. Awesome.

She thought she saw a flicker of movement ahead, near the entrance to the auditorium. Where was everyone? Even in the middle of the night, Guardians patrolled the building or spent shifts researching in the massive library or organizing worldwide operations. This was The Aegis's nerve center, and it was never this quiet.

She moved closer, and as she reached for the door, her foot slipped in something warm and wet. Her stomach did a flip-flop. She didn't have to look to know she'd stepped in blood, didn't need lights to know that the dark lump against the wall was a body.

Not good. This was so not good.

Something rustled behind her. Instinct kicked in, propelling her forward through the auditorium doors. It was set up like a large college classroom, with several rows of stadium seats and two aisles of steps. She moved as fast as she could to the stage at the bottom. If she could get to the exit on the far side, she'd come out near the reception desk, where she could sound the alarm—

A soundless blur streaked past her. She pivoted, stang at the ready, adrenaline coursing in a hot rush. Crimson eyes stared at her, and she swore she heard the sound of saliva dripping to the floor.

"Whore." The deep, masculine voice rumbled, and in her belly, the baby kicked.

"I don't know who you are," Regan said, "but you might think twice about insulting a Guardian inside her own house."

Rumbling laughter accompanied a snap of fingers,

and suddenly, the auditorium lights popped on. A vampire stood on the stage with her, over six feet of hulking, fangy, undead. His gaze fell pointedly to her belly.

"It isn't an insult if it's the truth."

She ignored the barb that hit a little too close to home. "Who are you? How did you get in here?"

At some point, Regan had placed her hand over the baby, as if doing so would keep it safe. *Idiot.* The stang in her other hand would do more—but only if she could cut the bloodsucker's head off.

The vampire moved so fast Regan didn't see it until its backswing connected with her cheek. Pain ricocheted from her jaw to her cheekbone and up to her skull as she slammed into the wall, her left shoulder taking the brunt of the impact.

"Who I am won't matter when you and the Horseman's bastard are dead." He hissed, his enormous fangs dripping saliva like a rabid dog.

There was something very...off...about this vampire. Not that most vampires weren't "off," but she'd noticed a subtle difference between Thanatos's daywalker vampires and your everyday variety nightwalker. Namely, Than's vamps seemed bigger, their fangs especially so.

"You're one of Thanatos's servants, aren't you?"

He snarled. "I belong to no one. I'm not one of the *Bludrexe*'s neutered pets." He came at her again, and as she struck out with the stang, she lost her balance and managed only a glancing blow that nicked his biceps.

The vampire's hand snapped out, catching her around the throat. Smiling coldly, he squeezed, cutting off her breath.

Panic wrapped around her, squeezing as hard as the

vampire's fingers. She might have had a chance if she weren't almost nine months pregnant, but even though she'd kept herself in excellent shape, she tired quickly, and her uneven weight made her awkward.

She couldn't die like this. She couldn't let this baby die. But as her lungs began to burn with a lack of oxygen, she knew this could be it.

Inhaling hard to find even a molecule of oxygen, she reached deep inside herself for the ability she'd kept tightly leashed for most of her life. The ability that had gone out of control the night she had gotten pregnant.

Not the time to dwell on that.

The tingle started low in her gut. Coaxing it as if it were a stray kitten, she called it forth, but it seemed to retreat, going from a pinpoint of light to a sickly glow. And then it snuffed out completely. What the—

"Die, bitch." The vampire hissed in her face.

Shit! Her power . . . she couldn't access it. Suddenly, the vampire inexplicably eased up on his grip, giving her a sweet gulp of air, and when he smiled, she knew why he'd done it.

To drag out her death.

"Fucker," she rasped. She clawed at his shoulders and kicked at his shins, but he didn't budge. Again she searched for her ability, the one that would drag his soul right out of him, but now it was as if it didn't exist at all.

Her mind went sluggish, her struggles weakening as oxygen deprivation took its toll. Images flipped through her brain, but not the ones she'd have expected while on the brink of death.

People lied about your life flashing before your eyes, because all she could see was Thanatos. She remembered

how he looked when he was coming, how his body strained
and his muscles bunched and rolled. She remembered the
sound of his voice, his laugh.

And she remembered the expression on his face when
he realized she'd betrayed him.

She was going to die, and it would all have been for
nothing.

In her belly, the baby kicked, harder and harder, as if it
too knew the end was near. The vampire smiled.

"I can sense the life within you," he said. "I'm going to
enjoy feeling it snuff out." His hand went to her swollen
abdomen, and in her mind, she screamed.

"Could you two be any louder?" A stranger's voice
joined the scream in her mind and the thud of her pulse
in Regan's ears, just as a breeze whispered over her skin.

In the next instant, the vampire flew sideways and she
was ripped out of his grip. She had only a split second
to see the other vampire who had joined the party before
he flung her aside. She hit the floor behind the podium
and sat there, gasping for air as the newcomer, one she
definitely recognized as one of Thanatos's daywalker
servants, attacked the vampire who had been trying to
kill her.

The newcomer slammed his fist into the first vamp's
head, sending him reeling into the wall. Before he could
recover, the new vampire shoved a splinter of wood—
where he'd gotten it, she had no idea—into the other
vamp's chest. The first vampire hissed even as his body
began to blacken and crack into dust.

The surviving vampire limped over to her, fury and
pain mingling in his eyes. "You betrayed Thanatos," he
growled. "You betrayed us all."

She wasn't sure about the "all" thing, but the rest was true enough. "Then why did you save me?"

"Save you?" The vampire gestured to the ashy mess that used to be his brethren. "He was merely going to kill you. I'm taking you to Thanatos." He grinned. "Trust me, I didn't *save* you."

Two

The only thing worse than being paralyzed and trapped inside your own skull, unable to move or speak, was being kept like that by your own brother and sister.

For eight and a half endless, insanity-inducing months, Thanatos, fourth Horseman of the Apocalypse, had been kept in a bed with nothing but a TV for company. Well, every twelve hours he was visited by someone from Underworld General Hospital to inject him with paralyzing hellhound saliva, change his hydrating saline IV bag, and give him a humiliating sponge bath before changing his sweat pants. But usually whoever visited was *wham, bam, thank you, ma'am* and all business. And sure, his sister, Limos, third Horseman, and Ares, second Horseman, hung out with him, but Ares wasn't all that talkative.

Limos was a chatterbox, but Than didn't really give a shit about what color nail polish she'd put on that morning or how she and her husband, a human named Arik, were planning a European honeymoon after the Apocalypse was over.

And seriously, a honeymoon? Wasn't it a little late for that? And it wasn't as if Limos didn't live on an island paradise anyway, so every freaking day was a honeymoon for them.

Bitter much, Than-boy?

Yeah, there might be some jealousy there. Because as sick as it sounded, the one thing that had kept Than sane over the thousands of years he'd been alive was the fact that Ares and Limos were as alone as he was. But now Ares and Limos were both married and happy, and he was left paralyzed, miserable, and ripping a massive hatred for the female who had put him here.

Regan.

Ever since he'd been cursed as the Horseman who would become Death when his Seal broke, he'd believed that his Seal was his virginity. He'd guarded his dick like it was the freaking Hope Diamond. He might have been an unpinned grenade ready to blow with sexual need, but dammit, he'd kept himself all virginal and shit.

Until Regan came along, with her seductive body, her devious plot, and her drugged mead. She'd managed to get him naked, get him immobilized, and get him off. The why of it still wasn't clear, since not once, in all of Limos's and Ares's ramblings, had they brought up the Aegis Guardian. And the fact that she was a Guardian, one of the human warriors who existed to rid the world of demons, only made her actions more mystifying.

Guardians didn't want to start the Apocalypse, so either she was secretly working against The Aegis, or she hadn't thought that fucking him would break his Seal.

But if it was the latter…why had she gone to extremes
to get him in bed? As a larger-than-life legend, he might
have starfucker appeal, and sure, he knew he was hand-
some, but resorting to drugs and her supernatural ability
in order to get what she wanted?

Fury slithered through him, as hot as the lust he'd felt
when he'd been beneath Regan, her wet heat clenching
around his cock. God, it had been good. For centuries
he'd fantasized about being with a female, had imagined
all the ways he'd take her. His favorite fantasy had always
been with her on all fours and him mounting her from
behind, his chest sealed to her back by their sweat, his
weight holding her steady for his thrusts.

For these past months, when his mind had drifted to
sex, Regan had been that female on her hands and knees.

His cock jerked in response to the direction of his
thoughts, pissing him off. His dick had no business getting
hard for her, and on his arm, his stallion, Styx, kicked,
sensing his master's emotions. The horse, currently in a
tattoo-like form, had been stuck on his skin, as paralyzed
as Than had been—

Wait. His cock was hard, his horse was stirring…
which meant the hellhound venom was wearing off.

Thanatos's heartbeat went double-time as hope shot
through him. Maybe his siblings were finally allowing
him to be free. Oh, man, if so…he had serious plans.
First, he was going to kick Limos's and Ares's asses. Then
he was going to have sex.

Lots and lots of sex.

Before Regan, avoiding sex hadn't been difficult
because he hadn't known what he was missing. But now
he knew, and his body craved it almost as much as it

craved revenge. And wasn't revenge going to be sweet. He couldn't decide if he was going to kill Regan or fuck her. Maybe both. Not in that order, though. He wasn't a complete sicko.

The door creaked open. Ares's heavy footsteps were accompanied by Limos's whisper-light ones and the click of hellhound claws on the floor.

"Hey, bro," Limos chirped, as if Thanatos was hanging out for fun. His hands began to clench, but quickly, he locked up his muscles, forcing himself to remain still.

Ares changed the channel on the TV they'd mounted above his bed. "Sorry about that," he grunted. "Someone must have bumped the remote. A cubic zirconia-fest on the Home Shopping Network couldn't have been too exciting."

Oh, no, really. I was just thinking about how great a gold filigree necklace and teardrop earrings would look on me, and at seventy-five ninety-nine plus shipping, it's a freaking steal. But damn, I missed the deal because, oh, that's right, I'm fucking frozen.

Limos's hand came down on Than's biceps, and he struggled to keep from twitching. "Hey...look...we have to tell you something." Her voice was low and serious, and shit, this couldn't be good. "I know you can probably feel the disruption in the world, and it's gotta be making you crazy."

Crazy? Try ceiling-licking, rabies-frothing, dish-ran-away-with-the-spoon in-fucking-sane. Limos and Ares had been keeping him up to date on Pestilence's exploits, but they hardly needed to. Thanks to his curse, Than could feel mass casualties around the globe, was drawn to them like a junkie to heroin. Obviously, being paralyzed had put the brakes on his ability to travel to them, but the pull was still there, swirling around his insides like smoke from a crematorium.

"It's about to get worse," Ares said. "Pestilence's plagues have caused war and famine and death all over the globe. It's why we haven't been around much. We've been spending way too much time at the sites of the worst of it."

Limos and Ares suffered similar curses as Than; Ares was drawn to scenes of large-scale battles, and Limos was tugged to famines. And yeah, Than had noticed that they hadn't been around to keep him entertained. At least Cara, Ares's wife, had been there. She read to Thanatos a lot, and he didn't think he could ever thank her enough for that.

So why is it about to get worse? He wanted to scream at them, could feel his left hand, which was concealed at his side, begin to curl into a fist.

"Last week, Pestilence claimed Australia in the name of Sheoul."

Oh, shit. Demons who were normally bound to Sheoul—what humans called hell—could now occupy Australia. A country that size could host millions of demons and allow for them to set the stage for a massive global attack. Demons had, since the beginning of time, desired to kick off the Apocalypse in order to defeat mankind and take the Earth as a trophy, and with Australia in their pockets, they'd just lobbed the ball that much closer to the end zone.

What about the humans?

Limos, who had always been in sync with his thoughts, answered as though she'd heard him. "Any humans who didn't evacuate are ... lost."

"We got a few out." Ares's voice turned bleak. "Kynan, Limos, Arik and I got a few."

"It's bad," Limos said. "But the good news is that The Aegis found a way to close the hellmouths. It's temporary...the magic they're using is being eaten away by demon countermagic, but it's slowed mass demon movement." She patted his arm. "Be patient, Than. Only a couple of weeks left to go, and we'll release you."

A couple of weeks? Why then?

Ares squeezed Than's foot. "Someone will be here in a couple of hours for your next injection. We'll be back when we can."

He and Limos left, and hell, no, Thanatos wasn't planning to be around for the next injection. For some reason, he could move again, and he was getting the fuck out of here.

Summoning all his willpower, he rocked his body until he built up enough momentum to roll out of bed. Hitting the floor hurt like a son of a bitch, but the pain only spurred him on. Something was tugging at his insides. Danger. Death. Both. Except the pull toward danger was a different sensation than anything he'd ever felt. It was almost as if *he* was the one in danger...but the feeling was distant. Whatever it was, it called to him, and he had to go.

He ripped the IV catheter out of his hand and dragged himself to the sliding glass door. Grunting, he shoved onto his hands and knees and crawled outside. Death and danger still yanked at him, two distinct ropes pulling him in opposite directions. The danger rope seemed more... urgent, but in his current, weakened state, he couldn't risk dropping himself into what could be one of Pestilence's traps. Death, however, filled him with energy.

Right. Death first, danger second.

Letting the tug to death guide him, he opened a Harrowgate and lurched through it. Instantly, hot, humid air hit Than like a furnace blast. The stench of rotting flesh and burning wood stung his nostrils. Weakly, he lifted his head and frowned at the sight of scorched earth and fallen trees. Than's internal GPS was telling him he was Down Under, but he'd never seen it like this before.

So much death. Explained why he'd been drawn here.

"Hey there, man." Thanatos jerked his head around to the shirtless male in skin-tight pants that kept shifting colors to blend in with the smoky gray and black background.

"Hades." His voice sounded like he'd swallowed shards of glass. "Is this... Australia?"

"Yeppers." Hades strode several feet, his boots crunching down on charred bones that appeared to be both human and demon. "Since it's been claimed in the name of Sheoul, I can hang out here."

Of course. Hades was as bound to Sheoul as a demon, although for a very different reason. A fallen angel, he'd been forced to run Sheoul-gra, the place where demon and evil human souls were kept, unless Azagoth, also known as the Grim Reaper, allowed him out.

"Azagoth let you... leave Sheoul-gra?"

"He gave me an hour," Hades said, his voice degenerating into a sarcastic drawl. "His generosity knows no bounds." He nudged Than with his boot. "Now I guess I'm stuck helping you. Recover quickly. I want to hit one of those new succubus whorehouses before I have to head back to the Gra."

A million pinpricks stabbed Than's muscles as he struggled to prop himself against a fallen tree. The blue-haired bastard just stood there and watched.

"Why...help...me?"

Hades's face went as hard as the landscape around them. "Because your fucking brother is pissing me off. While I can appreciate what he's trying to do, starting an Apocalypse and all, I get ticked off when he noses in on my business."

Thanatos wiggled his toes, relieved to feel them again. "What are you talking about?"

The blue veins that spiderwebbed Hades's pale skin grew brighter and started to pulse. "He's trying to dismantle Sheoul-gra and destroy Azagoth."

"Oh, shit." Without a Sheoul-gra, any demon or evil human killed in the human realm would be free to wreak havoc in their phantom form.

There was also a running theory that Azagoth might be the Horsemen's father, but so far, no one had been able to verify that. Until the rumor could be confirmed, Thanatos would rather the guy not be killed.

"Oh, shit, is right. Who'd have thought your screwball brother could have gone so serial-killer fucktwat insane?"

And that was the big problem. Reseph had been the kindest, most even-tempered of all of them. For him to have turned so evil did not bode well for Ares, Limos, and Than.

He became aware of a branch biting into his back, and at the same time, a low-level vibration started in the pit of his stomach. His body was coming to life.

And it was hungry.

Along with the hunger, the tug toward danger grew stronger, became a pulsing awareness in the back of his brain. What the hell was it?

"He grows stronger every day, Thanatos. The souls I

watch over are starting to reincarnate at rates I've never
seen."

Than frowned. "You think Pestilence is responsible for
that?"

"Maybe not directly, but as the Apocalypse grows closer,
souls are leaving me faster than they're coming in. Pestilence is getting a big boost in the demon population, and I'm
growing weaker. You need to kill him."

Thanatos rocked his head back against the tree trunk.
"I intend to repair his Seal, not kill him." Than had found
evidence that Reseph's Seal could be repaired, but only if
Than stabbed him with a specific dagger at a specific time.
Problem was that he hadn't figured out the "time" detail.

"Criminy. Whatever. Just do *something*. My very life
comes from those souls. I need them."

"Criminy?" Than stared. "Seriously? Big, bad, mohawk-
haired demon says 'criminy'?"

"Yes, criminy." Hades rubbed his bare chest. "And,
fuck off."

Than closed his eyes. "That's better."

The vibration in Than's core became a gnawing hunger, threaded with malevolence. The scent of blood hit
him, and he snapped open his eyes. Hades was on his
haunches next to Than, a knife in his hand. Blood flowed
from his slit wrist, and Than's fangs punched down as
the starvation that had been kept at bay for eight months
roared to the surface.

He lunged at Hades, but the male caught him around
the back of the neck and slammed his bleeding wrist
against Than's mouth. Thanatos's brain blanked out as
his body was hijacked by fierce hunger and pure animal
instinct.

"Ow, fuck." Hades's rough voice was a mere buzz in Than's ears.

At this point, he didn't give a hellrat's ass if he was savaging the male's arm. All that mattered was filling the hole inside him that, when emptied, led to indiscriminate feedings and a lot of death. Fortunately for Than, Hades was one of the few people who knew about Than's need, although he didn't know the extent of it.

Time swirled in multi-colored circles until finally, Hades pulled away and left Than leaning back against the tree, his body completely charged. The hunger was gone, but the other, odd tingle of impending danger still vibrated at the base of his skull. It was like a homing beacon, screaming at him to go.

"Thanks, man." Shoving to his feet, Than flexed his muscles, testing them after so many months of disuse. Out of the corner of his eye, he saw a flicker of movement in the burned-out forest, and knew he'd get a good workout in a minute.

They had company.

"No problem. I owed you one."

Keeping one eye on the creatures slinking from out of the shadows, Than casually flicked his finger over the crescent-shaped scar on his neck, and instantly, his bone armor snapped into place. Next, he summoned his scythe. "More than one. I've sent you a lot of souls, asshole." He was about to send Hades more.

"Yeah, fuck you."

He started to flip out his standard response of, "Can't have sex," but he remembered that yeah, he could. Thanks to Regan and her betrayal, he knew he could. But Hades was a dude, and Than wasn't that desperate.

20 Larissa Ione

But the urge was there, so powerful he suspected that it was similar to what Ares felt, a coil of tension that, if not released, resulted in death and destruction.

Good thing then, that Thanatos was in the mood for a little D&D, and not the role-playing game.

"So, what are you going to do now that you're not frozen solid?"

"First, I'm going to kill those demons and that fallen angel behind you." The scorpion tattoo on his throat began to sting his neck, its tail moving like a pulse, reminding Than that death was what he was meant for. Never one to argue with fate, he swung the scythe in a powerful arc, lobbing off one of the demons' two heads. He glanced back at Hades, who was looking like he might want popcorn to go with the action. "Then I'm going to do the same to the woman who betrayed me."

Three

Regan sat on the floor, staring at the vampire who had saved her from one threat and was planning to deliver her into the hands of another.

"You can't take me to Thanatos. He's incapacitated—"

"Stupid female," he barked. "I'm taking you to his keep until he returns. Several of us have come up with a plan to get him back." His voice softened. "And there are things you need to know, warnings I can't tell you here—" Blood spurted from his mouth, and he jerked forward, catching himself on the podium.

A crossbow bolt pierced his sternum.

"Get away from her!" Lance, one of Regan's fellow Elders, rushed toward them, crossbow in one hand, wooden stake in the other. More Guardians followed on his heels, including Suzi, who had moved into headquarters to assist Regan in her final months of pregnancy. From the side entrance, Elders Kynan and Decker burst through the doors.

"Don't kill him!" Regan shouted, but Lance ignored her, driving the stake through the vampire's heart.

"Dammit, Lance!" Kynan rounded on Lance as the vampire smoldered. "That's not how we do things."

"That's not how *you* do things," Lance said. "Not everyone in The Aegis agrees with your squeaky clean new way of treating the enemy."

Suzi crouched next to Regan. "Are you okay? Should I call your doctor? Oh man, I should have been with you—"

"I'm fine," Regan assured her, but Suzi wrung her hands, worry bleeding from her pores. "But you know, I could use a cup of your awesome honey chamomile tea." Suzi grinned, clearly relieved to be able to help. As she took off, Regan remained on the floor, gathering both her thoughts and her breath. "Why were Thanatos's vampires here? How did they get in?"

Juan, another Elder, kicked at the remains. "We captured them a couple of weeks ago. We needed to see the daywalkers ourselves. Somehow they escaped their cells."

"You morons," Regan snapped. "Don't you think we've done enough to Thanatos?"

"*We* didn't do it to the Horseman," Lance said, his expression so smug she wanted to slap him. "It was *your* report that brought his vamps to our attention. We needed to study them."

Oh, damn. Once again, she'd managed to screw Thanatos, just in a different way. Her guilt manifested into bitter anger, which she aimed at Lance.

"The Apocalypse is on our doorstep," she growled, "and you wasted time with vampires? Nice."

Lance scowled. "You're the one who volunteered to take over as vampire expert when Jarrod died last year.

You should have known that when you discover a new breed, we're going to want to dissect it." He cast her a nasty glance. "You aren't going to cry about it or some shit, are you?"

God, she hated when he did that. He and a couple of the other Elders seemed to think that as a woman, she'd break down into tears about every little thing. They'd been the negative voices when Regan's promotion into the Sigil was on the table, and now she never passed up an opportunity to show them she was just as capable as they were. She didn't have a chance to rip into him though, because Kynan intercepted and steered them back on topic.

"Dissect it." Kynan shoved his stang blade into its slot on his hip belt. "We have standard operating procedures for new species, and those include informing other Elders about plans to capture. They don't include dissection."

"You've been busy with your happy little demon family," Juan said. "We didn't see the need to make a big production out of capturing a couple of bloodsuckers."

Regan fought the urge to scream in frustration. "What if the Horsemen see this as yet another betrayal? Did you think of that?" The Aegis's relationship with Limos and Ares was already strained, thanks to what had gone down between Regan and Thanatos, and this could only make things worse.

"I'm more concerned about the impending Apocalypse than what the Horsemen think, but the fact that the vampires escaped is definitely troubling." Lance nodded at Juan. "Let's check the cells to make sure no other nasties are loose."

As they took off, Decker glared after them. "I hope they get eaten," he muttered.

"How are you feeling?" Kynan offered her a hand, but Regan refused it and pulled herself to her feet on her own. She'd had enough of being touched tonight.

"I'm feeling surprisingly good." She winced as a tiny foot caught her in the ribs. "When I'm not being kicked."

Kynan unzipped his leather bomber, revealing a weapons harness loaded to kill an entire legion of demons. "Gem said the same thing when she was pregnant." Ky's daughter, Dawn, was almost a year old now, and the cutest little dark-haired thing ever. Regan wondered what color hair her child—a boy, she'd learned a couple of months ago—would have, given that Thanatos's hair was blond and hers was dark brown. "I know we talked about this before, but if you need someone to talk to about pregnancy stuff, Gem is there for you."

Ugh. This had been an uncomfortable subject ever since Juan had brought up the fact that Regan didn't have a mother to share the experience with or to ask for advice. No, Regan's mother had committed suicide-by-demon after giving birth to Regan. As Lance had once put it, *"You should feel lucky she didn't off herself the second she found out her demon-possessed lover knocked her up."*

He was such a dick.

Regan offered a polite smile. "Thanks, Ky, but I'll be fine."

He nodded. "Offer still stands. When's your next doctor appointment?"

"Tomorrow. Dr. Rodanski is concerned about the baby's size, so he's going to do another ultrasound and decide if we're going to do a C-section instead of a natural delivery."

"You really should see—"

"No." She cut Kynan off before he could suggest allowing a demon doctor from Underworld General to take care of her. It was one thing to be working with demons to prevent the Apocalypse, but allowing one to touch her intimately? Not unless things got dire. *Way* dire.

"Regan," Ky said. "Your body reacts badly to medication. You can't have a C-section without meds and pain management."

"Rodanski said he'd figure it out." She hoped so, because what Ky, a former Army medic and physician at Underworld General, mentioned was a huge concern. The baby's delivery could be potentially dangerous. Still, she wasn't ready to deal with demon doctors and their alternative therapies.

Her stomach growled loud enough for Decker to hear. "Want me to get you something to eat?"

"I don't suppose you have a chocolate milkshake in your back pocket." She'd always been a bit of a health nut, but pregnancy had given her a major craving for all things ice cream.

He wrinkled his nose. "That crap will kill you."

An image of Thanatos popped into her head, and no, it wouldn't be the milkshakes that killed her.

"So," she said. "Tell me why you're here at this hour of the morning." The boys exchanged glances, and her gut twisted. "What is it?"

Beepers went off, three at once. Decker grabbed his phone first. "It's Lance. Fuck. Demons loose in the building."

Instantly, Ky and Decker drew weapons and closed rank around Regan. "What the hell is going on? If we hadn't come to discuss rousing Thanatos, Regan could be dead."

Regan gripped the podium so hard her nails dug into the wood. "You were thinking about rousing him? Now?"

"Long story, but yeah. We came across new information. We need to consider waking him right away."

"You're a little late for that, Aegi." The deep, rumbling voice from the doorway drained every drop of blood from Regan's face. She broke out in a cold, clammy sweat as she looked up to see Thanatos at the auditorium entrance, his big body radiating danger even his armor couldn't contain.

And she knew, without a doubt, that her nightmare was about to become reality.

Four

Regan couldn't breathe. Couldn't swallow. All she could do was stare death—literally, Death—in the face. Thanatos was going to kill her. His yellow eyes drilled into her, but when he spoke his words were for Ky and Decker.

"Leave us."

"Listen to me, Thanatos," Kynan began. "If you have a beef with someone, it should be me—"

"Shut up." Than's voice echoed through the auditorium, carrying as if he was talking through an amplifier. "Leave *now*. Last warning."

He moved toward them, his boots thumping like death knells on the carpeted floor, the bone plates of his armor clacking, the sword at his hip more menacing than she remembered.

"Go to hell, asshole," Decker drawled.

Regan reached out to grasp Deck's shoulder in warning, but it was too late. Shadows rose up around Thanatos, the souls of those he'd killed. Once released from the prison of his armor, they were deadly, nightmarish weapons Regan had no desire to encounter again. She had no idea if one of them could kill Kynan, seeing how he was immune from harm by anything but fallen angels, but Decker would be easy prey.

So would she. Her ability to rip souls out of a person... or to defend against an attacking soul, seemed to have been affected by the pregnancy. The loss would have been a relief not long ago. Now it left her vulnerable in a way she hadn't thought possible.

"Go," she said softly, never taking her eyes off those swirling souls. "I'll be okay." She hoped. Kind of doubted, really. But she would not be responsible for Decker's death.

"We're not leaving," Kynan said.

Thanatos smiled, and Regan shuddered. "I just killed a fallen angel." He threw out his hand, and one of the souls, its inky form sprouting wispy wings, darted toward Kynan. It halted mere inches away, straining as if tethered by invisible chains. "He can suck the life right out of you, human."

"Dammit," she hissed. "You guys go. Hang out in the hallway, but please...go!"

Ky and Decker both glared in stubborn defiance, but finally, they stalked off. When Ky got to the door, he turned around and shot the Horseman a deadly cold look. "You've got five minutes."

Five minutes? That would be an eternity, given that Thanatos could end her in under a second. The moment Ky and Decker were gone, Thanatos struck, wrenching her away from the podium and pinning her against the wall with his upper arm across her throat. She couldn't even reach for her handy-dandy anti-Horseman dagger.

"You betrayed me."

"Please," she whispered.

"Please." His voice was guttural. Low. Downright evil. "Say it again. It won't help, but I want to hear you beg before I kill you."

She would never beg for her own life, but she'd do anything for the child. She licked her lips, but she had no moisture on her tongue. "Please don't do this."

Closing his eyes, he inhaled, and a wicked smile curved his mouth. "The scent of your fear is intoxicating. How does it feel to be restrained and helpless, Regan?"

Horrific. It was horrific. "Do what you want to me," she rasped, "but don't... don't hurt the baby."

His eyes popped open. For a moment, he stared at her, his blond eyebrows pulled low over golden eyes. "Baby?"

How could he have missed the fact that she looked as if she'd swallowed a watermelon? The baby kicked, as if aware he was being talked about, and Thanatos looked down.

"What the—?" Thanatos leaped away, eyes wide and glued to her belly. "When?" He swallowed audibly. "Who's the father?"

Now she had to tread carefully. The plan had been to wait until after the baby's birth to rouse Thanatos and tell him about it... the hope being that if he came after Regan in a murderous fury, at least the baby would be safe. Now... shit. She wasn't sure what to do. Weird, since she'd always been able to think on her feet.

"Listen to me—"

"*Who?*"

She inhaled a shaky breath. "I'd feel better if Kynan was here—"

"*Kynan?*" Thanatos let out a godawful snarl, and she swore she saw the flash of fangs. "The Aegi is the father? He dared to touch you?"

Dared? "No—"

"Kynan!" His roar shook the entire building, and then his sword was in his hand and those creepy shadows were circling his feet.

"It's not Kynan," she blurted, but Than wasn't listening. "Kynan is a dead man."

"*Thanatos!* Yo, deaf Horseman. It's not Kynan. It's you." She smoothed her hand over her belly. "This baby is yours."

Thanatos had lived during the days when being poleaxed wasn't just an expression. He'd managed to avoid it... until now.

Now he knew exactly how it felt as he stood there like a dolt, staring numbly at Regan's belly. He dragged his gaze upward, to breasts that seemed larger than before, to her slender throat, and finally, he met her hazel eyes. They were as beautiful as he remembered, bright, with a warrior's hard ice behind fire. But they were also tinged with fear, proving she wasn't stupid.

When he'd first entered the auditorium, he'd been prepared to kill her. Now he just wanted a stiff drink.

He was going to be a father.

From virgin to dad in zero to sixty.

The door burst open, and both Kynan and Decker were there, pistols trained on Than. Bullets wouldn't penetrate his armor or kill him, but they'd hurt like hell if they struck exposed body parts. Like his head.

"Fire those guns," Than said quietly, "and every Aegi in the building will pay for it."

"We don't want any trouble," Kynan said. "Leave now."

"Leave?" Than laughed even as the souls in his armor spun like thousands of little tornadoes. Thousands? Why would there be so many? Didn't matter. Not right now. He took Regan's arm before she could scoot away. "I'll leave. But she's coming with me."

Decker's finger slipped from his pistol's trigger guard to the trigger. "No way in hell."

"It's all right," Regan said quickly. "I'll be fine."

"Presumptuous, don't you think?" Than said, and then felt like an asshole when she paled.

"Regan, you don't have to protect us." Kynan stepped closer, and Decker moved with him, their bodies in practiced sync. "Let's talk about this, Horseman."

"Stall until you can summon my brother and sister? I don't think so." He dragged Regan to the door at the other end of the auditorium, and when he slammed it open he wasn't surprised to find over a dozen Guardians, all armed to the teeth, waiting for him. Well, one female held a dagger *and* a menacing-looking cup of tea.

"First person who moves against me dies," he told them. "Second person gets you all killed."

Regan remained stiffly at his side. "Stay back, everyone. I'm going willingly."

All but one obeyed, and the one, the idiot who dared to swing a skinny blade at him, found out how fast Thanatos could launch a soul from his armor. The other slayers found out how loudly humans screamed when they were having their souls ripped from their bodies.

"Stop it," Regan yelled, but it was too late.

"I warned them," he said, as he hauled her out of the building. "And I'm not in the mood for second chances, Regan. Keep that in mind."

The second they were outside headquarters, Than threw a gate and tugged Regan through it. They came out at his Greenland keep in a marked-off area set aside specially for gates—the things had a tendency to slice people in half if they materialized next to or on top of someone.

Wind roared across the dark, barren landscape, carrying with it the faint tang of the nearby ocean and smoke from the fires inside the keep. Regan's ponytail fluttered as she stepped onto the grass, her cheeks pinking up from the cool breeze. It might be summer, but it was still cold, cloudy, and wet.

"Why are we here?"

He took her elbow and marched her toward the door. "I live here."

"I know that," she ground out. "But I figured you'd want to go someplace less obvious. Especially since you're now going to have the entire Aegis organization after you for kidnapping me and killing a Guardian."

"You figured wrong." He shoved open the door, and immediately his vampire servants came running.

"Master!" Viktor's dark eyes were wide, a grin splitting his face. "You're back. We didn't know or we'd have prepared—"

"It's okay. I'll be back to talk to you later." He led Regan down the stone steps to his dungeon, and when she resisted halfway, he swept her up and carried her. Oddly, where her belly touched his armor, her heat burned right through the bone plate.

"Let...me...go." She struggled in his arms, and he cursed, gripping her tighter while trying not to hurt her.

"Stop it. You'll injure yourself or the baby." A glint of silver flashed, and he blocked the blade before it bit into his cheek. With a snap of his wrist, he broke Regan's grip on the dagger and it clattered to the stone steps. "Let me guess. Coated in hellhound venom? Nice try."

"It's also imbued with a locator spell, you giant ass. The Aegis will be able to track me."

"Right," he drawled, "because they won't guess that you're at my place. Seeing how *I* took you."

She sank her teeth into his hand and he yelped, but he didn't put her down until they reached the first cell. Quickly, he shoved her inside before she bit him again. Not that he was opposed to biting, but there were more appropriate times for that.

Oh, look...you got laid once and you're already making everything about sex.

"You're just going to leave me here?" Regan asked, incredulous.

He slammed the cage door. "Yes."

Crimson splotches colored her pale cheeks, and she hugged herself, rubbing her bare arms. "Can I at least have a blanket?"

Fuck. Now he felt like a heel. She was dressed for summer in a gauzy white blouse, khaki capris, and bare feet, but it was freezing down here year round, and while it didn't affect him, she was human, and she'd succumb to hypothermia. He shouldn't care. In fact, he didn't. But he wasn't going to let her die while his baby was inside her.

"Well?" When he didn't say anything, because he was

actually considering taking her back upstairs, she sighed. "Look, I know you're angry—"

"Angry?" he spat. "You drugged me, restrained me, took my virginity, and then left me so pissed off that my siblings had to imprison me for over eight months. *Angry* doesn't even begin to cover it. Were you *trying* to start the Apocalypse? Does The Aegis know what you did, or were they in on it?"

"I didn't know you were restrained, Than. I lost control of my ability, and I didn't realize it was attacking you." She shivered... or maybe it was a shudder. "And I didn't drug you. I mean, obviously, you were drugged, but it wasn't my idea. One of your vampires gave me that wine."

"None of my vampires would betray me."

"Well, I hate to tell you this, but one did."

"Why?"

She shrugged. "Maybe he got tired of your grumpy ass and decided you needed to get laid. How the hell should I know?"

He ground his teeth. "They knew sex was off-limits for me. They wouldn't have done it."

"Fine. Whatever. Ask Ares or Limos. They know. The wine drugged me, too." She winced and palmed her belly, and before he even knew what he was doing, he was inside the chamber, his hands on her shoulders.

"Are you okay? Is it the baby?"

She blinked in surprise. "It was just a kick. Ponyboy is really active."

"Ponyboy?"

Again her cheeks colored, but this time with a soft, feminine blush. "Well, you're a Horseman... the father... so... Ponyboy."

He wanted to smile at that, but then he remembered he hated her and forced his expression to remain neutral. "I'll get you a blanket." He started for the door, but she stopped him with a hand on his forearm.

"I have to pee."

He gestured to the corner. "There's a chamber pot."

"Seriously? Eew." She recoiled in horror at the dusty clay vessel.

"Humans of your day are ridiculously spoiled. What do you think people did before toilets?"

"I don't really care. We *do* have toilets now, and I'd rather use one." She wrinkled her nose. "If I try to squat down on that, I'll never get back up."

"Fine," he muttered, taking her wrist. "You're a terrible prisoner, you know that?" She wisely kept her mouth shut as he led her back up the steps and to his bedroom.

When she saw where he was taking her, she ground to a halt just outside the door. "Um…"

"Would you prefer the dungeon? Your choice."

Her eyes flashed, and she shoved past him. "This will be fine," she said, as if she were a guest at a hotel who was dismissing the bellboy.

"Don't try anything, Regan," he warned. "I'm going to have a guard at the door."

"How long are you going to leave me here?"

"Until I figure out what to do with you." He bent to look her directly in the eyes. "But be clear on this; your life is now mine."

Five

A full hour after Regan had been snatched, Aegis Head-quarters was still in a state of chaos. Kynan was supposed to be heading home to New York to meet his wife and daughter so they could join their in-laws at Underworld General for the weekly family summit.

Today Kynan was going to be late. Shit, if he made it at all it would be a miracle.

"How did those vampires and demons escape, and how the hell did that Horseman find our headquarters?" Ian, one of The Aegis's Elders, was shouting. "We've never, in all our thousands of years of existence, been found. What happened?"

Kynan wanted to point out that The Aegis's headquarters had nearly been located by the enemy half a dozen times over the course of their history, and had they not moved locations, they would have been, but he kept quiet. Ian was a hotheaded asshole who wouldn't back down from any argument, and Kynan wasn't in the mood to knock him the fuck out.

Chad, another Elder with an attitude problem, rounded on Kynan and Decker. "And how could you have let that bastard just waltz out of here with Regan?"

"I didn't see you steppin' up to the plate yourself," Decker drawled, his usually faint Texas twang vibrating with every word. The more pissed off he was, the redder his neck got, as he liked to say.

"The Horseman couldn't have touched Kynan." Chad shot an accusatory look Ky's way. "You should have done something."

"Thanatos came prepared to deal with me," Kynan said, and damn if that didn't rankle. The guy had been smart enough to kill a fallen angel, and while Ky wasn't sure the soul of one could harm him, he hadn't been about to take any chances with his life or anyone else's...especially not Regan's.

"So what now?" Decker asked.

Ky eyed the coffeemaker, wondering if he should caffeinate. It was going to be a long day. "Valeriu, Lance, and Juan are already on the way to the UK to check out a site for our new headquarters." Now that Thanatos knew their current location, it, along with all of their libraries, secrets, artifacts, and weapons, was in danger if his Seal were to break.

"Hey!" Suzi burst through the door, even more frantic than she already was with Regan missing. "There's another Horseman here. I think it's War."

"Ares," Kynan muttered. He could never get it through these people's heads that the Horsemen would only be known as War, Death, and Famine *after* their Seals broke. "And it's about time."

Ian's green eyes nearly popped out of his head. "You told another one how to find us? Why don't you just put a neon sign on the building and upload our address to Yahoo?"

"I called him while Thanatos was still here," Kynan ground out. "I was hoping he'd be able to talk his brother down."

These fools truly had no idea how important it was to work with the Horsemen. Not only were they the only beings powerful enough to deal with Pestilence, but if humans pissed them off enough, they could wipe their hands of the fight altogether. Hole up in their residences and let humans fight Pestilence and his demons on their own.

Chad snorted. "Good plan. Maybe if you'd—"

Chad broke off with a strangled sound as huge hands came down on Suzi's shoulders to move her aside gently but firmly. Ares filled the doorway, his broad shoulders brushing the frame as he strode inside, a mountain of leather armor and attitude.

"Where is my brother?"

Kynan met the ancient warrior halfway into the room. "He left. Took Regan with him."

A river of curses fell from Ares's mouth. "How was he behaving?"

"Like he was in need of a rabies shot. He killed one of our Guardians."

"Just one? You caught him on a good day."

Ares was probably right. Than could have taken them all out and made it seem effortless. "I thought we'd agreed to keep him immobilized for a little while longer."

"We did, human."

"Then how did he get free?"

"I don't know."

Kynan scrubbed his hand over his face. "How helpful."

Ares stared at him. "Just get Regan back for us."

"I'll do what I can." Ares spun around on his heel and started out of the room, halting when Decker called his name.

"Your brother," Decker said. "He won't hurt her, will he?"

Ares's big shoulders rose and fell slowly, as if he were taking a deep, calming breath. When he spoke, his voice was deceptively soft.

"I hope not," he said. "For his sake, and the sake of mankind, I hope not."

Thanatos's chest was tight, his skin twitching as he paced the length of the great hall. His vampires had tried to bring him food and drink, had asked him if they could fetch him books, groom Styx—and currently, one of them was kneeling, exposing the throat that he'd slit by his own hand.

"Take it, sire." Artur, his oldest daywalker and the one who had been with Thanatos for over forty-five hundred years, watched him expectantly.

Fuck. "I've already fed."

"Then let me do *something*," Artur begged, his willingness to serve going into hyperdrive. Than's absence must have done a number on him. "Would you like me to tend to Regan?"

No one was going near Regan. Not even his most trusted servant. It was an irrational decision maybe, but right now Than was feeling pretty damned irrational. He yanked Artur to his feet. "If you want to do something for me, clean up the mess you made on the floor."

The vampire nodded. "Right away." He actually looked happy to have something to do. No doubt they were all hanging out in the kitchen, waiting nervously for Thanatos to explode.

He was close. Which was why he'd gotten away from Regan, who was one hell of a fuse.

He stopped in front of the fireplace and braced his fists on the mantel as he stared into the dancing flames. His mind was whirling in a stir of a thousand thoughts, and he couldn't focus. It seemed like every time he captured one, it led to another, and another. There was too much in his head, from the baby to Regan to The Aegis, to his siblings, to...everything.

It didn't help that his body vibrated with all the deaths around the world. He felt it all, like a million knives carving his muscles beneath his skin. And alongside the tremors that made him want to gate himself to the scenes of death and kill whoever was still standing was a spiraling storm of need that intensified in Regan's presence.

Always before, when he was worked up from death and destruction, his instinct had been to kill. The dark desire was still there, a throbbing, malevolent urge, but he also wanted sex. He wanted to drop Regan to the floor and drill into her until he didn't have the energy for violence.

She'd awakened something in him the night she'd taken him, and there was no putting it back to sleep.

The sound of footsteps rang out...heavy ones, which meant Ares had arrived. And he was armored. More footsteps, softer, but with the distinct click of hellhound claws on stone.

Drawing his sword, Than swung around. "Keep the mutt away from me, brother."

Ares's expression was stony. "Where is Regan?"

"Go to hell." The hellhound, a shaggy black beast that, only about half-grown, was still the size of a wildebeest, bared its teeth and crept forward. "I said, keep Hal away." The last thing he wanted to do was fight the hound. If he hurt Cara's beloved mutt, she'd have his ass.

"Then you need to go back to Greece with me."

"So you can lock me down again? Not happening."

"It's for your own good." Ares's tone was matter-of-fact, as if keeping his brother prisoner was no big deal. But then, Ares had always been a soldier, trained from birth to do anything and everything to win a battle at any cost...even if the price was his brother's life. Ares was fully prepared to put an end to Pestilence and had been from the beginning, so holding Than captive had no doubt been easy for him.

"My own good?" Than gritted out. "I spent *eight months* trapped inside my own head, going insane with boredom."

"That's why we gave you a TV. Movies. Music. Limos and Cara read to you—"

"You think that's enough? Do you know how many episodes of *Jersey Shore* you can watch before you want to gouge out your own eyes? I do, and it's probably a lot fewer than you'd guess." Than breathed deeply and paced, because the alternative would end in a lot of blood...both his and Ares's. "What were you thinking?"

"We were thinking it would keep you from going atomic."

"You wanna see atomic?" Than snarled and brought

his fist down on the trestle table, putting a seismic crack in the ancient wood. "You kept a big secret from me, Ares. A secret the size of a baby."

Ares paled, which was pretty damned satisfying. "Than . . . what did you do?"

Nothing much. I threatened to kill the mother of my child and half the Aegis Elders. "It's none of your concern."

"Where is she?"

Gripping his sword so hard his hand hurt, Than ignored the question. "Why didn't you tell me? For months, you and Limos sat at my bedside. And not once in that time did you say anything like, 'Hey, by the way, you're going to be a father,' or 'Yo, you knocked up the Guardian.' Would have been good to know."

Ares blew out a frustrated breath. "Dammit, Than. That's not something you say to someone who can't react. You'd have laid there with no way to ask questions and with who knows what going through your head."

"And whose fault is that?" he shot back.

Flickering light from the fire danced in Ares's dark eyes, obscuring any telltale hints of what his brother was thinking. "The plan was to wait to rouse you until the baby was born. At that point, we were going to decide what to tell you."

"Decide what to tell me?" Thanatos frowned, and then sucked in a harsh breath as realization dawned. "You weren't *going* to tell me, were you?" He felt the ground shift beneath him as the magnitude of Ares's and Limos's betrayal rocked him. "*You weren't going to tell me I was a father.*"

"Yes we were, but the rest of the plan isn't about you."

Ares held up his hands in a soothing gesture that was so *not* soothing. "If Pestilence finds out about Regan's pregnancy, the child's life will be in danger."

Son of a—Okay, yeah, there was that. He'd been out of his mind for a while there, but Ares was right. "Pestilence would love to hurt me through a child."

"More than that," Ares said. "We think the baby is your *agimortus*."

Of course. Than had spent the last months wondering why his Seal hadn't broken and trying to figure out what *would* break it. And now the warmth he felt when he was near Regan made sense. He was feeling his *agimortus*.

"How did you get free?" Ares asked. "You weren't due for another dose of hellhound venom for a couple of hours."

Thanatos glared at Hal, and he swore the mutt smiled. "I felt a pull that seemed to neutralize the effect of the venom. Turns out it was the baby." Than nearly stumbled over the baby word. So...foreign. "I didn't know what it was until I got to Aegis headquarters and found Regan. There were demons loose, and she and the baby were in danger."

"So you sensed the child?"

"Apparently." The sense had dulled now that the immediate danger had passed, but inside, he definitely vibrated with an awareness that had been with him for months but that he hadn't been able to identify. "You've always been able to sense your *agimortus*. Must be why I can feel the baby." He gnashed his teeth, frustrated by pretty much everything that had happened today. "By the way, I saw Hades. He said Reseph has his sights set on destroying Azagoth and Sheoul-gra."

"Not much we can do about that. We've got enough on

our plates in the human realm. Underworlders are on their own. Now, where is Regan?" Ares repeated.

"She's safe. That's all you need to know."

"Shit," Ares muttered. "You need to return her to The Aegis. That's the only way she'll be safe."

"You think I can't protect her?"

"Your temper—"

"My temper is under control," he roared, and yep, that display surely convinced Ares.

Ares smoothed his hand over the hound's head, calming the beast. What a huge change, given that only a year ago Ares had been gunning to destroy every hellhound in existence.

"You don't remember, do you?" he asked quietly.

Uh-oh. "Remember what?"

"The reason we incapacitated you in the first place."

Than's stomach turned over. He didn't want to know. He really didn't. The scorpion started stinging his neck, letting him know that what he'd done was poison to his very soul. "What . . . shit, what did I do?"

"You nuked the island, almost killed Arik, and very nearly damaged Reaver and Limos permanently."

Thanatos's mind spun with confusion. "What island?" The look on Ares's face said it all, and Than stumbled back a step. "No. Not *this* island. Oh, Jesus. How . . . how bad?" Than asked, but deep down, he knew. Vampires were immune to his death blasts, but few others were.

"Angels intercepted the shockwave, but they couldn't save many. You left few alive."

It all came back in a rush, a broken dam releasing so many memories. The thousands of the souls in his armor went crazy, evidence of what he'd done.

If a million angels descended on him right now and cast a million lightning bolts at him, the punishment wouldn't be enough. If it went on for centuries it wouldn't be enough.

"I was so angry at Regan... at her betrayal. The Aegis fucked us over, and then Reseph..." Thanatos had been riding Styx hard, chasing Regan across the frozen tundra, and Reseph... no, *Pestilence*... had come out of nowhere, had beaten Than to a bloody pulp and nearly killed Styx. If not for Cara, the stallion would be dead.

"That's why we didn't want to tell you about Regan and the baby. We mentioned her name once, outside the bedroom door. You must have overheard, because you let out a mini death wave that killed two of my Ramreels." Ares's voice warbled, just a little, but for him, that was a major show of emotion. "We didn't know what you'd do if we actually tried to talk to you about her."

"Shit, Ares. I'm sorry." Thanatos rubbed his sternum, but it didn't relieve the heavy crush of guilt. "Why did The Aegis do it? Regan claims she didn't drug the wine—"

"She didn't. The Aegis is still at the heart of it, but no, Pestilence arranged for the wine."

"How?"

"He replaced Atrius with a doppelgänger. We found the doppelgänger dead."

Which meant that Atrius was dead, too. Doppelgängers and the being they were created to replace shared life forces. Damn it! Atrius's sense of humor had lightened up the keep, and he'd been instrumental in keeping the rivalry between the nightwalker and daywalker vamps in check. Than would miss him.

"So Pestilence must have killed Atrius after the deed was done."

"Or one of your staff killed the doppelgänger, but they all denied it. We tested the rest of your staff to make sure no one else was a doppelgänger." When Than lifted a brow in question, Ares expounded. "We pulled a fang from each vamp. They all grew back."

A fang removed from a doppelgänger wouldn't be replaced. Than scrubbed his hand over his face.

"Speaking of fangs—"

"Don't." Thanatos cut off his brother. "Don't go there."

"I *am* going there, Than," Ares growled. "Reseph grew fangs when he turned into Pestilence. You grew fangs after your nuclear meltdown. Or after sex with Regan. Something's up, and I'm not letting it go."

"You have to. I won't discuss it." Ares was so wrong about when Than had gained his fangs, but Than couldn't tell his brother that he'd had them since they were cursed as Horsemen. It was a secret he was forbidden to share, even with his own siblings. He changed the subject, although he knew Ares wouldn't be deterred for long. "Do you think Regan is lying about being drugged, too?"

If Regan had truly drunk the wine instead of merely pretending, as he'd suspected, then much of his anger was misplaced. *He* hadn't been able to stand up to its aphrodisiac properties; a human stood no chance. And if she was telling the truth about losing control of her gift that incapacitated him... shit. Now he didn't know what to think.

"I believe her about the wine, but she did come here to seduce you."

A sickening feeling came over him. "To get pregnant. But why... wait. Don't tell me. I'm going to get it from the source."

Six

Your life is now mine.

Wrapping herself in the blanket at the end of Than's bed, Regan sank down on the mattress and concentrated on staying calm. It wasn't easy. She'd been in countless life-or-death situations, had nearly died twice, but she'd never been as close to panic as she was now.

All those other times, she'd never truly feared for herself. She'd feared more for her colleagues or for innocent bystanders, but even then, the fear had never interfered with her ability to think or fight. On the contrary; the fear had given her an edge. Now it was paralyzing, because all she could think about was the baby.

"Breathe," she murmured. "Just breathe."

She inhaled slowly for the count of three and then released the breath with the same count. It was a trick an Aegis doctor had taught her to combat her obsessive-compulsive attacks...attacks like this one, where she'd get something stuck in her head. It would play over and over, like a skipping record, until she either powered out of it, found a distraction, or found a ritual to ease her mind.

Right now, her ritual was to breathe, but it would only work temporarily. The moment she stopped counting, the panic would resurface, and a newer, worse thought would pop into her head, something completely out there, like if she didn't bounce a ball five times in a row, the baby could die.

Her struggle with OCD had been lifelong, and hers hadn't been a typical case at all. Doctors had never been able to get a handle on it, not only because her symptoms and behavior had been all over the place, but because she couldn't take any of the common medications used to treat it. Hell, she couldn't take any medications at all. Even before the pregnancy, she'd always had bizarre reactions to even mild over-the-counter meds, like aspirin.

Inhale. Exhale. Inhale. Exhale.

Think of a way to get out of here.

Inhale. Exhale.

Cell phone! Standing, she shoved her hands into her pants pockets. Nothing. It must have fallen out of her pocket when Thanatos picked her up like a caveman hauling off his kill to his lair.

Inhale. Exhale.

He'd also gotten the one weapon she could have used against him when he knocked the dagger out of her hand.

Inhale. Exhale.

What she wouldn't give for that bit of parchment on her nightstand.

The door opened, and there was no more inhaling or exhaling. Her breath jammed in her lungs as Thanatos strode into the room, his expression stormy, his body taut as a bowstring.

"You have some explaining to do." His voice was like rolling thunder.

As he slammed the door shut in Ares's face, she played nonchalant, when really, inside she was preparing for a possible EF-5 tornado.

"How about you start with the explanations?" she countered. "Like, how did you find me? Aegis Headquarters has always been kept secret, even from you guys."

He must have been grinding his teeth together something fierce, because the muscles in his jaws were leaping. "I sensed something that led me there." His eyes flicked down to her belly. "It was him."

She frowned. "You don't know it's a boy."

"You called him Ponyboy. But even if you hadn't, I knew. I can feel him."

Okay, she did not like that Thanatos had a stronger connection to her baby than she did. She'd read to the baby at night, played music for him, told him about the wonders—and dangers—of the world he was going to grow up in. How could Thanatos know the baby for five minutes and *feel* him?

On the other hand, maybe it was a good thing. If he could sense the child's life force, maybe he'd let them live. The baby gave her another one of those killer kicks, and she sucked air. Like earlier in the cell, Than moved forward, but this time, he stopped shy of touching her.

"It was just a kick," she muttered. "I think he might have hooves instead of feet."

His voice was as sharp as a stang blade. "Don't even joke about that."

"I wasn't." Well, she sort of wasn't. She hoped the kid wouldn't have hooves, but given that Thanatos's mother was a demon, and Regan's father had been...not a demon, exactly, but...yeah. Who knew what kinds of things could go wonky in the little colt's DNA?

Thanatos stepped back, his boot hitting the floor like a thunderclap. "Why did you do it? And don't lie to me, Regan. Ares told me you intended to seduce me in order to get pregnant. Why? And why not be upfront about it when you first came to me?"

Damn Ares. This whole thing had gotten so messed up and out of hand. "Because we found evidence that suggested that a child born of a Horseman and an Aegi could stop the Apocalypse, and it indicated that you couldn't know about the baby."

Thanatos narrowed his eyes until they were slits. "What kind of evidence?"

"The manufactured kind," she admitted. "We learned later that your scumbag brother planted it. Now we know he did it so we'd be fooled into thinking we needed to get you in bed, and he'd get what he wanted, which was for your Seal to be broken."

All kinds of curses fell from Than's mouth, some in languages she didn't know. "You are so damned lucky we were wrong about what would break my Seal." Cursing again, he dragged his hand through his hair. "But do you realize that you actually created my *agimortus*? You know that, right? You're aware that when a person is an *agimortus*, their death is what breaks a Seal," he said, and yes, she was aware of that. "So Pestilence failed to break my Seal by getting me laid, but he now has a real way to do it."

She wished he'd take off his armor. He was intimidating enough without it, but with it he was even larger, a sturdy wall of warrior with no vulnerabilities.

"We know that. But we're hoping Pestilence isn't aware that this child exists." A sick feeling rose up in her stomach when she thought about what had happened at headquarters. "But somehow, your vampires knew. One of them tried to kill me and the baby tonight."

Thanatos scoffed. "Impossible. None of my vampires would endanger a child they knew was mine."

"One did."

"Like I said, impossible."

Stubborn jackass. "Has it occurred to you that not all of your servants are loyal? One *did* give me the drugged wine."

"That was a doppelgänger. My vampires *are* loyal."

She stared upward, hating that she was going to give him ammo for his *my vampires are loyal* thing. "There were two daywalkers. One of them saved me from the other. He said he was going to take me to you."

Than smirked. "See?" Then his smirk fell away, replaced by a hard, grim line. "What were my vampires doing there?"

Crap. She'd walked right into this. "The Aegis captured them," she muttered.

"They what?" She took an involuntary step back at Than's shout. "You told The Aegis about my daywalkers?" He pinned her in place with a gaze as piercing as an arrow. "I guess I shouldn't be surprised, given your history of betrayal. You Aegi just can't stop looking for ways to fuck with us, can you?"

There was no arguing with that, because he was right. She wished she could change so much of what had happened, but the best she could do was protect the innocent life that had come as a result of The Aegis's machinations.

A fist pounded on the door and she jumped. Ares didn't wait for an invitation. He shoved open the door, and once he was inside the room became impossibly small. She hadn't seen either Limos or him since Limos's wedding night... all communication with the Horsemen had been through Kynan, and she had no idea how he felt about her. Oh, she knew he was on board with making sure the baby was safe, but he might very well hate her as much as Thanatos did.

"Is everything okay?"

"Obviously," Thanatos snapped, "I haven't killed her, so yeah, everything's okay. You don't have to hover."

Please hover...Regan casually shifted toward Ares. Maybe he'd get her out of here and back to headquarters. Although if Thanatos could sense the baby, he could find her wherever she went. She needed some sort of ward.

Thanatos's gaze zeroed in on her like a hawk's, and although he didn't move to block her, she got the impression that he was ready to spring if Ares tried to snatch her.

"We have to keep Regan safe." Ares held his hand out to Regan. "Now, let me take her back to The Aegis."

She started to move toward him, but Thanatos put himself between her and Ares. "She stays here."

"Not an option," Ares growled. "There's a reason you live out here in the middle of nowhere. Humans aren't safe around you."

"I would never kill my own child," Than said. "How can you think that?"

"I don't think you would," Ares said softly. "Not intentionally. But sometimes after you go to a scene of death, you return home still in a murderous rage. Do you remember how we had to get Cara away from you once?"

"This is different. Cara isn't my child." Thanatos hit the wall with his fist. "If the situation were reversed, if Cara was pregnant with your son, would you let her out of your sight? Would you let her go somewhere where she could be vulnerable to Pestilence?"

"Never," Ares admitted. "But there's no danger that I would accidentally kill her."

"Thanatos," Regan said, "The Aegis has protected me for almost nine months. They can handle another couple of weeks. Even with tonight's breach, I'm safer there than here with your vampires."

"I'll get to the bottom of that. My vampires won't touch you again."

She snorted. "Just let me go back. You said you can sense the baby, so I'll never be out of your reach."

"I'm not stupid, Aegi. You'll use Aegis magic or some shit to ward yourself so I can't sense my son."

She hoped the guilty heat in her cheeks didn't show. "That's silly."

"Than," Ares said, "let me take her. It's best that you don't get attached to the child."

"Why not?"

Oh, God, Regan did not want to do this. Not while he was so worked up.

"Why not?" he repeated, this time making his question sound like a threat.

"Because I'm not keeping it." Taking a deep, bracing breath, Regan stepped forward. "Someone else is going to raise this baby."

Unfuckingbelievable.

Thanatos stared at Regan and Ares in disbelief. He wasn't even sure he could find his voice. So instead of talking, he jammed his hands through his hair and paced. The awful tension was winding up to a fever pitch inside him, part anger, part global violence and death, part sexual need. If the way Ares was clenching and unclenching his hands was any indication, he was feeling the tension too. Battles must be on the rise somewhere.

Sure enough, as Than stalked around, trying to keep his head on his shoulders, Ares wheeled toward the door. "I have to go. I'll send Limos."

"I don't need a babysitter."

"We'll talk about this when I get back."

"Fuck that," Than bit out. "Why are you siding with Regan over me?"

Ares slammed his fist into the doorjamb, but he didn't turn back to Than. "Believe it or not, brother, we're doing all of this for you. What would you do if something happens to that baby, either because of you, or because it was vulnerable to Pestilence? I know what it's like to lose a child, and I swear by all that's unholy, I'll prevent the same from happening to you. You and that baby are our priority, and until Regan gives birth, she's part of that deal." Ares stalked out of the room, leaving him alone with Regan.

"Listen to me, Thanatos—"

"Tell me, who is this someone else you want to raise *my* son?" A long silence stretched, and the temper Ares was talking about cracked wide open. "*Who*?"

"There's no need to shout," she snapped.

He sauntered toward her, and although her eyes flashed with fear, she stood her ground, even as he came up against her so her swollen belly touched his. "You are carrying my son. You can't expect me to sit idly by while you throw him away like garbage after you're through with your scheming."

"How dare you assume that I'm throwing this baby away!"

"What else am I to assume? Do you want this child?"

Her mouth worked soundlessly for a moment. "I'm not mother material."

"That's not an answer. Let me put it another way. When you set out to seduce me, did you want this baby?"

She hesitated, glancing away before meeting his gaze. "No."

Her answer widened the fissure in his temper. No child, intentionally conceived, should be unwanted. "So the child is nothing but a tool for The Aegis. A pawn. And you're nothing but a brood mare."

"That's a little harsh."

"Then soften it for me."

She took a step back, and he moved with her, keeping the pressure on. "I volunteered to save the world."

"You volunteered to play whore for your colleagues," he growled, taking a perverse pleasure in her gasp of outrage. "So here's the deal. You will remain here until you give birth, and then you'll leave the child with me while I decide your fate."

"Go. To. Hell." She doled out the words like rare Neethul throwing stars, each barbed and edged with acid.

"You took my seed through trickery. You *won't* take

my child, too." He got down in her face. "Was it your idea? Or when The Aegis came up with the proposal, were you so desperate for a cock that you jumped at the chance to fuck me? How many men have you fucked for your job? How often has The Aegis whored you out?"

She slapped him so hard he took a step back. "How *dare* you?"

"How dare I?" He snared her wrists and flattened her against the wall, although he tempered his strength, unwilling to jostle her. "Are you really going to play the self-righteous, wounded party? You stole from me, Regan. You stole my virginity, and you stole my seed. You and your colleagues plotted to take this innocent baby, conceived as a means to an end, and dump him when his usefulness was over."

"That's not true," she ground out. "That means to an end makes him the most important person on the planet, even if it's not in the way we expected."

"He's important because if he dies, my Seal breaks. But in the Aegis's eyes, that's the only reason he's important. He was always intended to be a tool, and now he's also a plan gone wrong."

"Things might have gone wrong, but we'll make it right. I promise you. He'll have a mother and father who will love him, Thanatos. I'm giving him to Kynan and Gem. They'll keep him safe from Pestilence and give him the home and life and family I can't."

Well, if *that* wasn't just a punch to the gut. "*I* will give him a home and life and family."

"You're joking, right? Look around you, Horseman. You live in the middle of nowhere. You killed nearly everyone on the island. Are your vampires going to be his nannies? Are the souls in your armor going to rock him to sleep? And what happens if Uncle Pestilence drops by for a visit? Do you think he's just going to let you raise this child in peace? Every evil being on the planet is going to try to find and kill this baby in order to break your Seal, and the first place they'll look for him is here." She inhaled deeply, more fuel for her rant. "Or what if Pestilence somehow finds where Limos has hidden her *agimortus* and breaks her Seal? With two broken, the other two will break in a domino effect, right? So yours will follow. What happens to the child then?"

If Ares's and Thanatos's Seals broke in the domino effect following the first two broken Seals, both Cara and Than's son would have to deal with whatever being an *agimortus* involved.

And chances were that the "deal with" wouldn't be pleasant. From what he'd seen of Pestilence, evil Horsemen were eager to wipe out all evidence of their happy pasts.

"If my Seal breaks, it won't matter where he's living. And I can handle everything else. Including Pestilence."

"It won't work, Than. We've got to keep this baby secret and safe. He's going to Kynan."

"No, he's not."

"You blind fool," she spat. "This isn't about you or me. It's about what's best for the baby."

"Maybe you should have thought about that before you forced me to fuck you." He hurled the crude words at her like a weapon, and her almost imperceptible flinch said his aim was true. But a split-second later, she recovered, her chin up in stubborn defiance.

"I didn't *force* you. You said you wanted it." She

blinked hard, as if blinking back tears, but he knew better than that. Regan didn't cry. "You said you wanted me more than you'd ever wanted anyone, and that you were going to give in."

God help him, he *had* wanted her. And in truth, he wasn't upset about the sex…he was pissed as hell at the deception. But he wasn't ready to separate the two. "I was drugged."

"Were you drugged when we got hot and heavy in your gym? When you tore off my underwear and got me off with your hand? When you came—twice—in mine?"

A hot fever broke out over his skin at the memory, and his cock twitched at her words. "That was different."

"Well, how was I supposed to know? You were all over me. And then there was that…that Horsemen erotica book. The demon who wrote it bragged about how she'd hit the trifecta with you guys…" Regan blinked again. "How did she do that if you were a virgin?"

"My siblings and I can adjust memories. I made her think we'd had sex."

Her breath hitched. "I didn't know. If I had—"

"You'd what? You'd have given up your crazy scheme to take my seed?"

She stared at him for a long time before averting her gaze. "I'm sorry, Thanatos. I'd changed my mind. I didn't want to go through with the plan," she said, her eyes glued to the mattress. Maybe she was remembering what they'd done on it. "Not after I got to know you."

"An attack of conscience?" He snorted. "I'd be a little more forgiving if you hadn't run off. The truth would have gone a long way when I was lying there, exhausted and sated."

Exhausted, yes...but now that he thought about it, sated...not so much. His virginity had been taken and his Seal hadn't broken, so he'd been willing to go again. Hell, he'd have gone over and over if she'd climbed back on and rode him into the mattress.

"You wanted me to confess something like that after you threatened to break my neck? Telling you the truth wasn't an option."

Yeah, he remembered lying on the bed, pinned while his souls battled to free him from her soul-weapon, and telling her he'd wring her neck when he got free. Still, Regan could have spent a little more time explaining what had just happened.

"So your answer was to take off?"

"I admit," she murmured, "that I could have handled it better, and if I could change things, I would, but I can't."

Could have handled it better? It couldn't have been handled *worse*. "No, you can't change anything, but you *can* make it up to me."

Her head snapped up, her gold-spoked eyes flaring wide. "How?"

Smiling, he seized her shoulders and tugged her against him so he could speak directly into her ear. She wasn't going to miss a word of this.

"You," he said against the velvety perfection of her skin, "owe me eight months of life you stole from me. So starting now, you're going to give it back."

"I-I don't know what you expect me to do."

He pinched her earlobe with his teeth and inhaled deeply, taking in the scent of her nervousness and beneath it, Regan's soft, feminine vanilla spice. The very air in his lungs turned to fire as lust surged through his veins. He might be furious with her, might even hate her. But his physical reaction to her was the same today as it was the very first time he laid eyes on her.

"You're going to pleasure me." He got a dark, wicked thrill from her sharp inhale. "Whenever I want. At my every whim."

She jerked in his grip. "I don't think—"

"No, you don't think, do you. If you did, you wouldn't have gotten yourself into this mess in the first place. So for the next eight and a half months, you're going to be mine." He nipped her jaw before soothing the spot with his tongue. "Every. Night."

"You're crazy."

"No," he said, as he released her and moved toward the door. "I'm pissed. There's a difference. If I were crazy, you wouldn't have nearly as much to fear."

Seven

Every cell in Thanatos's body was vibrating with the familiar need to gate himself to a scene of death and add to it. What wasn't familiar was the new vibration, the one that throbbed in his groin.

He needed sex. Ares and Reseph had always been able to ease their destructive impulses by getting laid, which made sense, since their mother was a sex demon. But Than had never had that alternative, and instead of sex, he went straight for the kill.

Now, maybe, he had another option. The real question was which act—killing or sex—would give him the most satisfaction.

And the most guilt later.

He supposed it would depend on whom he killed or whom he had sex with.

You're going to pleasure me. Whenever I want. At my every whim. Right. He should storm back into the bedroom and get going on those months Regan owed him.

Except that in the mood he was in he didn't trust himself to be gentle...and even through his murder-lust haze, that frightened him a little.

"*Bludrexe?*"

Thanatos snarled, ready to take the head off the daywalker at the end of the hall. Before that happened, he clenched his fists at his sides. He demanded loyalty from his servants, and he got it because he'd never abused them. He couldn't—wouldn't—start now.

"What, Artur?"

"Should we prepare a room for your female?"

Thanatos was in Artur's face before he even knew he'd moved. "She's *not* my female."

"Yes, sir," Artur said, shrinking back.

"Fuck," Than breathed. "I'm sorry. I've got a lot of shit on my mind." Like the fact that Regan was certain one of his vampires had tried to kill her. His hackles rose at the very thought. "Regan said two of you were taken from here by The Aegis."

Artur, who was normally unflappable, shifted his gaze. Only for a second, but Than caught it, and in that instant, he went on high alert.

"Artur, tell me. Who?"

The daywalker swallowed. "Jacob, sire."

"And?" When Artur said nothing, Than stiffened. "Dammit, Artur. What's going on?"

Artur bowed his head, his long hair brushing the tattoo on his neck that all the daywalkers sported. "The other vampire was not one of ours."

Now Than understood Artur's reluctance to talk about

this. No vampire visitors were allowed here. His vamps had to go elsewhere for human blood and companionship.

"Who was he? How did he happen to be here for The Aegis to grab?"

"He was . . . a wilding."

A hiss escaped Than before he could stop it. "Why was he here?"

"I don't know, sire."

Than snared Artur by the throat and slammed him against the stone wall. "You're lying. You have your finger on every pulse here."

"The Aegis grabbed him and Jacob before he got a chance to tell us," Artur said quickly. "But I suspect it had to do with your son."

"How did this wilding know Regan was pregnant?"

"I don't know how he knew. Jacob and some others wanted to find her to bring her to you." Artur's lip curled. "We were angry at her deception, and we wanted her to be here when you returned."

The idea that a strange wilding had known of Than's child before Than himself did made the need to kill seethe wildly inside him. "Did you know where I was?"

Artur nodded. "Limos and Ares let us know you were safe. We wanted to rescue you."

So Thanatos's servants had wanted to release him from the prison of his own body, but his brother and sister, his flesh and blood, hadn't. Nice.

Thanatos stepped away from Artur, his body buzzing, his tattoos coming alive on his skin. The thump of his pulse pounded in his ears, drowning out the voice that demanded he return to the female he'd just told Artur wasn't his.

Demons. He'd find some demons to kill. Australia was crawling with them. New Zealand was a demon playground. But he didn't want to leave Regan.

He eyed the entrance to one of the spare bedrooms. Self-gratification had never worked to bring Ares down from battle rages—only full-on sex had done that—but at this point, Than was desperate to try anything.

"Tell the others that Regan is not to leave the keep," he told Artur. "Go."

The vampire scurried off, and Than shut himself in the bedroom. The darkness closed in on him as he turned into the wall and rested his forehead against the cool stone. It wasn't cool enough. If it were made of ice, it wouldn't be enough to ease the fever in his blood. Not when Regan was only a couple of doors down. All he could think about was her talented mouth, her warm hands, and the hot place between her thighs.

And as he untied his sweats and palmed himself, he prayed this would work. Prayed it would release some of the awful tension raging inside him, because if it didn't, someone was going to die.

Regan was forcing herself not to freak out.

Thanatos was beyond angry. Irrational.

Not that she could blame him. Even if things hadn't gone down the way they had that night, even if he hadn't been a virgin, even if he'd eagerly jumped into bed with her, he still had every right to be furious about being used.

Every night since then, she'd tried to come up with a way to explain it to him, to apologize, to do anything to make it better. But spending the better part of a year as his personal sex slave? She wasn't sure if the idea terrified her or thrilled her, but it definitely wasn't going to happen.

She needed to be with people she trusted, the only family she'd ever known. And she knew exactly how to get out of here. Thanatos kept a fleet of snowmobiles and ATVs outside his monstrous castle for his servants to ride to the Harrowgate a couple of miles away. If she could get to a phone, she could call Kynan and have him meet her there to get her through the gate. Sucked, but humans, unless they were special in some immortal way, died if they went through a stationary Harrowgate while conscious.

Once she was back with The Aegis, maybe they could spin up a ward for the baby so Thanatos couldn't find her.

But standing here wasn't going to get her anywhere. She needed a plan if she ran into vampire trouble.

I can sense the life within you. I'm going to enjoy feeling it snuff out.

Yeah, she definitely needed a way to protect herself, especially since Thanatos didn't believe her about how dangerous his vampires were. Unfortunately, the Horseman didn't have jugs of holy water or a bag of wooden stakes lying around. But she'd always been resourceful, and the wooden desk chair looked like just the thing . . .

It took one good smash of the chair on the floor to break one of the legs. She waited a minute to see if the noise brought anyone running, and when it didn't she gripped the wooden chair leg, pointy end all ready to stab, and slowly opened the door. Thanatos and his vamps were nowhere to be seen. The arrogant jerk probably thought she had nowhere to go and no way out.

She made it to his library without being seen. Quickly, she ducked inside, found his phone, and gaped in disbelief.

She'd spent entire days with her nose in his books, but she'd never noticed this.

He had a freaking rotary phone. Who still used those relics? Thanatos, apparently. Unbelievable. She dialed Kynan's cell number, but he didn't answer, and the stupid phone wouldn't let her *press one to leave a message*. She had to waste precious time waiting for the other option of holding, and when the voicemail finally picked up, she whispered that she'd meet him at the Greenland Harrowgate. Hopefully, he'd check his messages soon.

Distant clinking noises came from the kitchen, as well as the mouthwatering aroma of roast chicken, and her stomach growled. Leave it to her pregnant self to want food during an escape.

Later, she told herself. Later she'd gorge on an entire buffet, but right now, she had to make it outside before anyone saw her. With as much stealth as she could manage, she crept across the great room, her bare feet padding silently on the icy stone floor. She walked on rugs when she could, careful not to step on the silky tassels.

Yep, her OCD issues were out of control. This was the worst it had ever been, and while some of it was likely pregnancy-related, being kidnapped and held prisoner had definitely tripped her crazy-switch.

She made it as far as the front door. One of Than's vampires, a burly, ugly dude whose name escaped her—pregnancy-brain sucked—blocked her path.

"Our orders are to prevent you from leaving."

"I'm just taking a walk."

He bared his fangs. "And I'm a mermaid. Now go back to your room."

She raised her makeshift stake. "Get out of my way."

He laughed. "Stupid, fat human. You're no match for me."

"Fat? *Fat*? I'm pregnant, you walking corpse. I might be fat, but you're dead." With a lot less grace than she was used to, she lunged, but the vampire shifted, and her aim went awry. The end of the stake merely grazed his shoulder, but that was enough to piss him off.

He cursed, his hand snapping out to clutch her by the throat. She sucked hard, trying to gulp a breath. What was it with vampires and their habit of grabbing you by the throat?

Cursing in her head, she clawed at his neck, ripping his silk shirt at the collar. Her fingertips skimmed a tattoo there, and in an instant, the vampire's fury washed over her and her mind lit up with a vision, a strange one involving Thanatos bent over this vampire as the monster lay on a stone slab. The strange word the vampire at headquarters spoke, *Bludrexe*, blasted through her head, and then the vision was gone.

Clearly, her soul-sucking ability was gone, but her psychometric gift was still intact. Not that it could help her in this situation. No, old-fashioned dirty-fighting was all she had to rely on. As the vampire jerked his head back from her nails, his body shifted, allowing her to lift her knee and crunch it into his groin. He *oof*ed and released her, and she nearly fell when her feet hit the floor.

"Bitch!" he snarled, and grabbed for her again.

His fingers never touched her. A godawful roar shook the keep, and faster than she could blink, Thanatos had ripped the vampire away from her and had him on the ground on the other side of the room. She didn't waste time hanging around to see what was going to happen next.

Leaving behind the sounds of a violent smackdown, she scurried out into the gray morning dawn, heaved herself onto one of the 4-wheelers, and started it up with the keys left in the ignition. The big machine roared to life, and she was out of there. She gunned it, the wheels bouncing over the uneven terrain and jostling her badly enough that she had to slow down more than she'd have liked. Every once in a while, she risked a glance behind her, but so far, so good.

Until she reached the half-mile marker.

Thanatos stood there, his eyes like gold lasers, his arms crossed over his broad chest.

Shit.

She stopped the vehicle, but she didn't turn it off. She stared, and he stared back, and nope, she wasn't going to win this. Calmly—on the outside, at least—she turned the ATV around and started back toward the keep. Even over the rumble of the engine, she heard hoofbeats, and a moment later, Than's pale stallion, Styx, was next to her, his long-legged stride carrying him over the tundra at an easy gallop. Thanatos sat erect in the saddle, his watchful gaze on everything except her.

Great. She'd much rather he was glaring or yelling. She hated silence. Grinding her teeth, she sped up, desperate to get away from him. It didn't work. Styx kept pace with her, and she swore Thanatos smiled. It only lasted a second, but it was a smile.

And not a nice one.

"Regan, stop!" Than's voice cracked like an avalanche breaking loose on a mountain.

Startled, she let up on the gas as a massive white horse and an armored rider appeared in front of them. *Pesti-*

lence. She braked hard—too hard. The ATV fishtailed, its rear end popped up, and she flipped into the air before hitting the ground with a heavy, bone-jarring crunch.

The baby...oh, God, let the baby be okay. Regan pressed her hand to her belly, praying the fall hadn't hurt the little pony.

Groaning, she started to push up, and yelped when an arrow punched into the dirt an inch from her belly. Horses screamed, and the metallic clank of clashing swords rang out. *Shit, shit, shit!* Frantic to get out of the way of the flailing hooves, she scrambled, limping, toward the ATV.

Just as she reached the vehicle, an ice-cold puff of air flowed over the back of her neck, and with it, a snort... deep, growly...and a chill slithered up her spine. Very slowly, she turned, and froze solid at the sight of the thing standing there, its gaping mouth full of sharp teeth and its foot-long claws extended. The dragonlike creature was crystalline, like a giant rock-candy tree, all shards of ice, hard angles, and tiny, black, triangle eyes. Against a landscape of icebergs or glaciers, the demon would be invisible.

Invisible until it bit your head off with jaws the size of an alligator's.

Distantly, she heard Thanatos calling her name. Unable to look away from the monster, she stumbled backward, but it followed her, its scaly feet digging deep grooves in the earth as it moved. Then she heard the huff, felt the liquid nitrogen breath of a second creature at her back. Bone-chilling cold seeped into her flesh. Her nerve endings burned with white-hot fire. Pain stabbed her with evil little fingers, and shivers wracked her body.

Thanatos. He was trying to get to her, but he was

injured...so much blood. She took a step toward him—at least, she tried to. Her legs were numb and her coordination had fled with her body heat. Hypothermia? Yes, it must be hypothermia, because when one of the creatures breathed on her again, she didn't feel it. No, there really was no more cold. She was tired, though. So exhausted.

She blinked. Where was she? Screams rent the air, horrid, pained noises. All around her, shadows swarmed over the ice monsters, who shrieked until they blew apart, sending icicles blasting like shrapnel.

Where was Thanatos? Didn't matter. She just wanted to sleep, and the ground looked so soft...

The world spun as her legs gave out and she hit the earth. She didn't know where she was, couldn't remember her name, but at least she was finally warm.

Eight

"Regan!"

Thanatos watched helplessly as she went down and lay motionless. He'd released his souls to destroy the frost demons, but he'd wanted to kill the beasts himself. Instead, he was engaged in battle with Reseph, who had grown much more powerful in the last eight months.

Reseph—Thanatos still had a hard time thinking of him as Pestilence—sat atop Conquest, his ice-blue eyes gleaming with bloodlust. Both horses were bleeding, gashed from teeth and hooves, and Than had taken a glancing blow from his brother's sword across his temple, but Reseph remained uninjured.

"Your Aegi whore doesn't look so good," Pestilence said. "Pregnant chicks are so fragile. But you *know* they put out."

Thanatos didn't dare go to her aid. Not while Pestilence was here. "What do you want?"

"I was hoping to rail your woman and then kill your son, but you went and fucked that all up."

The question of whether or not Pestilence had known about Regan's pregnancy was now answered. "How long have you known?"

"That the whore was knocked up? For a lot longer than you." Pestilence winced. "Ouch. That must hurt, huh?"

Fucker. "If you so much as touch either of them, there will be no saving you from me. Now get off my island."

Pestilence grinned. "You got it, bro." He threw open a gate. "Later."

That had been too easy. Pestilence was definitely up to something, but right now, Than's priority was Regan, and the second Conquest carried his brother through the gate, Than was off his stallion and at Regan's side.

Gripping her shoulder, he shook her gently. "Regan. Hey, can you hear me?" She didn't stir, and fear clogged his throat. Her normally tan skin was white and ice-cold, her lips blue. The frost demons hadn't ripped into her with their claws or teeth, but their breath could freeze a living thing into a solid block of ice in seconds.

"Styx. To me." The stallion poofed into smoke and settled on his forearm as he scooped Regan into his arms and opened a Harrowgate. He stepped out inside Underworld General's emergency department. Which was in chaos.

The hospital was brimming with injured demons, so many that nearly every inch of space was taken up by bodies. Outside the sliding glass doors that led to the underground parking lot, more patients waited to get in. Jesus…there had to be two hundred demons in the parking lot, some lying in pools of blood. Medical staff were running around wildly, overwhelmed and clearly exhausted.

These people would not be able to help, and Regan didn't have time to wait. Cursing, he turned back to the gate inside the emergency department, but froze when the ambulance bay doors slid open and a tall, black-haired vampire strode inside. His face was familiar, but that wasn't what tripped Thanatos like a taut wire.

The vampire was a daywalker. Damn. How? Thanatos had spent countless centuries searching the world for them, and although he knew a handful of them existed in the wild, blending in with the nightwalkers, they generally laid low, not wanting Thanatos to get wind of their existence.

No, Than was, to many daywalkers, their personal nightmare.

This one walked into the hospital with an arrogant gait, seemingly not worried that Thanatos would find him. And when the daywalker halted mid-stride and met Than's gaze, there was no fear there. Curiosity, but no fear. The other male broke eye contact first, and made a beeline for a female in scrubs.

Later. Than would have to solve the mystery later. He stepped into the Harrowgate and gated himself back to his keep. Regan flopped like dead weight in his arms as he ran inside and shouted for his vamps. Artur was there in a heartbeat.

"Warm some blankets and tea, and start a fire in my bedroom. Hurry!"

While his servants scrambled to obey, he whisked Regan to his room. Gently, he placed her on the bed and then stripped her of her damp clothing. He angled his body to prevent the vampires starting the fire from seeing her as he removed her bra and left her only in her underwear. He wasted no time in tugging up the blankets and then stripping himself and climbing into bed with her.

He eased behind her, his chest plastered to her ice-cold back. It was like snuggling up to a slab of beef in a meat locker. Viktor entered with two lightly warmed blankets, which Than draped over her bare skin before resettling the covers over her.

"Bring more warm blankets in fifteen minutes," Than said. "And contact Ares or Limos to get a doctor from Underworld General here."

Viktor nodded and slipped from the room, leaving him alone with Regan.

He wrapped his arms around her, letting one hand drift up to her throat so he could monitor her pulse, which was too sluggish. Her breaths were too shallow. Worry washed over him like a tsunami, first crashing in one big swell, then rippling through him and piling more fear on top of the first wave.

"Dammit, woman," he muttered. "You just had to run off like that."

Briskly, he rubbed her shoulders, working his way down her arms. His fingers brushed her belly, and his breath hitched.

Somehow, it seemed like a violation to touch her there, which was ridiculous, given that he'd touched her everywhere else, and besides, the baby inside was his. Was the child okay? Had the cold and the fall affected it even worse than they had affected Regan?

Shoving aside the sense that he would be doing something wrong by touching her, he lay his hand on the taut skin just below her navel. For a long moment, all he felt was cold. Then, movement. Something rolled against his palm—a foot, maybe.

Fierce pride bubbled up inside him. Obviously, Regan was pregnant, but it truly hadn't sunk in until now. He was going to be a father. He was going to have a son.

Terror tangled with the pride and joy. What if he sucked as a father? What if he couldn't protect his child? He'd been there the day Ares had lost his sons, and he could still remember Ares's screams, could remember how long it had taken for him to recover.

And if they didn't neutralize Pestilence, he'd forever be a danger to Than's son. Regan was right about that, even if he hadn't wanted to acknowledge it at the time.

He tugged Regan closer so he could wrap his arm around her and his son, shocked by the intensity of what he already felt for the child. He'd always wanted kids, had wanted to pass on the kind of love his parents—the humans who'd raised him—had showered him with. The kind of love he hadn't gotten from his demon mother or the angel who had sired him.

If he could create and raise a child who was decent, who didn't cause pain and suffering the way Thanatos had, then maybe some of his life would make sense. Would mean something. And maybe, just maybe, a child would give him something to fight for. He'd grown so numb to the human world around him, but this baby was already a bright spot in his foggy gray world.

What color eyes would he have? Would his hair be fine and silky like Regan's, or thick like Than's? Would he have Regan's rounded cheeks, or his high, sharp cheekbones? Not that any of it mattered. The child would be perfect regardless of who he took after.

There was a tap at the door, and Viktor entered with two more warm blankets, which Than used to replace the others. Regan's skin was starting to feel less icy, but she still wasn't stirring.

"Come on, Regan," he said into her hair. "Show me some of that fire inside you. Show me what you're made of. I won't let you die. No one is allowed to kill you but me." He meant that last as a joke, but it wasn't funny, was it? He'd been prepared to kill her a few hours ago, and if he'd succeeded, if he hadn't come out of his death-fury...

Shit. He could have made the biggest mistake of his life.

It was reminder that he needed to work harder at keeping his temper in check. Because he would prove to Ares that he wasn't a danger to his own child. He would never be a danger to those close to him.

The scorpion on his neck stung him, calling him out. *You killed the man who raised you as his son. You've murdered friends. You slaughtered a servant today when jacking off didn't relieve your urge to kill. You kill everyone.*

You. Are. Death.

"Have you found any suitable sites for a new headquarters?" Kynan spoke to Valeriu via a teleconferencing app on his iPhone.

Now that their location had been compromised, moving as quickly as possible had become their top priority. The non-evil Horsemen might be allies—although that designation was a little questionable in Thanatos's case—

but if their Seals broke, they could wreak some catastrophic havoc with their knowledge of the current Berlin
headquarters' location.

"I'm looking at one in Scotland now. It's a castle with
connections to the Templars, and it features an extensive
network of underground passages. I think it might be our
best bet. How are you guys doing there?"

Kynan glanced at Chad, Malik, Zachary, and Ian,
who were listening in on the conversation from where
they were sitting around the conference table. "Decker
just landed in DC to meet up with Arik for some sort of
military project. Lance and Omar are on a flight back
here from Australia. Takumi and Juan…I don't know
where they are. They're supposed to be coordinating a
strike against Pestilence's demons in the Philippines, but
I haven't heard from them." The Aegis message symbol
was flashing on his phone though, so he might have word
from them when he was done with this conference.

"Any news about Regan?"

Ky blew out a breath. "I haven't heard from her. Ares
texted me on his way to a battle somewhere. He found
them at Thanatos's place. Regan's fine, but I'll head there
as soon as I can. See if I can talk him into letting me bring
her back."

"What about your in-laws? Anything from them?"

Ky nodded. "The war between the born wargs and the
turned ones has escalated. Their Council has dissolved,
and—"

"And we care about werewolf fallouts…why?" Ian
interrupted.

"Because," Val replied, "their Council is as old as we
are. If they can break, anyone can."

Ian rolled his eyes. "*We're* not animals. We can govern ourselves."

"It's not just about that," Kynan said. "We care because the born wargs have aligned themselves with Pestilence. They're looking to start the Apocalypse. My brother-in-law, Con, managed to bring the turned wargs together and get them on our side."

"So it starts," Chad mused. "The underworld is organizing and starting to take sides."

Kynan braced his elbows on the conference table. "It's only a matter of time before those who can walk hidden in the human world start a war against humans."

"It's not a matter of time," Val said. "In the last hour, I've gotten dozens of reports of organized forces all over the world attacking embassies, police stations, military installations."

"They're going to start an Apocalypse without the damned Horsemen." This was exactly what they'd been afraid of. The true, Biblical or *Daemonica* Apocalypse wouldn't start, but the technicalities hardly mattered. If they saw decades or even hundreds of years of war between humans and demons, it would feel apocalyptic enough. Kynan stood. "We need to contact all Aegis cells and start emergency recruiting."

He thumbed the Aegis symbol flashing on his phone's screen, and when he brought the cell up to his ear, Regan's whispered voice, saying she was heading to the Harrowgate outside Than's keep, sent his pulse into critical overdrive. *Shit.* The message was old—A bloodcurdling scream from outside the conference room cut into his thoughts, and half a second later, it was joined by more screams, shouts, and gunfire.

"What the fuck?" Chad leaped out of his chair and threw open the door.

The next few seconds were a blur of blood and gore, as Chad rocked backward and hit the floor, an arrow piercing his eye and blowing out the back of his skull. Pestilence stalked inside, his armor splattered with blood and bits of flesh and hair, and when Ian swung at him, the Horseman swatted him aside as if he was a fly.

Outside the room, the sounds of battle escalated. Kynan drew his stang and went after Pestilence, but the big male ducked out of the room and was gone.

"Ian! Zach!" Ky helped Ian to his feet. "We've got to protect the artifact chamber." The tens of thousands of items The Aegis stored there—some historical or religious, some imbued with magical or demonic powers—could become devastating weapons in the hands of someone like Pestilence.

The three of them sped down the hallway, their path impeded by demons and fighting Guardians.

"They released the prisoners." Kathy, Regent for one of the Frankfurt cells, dropped a spindly Croucher demon with a roundhouse kick to the throat before stabbing it in one of its three eyes with the silver end of her stang.

That explained all the pissed-off demons, many of whom they'd re-captured after they'd escaped containment with the vampires who attacked Regan.

A Cruentus demon, an ugly motherfucker that lived to kill, rounded the corner ahead and came at them at a lumbering run. Ky and Ian met it, both of them slicing deep into its skeletal chest. Its claws struck out, raking Ian across the abdomen. Blood welled, but the cuts were shallow, and only pissed off Ian more.

"Kynan!" The shout came from behind, and he whirled just in time to see Pestilence bury his fist in Zach's gut and brutally rip out a bloody mass of organs.

Smiling, Pestilence left the dying Elder and strode toward Ky and Ian. Kathy, who had dispatched the Croucher, did her best to become a part of the wall, but as Pestilence walked by, he casually slammed his palm into her throat, killing her instantly.

He hadn't even looked in her direction.

"Run," Ky snapped, giving Ian a shove. "I'll stall him. He can't hurt me."

"He can't," came a deep, dark voice, "but I can."

Kynan didn't need to turn to know that a fallen angel was standing behind him. Didn't need to turn to know that while he planned to fight until he couldn't fight anymore, the angel was going to win.

Nine

"I want you, Regan. More than I've wanted anyone, and damn you, I'm about to give in."

Thanatos's sexy, deep voice rumbled through Regan like a drug, turning her bones liquid and her brain to mush. Somewhere inside her mind, she knew this was a dream about the night she got pregnant, just like she knew it was useless to try to wake herself up. Every time she had this dream, she tried to change it, as if doing so would also change the outcome in real life.

"No!" Thanatos's lips moved, but the buzz in Regan's ears drowned out the sound. The mead. She shouldn't have drunk the mead…

Shifting, she poised her naked body over the head of his cock.

"Don't do this. Regan!"

Don't do what? She heard him, but the words didn't compute. Not when her body vibrated with need. She sank down on him, taking him all the way to the root. Pleasure roared through her, almost orgasmic already, and they'd only begun.

She moaned, grinding on him, loving the feel of his hard shaft sliding over all her sensitive spots. She wished he'd touch her, wished he'd reach up and caress her breasts or better yet, grip her hips in a bruising hold and anchor her against him. Why didn't he do that? Why wasn't he touching her? She wanted him to give himself to her with so much force that she'd feel him forever, because this would be the last time with him.

But wait...why would it be the last time? Hazy thoughts filtered through her brain...something about having to leave here after this. Leave? No way.

Ecstasy burned in her veins as she pushed all thoughts of anything except sex aside and lunged forward to score her nails on his chest, marking him. Claiming him. She threw her head back and cried out as his hips came off the bed to take her deeper. Faster...she had to move faster. Her body was no longer her own. It had taken the reins and she was letting it run.

"Stop," he rasped, but Regan's brain heard it as "more," and she moved faster. She wasn't going to slow this down, drag it out. There would be time later for decadent, leisurely sex. "Regan, stop now!"

More now!

More? She couldn't do any more than this. "No way... oh, oh, yes." Her body convulsed with pleasure, and at the same him, his orgasm took him, his big body bucking beneath her. She came again, before the first climax had even waned, and she had to cling to his shoulders or go flying.

So good… that had been so… good.
You took my virginity.
Regan blinked.
You drugged me and defiled me.
Horror welled up. No…I…
You traitor!
He was yelling at her, threatening to break her neck, and then she was running out into the snow, where Pestilence and ice trolls were coming at her—

Fighting a scream, Regan opened her eyes. She wasn't stuck in the nightmare anymore, but she *was* in Thanatos's bed. She drew in a controlled breath, taking in Thanatos's earthy, masculine scent, and knew she was safe.

At least, she was safe until she gave birth, and then Thanatos would likely kill her for what she'd done.

He stood near the fireplace, his muscular upper body bare except for the tattoos that depicted scenes from his past, his lower body covered in a pair of baggy workout pants that sat dangerously low on his hips. His head was bowed, the braids at his temples falling over sharply defined cheeks, the tendons in his neck standing out in stark definition. She had a feeling his eyes were open.

This was Than's bedroom, but how had she gotten here?

Her mind was sluggish as she searched her memory, and when it came back to her, she whispered a curse. Thanatos whirled around and was at her side in a heartbeat. She hadn't even seen him move.

"Regan." His voice was a deep rumble. "You're awake." He palmed her forehead. "How do you feel? Are you cold?"

She pushed up on one elbow, which wasn't easy, given

that she must have fifty pounds of blankets on top of her. "I'm hot, actually."

Thanatos peeled away several layers of blankets and propped some pillows against her to help brace her as she sat up. Surprised by his attentiveness, it took her a moment to find her voice again. When she did, she had to struggle to find the words to ask what she needed to know.

"What happened? With Pestilence. The demons." Lame. She'd struggled for those *six* words?

"The demons will never bother you again." His answer was little more than a growl. "Don't worry about Pestilence. I'll keep you safe." The way he said it, as if he were pledging his very soul to the cause, eased her fears, at least for now. "Are you hungry? Thirsty?" He gestured to a covered platter and a carafe. "I had my staff prepare hot broth and sandwiches for when you woke up. Artur remembered how much you loved his ham and cheese subs."

"I'm starving." Regan might not trust vampires, but Artur had been nice to her, and he made the best freaking subs. Her mouth watered at the sight of the food. "I love the way Artur toasts the bread."

"I do too." The barest hint of a smile touched his lips. "With just a smear of butter."

She nodded. "He said the secret is real Irish butter with a touch of—" A sharp, shooting stab of pain nailed her in the belly, and she hissed.

"What is it?"

"Baby," she gasped. "I think I just had a contraction."

His hand came up to her cheek in a tender gesture that nearly made her gasp again. "Is it time?"

"I think...I think it's a Braxton Hicks."

"A what?"

"Sort of pre-labor pains. I've been having them for the last week or so."

The Horseman didn't look satisfied with that answer. "You shouldn't have tried to run." He dropped his hand, and she hated the way the lack of his touch left her feeling cold again.

"I'm in danger here," she insisted, but Than shook his head.

"The vampire who tried to kill you at headquarters wasn't one of mine. And I promise you, the vampire who tried to stop you from leaving won't touch you again. None of them will."

Regan wasn't so sure about that, but she had nothing to go on but a gut feeling. And while she trusted her instincts, Thanatos was another story.

At a tap on the door, Than unfurled to his full, impressive height. "Enter."

The door opened, and one of the vampires entered with a huge, dark-haired male wearing a black paramedic uniform. He carried a red duffel, and his right arm was encased in tattoos. This was Shade, one of the demon brothers who ran Underworld General. And the one who had used his incubus gift to ensure she was pregnant, even though she'd changed her mind.

He strode across the room, passing through a splash of shadow where the firelight didn't reach, and maybe Regan's eyes were tricking her, but he seemed to disappear until he stepped back into the light.

"Showoff," Than growled. "And it's about time."

The demon shot the Horseman an annoyed glare. "You might not be aware that we're teetering on the end of the world, but we're overflowing with casualties. We don't have time for house calls."

"You need to make time for this," Than said. "The baby Regan carries could trigger the Apocalypse if he dies."

"I know that. But I haven't even been to my own home in two weeks." Shade dropped the medic bag. "So fuck off. I got here as soon as I could." He strode over to Regan. "The message I got was that we're dealing with hypothermia?"

"Obviously," Than said, "she's better. No thanks to you. But she's having…what are they called? Breaking Dicks?"

"Braxton Hicks," Shade muttered. He went down on his heels next to the bed. "How are you feeling?"

Regan hesitated. Kynan might trust his demon in-laws, but she was not only less trusting, but she'd literally been born to fight them. A hatred of demons was in her DNA.

"Human." Shade's tone was no-nonsense, but not unkind. "You trust me as much as I trust you, but we have a common goal here. I like the planet the way it is. If that means making sure you and the little foal are medically sound, I'll do everything I can. Now, tell me how you're feeling."

She bristled, but ultimately, Kynan was a good judge of character, so she supposed she could suck it up, just this once. Besides, the baby was half…whatever Than was, so a demon medical specialist could only be an asset.

"I feel a little weak, but okay."

"How did you treat her?" Shade asked Than.

"Warm blankets. Body heat."

She sucked in a breath, her gaze flicking up to the

Horseman, who looked at her as though daring her to bring up the body heat thing. Yeah, he didn't have to worry about that. The idea that he'd put that hard, lean frame against hers...she shivered at the forbidden image.

"How long was she unconscious?"

"About six hours. She roused enough to drink some hot tea and went back out."

She had? She didn't remember that at all.

"Did you get her temperature?" When Thanatos shook his head, Shade sighed and started to peel back the covers.

A rumbling noise came at the same time that Thanatos's hand came down on the comforter. "She stays covered."

With horror, she realized she was naked except for underwear. Nudity had never bothered her, but again, the idea that Thanatos must have undressed her, and that this strange demon might be touching her like that...well, it made her want to hyperventilate.

"I can't examine her if she's covered up, asshole," Shade said.

"I'll get her some clothes." Than went to the huge wardrobe at the end of the bed.

Shade, his nearly black eyes glittering, turned back to Regan. "While he's being a dick, I'll take your vitals. Give me your wrist."

She held out her arm, and Shade took it. The baby did some sort of somersault in her belly, and Shade flew backward as if he'd been shot out of a cannon.

"What the—" Shade slammed into the wall and sat there, dazed.

Regan sat up, clutching the blankets to her chest. "Are you okay?"

"Hell's rings." Shade shook his head as if to clear it, and shoved to his feet. "That was like a billion-jolt shock, but without the electricity. Like I got a full body punch from a Gargantua demon."

Thanatos moved over to the bed and took her hand. "Nothing happens to me."

Regan eyed the shirt in his other hand. "Can I have that?"

He gave it to her. The black T-shirt was three sizes too large, but it would work as temporary maternity wear.

She gestured to Shade, Than, and the vampire standing near the door. "Turn around."

They did, and she slipped on the T-shirt. She still had no pants, but this would have to do. She tugged the blankets across her lap. "You can turn around now."

Shade walked over. "Take her hand again, Horseman."

Although he looked oddly uncomfortable, Than put his hand over hers. "Nothing."

Nothing? Maybe not for him, but she got a hot rush from his touch. Obviously, her body remembered the pleasure he'd given her with those hands. Annoying.

"I'm going to try again." Shade, his *dermoire* glowing, lightly pressed his fingertips to her forehead. Same result. Well, similar. This time he cartwheeled backward and landed in a heap next to the fireplace. Thanatos smirked.

"What's going on?" she asked, as Shade groaned and got to his feet, a little slower this time.

"I think your kid hates me." He rolled his shoulders, wincing a little. "Before I got suckerpunched that time, I got a thread of my power into you, and I felt him." He eyed her. "Hope you knew it's a boy."

"Yeah, we did," Than said. "So did you get anything else?"

"Not a lot. But I can tell you that the kid is big. You've easily got a nine-pounder in there. He's ripping some sort of powerful ability, and he's obviously picky about who he lets touch his mom." Shade looked over at Thanatos. "Or not picky."

Thanatos arched a blond eyebrow. "That's not very professional."

Shade gave Than a droll stare. "I'm a demon. You want professional, haul her over to the Mayo Clinic."

Thanatos snorted and gestured for the daywalker vamp to come over. "See if you can touch her."

Doing her best to not recoil, Regan held out her hand. The vampire's fingers skimmed harmlessly over her knuckles.

"Weird." She frowned. "I had a doctor appointment just last week and there were no issues. Maybe the baby only reacts to demons?"

"Maybe." Shade held out his arm. "Can *you* touch someone? Try me."

Couldn't hurt. At least, couldn't hurt *her*. The demon might not be so lucky. Tentatively, she placed her fingers on his forearm. Nothing happened.

"Interesting." Shade handed Than a thermometer. "Can you get her temp?"

Thanatos stuck the thing in her ear, and a moment later, it beeped. "Ninety-eight point eight. Is that bad?"

"Perfectly normal. Looks like the baby protected you from the frost demons. Regan, what's your due date?"

"August twenty-ninth."

Shade glanced at his watch. "Ten days. You're close."

He went down on his haunches beside the bed and lowered his voice. "Are *you* okay? Any concerns you want to share? Do you want to talk in private?"

Her opinion of the demon shot up about a million points. Somehow, she hadn't expected him to be sensitive to her needs or considerate of her privacy.

"I'm fine," she said. But *ten days*? How did the time sneak up on her like that? "But if you could get a message to Kynan to let him know what's happened, I'd appreciate it."

Shade nodded. "Any medical concerns? Has the pregnancy been normal?"

"There was a minor incident at the beginning of my sixth month. Some cramping and bleeding." When she saw Than stiffen out of the corner of her eye, she added quickly, "Everything's okay. The docs suspected placenta accreta, but the ultrasound didn't reveal anything."

"What is that?" Than asked.

Shade frowned. "It's when the placenta attaches itself too deeply into the wall of the uterus. It can require surgery after the baby is born to remove it." Shade stood. "Are you on any special treatment?"

"Bedrest for a while, but it was just a precaution."

"Okay," Shade said. "Since I can't do much more here, get some rest and food, and call if you need anything. I'll have Eidolon come by when he gets a chance." He shouldered his medic bag, but before he could leave, she shocked herself by calling out his name.

"Shade, wait." When he paused at the door, she chewed her lower lip.

She wasn't used to having civil conversations with demons, and besides, the first time she'd met Shade, a couple of years ago in Egypt, he and his brothers had been antagonistic sons of bitches with no respect for The Aegis. They'd all gotten off on the wrong foot, for sure.

"Was there something else?" Shade finally asked.

"Yeah. Um...thank you."

Shade grunted. "Look at that. A thank you from a slayer. The Apocalypse really is here."

"I take it back," she muttered, and fell back into her pillow as he stalked out, not even bothering to smother his laughter. Thanatos followed him, leaving her alone.

Normally, she'd be grateful. She'd always been comfortable with her own company. But for some reason, she didn't want to be alone right now. What she wanted was to go home. To the only home she'd ever known.

The Aegis.

Thanatos followed Shade out of the room and stopped him when they reached the great hall. "Tell me the truth, demon."

Shade's expression shuttered. "What makes you think that anything I've said was a lie?"

"I don't think you lied. I think you omitted." Than smiled grimly. "I deal in death, and I sensed your fears for Regan."

"I'm a paramedic," Shade said as he adjusted the medic bag on his shoulder, "not a doctor. You need Eidolon."

"Yeah, well, he's apparently not available, and don't give me the paramedic bullshit. You know more about medicine than most human doctors, so spill."

Shadows flickered in Shade's eyes, and Than wondered what gifts this Seminus demon possessed. "The baby is fully formed and ready to be born, but he's big. It could

be a difficult birth, made more so by her earlier problem
and the fact that right now it appears that there can't be
any medical intervention as long as no one can touch her."

Women had been giving birth since the beginning
of time, and although Thanatos knew how dangerous it
could be, he tried to comfort himself with the fact that
females were designed for reproduction, and there was
nothing more natural than having a baby.

"If she were able to be touched, what would a human
doctor do in this situation?"

Shade shrugged. "Monitor closely. Probably induce
labor by now to make sure the baby doesn't grow any
larger. Maybe schedule a C-section to be safe." He
shrugged again. "I haven't kept up on human obstetric
medicine, so I could be talking out my ass."

Thanatos suspected the demon was *covering* his ass.
"You have non-demons on staff. Maybe one of them can
handle her case. A vampire at least, since we know vampires can touch her."

"We do have a vampire medic," Shade said. "And we
have a lot of non-demon doctors. It's possible one of them
can deal with this."

"What can I do in the mean time? What would you tell
me to do if things were normal?"

One black brow arched. "Fuck her."

Than wasn't sure he heard that right. But the demon
couldn't have been clearer. "Ah . . . what?"

"Have sex with her. It can help induce labor." Shade
smirked. "And unless you're jumping up and down on her
belly, it's not going to *hurt*."

Thanatos rolled his eyes. Stupid sex demons. "Tell
Eidolon I want to see him immediately."

"Yeah, that's the thing, Horseman," Shade drawled. "You don't order Eidolon to do anything."

Most demons had more respect for the Four Horsemen of the Apocalypse, but not these Seminus brothers. It was annoying as shit. The only one Thanatos liked was Wraith, but that might be because in a lot of ways, the laid-back demon reminded Than of Reseph.

"You said you like the planet the way it is. You sure about that? Because the female in my bedroom is carrying a child that could make or break the world. And I probably don't need to remind you that *your* sister started this all."

"No, please remind me, asshole. There's never enough blame to throw around." Shade paused, oddly hesitant. "Ah... speaking of blame, you should probably know that I'm the reason Regan is pregnant."

Thanatos jerked as if he'd closed his hand around a live wire. Teeth clenched, he growled, "Explain."

"I hooked up her egg and your sperm. I didn't know any details about the situation at the time, and I'm guessing Kynan kept them from me so I wouldn't have to go through some overly moral internal struggle." He shrugged. "Humans. Anyway, there you go."

Than wasn't sure if he should kill the demon or give him props for admitting what he'd done. Took balls, for sure. "If you'd been aware of the situation?"

"Does it matter? It's done. But I will say that when it comes down to it, I'd sell my soul—hell, I'd sell *your* soul, to keep my mate and kids safe. I'd do whatever it took. I don't know anyone who wouldn't. You've got a kid on the way, so think about how far you'd go to protect him." Shade spun on his heel. "I'll tell E to come by. In the meantime, keep Regan safe." The demon disappeared through the front door.

Keep Regan safe? What did Shade think Thanatos was trying to do?

Needing to make sure she was still okay, he quietly pushed open the door to peek into the bedroom. Regan was sitting on the bed, one hand clutching a sandwich, the other stroking her belly. A hint of a smile curved her lips as she looked down, and no, that wasn't the picture of a woman who was prepared to easily give up a baby she didn't want. That was the picture of a mother, and even if she didn't admit it to herself, Regan loved the child.

The knowledge was both a relief and a fist to the gut. How could she love it, yet be so willing to give it up? Was it because the baby was his? Did she hate him so much that she didn't want the reminder toddling around behind her?

Cursing, he stalked into his library. In a fit of temper, he swiped his arm across one of the shelves. Books, baskets, and baubles crashed to the floor. Something metallic clattered across the tiles. Reseph's iPod.

Thanatos scooped it up, the smooth, black case so cold in his hand. Reseph had loved the thing, which was why it had been buried in the leather basket—Than had hidden it from him as a joke. Well, sort of. Reseph had often driven them all crazy by singing country songs at the top of his lungs. Sure, he'd actually had a great voice, but one could only take so many hours of twang.

"What are you doing?" Regan's voice came from behind him, and crazily, his pulse jumped.

Thanatos gave a casual shrug, but his body wasn't fooled, not when he saw her in the doorway, still in his T-shirt and a pair of his sweats she'd cinched beneath her belly. No female had ever worn his clothes, and an oddly primal instinct got him all growly and possessive at the idea that something of his was both on her and in her.

"Nothing," he muttered, tossing the mp3 player onto his desk.

"'Nothing' involves making a mess of your library?" She walked over to the desk, her bare feet not making a sound on the stone floor. Even as pregnant as she was, her confident grace wasn't diminished.

"You need socks."

She blinked. "What does that have to do with the messy library?"

"Nothing. But I don't want your feet to get cold."

A soft smile curved her lips, and he wished she wouldn't do that, because a smile like that could disarm him eventually. "You're an odd man, Thanatos Horseman." She picked up the iPod. The screen lit up, and her eyebrows lifted. "I wouldn't have taken you for a country music kind of guy."

"I'm not. Reseph is. Was. And you should be in bed."

"I feel fine, and if I lay down for too long, my hips hurt." She eyed the iPod again. "Alan Jackson. George Strait. Jimmy Buffett. Conway Twitty. Wow. Not a single rock band."

"Reseph was the flightiest person I've ever met, but when he latched onto something, he went all out. Totally single-minded. He even had a couple of favorite country bars where he'd go to dance. He loved to two-step."

Regan's nose wrinkled. "I can't imagine him doing anything...normal. Or nice."

"In a strange way, he was the most normal of all of us. He was definitely the nicest."

"I'm having a hard time believing that." She shot him a sideways glance. "You know, seeing how he tried to kill me today."

If that had happened...Thanatos couldn't even go there in his thoughts. He was intimate with death the way regular people were intimate with their lovers, but it had been four thousand years since he'd experienced a personal loss. He was pretty sure he would react...badly.

"If Reseph had wanted you dead, you would be," he said levelly. "His arrows don't miss."

"Maybe the baby was protecting me."

Than frowned. He hadn't thought of that. "Doesn't matter. If you hadn't taken off like that, he wouldn't have had an opportunity to try."

"Well, maybe you shouldn't have kidnapped me."

"Maybe you shouldn't have seduced me," he shot back, fully aware that they sounded like a couple of children.

Taking her bottom lip between her teeth, Regan looked down at her bare feet. "I really am sorry, Thanatos. I know you don't believe me, but I am."

Bitterness welled up like bile. "I told you how you can make me believe you, and since you have no trouble whoring for The Aegis, whoring for me shouldn't be a problem."

Something sad flashed in her eyes, and his bitterness boomeranged back at him, filling him with regret. Especially when, instead of snarking at him like he expected, she turned away.

Dammit. He tempered his voice so they could continue without the schoolyard squabbling. "Why did you do it?"

"I told you, we got information—"

"Yeah, yeah, save the world. But I mean, why did *you* do it? What made you agree?"

"Saving billions of people isn't enough of a reason?"

"There's always a personal consideration. I don't care how selfless anyone's actions are. There is *always* another reason."

She turned to him, her fingers fluttering over her belly. "I was the only one who *could* do it. My colleagues figured that my ability to rip souls from people could protect me from the ones in your armor."

"Even if that were true, it's still not answering the question about your personal angle. What was it?"

"Nothing—"

"*Bull. Shit.*"

The scars at her temple and chin, scars he found so sexy, darkened like barometers for her temper. "Maybe I was desperate for a cock, like you said. Maybe the idea of screwing a legend tempted me."

She was lying, although he couldn't say how he knew. What was clear was that she wasn't going to tell him the truth. Fine. He'd fling the crap right back at her.

"Good. Being desperate to fuck a legend will make the coming months go much better for you."

Once again he expected her to snark back, and once again she did the opposite. But this time, instead of falling silent, she changed the subject. "What happened to the vampire who tried to stop me from leaving?"

Instant anger flamed hot at the memory of Serkhama launching an attack on Regan. The daywalker had deserved punishment for that, but Than had been too crazed to consider any option but death. His little self-gratification session hadn't done a thing to dial back his tension. Only killing Serkhama and the frost demons had done that.

"He's gone."

"Gone as in dead or gone as in no longer here?"

"Yes."

"You're such a jerk sometimes."

"You think I haven't heard that before?"

She smiled sweetly, but her words were tart. "I'm sure you have."

There was the fire he'd been looking for. He hated that he liked it. That he found it intriguing. His brain searched for a suitable retort, but when she winced and reached behind her, he passed on the comeback.

"What is it? What's wrong?"

"It's just my back," she sighed. "Back pain is a pregnancy thing, apparently."

Without thinking, he crossed to her and nudged her hand out of the way, replacing it with his. "Let me." She tensed, but as he began to massage her lower back, alternating a kneading motion with lighter strokes, she relaxed with a groan.

"Oh, that's good," she moaned.

He loved that sound. Loved the way it both eased his mood and stirred his blood. He wanted to purr like a big cat. And then rub himself all over her.

Fucking idiot. Rubbing was what got them into this mess.

She arched her spine, pushing back into his massaging fingers, letting out a purr of her own. And yeah, that caused an instant hard-on. And how messed up was it that he was wanting to get naked with her?

Yes, he'd told her she owed him sexual favors, but he'd been pissed, confused, and still reeling from the shock of coming out of hibernation to find out he was going to be a father. He'd lashed out like a teenager who'd been dumped by his first girlfriend. Five thousand years of maturity had gone out the window in a matter of minutes.

He was such a dumbass.

The sound of a cleared throat startled him, and he jerked away from Regan. "What is it, Viktor?"

The vampire stood stiffly at the library entrance. "There's an Aegi here to see you."

Regan wheeled around so fast she lost her balance. Than leaped to catch her before she hit the desk, and for a split second, her grateful smile completely erased the tension between them.

And then Kynan staggered inside, a mass of cuts, bruises, and *really* wrong angles. One eye was swollen nearly shut, and his nose was badly broken. Than had a hard time feeling sorry for him, given that the human wanted to take Than's son.

Regan gasped. "My . . . God. What happened?"

Kynan halted a dozen feet away, his icy gaze locked with Than's. "He happened."

"I haven't left the keep, human. And even if I had, you know I can't harm you." Which sucked, because there were times that Than really would like to pulp the guy.

Except someone had already beaten him to it.

Kynan's split lips peeled back in a snarl that revealed blood-streaked teeth. "How did you find our headquarters, Horseman?"

Thanatos curled his hands into fists to stop a punch that wouldn't land anyway. "I sensed the child you were hiding from me. The child you will not have."

"Now isn't the time to discuss that." The human kept his eyes on Thanatos, but his words were for Regan.

"Thanks to your baby daddy, Pestilence found headquarters. He tracked Than's Harrowgate." Kynan's voice went low, and Than's gut went with it. Pestilence's easy capitulation during the battle earlier made sense now. He'd said he had something to do. Now Than knew what. "The building is all but destroyed. The son of a bitch brought a fallen angel with him. Between the two of them and the demons they turned loose..." He scrubbed his hand over his face to wipe blood out of his eyes.

"What?" Regan's voice was soft, a thread of worry woven into it. "Between the two of them...what?"

Ky met her gaze. "They killed everyone in the building but me."

Ten

Regan stood there, her brain unable to process what Kynan had just told her. "Who?" she rasped. "Who's dead?"

Kynan's red-rimmed eyes flashed. "Malik, Chad, Ian, Zachary, Kathy, Hans, Shylon, everyone in the personnel department, two dozen Regents who hadn't gone back to their local cells yet... Suzi."

Oh, God. Regan slapped her hand over her mouth and fought the urge to cry out. She'd always been calm and logical, even in the face of losing those she cared about, but the pregnancy hormones had her crying during freaking car commercials. Four Elders dead, several soldier-level Guardians. And she'd really liked Suzi, who had been one of her few friends. Her only friend, really.

The room spun, and she stumbled toward the sofa. Instantly, both Kynan and Thanatos were there, one on each arm. She jerked away from Thanatos as the faces of the dead flipped like playing cards through her brain.

"Don't touch me," she snapped. "This is your fault." But even as he backed away, so did Kynan...with a grunt.

Her support gone, she crumpled. Before she hit the floor, Than had her again, sweeping her up in his strong arms, and this time, she allowed him to help her to the sofa.

"What..." Kynan stared at his hands. "It felt like I got punched."

Thanatos eased away from her, although he remained close, propping himself against the wall, one knee bent, foot planted on the wall behind him. "Guess we can add humans to the don't-touch list."

"The baby has suddenly decided that no one but Thanatos and vampires can touch me," she explained, and then she stiffened at the sound of raised voices and pounding footsteps.

A split-second later, Limos, Arik, and Decker filed into the office. Limos tossed a duffle bag to the floor. "I went on a quick shopping spree for Regan. Figured she left before she could grab anything."

Still reeling from Ky's news and too flustered by Limos's kindness to speak, Regan nodded her thanks as Arik glanced at Ky and barked out a curse. "You need a doctor, man."

"You think?" As if the air had been let out of him, Kynan sagged against a bookcase. "I'll head to UG after this. Obviously, you guys all got my text."

"I was with Arik and Limos when it came. Hitched a ride with them." Decker angled his body closer to Ky, within reach if the other man collapsed. "How bad was it?"

"Bad," Ky replied. "Real bad. Pestilence and a fallen

angel came in like they owned the place. Forced Rebecca to open the door to most of the chambers before he killed her. She died quickly. Few were as lucky." He paused. "Chad, Malik, Zachary, Ian, and I were in the conference room when we heard the battle and screams. The bastards...shit...we never had a chance."

Limos wrapped her arm around Arik's waist in a comforting gesture that Regan would have gagged at just months ago. Now her stupid hormones had her thinking how sweet it was.

And how she'd never have that.

"What happened?" Limos asked.

"They toyed with us for hours, some of it just for the fun of hearing people scream. The things they did..." Kynan shuddered, his eyes haunted. "Their main goal was to get us to open the artifact chamber. I opened it, but I did it to get a *qeres*-coated blade."

Regan blew out an unsteady breath. "You took out the angel with it?"

"And not too quickly." Ky's gaze hardened with hints of how much he'd enjoyed that. Kynan was one of the most level, compassionate people Regan knew, but he was also a soldier who would do what was necessary. And he was even more dangerous when he was pissed.

"What's *qeres*?" Decker asked.

Regan shifted on the couch to keep her ass from going to sleep. "It's a weapon developed by ancient Egyptians to combat angels. Well, fallen angels."

"Why doesn't the R-XR know about it?" As a member of the U.S. Army's paranormal unit, the R-XR, Decker wasn't intimately familiar with everything The Aegis knew and possessed, even though he had been inducted into The Aegis and made an Elder. His Guardian status was too new, and he had a lot of catching up to do.

"Because we don't have enough to share," Regan answered.

Arik stroked Limos's back. More sweetness. "What happened to Pestilence?"

"He took off. He was furious that he couldn't get into the artifact room and worried his siblings would show up to try to stop him."

"He'll be back." Than's voice was grave. "The Aegis holds too many powerful objects. He'd love to get his hands on anything, but was there something in particular he was after?"

Kynan gave the barest nod, as if his neck pained him. "He said something about Wormwood. It's most notably a star mentioned in Revelations, but it's also the name of a dagger The Aegis appropriated in the late 1300s."

"Why would he want that?" Regan asked, more in general than to anyone specific.

"No idea," Than said. "I remember the dagger. It supposedly belonged to an influential archbishop."

Limos tapped her chin. "Wasn't it rumored to have been forged by a demon?"

"The archbishop claimed it was a heavenly relic," Kynan said. "Originally worn by an angel. We've never found the truth about it, but maybe Pestilence knows something we don't."

"We've got to move all the artifacts," Decker said. "We can't allow him to get anything, especially something he wants."

"It'll take forever to transfer the items to a new location." Regan's head ached just thinking how long it would take and how much effort would be involved. "And they'd be vulnerable during the move."

Kynan sighed. "I know, but we don't have a choice. Val is securing a new headquarters, and once that's done, I can use Harrowgates to transport the most important things quickly."

The most important things? Everything in their inventory was important. The Aegis was the largest collector of historical, Biblical, and demonic artifacts in the world, holding one-of-a-kind spell books, summoning crystals, and documents that could obliterate entire religions and destabilize governments. Heck, although Regan hadn't seen it herself, the Ark of the Covenant was supposed to be locked away at Aegis Headquarters.

God, this was a disaster. And wait... "If Pestilence was able to track Thanatos's Harrowgate, can his gates also be tracked?"

"Once Reseph's Seal broke, we lost that ability." Thanatos's expression was contemplative as his gaze traveled between her, Arik, and Decker, and then finally returned to Ky. "You said you have *qeres*?"

"Very little," Kynan replied slowly. "The recipe has been lost, so we can't make more. What we have is *all* we have."

"Give me a minute." He strode away, and Limos went with him, leaving Regan with Ky, Arik, and Decker.

Decker sprawled out in one of the fat leather chairs while Arik remained standing, and Ky limped over to Regan and sank down on the sofa next to her.

"Are you okay?"

I've been kidnapped, nearly impaled by an arrow, almost frozen solid, but other than that... "I'm fine."

Kynan glanced in the direction Than had gone and lowered his voice to a discreet murmur. "I got your message about escaping just before Pestilence arrived. Has Thanatos hurt you?"

She gave a sharp shake of her head. "He won't let anything happen to this baby."

"That's not what I asked." Ky shifted in his seat, careful not to touch her. "If you tried to make an escape, why are you still here?"

"Thanatos stopped me before I could get anywhere. On the way back Pestilence attacked us and sicced some frost demons on me. I got a little chill. As you can see, I'm fine. Thanatos took care of me. He won't risk injuring me."

"And what about after the baby comes? What then?"

That was the question of the century, wasn't it. The recurring nightmare of Than killing her popped into her head, and an ice-cold stab of dread shot up her spine. "We can worry about that later. Obviously, Than knows the plan for the baby, and he's not happy. I'll work on him." Ha. She had a feeling Sheoul would freeze over before he changed his mind. "Do you think Pestilence's attack on headquarters is related to the release of the vampires at headquarters?"

No doubt Kynan recognized her diversion tactic, but the new subject was too important to ignore. "It's too early to know, but it's one hell of a coincidence."

"I can't believe this," Regan whispered. "Things just keep getting worse."

"It's not all bad," Ky said. "Remember how you asked why Decker and I were at headquarters when you were attacked?"

"You said you were there to discuss waking Thanatos."

"That's because we've come across some new information just in the last couple of days." Decker dropped his gaze to Regan's belly. "Has Thanatos confirmed that the baby is his *agimortus*?"

She nodded. "Why?"

"We think that the baby might be the key to the end of the world...but he might also be the key to saving it, just like we were led to believe in the first place." There were some exchanged glances before Ky spoke. "We've put together everything we've found regarding Thanatos and his role in ending the Apocalypse, including a mishmash of texts about a birth weakening Pestilence's heart. And you know the part in Thanatos's prophecy about a cry?"

She nodded. Than's prophecy, which was part of the *Daemonica*'s apocalyptic prediction, was burned into her brain like a brand. *Behold! Innocence is Death's curse, his hunger his burden, a blade his Deliverance. The Doom Star cometh if the cry fails.*

"Well," Kynan continued, "it fits with a passage from the *Torran*."

Arik frowned. "What's a Torran?" Like Decker, Arik was both an Army R-XR member and had only recently been named a Guardian. Regan hadn't yet had the opportunity to go through the thing, but she'd love to get her hands on it. "You know how humans have a bazillion different religions, and each of those religions breaks off into smaller denominations? Like, within the designation of Christianity, there are Catholics, Baptists, Protestants... and even those branch off into sects of varying ideology. Well, demons have something similar. The *Daemonica* is their bible for the largest of their religions, but they have others. One of the religions, Bletouth, broke apart into two very different ideals. There was a nasty war, and in the end, their religious book was torn in half, and each given a name. The *Torran* and the *Toreign*."

"We've had a copy of the *Toreign* for centuries, but we didn't procure a *Torran* until a couple of months ago, so we're only now uncovering useful info." Ky rubbed the back of his neck. "So anyway, inside the *Torran*, we found a passage relating to the Horsemen and the Apocalypse. It says, 'First cry weakens the heart...a plunge of the blade ends it.' Basically, we think that the baby's birth will turn Pestilence mortal for a short period of time, allowing 'the blade,' Deliverance, to kill him."

Deliverance was a dagger forged thousands of years ago as a weapon against the Horsemen—the only weapon believed to hold the power to kill them. Unfortunately, as they'd learned eight months ago, the blade wasn't effective against Pestilence.

"That's why you came to headquarters the night I was attacked by the vampire. To discuss rousing Thanatos so he could be there for the baby's birth," she mused. "So what about the part of his prophecy that mentions the Doom Star?"

"Some of us believe the Doom Star is Halley's Comet. The comet has been associated with everything from godly messages to the devil's tool to the Star of Bethlehem. We think that if Pestilence isn't killed at the baby's first cry, the next opportunity won't happen until Halley's Comet next appears."

She could predict where this was going. "And I'll bet it won't show its comet-y face anytime soon."

"The year twenty sixty-one."

Jesus. By then there might not be much of a world left to save. She considered everything Ky and Decker had told her. "Why didn't you guys tell me any of this sooner?"

Kynan wiped a trickle of blood from his temple with the back of his hand. "You've got enough to deal with. We didn't want to get your hopes up before we got everything figured out."

Regan didn't like being kept out of the loop, but at this point, it hardly mattered. Not when the world was collapsing around them.

Something beeped, and Ky dug a cell phone out of his pocket. After pushing a button, he propped the phone on Than's desk, and both Lance and Val offered greetings over the speaker.

"Are we clear to talk?" Val asked.

"Right now there are only Aegi in the room," Ky said.

"Good," Val said. "What's going on on your end?"

Regan sat up. "I was about to tell these guys to take me back with them. You'll all need my help—"

"The best thing you can do right now is stay safe," Kynan said. "Never thought I'd say this, but I think you're better off here with Than."

Regan's stomach rolled. "What? Are you kidding me? I can't stay here."

"Kynan's right," Decker said. "As much as I hate it, we can't risk moving you around."

"Yes, you can." Her voice cracked. "You have to." *You're going to pleasure me. Whenever I want. Every. Single. Night.* Oh, God. "I can stay at a regional headquarters."

"Regan." Kynan's military bark snapped her to immediate attention, and she realized she'd been panicking.

Babbling. "If Thanatos can sense the baby, he can find you. We can't risk him coming for you and Pestilence tracking him."

"He'll agree to not go after me. He'll understand."

Arik snorted. "Thanatos? Understand? Have you even met him?"

"I agree," Kynan said. "If you were Gem, I wouldn't let you out of my sight. He's not going to let you go."

"This place is crawling with vampires," she reminded them. "And in case you forgot, one of them tried to kill me." Yes, Thanatos had explained that the vamp hadn't been his, but right now, she'd take any argument to get away from here.

"*Tried*," Decker said. "You could have killed him with your power. You can defend yourself."

Did she dare tell them that her defensive ability had failed? Maybe it was just a fluke. And it wouldn't change anyone's mind, anyway. Ultimately, they were right. As much as she hated to think it, she probably was safest here, at least for now.

Val's voice crackled over the airwaves. "This will also put you in a unique position to study the daywalkers."

"Yeah," Lance chimed in. "Give you something useful to do."

She glared at the phone as if Lance could see her expression. "As if gestating a baby that might save the world isn't enough?"

She could almost hear Lance's shrug. "Once the kid pops out, you'll be dead weight again."

"Shut up, asshole." Kynan said.

Decker shoved to his feet as if ready to go through the speaker and kick some ass. "You're such a dick."

"It's okay," Regan said. "We're all stressed." But damn, Lance had struck a nerve.

Oh, she was used to his clumsy barbs, but this one was actually spot on. She'd never felt as if she had as much to offer as the other Elders, and she suspected that her abilities were the only reason she'd been promoted. That, and the fact that Lance had once told her that they wanted to keep an eye on her. The soul-sucking ability was dangerous, and they wanted her leashed.

"Fuck you," Lance muttered. "I was just trying to make sure she had something useful to do. Don't want her going the way of her Mama."

The room exploded in curses, so many insults flying at Lance that Regan couldn't separate them. She wasn't her mother. Yes, she may be giving her child up for a better life, but she wasn't going to kill herself. Even in the first two months after that horrible night with Thanatos, when she'd nosedived into such a deep state of depression and guilt that she could barely leave her bed, she hadn't thought about suicide.

Granted, she might have considered dropping back into the fighting ranks again after the baby was born, because dying in battle wasn't killing yourself, right? Not if dying wasn't the goal, the way it had been for her mother.

Her stomach turned over again, threatening to spill, and she shoved to her feet and brushed past Limos, who was just entering the room. "I . . . um . . . I need to go."

Decker moved toward her. "Regan?"

"I'm okay." She held up her hand to hold them off. "I just need a minute."

With that, she ran as fast as she could to the bedroom, where she dashed into the bathroom and lost her last meal.

Eleven

The tap on the bedroom door came as Regan finished brushing her teeth with one of the spare toothbrushes she'd found in Than's master bathroom cabinet.

"I really don't want to talk to you, Thanatos," she called out, realizing how stupid it was to say that before the sentence was even out of her mouth: Thanatos wouldn't have knocked. He'd have barged in like a pissed-off bear awakened from hibernation.

She put away the toothbrush as Decker's muffled voice came through the door. "It's not Thanatos."

"Oh." She waddled into the bedroom and sank onto the bed. "Come in."

Decker slipped inside, silent as a ghost. For a big guy, he was remarkably agile. Then again, so was Thanatos... agile in ways her body warmed to think about.

"You okay?" Decker asked.

"Yeah."

"Don't let Lance get to you. I think his mama's milk was curdled."

She sighed. "It's not Lance. It's everything. I feel so useless. I should have been there today. I could have helped."

"Sounds like no one could have helped. You'd have just gotten yourself killed."

Her breath shuddered out of her. He was probably right, but that didn't lessen the guilt of not being with her colleagues when they needed her. It also drove home the fact that the crisis was worse than she'd been willing to admit.

"You know, all this time, even when things looked like they were at their worst, I never doubted we'd beat Pestilence and stop the Apocalypse."

"We will," Decker said fiercely. "We'll find a way."

"I'm not so sure anymore." It hurt to say that, and part of her couldn't believe she *had* said it. Defeat had never been an option for her. She'd fought for her very life from the day she was born. Now it seemed as if fighting might only drag out the inevitable. "With headquarters compromised, Pestilence has not only hamstrung us, he's crippled our ability to organize and command, not to mention that this has to be a huge blow to every Guardian's confidence."

"Stop." Decker sat down next to her. "We have to maintain hope." He looked down at her belly. "And that peanut in there is hope."

She offered him a thin smile. "You're one of the only people besides Kynan who can say that without cringing."

"Because it's a baby. It's not a monster, no matter what anyone else thinks."

"Thank you." She eyed the bed pillows and fought the urge to straighten them. "Not to be rude, but…is there a reason you're here?" No one but Suzi had ever bothered to keep Regan company.

"That's what I've always liked about you," Deck said. "No bullshit." He sobered, and she braced herself for whatever was coming. "I wanted to give you a heads up on a call Kynan just got from Sammara in the Tech Department. She ran a check of headquarters' computers."

Alarm bells clanged in her skull. "Don't tell me Pestilence got our personnel records."

"He did." Decker's tone was weary, his eyes tired. "And worse, he got the locations of every Aegis cell worldwide."

"Oh, Jesus," she rasped. "The slaughter is going to be off the charts."

"The good news is that the information is encrypted," Decker said. "We have time, but maybe only a matter of days."

And after that, Guardians could very well become an endangered species.

Thanatos stalked into his library and went on instant alert. Arik and Limos were on the couch, and Ky was draped bonelessly in one of the armchairs. Someone, probably Arik, had found Than's med kit and tended to Kynan's wounds, but he was the grayish color of a dead bile slug, and he clearly needed medical attention.

But where the hell was Regan? "Where is she?" The question came out as more of a bark, but Thanatos didn't give a shit if he sounded hyper and grumpy, and maybe a little too freaked out that Regan was missing.

"She's in the bedroom," Limos said calmly. "I think she had to puke."

Thanatos started out the door, but Arik called him back. "Don't, man. Give her a few minutes. She just lost a bunch of colleagues and friends, thanks to your brother."

"My brother. Not me."

"Idiot." Arik beaned Than in the chest with a pencil. "You're five thousand years old and still don't know anything about humans."

Than looked down at the pencil and considered kabobbing his brother-in-law with it. "Because I don't hang around with humans."

"Just trust me on this," Arik said, and Limos nodded in agreement. "Your brother, who you want to save, just destroyed Regan's world. You're probably the last person she wants to see right now. Well, second to last. Pestilence wins first place."

Than still didn't understand why he should be held responsible for Pestilence's actions, but he'd listen to the human, since Arik knew Regan better than he did. Which rankled.

Limos leaned forward on the couch, bracing her forearms on her knees. "These guys just filled me in on some important shit about your prophecy." She blew out a long breath. "Damn, Than, there might be an end to all of this in sight."

Than listened as Ky laid out the prophecy about the baby's cry—and the fact that burying Deliverance in Pestilence's heart while it was weakened would kill him.

Made sense... but Than didn't like it. He didn't want to kill his brother. He wanted to save him.

"What about the Halley's Comet Doom Star thing?" Than asked. "I found something in one of my shrines that indicates I can save him by using Deliverance at a particular time. What if that's what the Doom Star part of the prophecy is about?"

Ky rubbed his eyes and swore. "Hadn't thought of that."

"Doesn't matter," Arik said. The comet won't return to Earth until twenty sixty-one. We can't wait that long."

The easy way Arik said it, as if waiting to save Reseph wasn't even an option, pissed Than the hell off. Yeah, he got it. He did. Dicking around for half a century waiting for a damned comet while Pestilence ravaged mankind and demons warred with each other wasn't exactly an option. But dammit, Reseph was Than's brother, and the male he'd once been deserved a little more respect.

Instead of knocking Arik across the room, Than swung around to Kynan and held out the book he'd fetched from the vault in the dungeon where he kept his most priceless items. "It's a history of angels. I flagged some passages about *qeres*."

"Damn." Kynan took the book. "We don't even have this. Where did you get it?"

"Found it in a burial chamber outside Babylon."

Ky cocked a dark eyebrow. "Long time ago."

"You could say that." Than glanced at everyone as he spoke. "It says *qeres* incapacitates angels, which you know. But it also lists one of its ingredients. 'Poison like the hounds of hell.'"

"You think it's made of hellhound saliva?" Arik asked.

"I don't know. But if it works like it, *qeres* could, potentially, work on us."

Limos's head whipped around. "Pestilence. We could use it on him."

"Exactly. He's become nearly immune to hellhound venom, but *qeres* has other properties. He may be vulnerable to it."

"And then what?" Kynan smoothed his long fingers over the leather binding. "You incapacitate him, but what if the effect is only temporary? We don't have much of the stuff, and once it runs out, there's no way to hold him."

"What about Regan?" Limos asked. "Her power held you for a few minutes. Maybe it would work on Pestilence."

The reminder made Than twitchy, not because he'd been held immobile and helpless, but because all he could think about was Regan on top of him, her naked body undulating, her panting breaths matching his as they neared orgasm.

"Even if she can hold Pest while in freaking labor," Arik said, "what then? If we miss the incredibly narrow window of the baby's cry, Deliverance won't kill him. Then we definitely have to wait for the comet."

Thanatos's pulse pounded in his temples at the thought of killing his brother.

"What if we freeze him?" Arik asked. "You know, like Han Solo."

Thanatos shot Arik an are-you-kidding-me look. "Yeah...carbonite freezing machines might be a little hard to come by, given that we don't live in the *Star Wars* universe."

"Ass," Arik muttered. "I'm talking about ice. Flash freeze him with liquid nitrogen or something."

Limos toyed with the orange flower in her hair. "Even if you could lure him into a trap like that, he'll unfreeze in minutes."

Kynan shifted in his chair with a wince. No doubt his massive injuries were agonizing. They were also leaving blood all over Than's furniture. "So what we're left with is trying to hunt him down and incapacitate him while we wait for your son to cry."

Son. Than wondered if he'd ever get used to hearing that. "Yeah, and you wanna explain why the fuck you believed this evidence you found that said my kid would save the world?"

"Because Regan inspected the scroll your brother planted for us to find," Kynan said. "At the time, we didn't know it was a setup, but Regan discovered that the author believed the prophecy they wrote."

Thanatos picked up Reseph's iPod for no other reason than to remind himself that the male who had loaded the mp3 player with country music would hate himself for what Pestilence was doing. "So we know Pestilence didn't write it. It was his trick to take my virginity."

"And that's what's so weird about the situation," Ky replied. "*He* thought it was a trick, but the author thought it was true, and it might be true after all. So did the author believe your son will save the world because they know something we don't? If that's the case, they may be working against Pestilence rather than with him."

Thanatos really wanted to have a chat with this mysterious author. "We have to find whoever penned the baby prophecy. Have you talked to Reaver or Harvester? Maybe they can provide some insight."

Limos tucked herself more fully against Arik. If she got any closer she'd be up his nose. "The last time I talked to them... what, a month ago? They said they didn't know anything. Or if they do, they aren't talking because it's against their stupid Watcher rules."

"And don't get them in the same room together," Arik said. "Christ, we had to rebuild half of Limos's party house after our last conversation with them."

"Why?"

Limos studied her nails, painted yellow and pink today. "They got into a fight. It was like two jumbo jets colliding in mid-air."

Harvester and Reaver had never been fond of each other, but they didn't usually get physical. "What were they fighting about?"

"Dunno." Arik lifted one shoulder in a shrug. "They didn't say a word. We were talking to Harvester, and Reaver showed up and they went at it."

"And that's the last time anyone has seen them?" Than asked.

"Yep."

Those damned angels. Yeah, the Horsemen could summon them, but that didn't mean they'd arrive in a timely manner. They seemed to delight in showing up only at their own convenience. Did Reaver know about Pestilence's attack on the Aegis? Did he even know Regan was pregnant? Speaking of which, she'd been gone too long for his comfort. And, wait... "Where's Decker?"

"He went to check on Regan—" Limos hadn't even finished her sentence before Than was halfway down the hall.

Insane, possessive anger clawed at him as he threw open the bedroom door. The sight of Decker sitting so close to Regan spiked Thanatos's anger meter up to critical. Before he knew it, he had his fist in Decker's T-shirt collar and had thrown the human across the room. In the next instant, Regan was on her feet, putting her body between them.

"Stop it! Decker was only talking to me."

Decker picked himself up, calmly brushed himself off, and shot Thanatos the bird. "You know what you need? An old-fashioned ass-whupping."

"You going to be the one to give it to me?" Than taunted.

Decker shook his head. "As much as I'd like to, I'm not stupid. But I'm also not leaving unless Regan tells me to go."

Thanatos's respect for the male went up by a point. Which gave him a grand total of one point. On a scale from zero to a hundred. Still, you had to credit a guy who knew how to check his testosterone at the door and not try to beat down a male who could squash him with a finger.

"It's okay, Deck," Regan said, with way too much familiarity and affection than Thanatos liked. "You can go."

"You sure?" Decker gave Thanatos the evil eye.

"She's sure," Than growled, at the same time Regan said, "I'm sure."

Decker shot Thanatos another hateful glare as he moved to the door, and the second he was gone, Thanatos swung around to Regan. "You are never to be alone in a bedroom with a male."

She snorted. "You have no say over who I have in my

bedroom. If I want to invite the entire Miami Dolphins team into my bed and have a big orgy while covered in chocolate sauce, you have no say in that whatsoever."

The brief image set fire to his blood, but he kept his temper on simmer, unwilling to let her bait him. Still, he kind of wanted to hunt down every player on the football team and turn them into stains on the Astroturf.

"My house," he gritted out, "my rules. No chocolate NFL orgies in my keep. I think that's a reasonable request."

"For Christ's sake," she said, throwing up her arms. "Do you seriously think my mind is set on getting Decker into bed?"

"He wants you."

"No, he doesn't. And even if he did, it's not like I'm a real prize right now. My feet are swollen like overcooked hot dogs, I have stretch marks, I'm fat and ugly and awkward—"

"Stop." He clenched his fists at his sides to keep from reaching for her. She was so pretty in her indignation, her cheeks pink with a delicate blush, her dark hair framing her face in tousled waves that gave her a wild fierceness that wasn't diminished by her pregnancy at all. "Never say that to me again. You aren't fat or ugly. There's nothing more beautiful than a woman carrying her mate's child, and—" He broke off with a horrified grunt. Mate? What an idiot. "Not that you're my mate. It's just that breeding women are—"

Once more, he broke off, aghast at his rambling, moronic self. Humiliation turned his cheeks hot, and he spun around, intent on leaving, but her soft voice stopped him, and he swung back around.

"Breeding? Look, if I'm going to stay here, we'd better set some ground rules."

"Like?"

"Like you aren't going to order me around. And I get my own bedroom. And I want ice cream. The good stuff, not the icky ice milk crap."

He cocked a tawny eyebrow. "Anything else?"

His sarcasm wasn't lost on her, but she ignored it. "Yes. While we're at it, I want some Guardians here with me."

Regan held her breath, wondering if she'd gone too far as he moved toward her, his big shoulders rolling, his eyes flashing. When he was close enough that their bellies touched, he dipped his head so low she thought he was going to kiss her.

Crazily, she didn't know if that would be a good thing or a bad one.

"Here's how this goes. No Guardians. I don't trust any of them, including you. You can have as much ice cream as you want. I doubt I'll stop ordering you around." He turned his face away and put his lips to her ear. "And you don't get your own bedroom. You sleep here. With me. Remember what I said."

How could she forget? *For the next eight and a half months, you're going to be mine. Every. Night.*

Reaching up, she fisted a handful of silky hair and forced his face back toward hers. His firm lips were a mere inch from hers, and she went up on her toes to get even closer, so close his heat caressed her skin.

"Yeah?" she murmured. "Want to wager on that, Horseman? You'll be dying to get rid of me long before eight and a half months comes around."

He brushed the tip of his finger along her jaw, a teasing, sensual touch that didn't match up with what he said next. "I already am."

There was no reason, none whatsoever, for the sting of rejection Than's words brought. But there it was. Dropping back down on her heels, she released him.

"Then let me go. I get why I can't leave right now, but when The Aegis has a new, secure headquarters, let me go."

"Do you know how often I pleaded with Ares and Limos to do the same to me over these last months? Not aloud, since I couldn't speak, but in my head."

What did one say to that? Regan could only think of one, lame thing. "I'm sorry—"

"You're sorry? Really?" His voice became a low, silky whisper. "Then prove it."

His hand snapped to up to grab hers, and as her heart pounded out of control against her rib cage, he slapped her palm against his chest. Slowly, so slowly, he dragged her hand down. She tried to stop him, but she was no match for his strength. Her palm slid over hard, rolling abs and, guided by Thanatos, slipped lower, to the thick length behind the fly of his pants.

God, he was so gloriously hard, his cock pressing so firmly against the fabric that she could feel the curves that defined the smooth blunt head and the rigid shaft.

Clearing her throat, she managed a raspy, "You're insane."

"Yeah?" He stared down at her, his guttural words rumbling through her in a wave of heat. "I was a virgin before you. You woke a sleeping demon, Regan. I tried to sate it myself, but failed. Now you're going to deal with the consequences."

With that, he broke away from her and strode out of the room, leaving her confused, pissed off, and...really, *really* achy.

Things were getting hairy.

In the last nine months, the human realm had become a battleground, and Reaver had spent much of it in training, working to hone his battle and healing skills in preparation for Armageddon. But for the last month he'd immersed himself in the heavenly Hall of Records, desperate to find any scrap of knowledge that might reveal something about Harvester's history.

He'd been gunning for her for nine months, ever since she'd taken him captive in Sheoul, cut off his wings, and tried to get him addicted to marrow wine. He couldn't kill her, not while she was assigned as the Horsemen's evil Watcher, but he suspected she'd been involved in the deception that had led to Regan's pregnancy, and if so, she'd be fired—likely with actual fire—and destroyed.

Smiling at that thought, he popped into Than's place, and instantly the smile disappeared. If the grim expressions on everyone's faces hadn't been a clue that something was wrong, the fact that Kynan was torn up was proof.

"What happened?"

Limos attacked him with a huge hug, as usual, and as soon as she stepped back, Kynan stood with a wince. "You don't know?"

Reaver crossed to him and gently palmed his shoulder. Divine energy flowed through Reaver and into Kynan, and in an instant, he was partially healed. As a battle angel, Reaver's healing abilities were limited, but his recent training had given him some small talent for repairing damage caused by fallen angels.

"If I knew what happened, I wouldn't be asking," Reaver said wryly.

"Where have you been?" Limos interrupted.

"In the Hall of Records."

"For a month?"

"It was only hours for me. Time runs differently in Heaven." He focused on Ky. "Now, what happened? And why is everyone here? Where's Thanatos?"

"I'm right here." Than emerged from the dark shadows of the hallway, a hot flush coloring his skin.

"The baby has been born?"

Than snorted. "Great. You were in on it, too? You knew they were planning to give my kid away?"

"Someone had better tell me what is going on," Reaver said slowly. "Right freaking now."

"Regan is here," Limos said brightly. "Than kidnapped her."

Thanatos folded his arms across his chest as if waiting for Reaver to dig into him. Reaver wasn't going to waste the time. "And the baby?"

"Still percolating," Than said. "They're both safe in my bedroom. The baby seems to be offering her some protection."

A blast of rare anger vibrated the very air around Kynan. "She wouldn't need that protection if you'd left them at headquarters instead of kidnapping them like a caveman. Pestilence would never have found HQ if not for you."

Reaver whipped his head around to Than. "You were at Aegis HQ?"

"Yeah," Ky gritted out. "And now, thanks to him, Pestilence was, too."

"The damage?"

"We're fucked." Ky ran his hand through his dark hair, leaving behind spiky grooves. "Dozens dead. Prisoners loosed. Possible compromise of our regional cells."

"Damn," Reaver breathed.

Kynan flexed his fingers as if testing them. At least one had been broken before Reaver arrived. "Do you know why Pestilence would be looking for a dagger called Wormwood?"

"No, why?" Reaver replied.

"Pestilence had a bug up his ass about it," Kynan said. "It's not all bad news, though. We've got some new leads on a way to stop Pestilence." Kynan filled in Reaver about the discoveries they'd made in the *Torran*.

"But there's no way to know if the writings are just ramblings," Reaver said. "Just because someone wrote it doesn't make it true."

Kynan scrubbed his hand over his face. "We have to proceed as if it's true. We don't have a choice."

The timing of the baby's cry had been confirmed to both Reaver and Harvester by their bosses soon after Than's baby was conceived. Pestilence could, indeed, be stopped at that moment, but Reaver had no idea what was up with the Doom Star part of the prophecy. Not that he could discuss it with the Horsemen even if he knew.

"Do you know how to incapacitate Pestilence so you'll have him for the birth?" he asked.

"The Aegis might be the answer to that," Than said. "They have *qeres*."

Of course. Pestilence, being half angel, might be susceptible to the substance.

"Do you know if it'll work?" Ky asked.

Reaver shook his head. "I don't know, but even if I did—"

"Yeah, yeah," Limos muttered. "You couldn't tell us. Stupid Watcher rules."

"Speaking of rules," Reaver said, "be careful what you say in front of Harvester."

"Why? What's going on with you two?" Arik asked.

"Nothing you need to worry about." Reaver glanced over at Than. "What's going on with the baby? You mentioned it's protecting her?"

"Looks like," Than said. "Demons and humans can't seem to touch her without getting tossed, and a frost demon's breath attack should have caused a lot more damage."

Reaver frowned. "Did this all start recently? Within the last week or two?"

"Yeah," Than said. "How'd you know?"

Smiling, Reaver clapped Than on the shoulder. "Because the baby is part angel. And angels, at around the eighth month in the womb, start showing signs of the powers they'll have. Cool. Sounds like kiddo is going to have some battle angel in him."

Thanatos beamed, and Reaver nearly choked on the good kind of surprise he never got from that Horseman. It was nice to see him glowing with such pride in his offspring.

"Is there any way around it?" Than asked. "I mean, it's cool, like you said, but he could interfere with people trying to help Regan. Like doctors."

Yes, there was, but neutralizing an angel infant meant using evil magic and blood sacrifice, which also carried a risk to the infant and could do massive damage to the mother. Even if Reaver could share the information, he wouldn't.

"I can't say, but I can tell you that you're better off using your time to capture Pestilence." Reaver nodded toward the hallway. "Speaking of the baby, I'm going to see Regan."

That fast, Thanatos lost the happy-happy and moved to bar Reaver's path.

"Don't take her from me, Reaver." Than's stance was rigid, aggressive, but his voice revealed something Reaver had never heard from the Horseman: vulnerability.

"I won't," Reaver assured him. "I swear." With The Aegis compromised, she was probably safest with Thanatos anyway.

But in a way, that was like saying she was safer with a python than a cobra.

Twelve

Regan spent a few minutes pacing, breathing, and counting through the OCD attack that was screaming for her to take control of her immediate situation. Even if all that meant was that she rearranged the bedroom to suit her, the desire to *do something* was stretching her like a rubber band on the verge of snapping.

A tap at the door broke her out of her thoughts. She opened the door...and gaped.

Standing in the doorway was an angel. A perfect specimen of a male, his shimmering golden hair falling in immaculate waves around his broad shoulders, his piercing sapphire eyes sharp with intelligence. He was stunning.

She'd been hearing stories of the infamous Reaver for years, had even seen him and another angel named Gethel a couple of years ago in Egypt. Back then, he'd been a fallen angel, but he'd been redeemed before her very eyes after a near-apocalyptic battle in which another fallen angel had very nearly opened the gates of Heaven to the evil forces of Hell.

He smiled, and she swore he sort of ... glowed.

"Hi, Regan." Reaver stepped inside the room, and she wondered if Thanatos was going to have a cow about *this* male being in a bedroom with her. "How are you feeling?"

Voice. She had to find her voice. "Ah ..." She cleared her throat. It wasn't every day you spoke to an angel dressed in expensive slacks and a silk shirt that matched his eyes. "Fine." *Fine?* Dolt.

"And the baby?"

Her hand fell automatically to her belly. "Hungry."

Cocking his head, Reaver eyed her stomach. "He won't let me touch you."

"The baby seems to be a bit protective."

Reaver's jewel-like eyes flicked up. "Not the baby. Thanatos."

"I—what?"

"Not that I would touch you. I'm just saying. He's as protective of you as the child is."

Her mouth fell open again, but she snapped it shut and shook her head. "Thanatos hates me."

"He might tell himself that, and he might even believe it," Reaver said. "But it's not true."

She sighed. "For an angel, you're sort of ... um ..."

"Naive?" His smile got wider. "Trust me, I spent enough time with demons to not be naive about anything ever again."

Could Reaver be right about Thanatos? Between his fits of being angry with her, he did have moments of ... well, she could almost call it tenderness. Tenderness that always made her lower her guard when she should be not only raising it, but fortifying it. But what if Reaver was right? Could he get past what she'd done to him? Could *she* get past it?

The answer to those questions came quickly. The pain she'd caused was a monumental hurdle they'd never clear. No amount of revenge he extracted from her was going to ease her guilt or heal his wounds.

No, Reaver wasn't right about Thanatos. She met his gaze steadily, too mentally exhausted from the day's events to keep circling around whatever the angel had come for. "Forgive me, Reaver, but why are you here?"

"To the point. I like that." His voice was soft, but firm. "I'm here because technically, I can't help the Horsemen with anything that relates to the Apocalypse. But I can help them with other things."

"Other things?"

"Relationships."

She barked out a laugh. "Thanatos and I don't have a relationship."

"You're about to be parents. That's the most intimate relationship there is."

Maybe for normal people. But there was nothing normal about Thanatos or the way this child had been conceived. "This baby belongs to Kynan and Gem. Didn't anyone tell you?"

"I know what the plan was," Reaver began, "and Kynan and Gem would be wonderful parents to your son. But you and Thanatos together would be even better."

Regan nearly choked. "We'd kill each other." Besides, she knew nothing about being a mother, and the baby deserved better. And what would happen when he got older and learned what she'd done? He'd hate her. He wouldn't want her. An awful sorrow clawed at her, and she had to force herself to speak without a hitch in her voice. "Trust me, the plan with Gem and Ky is for the best."

"Is it?"

"Yes. I—"

Reaver held up his hand, the simple but commanding gesture shutting her down instantly. "I know the arguments. I know the reason for giving the baby to Ky and Gem was to keep it hidden from enemies. But I also know Thanatos. He doesn't let things go easily."

Great. Just great. She didn't know what to say to that, but it turned out she didn't need to say anything. Reaver moved to the door.

"Take care of yourself, Regan. And be...gentle... with Thanatos."

"Gentle?" There she went gaping again. "He's a five-thousand-year-old warrior named Death. I can't think of anyone who is in less need of kid gloves."

A small smile ruffled the corners of Reaver's mouth. "Of all the Horsemen, he's the one most in need."

"I don't understand."

"You will." He opened the door. "Be safe."

Be safe. She was living with a man named Death, his evil brother Pestilence was trying to kill her, The Aegis was under attack and its members were walking around with prices on their heads. *Safe* seemed like a pipe dream right now.

Everything was falling apart. Her friends were dead, her guilt about what she'd done to Thanatos was raging, and now that Pestilence knew she was pregnant, her baby was in terrible danger. Regan sucked air, trying to keep from hyperventilating.

Didn't work.

She pinged around the room like a ricocheting bullet, her mind a whirlwind as she tried to focus on something to alleviate her racing mind. When her gaze lit on a scattered collection of tiny pewter soldiers on Than's dresser, that focus sharpened into a plan.

She fell on the little soldiers like a cat on a flock of chicks.

"They're out of order," she whispered, as she grouped the toys into trios, all perfectly spaced an inch apart. Next, she hit the wardrobe, where she rearranged Than's clothes by color...which was easy, considering most everything was black. She spaced his hangers so there was an inch between each, and then she lined up the boots, running shoes, and flip-flops at the bottom of the wardrobe.

The bed. The bed was off-center in the room. And it was facing the wrong direction. The headboard needed to be beneath the window.

She shoved at it, but the thing must have been made from solid logs. She marched over to the door, whipped it open, and as suspected, there was a vampire standing guard a few feet away.

"What's your name?"

"Peter."

"Peter?" What kind of scary vampire name was that? His accent, Russian, she thought, was scarier than his name. And his slicked-back blond hair. Whatever. "I need your help," she said crisply.

"I can get Thanatos."

"I just need help moving the bed."

He looked at her like she was a nutcase, but he shoved the giant thing where she wanted it. "The dresser, too. It needs to go three inches to the right." She got another *you're insane* look, but he moved the dresser.

When he finished, he hightailed it toward the door. He moved fast, too fast for her to shift out of his way, and his arm slammed into her shoulder on his way past. The next thing she knew, he was sailing through the air. At least, he was until the wall interrupted his flight and he crumpled to the floor.

"Oh, crap." Regan started toward him. "Sorry. That hasn't happened to any other vampires."

Peter came to his feet, fangs bared. Fangs...wait, they were big, but not super-sized.

"Are you a daywalker?" she asked.

"Fuck no." The way he said it, as if it was an insult, was curious.

"The one who tried to stop me from leaving earlier... is he a daywalker?"

"*Was* he, you mean? Yes, he was."

Okay, well, that answered the question about whether or not Thanatos had killed him. But why would day-walkers be able to touch her, but not the common night-walkers?

"I should thank you," Peter said. "He was a bastard. But watch your back, slayer. There are daywalkers who aren't as thrilled about his demise as my night brethren and I are." Peter left, this time giving her a wide berth. He might not be a scary vampire, but he was smart.

Regan pondered the new information and the fact that Peter had helped her by giving her a warning as she went to work on the drawers—dresser drawers, bathroom

drawers...everything she could find. She didn't come up
with any reasonable explanations for the difference in the
baby's reaction to the vampires, but hey, Thanatos got his
socks folded properly and his toothpaste tube rolled so
there were no dents.

She set her sights on the window next...a window that
was narrow, filled with thick, medieval-style glass. The
bubbles in it, unevenly spaced and multiple sizes, were
going to give her seizures. She couldn't fix it, but she
could hide it. Oh, it would still bother her, but hopefully if
it was out of sight, she'd be okay.

She grabbed one of Than's T-shirts from a drawer and
stuffed it into the recessed sill against the window.

But when it fell, wadded up and wrinkled onto the bed,
to the exact spot on the mattress where she and Thanatos
had had sex, it struck her that no, nothing was ever going
to be okay again.

Once everyone was out of his keep, Thanatos considered
his next move. The last twenty-four hours had been a
nightmare whirlwind, and unfortunately, he had a feeling
that the nightmare was only just beginning.

Pestilence had managed to outsmart all of them, and
if they couldn't stop him, Than wouldn't have a chance to
enjoy fatherhood. And he definitely wanted to be a father.
It was something he'd never thought he'd be, and as furious as he was with Regan for using him to get pregnant,
he was just as thrilled that she *was* pregnant.

It was so fucked up. Her betrayal was giving him what
he'd most wanted in life. Even more fucked up was the
fact that he was stung by her betrayal, but still so damned

possessive. He'd come uncorked when he'd seen Regan with Decker, and his inner caveman had done a cock-blocking, chest-pounding, you-mine bunch of bullshit with some growls and threats thrown in for good measure.

Then he'd compounded his stupidity by bringing sex into the situation again. But dammit, he'd been pissed when she'd begged to go back to The Aegis. She was pregnant, and it was *his* job to take care of her. He'd missed so much that he should have been a part of, and all he wanted was these last few days.

On his arm, Styx bucked, sensing Than's agitation and still restless after months of inactivity. "Styx, out."

The stallion materialized in the middle of the room and did a playful crowhop before looking around for his Jolly Ball. Styx loved to fling the thing around by the handle, especially inside the keep, where his aim—for breakable objects and vampires, was impressive.

Than left him to find his toy and went in search of Artur, whom he found in the kitchen, supervising the final touches on dinner.

"Sire." Artur inclined his head in greeting. "I hear Styx. Shall I take a beer to him?"

The horse loved cheap beer, and Than figured giving him a can now and then wouldn't hurt, seeing how Styx was pretty much immortal. "Send someone else. I need to talk to you."

Artur assigned Viktor to beer duty, and followed Than outside into the courtyard just off the kitchen's side entrance.

"Yes, *Bludrexe*?"

"Artur, I need baby things."

From the way Artur's brows shot up, what Than said

was not what the vampire had been expecting to hear. "Baby things?"

What a weird conversation to be having with an ancient vampire. "You know, things babies need. Clothes and bottles and diapers. Stuff like that. Oh, and books. Definitely books. Can you do some shopping?"

"Ah...yes, sire."

"Not too much," Than said quickly. "Just the basics. I want to buy the other stuff myself." Man, he was going to look like a fool in Babies "R" Us, wasn't he? "And..." He trailed off, his cheeks heating. "And could you get some lotion? Something pregnant women use for stretch marks? And back rubs?" Regan had mentioned the stretch marks, and although Than hadn't noticed any, he had seen the way she winced when she reached behind to her back.

"Yes, sire. Is that all?"

"I think so. Oh, wait. And something for swollen feet."

"I'll take care of it. Will you be killing any more of us today?" Artur's tone was so deadpan that Thanatos had to rerun that last sentence in his mind a couple of times to make sure he'd heard it right. Of all Than's vampires, only Artur would be brave enough to say that.

"No plans right now," Than said. "But that could always change. Why? Are the others concerned?"

Artur inclined his head. "No one disputes your right to protect your female and son, but it's not like you to be so out of control with us in your own home."

Yeah, that was weighing on Thanatos, too. He'd snapped, had hardly realized what he'd done until it was over and Regan was gone. Had he kept his cool, the vampire would have been in the dungeon and Regan would never have been able to get out of the keep to get attacked by the frost demon.

The kitchen door opened, and Peter stepped out. "Your, um, *the* Aegi female is acting crazy."

"You have to be more specific," Than sighed, "since that seems to be her natural state."

"She's rearranging your room as if her life depends on it."

Rearranging his room? No, not even close. Regan was rearranging his entire freaking *life*.

Thirteen

"Woman, what are you doing?"

Choking on a startled scream, Regan spun around to Than, who stood in the doorway, looking utterly perplexed. At some point, he'd changed into a pair of black leather pants and a black turtleneck that emphasized his hard, masculine body. Every feminine instinct she had came awake and started panting despite the inappropriateness of the situation.

"I'm rearranging." At least her voice didn't sound as breathless as she felt. "If I'm going to be a prisoner, I want to be a comfortable one."

"You aren't a prisoner."

"Really?" She crossed her arms over her chest. "Can I leave?"

He folded his arms across his chest in blatant mockery. "No."

"So I'm curious about how that doesn't make me a prisoner."

"You're here by necessity now, Regan."

Grudgingly, she had to admit he was right. Not out loud, of course. Not when she knew damned good and well he'd keep her here even if she didn't need to be for her own safety.

"So why are you here?" she asked. "To tell me more about the demon I woke in you?" The one he wanted her to...sate.

That thought shouldn't make her pulse pick up the way it did.

His eyes flared with heat, and she waited for the raunchy comeback. "We need to talk. We can do it over dinner."

Well, that wasn't the response she'd expected. "Dinner?"

"Yes. It's an interesting concept that's been around as long as I can remember. Food is served at a table, and we eat it."

She narrowed her eyes at him. "There is something seriously wrong with you." When he said nothing, she followed his gaze. Her belly. He was looking at her belly, and the expression on his face, one of tender longing, touched her someplace deep inside. Someplace she hadn't even known existed, but it was now all mushy and warm. "Than?" She said quietly, remembering Reaver asking her to be gentle with him. "You can touch, if you want."

His gaze snapped up. "No. I...ah..."

"It's okay." Slowly, she took his hand and brought it toward her.

The moment she put his palm to her stomach, the baby kicked. A slow smile spread across Than's face. God, she'd never seen anything so beautiful or sweet. This deadly, powerful warrior was lost to a tiny, unborn infant.

Heat swamped her... a strange heat that wasn't entirely sexual. There was a connection between them, like a circuit that had been completed when Thanatos put his hand on her belly. The current surged through her veins, delivering a powerful punch of energy that made her vibrate. It was so corny, but Thanatos must have felt it, too, because his eyes were fastened on hers, their color shifting from yellow to gold, and the tattoos on his neck pulsing to the beat of her heart.

She swallowed as a tense, wonderful thrill charged the air between them. It was as if they were in a bubble where only they existed, the three of them somehow becoming a single unit.

His watch beeped, and as if startled out of a spell, he stepped back, breaking contact. The lovely energy cut off like a switch had been thrown, and the cool air swept in again, leaving her feeling oddly exposed. The baby made his displeasure known by doing something that felt like a karate lesson.

"So." She cleared her throat of the sand that had settled in it. "What are we having for dinner?"

Thanatos gestured for her to follow. "Come see." His voice was rough, edged with emotion, and she was happy she wasn't alone in that. It was truly shocking how much she enjoyed the way his touch made her feel.

Eagerly, because she was starving, she followed him into the great room, which was empty except for a couple of Thanatos's vampires. "Where is everyone?"

"They've been gone for a while now. You were rearranging my room for over two hours."

"Nesting instinct." She pretended not to notice Than's dubious glance.

Regan inhaled, taking in the savory aromas coming from the kitchen. The trestle table along the far wall was set with two plates, one at the head and one at the corner. So many covered trays loaded one end of the table that, they could have been expecting a dinner party of twenty.

"How many people do you think I'm eating for?" she muttered as she approached the table.

"I didn't know what you like, so I had my staff prepare several dishes." He pulled out the side chair for her. She didn't know why she was surprised by his manners, but she was.

She sank awkwardly into the seat, and when Than gripped her upper arm to help her, she was once again surprised. And flustered.

"Um, thank you." She glanced at the huge spread. "But you didn't have to go to all this trouble."

He sat at the head of the table. "My son is inside you," he said simply. "You need to eat."

Right. Of course this was about the baby. Not that she'd expected anything else, but... it still smarted. And what was it Lance had said? That once she delivered the baby, she'd be nothing? He was being an ass, but what he'd said had gone to the very core of why she worked so hard at The Aegis, why she volunteered for everything, why she'd tried to become their expert on vampires and dhampires...all so she'd be useful. All so she'd be needed. They'd kept her close because of her soul-sucking gift, but now that it was gone, what if Lance was right?

The sudden urge to rearrange the silverware and food platters made her fingers twitch.

"Regan?" Thanatos gripped her hand. "Hey. What's wrong?"

"Nothing," She offered a shaky smile, and was relieved when one of his vamps strode out of the kitchen with a steaming bowl. He stopped next to her and used a pair of tongs to lift a hot, wet towel into her hands. The light, lemony scent should have sparked her appetite, but somewhere in her head, her hunger had died.

As the vampire removed the lids from the dishes, she watched him, uncertain about his night or day status. He was big, but she didn't get the daywalker vibe from him. Was it rude to ask?

She waited until he left to lean close to Than and ask quietly, "Was he a day or night vampire?"

"He's a daywalker. Why?"

"Because earlier in my room, one of your night guys, Peter, brushed by me and got blasted across the room. I think only you and the daywalkers can touch me. Do you know why that would be?"

Thanatos's expression shuttered, and when he spoke a flat, toneless, "No," she got the distinct impression he was lying. Okay, new tack. "One of the vampires at headquarters...he called you *Bludrexe*. What does that mean?"

"I have no idea." His tone was as bland as his expression.

"Well, I also got the same word from the vampire who tried to stop me from leaving. And I've read it somewhere before."

Than gave a vague shrug. "Why the questions?"

Because I need The Aegis to need me. "Because I'm The Aegis's resident vampire expert." She turned her plate an inch clockwise so the Italian grape design was sitting straight. "Do you know how the daywalkers came into existence?"

"Why the hell would I know?"

"Maybe because you're employing the only daywalkers we've ever come across."

"And that's why you kidnapped them? To find out how they came into existence?" His voice was as hard as the look he gave her. "What was the plan? Torture? Dissection?"

Yikes. He'd hit that nail on the head. "I didn't know about their capture, Than. Neither did Kynan. He was just as pissed as I was. It was stupid of us to do that."

He stared at her as if gauging the truth of what she'd said, and then he jerked his head toward the food. "Eat."

Resigned, she turned her attention to the food, and now that she got a good look at everything, her eyes nearly bugged out of her head.

The table was a buffet of roast beef, fried chicken, spaghetti, enchiladas, a variety of side dishes, including a leafy green salad, pasta salad, steamed vegetables, macaroni and cheese, three kinds of breads, and two soups.

"This could feed an army," she said, even as she dug into the mac and cheese—her favorite.

She loaded her plate with a scoop of everything except the roast beef, and it was only after she'd taken a dozen bites that she realized Thanatos wasn't eating. He was just...watching her.

"Aren't you hungry?"

His eyes darkened, and again, she expected some typical male answer full of subtext, an "Oh, yeah, I'm hungry, all right," but this man was full of surprises.

"I'll eat after I'm sure you've had enough."

"Why?"

He glanced down at his empty plate and then back at her. "Because my people...the people who raised me... made sure pregnant women ate first and got the best food."

Something fluttered in her chest. How could he be so rough and angry one minute, and yet respectful and attentive the next? She felt her guard slipping with every caring gesture and word, and it occurred to her that the danger he presented to her might not be merely physical.

She forced herself to concentrate on the food before she let her mind wander into places it didn't belong. "But there's so much here. Far more than I could eat in a month." The baby wriggled, and she revised that thought. "A week, anyway." When Than didn't seem inclined to budge, she gestured to the platter laden with roast beef slices. "Beef hasn't sat well with me for the last couple of months, so please, go ahead."

Thanatos inclined his head in a polite nod and loaded his plate with beef and gravy. "Do you have cravings?"

"Food," she said, and there went the fluttering again at his low chuckle. "Any food. You name it, I want it." She stabbed a piece of chicken with her fork. "I try to eat as large a variety as I can so the little guy develops a taste for lots of different ethnic dishes. I read somewhere that a varied diet can prevent picky eaters, both in the womb and then later when toddlers are eating solids." Than looked at her as if she'd grown another head. "What? Why are you staring at me like that?"

"It just seems odd that you'd care about the baby's diet when you don't intend to have anything to do with him once he's born."

Ouch. "I care more than you can know, Thanatos."

She cared so much that she intentionally didn't think about the day she'd have to hand the baby over for his own good, because if she thought about it, she'd break down. The baby was her entire focus...keeping it safe, keeping it healthy, and making sure it was loved. But she didn't bother to explain, because he wouldn't believe her, and he'd made it clear he didn't want to hear it.

He gave her another strange look, as if he were again weighing her words for a measure of truth. Finally, he gestured to her plate, and when he spoke, his tone was almost friendly. "Then eat. And later, make a list of your favorite foods. I'll have them prepared for your meals. You can also use the kitchen anytime you want."

Again, his thoughtfulness made things flutter. Beneath all that physical and emotional armor was a decent man who had been dealt a crappy hand.

"So if I want to make chocolate chip cookies at two in the morning, I can?" Not that she knew how to cook, but she could learn. That's what cookbooks were for, right?

"Yep."

"Brownies?"

"Yep."

"Pineapple upside-down cake?"

His smile took her breath. "Only if you share."

"You like pineapple-upside down cake?"

"It's my favorite."

Once, she'd seen a Valentine's Day issue of a women's magazine with a heart-shaped pineapple upside-down cake on the cover, and inside the magazine was an article about romance and food and creating the perfect evening. A picture showed a couple sitting at an intimate table for two, lit by candlelight, and the cake between them.

Now her runaway imagination plugged her and Thanatos into the picture, him leaning across the table, his mouth inches from hers, the soft glow from the candles highlighting the sharp angles of his jaw, the sensuous curves of his lips.

His voice was husky as he whispered, *"For the next eight and a half months, you're going to be mine. Every. Night."*

Regan's hand shook as she hastily shoved a forkful of spaghetti into her mouth and shoved the vision out of her head. Reaver was wrong. Thanatos might want her, but only because of what she could give him: a son and several months' worth of sex, after which he'd either kill her or kick her out the door.

Some secret, guilty part of her even thought that maybe she'd deserve whatever he did to her.

So no, she wouldn't be making Than pineapple upside-down cake.

Ever.

Thanatos loved watching Regan eat. There was just something...pleasing...about watching a female feed her young, whether the infant was in her arms or in her womb.

What wasn't pleasing was how she suddenly seemed to have lost her appetite, and he thought he'd seen a subtle trembling in her hand. He probably shouldn't have needled her about the Aegis taking his daywalker, Jacob. Idiot. Upsetting a pregnant female when she should be eating was foolish.

But he had to admit, he'd been shocked by what she'd said about feeding the baby. There were pregnant women out there who intended to keep their babies but didn't give a second thought to what crap they ate, drank, snorted, or smoked. And yet, Regan, who was prepared to give hers up, was concerned about his future diet.

He'd believed she cared about the child, but only because the fate of the world sat on the innocent baby's shoulders. But the more he saw, the less sure he was that she viewed the child as nothing more than a tool.

"More?" He pushed the dish of macaroni and cheese closer.

"Oh, heck no." She eyed the casserole like it was an enemy. "I'm going to pop." She rubbed her belly. "Actually, I kind of wish I would. Though I guess now we have to hope he takes his time so we can nab Pestilence."

It was on the tip of his tongue to get nasty, to ask, "And then what? You give the baby to Kynan?" Instead he reminded himself that he'd just given himself a mental lashing for upsetting her and kept the conversation light.

"Do you cook much?"

"I don't know how." Her long sable lashes fluttered downward with her gaze, as if her admission embarrassed her. "Not that it matters. I don't have a kitchen."

No kitchen? "Where do you live?"

"I've had a room at Aegis headquarters since I was sixteen. It's like a studio apartment. At least it has a bathroom, so I can't complain."

"Doesn't sound like you have much space."

She shrugged. "Don't need it. It's not like I throw a lot of parties or hold holiday gatherings or anything."

"Sounds lonely." The words were out of his mouth before he could even think about what he'd said...or how much it revealed about himself, given that he lived a solitary life, too. He recognized loneliness far too well.

"I keep busy," she said, and yeah, so did he, but busy didn't change the fact that he still slept alone at night.

"What about when you aren't working?"

"I'm always working."

"Don't you take time out to enjoy human holidays and celebrations?"

"Someone has to work. Demons don't stop terrorizing people just because it's Christmas." She arranged her silverware carefully on her empty plate. "Kynan and Val used to invite me to their houses for Thanksgiving and stuff, but it's awkward to intrude on family gatherings, you know? So I work. The Aegis has a never ending list of documents they need me to feel up for authenticity, so it's cool."

No, it wasn't cool. She had no real family or friends, did she? But why? And a never ending list? Didn't The Aegis have anyone else to verify the authenticity of the texts in their library?

"So what—they keep you locked up at headquarters and force you to do their bidding?"

Regan jerked as if he'd jabbed her with a cattle prod. "Of course not. I volunteer for work. I'm lucky to be there at all. The Aegis usually kill people like me."

"People like what?" When she looked down at her plate, clearly uncomfortable, he tempered his voice. "Regan? You can tell me. There's nothing I haven't heard."

For a long moment, she sat there, her body tense, and he knew she was ready to bolt from the table. Very slowly, he reached out and settled his hand over hers, stroking with the same motions he used to calm Styx. Sad, maybe, that all he had to reference was his ability to ease his horse, but women were so foreign to him. His only experience was with Limos, and she wasn't exactly a typical female no matter how much she wanted to be. Besides, when she'd needed comfort, she'd generally gone to Reseph.

Gradually, Regan relaxed. "My birth parents were Guardians. But my father was possessed by a demon, and while he was under the demon's influence, he impregnated my mother. I'm not a demon," she added quickly, and he smiled.

"I know that. You're a *camborian*."

Her head came up. "I'm not a cambion."

He shook his head. "A *cambion* is a child born of a demon-human union. You're a *camborian*. Basically, your father's very human seed was infused with demonic energy. So you aren't a demon, but you possess some of the demon's traits and abilities. And you probably have some of the demon's sensitivities."

She frowned. "I can't take most medications."

"I've heard that a lot of demons can't tolerate human medicines. So it would make sense that you'd have some abnormal allergies."

"I find it odd that The Aegis didn't know the term for what I am."

He snorted. "The Aegis doesn't care. If they kill babies born of a possession, do they really need a name for it?"

Her glare told him she wasn't ready for criticism of her people. Especially not by him. "We have a name for them. It's just not the one you use."

"Yeah? What do Guardians call people like you?"

She averted her gaze, and an instant rage came over

him, so strong that he felt the souls inside him begin to stir even without being armored up. "Shitspawn."

He couldn't contain the rattling growl that rose up in his chest. "They call you *shitspawn*?"

"No." She shook her head hard, her denial too violent. "I mean, not...it's been a while."

"They might not say it to your face, but the term is there. You hear it, but then they look at you and say, 'Oh, I didn't mean *you*.' Isn't that right?"

Again, she denied it with a shake of her head. "You don't know—"

"Yes," he interrupted. "I do know. No one has fucked with me like that and lived to regret it, but I've seen it a million times in my life."

"Thanatos? *Thanatos.*"

"What?" he snapped.

"Your eyes are glowing and the table is shaking."

He wanted to tear apart every Guardian who had hurt her. It didn't make sense, given that at one point he'd wanted to hurt her, too, but so much of what he was feeling didn't make sense.

Christ, no wonder she kept busy working instead of socializing. Hanging out with her colleagues in her spare time would be about as fun as unclogging a toilet with a spoon.

Figuring that the way she was frantically folding her napkin in perfect squares was an indication that the subject was right up there with unclogging toilets, too, he reined in his temper and reached for one of the three desserts on the table. "Cake?"

Her eyes lit up. "I shouldn't...but I swear, this kid instantly makes room for sweets no matter how full I am."

"So . . . strawberry cheesecake, red velvet cake, or chocolate mousse?" *Your colleagues' heads on silver platters?*

"Yes, please." She practically bounced in her chair, and Than couldn't help but laugh, partly at the heads-on-silver-platters thing. That shit would be *funny.*

"There's also five different flavors of ice cream in the freezer."

She grinned. "I'll save the ice cream for later. Right now . . . those."

He dished up a serving of each of the desserts and pushed the plate to her. "Eat up."

"You're having some, too, right? This isn't another *not until you're done* thing, is it?" Her chin came up as she shoved the plate away. "I'm not eating dessert alone. You want me to eat it, you eat with me."

Stubborn woman. Fine. He could play that game, too. "I'll have a bite," he said silkily. "But you have to give it to me."

It amused him that she narrowed her eyes at him but she still, with jerky, huffy motions, cut a bite of cheesecake with the edge of her fork. She held it out, handle toward him.

"Here."

"What, not going to feed it to me?" He wasn't one to tease, or flirt or play, but he'd do whatever it took to get her to eat. *Keep telling yourself that, Than-boy.*

"I'm pretty sure you're capable of feeding yourself."

"You're right." He took the fork, covering her fingers with his as he did so. "I should be feeding you." Gently, he pushed the tines toward her mouth.

"You said you'd have some if I gave it to you," she protested.

He grinned, putting the dessert to her lips. "You eat this, and I'll take a bite."

She made a small growling noise that worked like instant Viagra on him. The sexy rumble went straight to his groin, and he shifted to make more room in his pants. When she grudgingly opened her mouth to take the morsel, he nearly groaned. She was wearing his clothes, carrying his son, and taking food from his hand. In the clan he'd grown up in, she'd be considered his.

Mine.

It was a word he'd never thought he'd use. Never thought he'd have an opportunity to use. And he still shouldn't. Regan wasn't his. Even if she hadn't deceived him, she didn't want him, she didn't want his son, and she clearly couldn't wait to get away from him.

No, she definitely wasn't his.

Mood effectively dampened, he released the fork and her hand. "There. That wasn't so hard, was it?"

Confusion flashed in her eyes at his tone, sharper than he'd intended, but he hardened himself against it as he took a slice of red velvet cake. They finished the meal in tense silence, though Than didn't eat the last of his food until Regan had pushed aside her plate and leaned back in her chair with a satisfied sigh.

As he washed down his final bite with a Mountain Dew, she yawned. Instantly, he was on his feet and pulling her to hers. "I'll help you to bed."

"What?" She allowed him to take her a few steps, but then she jerked to a halt. "Why?"

Honestly, he had no idea. So much had happened to her today, and she must be exhausted…so his first instinct when she yawned had been to take her to bed. But hell if he was going to tell her he was so addled by her pregnancy and so eager to have a child that all he could think about was making sure she was taken care of.

He glanced at his watch for help. Midnight. Excellent. "It's late. You need to go to bed."

"I don't need you to tell me when it's time to go to bed, you know."

Of course not. She didn't need him for anything. He'd been locked out of her life and his son's life for over eight months with absolutely no input and no way to provide for them. A twinge of hurt put him right back into defensive mode, and he smiled coldly.

"I didn't say we'd be sleeping."

Regan shoved past him and started down the hall. "You're an ass."

"You didn't think that when you were panting my name."

"As you like to point out, it was my job," she said over her shoulder.

The reminder was a kick to the gut, but he refused to let it show. "Clearly, you liked your job. A lot."

She stepped into the bedroom and wheeled around, her jaw clenched. "Clearly." She let out a bitter laugh. "What, you're surprised I admitted it? You're not hard on the eyes, and you do have a certain dangerous-guy sex appeal."

"Wow. Talk about a ringing endorsement."

"Endorsement? I'm not writing a testimonial to get you a date or something. I'm just saying you aren't a total loser."

"You missed your calling. You really should be writing bios for EvilLove.com."

For a moment, she glared. And then, unexpectedly, she

laughed. A real gut-buster that caught him so by surprise that he stepped back. "Why are you laughing?"

"Because you can be such a dick that I never expect you to have a sense of humor."

"Truly, your praise leaves me glowing," he said dryly.

"'Glowing' is not a word I'd use for you." She shot him a snarky smile and did a one-eighty, which resulted in him dropping his gaze to her shapely backside.

Pregnancy had put a little extra padding there, but he didn't mind. He'd liked her hard, toned warrior body before, but the new, slight roundness gave her a softer appearance that suited her, although he'd bet his left fang that she'd kill anyone who told her that.

"Where are you going?"

"To shower," she said over her shoulder. "Or is that something else I'm not allowed to do?"

He shrugged. "You can shower."

"Gee, thank you." She strode into the bathroom and slammed the door, and he finally allowed himself a grin. He hadn't had this much fun in a long time, and he was only going to enjoy himself more when she climbed into bed.

No, he wasn't going to require sexual favors...even though it was tempting. She'd lost friends and colleagues today, and he wasn't a complete bastard. All he wanted was for her to plead a little. To know what it was like for him to lie frozen in Ares's house, pleading silently to be released. At least Than was giving Regan a chance to use her voice.

She'd beg for him to leave her alone, and he would. Hell, he'd give her whatever she wanted. He just wanted... what, an apology? Yeah, maybe that was it. Oh, she'd tried, had thrown him token "I'm sorry" lines, but he didn't buy it. She'd done The Aegis's bidding like a good little soldier, and an innocent child was going to suffer the consequences.

But not if Than could help it. If the child could, indeed, save the world, well, that was a bonus. But even if not, Thanatos would make sure his son was cared for and loved. Because he might have known about the baby for less than forty-eight hours, but he already loved it. He'd long ago given up on the idea that he'd ever have a child, but while the dream had died, the longing hadn't.

Now his dream had risen from the dead, and he wasn't going to let it slip through his fingers.

Fourteen

Regan showered, her stomach churning at the thought of what was to come. Was Thanatos really going to demand sex?

As much as her body got all hot and achy at the idea, her mind went cold and panicky. Oh, she wanted to touch him, to feel his skin sliding against hers, but every time she got too far into the fantasy, *that night* came back to her, and his pleas for her to stop worked like an icy shower on her libido.

Funny how she could hear him tell her no *now*, but at the time, his words hadn't computed. It made no sense, and only added to the muddled emotions that coursed through her.

She dried off slowly, hoping that by some miracle he'd grown tired of waiting for her. But when she opened the bathroom door, her heart leaped into her throat at the sight of him stretched out on the bed, shirtless, hands behind his head, an expectant gleam in his half-lidded eyes.

Good God, he was gorgeous.

She was in so much trouble.

She stepped out of the bathroom, her legs wobbly, her fist wound tightly in the towel around her.

Than's lips quirked. "Waste of time to cover up, when you'll be losing the towel in a minute."

An awkward kind of terror seized her. "I-I don't think this is a good idea." No, she didn't think it. She *knew* it.

"Are we really going to do this again?" Thanatos shifted slightly, making the tattoos on his bare chest writhe. They were amazing ... layered on top of each other and yet each distinct. They'd been taken from his thoughts by a demon who imbued each with emotions so powerful that Regan hardly needed to use her psychometric gift to read them. Although when she'd used her tongue on them that once, all she'd felt was lust, and the memory dried her mouth so thoroughly she might as well have gargled with sand. "I told you what was going to happen."

She had to clear her throat to speak. "Because I owe you."

"Yes."

That he was right sat like a stain on her soul, and there was nothing she could do about it but snag the maternity nightgown out of the bag of clothes Limos had brought her, return to the bathroom, and throw it on. When she emerged, Than was in the same position, his eyes predatory, tracking her as she flipped off the light and used the dim glow of the embers in the hearth to guide her to the bed. The moment she climbed onto the mattress, his fingers circled her wrist.

"You ready? Not that it matters." His voice, sensual and as rich as dark chocolate, made her stomach clench with hunger that had nothing to do with food.

"You really aren't going to give up on this, are you?"

"One thing you might as well learn about me now, considering you'll be here for a while, is that I'm stubborn as hell and I never give up. In a contest of wills, I'll win every time, Regan."

"Why?" she asked bitterly. "Because you're a man and I'm a mere woman?"

His fingers tightened on her wrist. "Have I ever given you the impression that I'm misogynistic?"

Actually, no, he hadn't. The whole "males must be better than females" shit was Regan's issue, not Than's. She'd had to fight for everything she got in The Aegis, including her spot in the Sigil, which had been a Males Only club for most of its existence.

"I'll take your silence as a no," Than said. "So ask me again why I'll win a battle of wills."

"Fine." She jammed her feet under the covers. "Why?"

"Because I'm immortal and you're a mere human. I have an eternity to out-stubborn you."

"Oh, good. So it's not the fact that I'm a woman that makes you feel superior—it's the fact that I'm a human. I knew something *mere* would come into play."

She felt his amusement more than saw it. "You're stalling."

"I don't know what you're talking about."

He dragged her hand across the space between them and laid it on his crotch. "I'll give you an out, Regan. All you have to do is ask me not to do this."

"Don't do this."

"That was a demand," he said, his voice rough and dark. "I said ask. Very nicely."

A chill settled over her skin despite the roaring fire. "Beg, you mean."

When he didn't reply, her first instinct was to yank her hand away, but her second, stronger instinct was to leave it there.

He wasn't hard.

The realization...bothered her. Why would he want this so badly if he wasn't turned on? Was it truly only to punish her? To get even? To have the satisfaction of hearing her plead?

Following her first inclination, she started to pull away. Than's grip loosened and his amusement washed over her again. He'd expected her to refuse, and by refusing, she'd play right into his hand—or her hand, as it were. He'd have more ammo to use against her, more reasons to make jabs about her sleeping with him only because it had been her job.

No way. It was time for an injection of steel into her spine, and it was time for this Horseman to learn a little about expectations.

She cupped him firmly, and to *her* amusement, *his* air of amusement left him. And when she began a slow, sensual massage, his entire body stiffened. Beneath her palm, his cock swelled.

Ha! She supposed she shouldn't feel too victorious— what man wouldn't get hard if a woman was stroking him like this?

Shifting onto one elbow, she unzipped his fly, and as his erection sprang out, he snared her wrist.

"What are you doing?"

She gripped him, and he hissed a breath through his teeth. "What you want me to do." Feeling a measure of control she'd so badly needed, she slid her hand down his length, loving the velvety smoothness of his skin. "Seems to me you gave me a choice. Pleasure you or beg. I don't beg."

She also didn't know how far she could take this. If he wanted her to mount him the way she had that night... she suddenly couldn't breathe. And yet, her hand was still moving, more evidence that her mind was very much divorced from her body when it came to this man.

His groan rumbled through the darkness. "Regan..." His voice was tortured, the sound so deep and male that it eased her anxiety about full-on sex. Maybe this would be enough for him for now. She hoped so, because she couldn't go any further, not with those memories lurking so painfully in her mind.

He was so hot in her palm, steel and silk, and she took her time sliding her grip from the thick base to the broad head. Each stroke brought a raspy breath and a slow, seeking churn of his hips. Maybe this would be a step in the right direction for them. There had been so much hurt between them, and they could both use a positive encounter to begin to balance the negatives.

She stole a glance at him, and in the fading halo of orange firelight, he was magnificent. Shadows created hard lines along his jaw and cheekbones while the light accented his full, lush lips as they parted to release a harsh breath. His lust-glazed eyes watched her with such intensity that heat licked her everywhere his fevered gaze came to rest on her body.

A bead of moisture formed at the slit in his penis, and

when she swiped her thumb through it and smoothed it over the cap, his lips parted more, revealing hints of glinting teeth. A sound escaped him—a low, desperate gasp that brought a thrill of excitement to her heart.

Gently, she squeezed his shaft, eliciting another gasp of pleasure. More. She wanted more from him. This might have started as a power play between them, but now...oh, this was delicious.

She pumped her fist down the length of him, to the broad base where the edge of her hand hit his zipper, then back up to the firm tip of the head. When she moved her hand down again, she worked her fingers to caress his sac, and he groaned. The sound of a male in ecstasy sent a visceral ache straight to her core, and wetness bloomed between her legs.

She brought her hand back up, squeezing firmly and using her thumb to rub slow circles on the sensitive skin just under the head.

"Stop." Than caught her forearm and stilled her movements. "I'm going to come."

"Isn't that the point of this?"

He reached out, and she could have sworn his hand trembled as he lightly touched her face. "What do you want?"

Was this a trick question? Would he refuse whatever she said? If that was his game, she supposed she could play.

"I want to finish you," she said, daring him to refuse this. "I always finish what I start."

His yellow eyes drilled into her, and he dropped his hand from her cheek. "Yes, you do, don't you. No matter the consequences."

Ouch. Again. He was full of venom tonight. Unexpectedly stung, she averted her gaze, refusing to let him see how his words affected her. More roughly than she intended, she went back to stroking him. As if she'd struck a match to gasoline, he let out a hoarse cry and arched into her grip.

His head punched back and his entire body strained with leashed power as she took the cue and pumped her fist harder, faster. He liked it rough, she thought, and for some reason, that knowledge made her dizzy with want. She crowded closer to him, desperate for more contact.

"Regan," he gasped. "I'm going to—" He broke off with a guttural shout as his body convulsed and wet, hot spurts splashed over her hand and onto his stomach.

She kept up the hand action until he stopped her by putting his hand over hers. For several heartbeats, he lay there, eyes closed and his fingers stroking her skin. The darkness between them settled into a comfortable calm, even though her heart was beating a mile a minute and her feminine parts coiled tight with unquenched desire.

An odd pang in her gut unnerved her, coming so quickly on top of the arousal. The pang intensified, and the desire coursing through her shifted. Her stomach churned, and a burning sensation spread up her torso. She sat up with a wince as a massive cramp tore through her midsection.

"Oh, no." Thanatos grabbed her wrist as an oily, malevolent agony swamped her body, locking her muscles and turning every nerve ending into a live wire. "You aren't running away from me again. I didn't threaten to break your neck this time. Not until the eight and a half months are over, anyway."

There was a teasing note in his voice, but now was definitely not the time for that. Nausea bubbled up in her throat and icy sweat broke out over her skin.

"Let me go," she whispered. Blades of molten steel stabbed her in the eyes, blurring her vision so badly that Thanatos's face became nothing but a smudge.

"Why?"

Bile soured her mouth. "Because I think..." She cried out as a lightning bolt of searing, twisting pain shot through her spine. "Oh, God, I think I'm dying."

Dying?

"Regan!" Than leaped out of bed, catching Regan as she tumbled off the mattress.

"Bathroom," she gasped.

He scooped her up and got her to the toilet just in time for her dinner to come back up.

Her entire body shook, and her skin was hot and slick with sweat. She moaned between sharp, labored breaths as she braced herself over the toilet seat, her trembling arms threatening to collapse. A drop of blood plunked from her nose onto the toilet seat.

Fuck. He went down on his heels next to her and swept her silky hair away from her face. "I'll get help. Just... stay here."

Stay here? Where else was she going to go? *Dolt.*

It took him five seconds to get to his cell phone and dial Underworld General, five more to bark into the phone that he needed Eidolon, and another five to get back to Regan who, in that fifteen seconds, had slid to the floor and was curled up in a ball.

Shivers racked her body, made worse by her labored breaths. A rare terror made his motions jerky and he tore a blanket off the bed and wrapped her in it, which wasn't easy, since she'd stiffened up as if her muscles had turned to cement.

Feeling way too helpless, he sank down on the floor and dragged her into his lap, holding her to his chest to brace against the tremors. "Can you talk to me?" She was burning up, fire on his palm. "Hey, I need you to say something." If she didn't, he'd scream. Jesus, he was terrified.

"Hurts…" Her spine bent impossibly back as she seized and cried out.

"Is it the baby?"

"No," she gasped, and then scrambled away from him to vomit again. When she was finished, she collapsed, and he caught her, drawing her back against him.

What the hell was this? A sudden flu? Or a pregnancy thing? He ran a massive list through his head, but as an ominous webbing of blue veins began to spread across her waxy skin and black splotches bloomed under her fingernails, he knew this was way out of his frame of knowledge.

By the time Eidolon and a blond vampire medic arrived, Than hadn't come up with anything that made him feel any better about this. All he knew was that she was in pain, and he'd do anything to change places with her.

Eidolon, dressed in wrinkled scrubs that spoke of non-stop work shifts, tossed his medic bag on the floor and kneeled next to Regan. "What's going on?"

Regan tried to answer, but her teeth were chattering

too hard to speak, so Than did it for her. "She said she was dying, and the next thing I knew, she was throwing up. She's hurting and burning up, Doc." He seized the demon's wrist. "Help her."

Fear and desperation made his plea a command, but the doctor took it in stride, the markings on his arm—glyphs known as a *dermoire*—began to glow as he summoned his healing power.

"I'm going to attempt to touch her. Shade warned me, but I've got to try. I brought Con in case." The demon gripped Regan's shoulder, and a split-second later, he exploded backward, landing in an awkward heap against the bathtub. "Son of a...fuck." Groaning, he sat up as Con took his place at Regan's side.

"When did her breathing become labored?" Con asked.

"Right after she threw up the first time."

Con nodded. "I'm going to take her pulse—" The vampire didn't finish his sentence. He didn't even get more than a finger on her wrist before he joined Eidolon next to the tub. "Guess not," he croaked.

"Dammit," Than breathed. Regan had said Peter, a nightwalker, hadn't been able to withstand contact with her, either. He'd hoped Peter had been an isolated incident, but once it got out that only Than and the daywalkers could touch Regan, there would be questions he couldn't answer. At least, he couldn't answer them with the truth.

Eidolon rubbed his shoulder and moved closer. "The raised veins, discolored fingernails, and nasal bleeding are indicative of a demon poisoning. Is it possible she ingested something? If so, we need to find out what. I have antidotes for most demon toxins, but we need to act fast."

"No one in my household would poison her." Than closed his eyes, his denial sounding childishly vehement. He didn't want to go there, didn't want to think one of his vampires could have done this, but he also couldn't waste time with denials.

Nor would he deny that if someone did poison her, they'd suffer in ways that would make the horrors of Sheoul-gra look like amusement park rides.

"She could have eaten something at dinner..." He trailed off, wondering why he wasn't sick. Granted, poison didn't affect him the way it did mortals, but he should still feel a twinge of discomfort. Unless... "The chocolate mousse. It was the only thing she ate that I didn't at least taste." Rage coiled like a venomous snake inside him, but as murderously pissed as he was, he gently eased her off of him.

"Hurry, Horseman," Eidolon said, his voice quiet but grave. "She and the baby are both in danger if I can't touch her to help."

"Save...the baby." Regan's raspy voice was barely audible.

"We will." Than shoved to his feet, hating that he had to leave her. "We'll save you both."

Regan peered up at him with dull, unfocused eyes, her beautiful brown hair fanning like spilled blood on the tiles. "Kill me. If I'm dead, you can get the baby out to help him."

She was serious. Dear...God, she really wanted him to kill her. "It won't come to that," he croaked. "Just hold on, Regan. Damn you, *hold on*." He raced out of the room and into the kitchen, a black, inky fury pumping out of his very pores.

The vampires scattered before the storm cloud of souls billowing around him. "Who made the chocolate mousse?" When several vamps exchanged wary glances, he fucking lost it, grabbing two of them by the throats and slamming them so hard into the wall that bits of stone rained down to the floor. "*Who*?"

"Dariq," one of them gasped.

Than dropped them, whirling to Dariq, who had gone sheet-white and was slinking toward the door. Before Than could pounce, Dariq darted out of the kitchen.

Snarling, Than produced his scythe and in one smooth movement, hurled it across the great room. Dariq dove for the front door, but the weapon caught him between the shoulder blades and pinned him to the wood.

"What was in the mousse, Dariq?" Than crossed the room, aware that every vampire eye in the house was on him. He caught the scythe handle, but instead of yanking the blade free, he twisted it, reveling in the vampire's scream. "Tell me, or the next thing I do with this blade is castrate you." Actually, that was going to happen anyway, at some point.

Dariq hissed, spitting blood. "Neethul mucosa."

Thanatos's chest went cold. That shit was fatal within minutes for most creatures. Than whipped his head around to Artur. "Tell Eidolon. Hurry!" Artur took off in a blur, and Than returned his attention to Dariq. "Why? Who else is involved?"

Out of the corner of his eye, Than watched for a reaction from the spectators, but so far, no one seemed unduly concerned that they'd be outed.

"Not...saying anything...else," Dariq growled, and he was so wrong about that.

Than shoved his fist right through the male's back and palmed a wet, smooth kidney. The organ no longer worked in the capacity it had when Dariq was human, but it still was a massive source of pain.

"You will tell me, vampire. If I have to spend the next month doing nothing but making you scream, I will." Thanatos squeezed the organ so hard his fingers punctured the slippery surface.

Dariq's shriek echoed off the castle walls, and the scent of his blood had Than's fangs punching down like knives.

"Tell me."

"F-uck . . . you."

Than leaned in close, so close his breath condensed on the vampire's ear. "That's fuck you, *Bludrexe*." He ripped out the organ, relishing Dariq's agonized bleats. Before the male even stopped making noise, Than dragged him down to the dungeon and hurled him into the cell Than had once intended for Regan. Now to get some answers—

"Thanatos!" Artur leaped down the steps, landing in a lithe crouch at the base. "The doctor needs you. Hurry."

Shit. He slammed the cell shut and jabbed his finger at Dariq. "I'll be back, and I promise you'll spill your guts. Or I'll do it for you."

Leaving the vampire sprawled on the floor in a pool of his own blood, Than sprinted to his bedroom, where Eidolon was filling a syringe. The doctor looked up as Than skidded to a halt at Regan's side. She was pale, so pale. Even her lips were winter white, tinged with ice blue.

"Just in time. This antidote, when it works, works in seconds. When it doesn't work, it prolongs the inevitable." Eidolon thrust the syringe and a rubber tourniquet in

Than's hand. "Inject this into her cubital vein. I'll show you where and how."

When it works? Than's heart pounded so hard against his ribs it hurt. Regan was motionless, her chest barely rising with her breaths. "This usually works, right?"

"Usually," Eidolon said, but Than didn't like the doubt in his voice. He also didn't like that the doctor lowered his voice to say the rest. "That's a nasty toxin she was dosed with. The good news is that its effects on the baby should be minimal, so if . . . the worst happens . . . we have a good chance of saving him if we can deliver him quickly."

Meaning that if Regan's agony and life was prolonged by the antidote, Than might still have to kill her to save the baby. "It won't come to that." Holy shit, it had better not come to that. "Tell me how to do this." Than followed the doctor's instructions, and as he pulled the needle free of Regan's vein, she moaned.

"Than?"

He tossed the syringe aside and gripped her hand. "I'm here. It's going to be okay."

Her eyes clung to his, brighter than they had been. "I'm sorry."

"Not this again," he murmured. "Not now. We don't need to talk about it—"

"Not that. About your vampires." Color spread into her skin, and the cherry tint that made her lips so luscious infused them once again. "I'm sorry someone betrayed you." The sincerity and pain in her voice put a lump in his throat. Dammit, he was softening toward her, wasn't he?

Kill me. If I'm dead, you can get the baby out.

Yes, he was.

He couldn't.

"I guess it's no surprise that you recognized betrayal before I did." The words were sharper than he'd intended, and pain flashed in her eyes before she closed them, effectively shutting him out and withdrawing into herself. And damn her for making him regret his harsh words. Damn him for saying them. And damn this entire fucking situation.

Eidolon stood. "Can I have a word with you outside?" The demon didn't wait for an answer. He strode out of the bathroom and bedroom with the arrogance of someone who expected to be followed.

Once in the hallway, Than crossed his arms over his chest. "Is there a problem? Did the antidote work?"

"It did. The clearing of the discoloration under the fingernails indicates complete reversal of poisoning. But that's not what I wanted to talk to you about." Eidolon pegged him with serious black eyes. "I don't know what's going on between you two, but that female in there is carrying your child, and she's had a number of close calls. She's fragile physically, and probably emotionally. Quit being a dick."

Than clenched his fists at his sides to keep from knocking the demon's teeth out. "You have no idea what she did to me."

"And I don't give a shit. As a doctor, my concern is her health, and the health of the baby. As a father, my concern is the health of the world. I'm not saying you have to forgive her, or make her your mate or put a crown on her and call her Stallion Queen. I'm saying you need to keep from stressing her out until the baby is born. After that, take your revenge, kill her, do whatever the fuck you Horsepeople do. But if you want a healthy baby, get your head out of your ass and don't make things worse for her."

"You Seminus demons have a hell of a lot of balls to talk to us the way you do," he growled.

Eidolon smirked. "You have no idea." The doctor nodded at the bedroom door behind him. "Regan should be fine after some rest. Do a better job keeping her safe, because from what I've seen and heard, you're not so good at it. Tell Con I'm heading back to UG."

Thanatos really did not like that doctor, and if he wasn't the best hope for Regan and the baby when the time for the birth came, Than would kill him for what he'd just said. Asshole.

The fact that Eidolon was spot-on in his assessment only made it worse. Not so good at it. Yeah. Than's own words came back at him as if they'd been launched from a slingshot. *I'll keep you safe.* He'd promised Regan, and he'd failed. Then he'd compounded his failure by kicking her while she was down.

Down because of you, dickhead.

Than opened the bedroom door and was surprised to see Con walking toward him, medic bag slung over his shoulder. "E left?" When Than nodded, Con gestured to the bed, where Regan was curled up, the covers bunched around her feet. "She made it to the bed herself and conked out the second her head hit the pillow. Someone will call you in the morning to check on her."

"Thanks, man." Than grabbed Con's arm as he prepared to leave. "Hey, do you have a vampire working at the hospital who can walk in the daylight?"

One blond eyebrow shot up. "Never even heard of one."

"Bullshit."

Con lowered his voice and shifted his silver gaze to the bed. "You really going to make a big deal of this right now?"

No, he wasn't. Regan and the baby were more important than a random daywalker with UG connections. For now.

Taking Than's silence as a no, Con clapped him on the back and strode out, leaving Than alone with Regan and his guilt. He moved to her, noting the steady rise and fall of her chest, the soft snores that fell from her parted lips.

One hand was tucked under the pillow, and the other rested over her belly as if she was trying to protect the baby even in her sleep. She was so adamant about giving the child up, but clearly, she cared. Goosebumps prickled her skin, and he drew the covers up to settle over her shoulders. With a soft sigh, she tucked them under her chin and curled into a tighter ball.

"I'm sorry I'm such a dick," he muttered. "You just... you piss me off sometimes. I want to hate you, but I can't." He didn't know what he wanted to do with her. Well, scratch that. Right this minute he wanted to climb into bed with her. To tuck her against him and protect her the way he should have been doing.

No doubt she'd hate him more than she already did if she woke up in his arms. And dammit, why was he thinking like this? He couldn't let himself grow attached. What if she betrayed him again? His temper was too volatile, his fuse too short. And honestly, the anger he was holding onto was starting to worry him. He'd never been a load of laughs, but he'd also never been intentionally cruel... especially not to women.

So yeah, he didn't know what the hell was wrong with him, but one thing was certain: Until he found out the extent of who was involved with wanting Regan dead and why, he wasn't leaving her alone. As much as he wanted to release some fury by paying a visit to Dariq, he couldn't do it until he got some extra protection for Regan.

Which included protection from himself.

So instead of climbing into bed with her or torturing the vampire who'd betrayed him, he texted Ares and Limos and fetched the dagger he'd relieved her of on the day he'd brought her here. Then he settled himself in the corner chair, crossed his legs at the ankles, and closed his eyes. He'd slept in worse places. He'd survive.

Whether or not he'd survive Regan…that was the question.

Fifteen

The screams reached Reaver's ears first. Then, as he got closer to the closed door at the very center of the abandoned nuclear power plant, he heard the moans.

Gethel was behind that door, torturing who knew how many demons for who knew what reasons. Right now, Reaver didn't give a crap what she was doing or why. The three realms—Heaven, human, and Sheoul—were at war, and Reaver had never been above doing what was necessary to win.

He threw open the metal door, and Gethel, standing in the center of the gym-sized room, turned to him. Her white tunic was splattered with blood, and in her hand was a *treclan*, a glowing spike that was effective only against other angels, including those of the fallen variety.

Which meant that the naked female on the table, her face and body partially hidden by Gethel, was some sort of angel.

"Reaver." Gethel's wings flared out before folding against her back, a show of dominance. Angels had hierarchies, and the high-level ones liked to flaunt their status whenever possible. The high-ranking pricks also rarely tucked their wings away, as if they needed to remind everyone that they had them.

Reaver generally kept his hidden, but he flapped them in defiance, letting the sapphire-tipped white feathers whisper against the air.

Gethel's mouth ruffled in amusement. "I wonder if you were so rebellious before you fell."

He tucked his wings away. "I'm going to throw out a wild guess and say yes." And it was a guess, given that he didn't remember anything before the event that caused his fall thirty years ago, and the weird thing was that no one else remembered him, either.

His lack of a past left him at a distinct disadvantage when it came to the political maneuverings of his angelic brethren, but ultimately, it didn't matter. He'd earn a place at the top of his Order, but he'd do it without resorting to games.

"I'm not here to chat. I want to know if you have any information on Wormwood."

She arched an eyebrow. "The star?"

"The dagger. Pestilence wants it."

She waved her hand. "It's a silly relic that's been attributed to angels and devils, saints and sinners. It's just a dagger. If Pestilence wants it, he must think it has power. It doesn't."

Damn. "You sure?"

Gethel shot him an arrogant *of-course-I'm-sure-you-peon* look. "How is Regan?" Gethel ran a long finger over the smooth surface of the spike she was holding. "And the child?"

As the Horsemen's former Watcher, Gethel kept up on Horsemen business, and as an angel invested in the fate of the world, she kept up on prophecy and minor things like a baby who could bring about the end of human existence. Sometimes Reaver thought she was a little too involved, but then, he supposed he wouldn't be able to easily step back from people he'd known for thousands of years either.

"They're both fine. And since Aegis Headquarters has been compromised, they'll be staying with Thanatos until the baby is born."

She tapped the spike against her chin as if deep in thought. "Do you find it odd that Pestilence just happened to trace Thanatos's movements at the right time to find headquarters?"

Yes, actually, he did. The Horsemen could cast a gate to take them to the last place a sibling had gone to, but by all accounts, Thanatos hadn't been at headquarters for long. Pestilence would have had maybe a five minute window in which to trace Than to headquarters.

"Why?"

Gethel's gaze locked on him, and her voice lowered, as if she were letting him in on a secret. "I believe it was Harvester who told Pestilence to trace Thanatos to Aegis Headquarters." She turned back to her gruesome work, and Reaver drew to a shocked halt at the sight of Harvester strapped to a table, her body impaled by five *treclan* spikes. "But I don't think she's going to admit to it. She also won't tell me who ordered her to hold you prisoner nine months ago." She jammed a sixth *treclan* into

Harvester's pelvis, and the scream that came out of the fallen angel's mouth made the entire building quake.

As much as Reaver wanted revenge, this wasn't the way.

"Why are you doing this? You aren't the Horsemen's Watcher anymore."

Black storm clouds passed over Gethel's expression, disappearing almost as fast as they'd blown in. "This goes beyond Watcher business. Her treachery is expediting the Apocalypse."

Bullshit. This was personal somehow. "And? There's something you aren't telling me."

"I don't owe you an explanation." Gethel summoned another spike. "Harvester and I have...history. But trust me, she knows *exactly* what this is about."

Reaver wondered how much trouble he'd get into if he popped Gethel a good one. "Do you have permission to kill her?" As the Horsemen's evil Watcher, Harvester was in a protected position, subject to execution orders only by mutual consent from agents of both Heaven and Sheoul.

"Unfortunately, no." Gethel said. "I have to release her when I'm finished."

"Release her now."

"I don't think so."

"You said yourself you won't get anything from her. Release her."

Gethel rounded on him. "She tortured you. Held you so Pestilence could maneuver The Aegis without interference. Because she kept you out of the game, Regan is pregnant, and the Apocalypse may be only days away. Yet you want this evil...*thing*...released?"

"I want you to release her because *I* want to be the one

to make her suffer. Her suffering, and her death, when ordered, will come at *my* hands. No one else's."

For a long moment, Gethel stared at him, her eyes burning into him as if trying to see all the way to the truth. Which was that yes, he wanted revenge against Harvester, but they would battle it out as equals. She'd been horrible to him, but she'd also been oddly...tender at times, as if she'd regretted her actions. He wouldn't afford her the same tenderness, but neither would he torture her while she was helpless.

Finally, Gethel shoved the spike into his hand and flashed away in a huff. Harvester, her eyes too swollen to open to more than mere slits, shuddered so violently that the table shook.

Holy hell.

Warring with the side of himself that wanted to leave her to rot and the side that wanted to relieve her suffering, he tugged free five of the *treclan* spikes, leaving the last to hold her in place while he unbuckled the straps that secured her arms and legs to the table. Once those were removed, he yanked the last spike from her shoulder.

Before he could stop her, Harvester rolled off the table and landed in a heap on the floor. As he came around the table, she dragged her body toward a dusty desk in the corner of the room. When he reached for her, she scrambled beneath the desk and curled into a ball.

"Fallen." Reaver used the derogatory nickname for fallen angels as a command, putting an edge on it to piss her off and bring her back to her normal nasty self.

Instead, she cried out at the sound of his voice, and her entire body began to tremble. Gethel had done a number on her.

Sinking down on his haunches, he reached for her. "Harvester?" This time, his voice was softer, but she still flinched, and he drew his hand back.

"I'm not going to hurt you."

She hissed. "Why not?"

"Because it looks like Gethel has done enough already."

"She's not . . . right."

"If she *is* right, you'll be destroyed for helping Pestilence."

"No, I mean . . ." A tremor racked her and her gaze turned haunted. "Never mind." Her voice was a raw rasp, shredded from screaming. "You must be loving this."

Strangely, no, he wasn't loving this. He wished he could, and maybe if she'd launched herself off the table and freaked out on him, he would have. But he disliked seeing anyone as powerful as Harvester reduced to a helpless puddle.

"Come out. I won't hurt you."

"As if you could," she shot back, but the shivers traveling over her skin negated her bravado.

"So defiant," he murmured.

A tangled lock of hair had fallen across her face, and without thinking, he reached to brush it back. The moment his fingers touched her, she curled up even tighter, her hands coming up to shield her head, but not before he saw a single tear form in one eye.

That one tear took Reaver down hard. Harvester could be faking her pain and fear, trying to play it all up to gain his sympathy, but he doubted it. She was truly afraid for her life.

"What was Gethel talking about when she said you knew exactly what this was about?"

Harvester flinched, a barely noticeable tightening of her muscles, but Reaver didn't miss it. "Nothing," she rasped. "Leave me. If you're not going to kill me, go away."

She didn't want him to see her in this state, exposed, weak, and terrified. Reaver couldn't blame her. "I'll go," he said, standing. "But Harvester? Fuck with me again, and next time, I won't stop Gethel. And if I find out that you were in any way involved in trying to break Thanatos's Seal or leading Pestilence to Aegis Headquarters, I'll be the one holding the *treclan* spikes."

The baby woke Regan with a series of kicks. No doubt he was annoyed by her growling stomach. She was just happy the little pony was kicking. Last night had been terrifying, and as she'd writhed on the floor, all she could think about was the baby. Had he been in pain? Had he been afraid?

And when she'd told Thanatos to kill her in order to save the baby, her one regret was that if she died, she wouldn't have ever been able to hold her son.

Her son. Dear God, she couldn't afford to think like that. If she did, she wouldn't be able to do what was best and give him to someone who could keep him safe.

The baby rolled, and a warmth settled into her heart. Had her mother felt Regan moving around inside and smiled every time, the way Regan caught herself doing? Or had her mother been afraid of the baby conceived with a demon-possessed Guardian? Had it been easy for her to give up Regan? Because for the first time, Regan was imagining handing over the child . . . and already her eyes were stinging. Could she actually do it?

If Thanatos was able to destroy Pestilence, Regan wouldn't have to give up the baby, though. Right? Maybe she and Thanatos could...could what? Share custody? Not likely. He wasn't exactly the sharing kind.

A buzz started up in her brain as her OCD switch flipped on. Everything was so out of her hands right now, and she had no idea how to harness even a little control.

Breathe. Count. Breathe.

The baby jammed a foot in her ribs at the same time her stomach growled, breaking her concentration. Cradling her midsection in an attempt to still both the baby and her rumbling gut, she opened her eyes. Even though she'd known where she was, her heart sank a little. She'd never again wake up in the room she'd kept at Aegis Headquarters. Then again, maybe that was a good thing. When The Aegis moved to their new location, maybe this time she'd take an apartment of her own.

Of course, if Thanatos had his way, a move wasn't going to happen for another eight months.

Where was he, anyway? The other side of the bed was undisturbed.

I guess it's no surprise that you recognized betrayal before I did.

Well, that explained why he wasn't in bed. She'd really thought, when he held her so tenderly and didn't jump on the offer to kill her for the sake of the baby, that his hatred had eased. When her agony had been at its worst, she'd taken comfort in his change of heart.

Clearly, she was a fool.

Sighing, she sat up and drew a startled breath when she saw him in the corner chair, his long legs stretched out in front of him, his arms folded across his bare chest, an open book cradled in his hands. His eyes were closed, but on his arm, Styx was tossing his head. Maybe the stallion was as impatient to be fed as the baby was.

Wait...did Styx even eat?

With as much grace as she could muster, she stood on feet that were swollen and would no longer fit into her shoes.

As she padded over to Thanatos, the floor was as freezing as an ice rink on the soles of her feet, but after the agonizing fever from the poison she welcomed the cold.

"Thanatos?" She knelt next to the chair, but he didn't stir. Styx bucked...maybe he'd heard her? Very gently, she stroked her fingertip over the stallion's shoulder. The horse stopped tossing his head, but as she traced the line of his back, he stomped his foot. Did that mean he was annoyed? He was as hard to read as his master.

She drew away from the horse, letting her finger drift up Than's arm. His body was covered in tattoos, most of which he hadn't allowed her to touch. Probably a good thing, since she felt emotion in ink...and Thanatos's tattoos were emotion transferred to skin.

Maybe...maybe this was how she could begin to make things right between them and show him that while he might not care about her, she cared about him and had since before that awful night. If she could learn more about him, learn what he wanted and needed...

Tentatively, she put the tip of her finger to an outline of a skull engulfed by flames above his right pec. Instantly, heat licked up her hand, and as she opened herself to her gift, images swamped her brain. Thanatos, in pain as fiery arrows punched through his armor and into his body. Demons came at him from across an open, grassy

plain that was soaked in blood and littered with human
and demon corpses. Thanatos's thoughts raced through
her...his unimaginable agony, his fury as he swung his
blade, his regret at having released all the souls in his
armor, leaving him vulnerable to the fire-arrows.

She recoiled, her skin burning, as if sympathizing with
what he'd gone through. She'd always assumed he was
immune to harm and physical pain, but he'd experienced
his flesh burning all the way to the bone, and his misery
had been genuine.

"Oh, Thanatos," she whispered. "I'm so sorry."

Her hand quivered a little as she moved it to his left pec
and feathered her fingertips over the exquisite hellhound
design. As if she'd been dropped into a movie, nasty
snarls rang in her ears and razor-sharp teeth snapped in
her face. Thanatos was in a dark cavern, surrounded by a
pack of hellhounds. His souls had already killed a dozen
of them, and another dozen lay in pieces on the ground,
victims of Than's massive sword. Behind him, a mountain of bones and bodies formed a grotesque feeding sta-
tion, and Regan's stomach heaved.

She shuddered and braced herself to touch the tip of a
Celtic-designed sword dripping with icicles on his breast-
bone. A faint vibration shimmered along her skin, and icy
cold seeped into her bones. A stark, wintery landscape
opened up before her, and rage...so much rage, rushed
through her veins. In the distance, a bizarre forest rose
up out of the ice. What kind of trees were those? She
squinted, and when the truth hit her, bile washed into her
mouth. Not trees—giant wooden stakes, each impaling
a body. Good God, hundreds—no, thousands—of men,
women, and children had been skewered.

Between the stakes were more dead—soldiers, hacked to death and lying in pools of blood.

"You went too far, Thanatos. Too far." Gethel stood nearby, her eyes sad as she looked from Thanatos to the forest of dead.

But Than was beyond reason, and with a roar, he launched at the angel, his bloody sword flashing in the streaks of sunlight that penetrated the clouds. Gethel flashed away in a flicker of golden light, but another voice came from behind, and he whirled, sinking his blade into the belly of a female Regan swore hadn't been there a moment before.

The female demon gasped, her blue lips and frosty skin going even paler. Regan didn't know her species, but she was definitely a demon.

A silver tear dripped from one gray-blue eye as she looked at Thanatos in shock. "Than..."

Thanatos let loose another angry roar, and in one smooth, powerful move, he jerked the sword out of her body and swung it in a massive arc, separating her head from her body.

Thanatos stood silently, staring at the dead demon as her body disintegrated the way most of them did when they died in the human realm.

And then, as Thanatos's murderous fury melted away, the reality of what he'd done sunk in. Horror replaced the anger. Sorrow and pain clenched at Regan's heart as his emotions became hers. The demon had been his friend. In his death-haze, he'd killed his friend.

Tears stung Regan's eyes. She pulled away from Than, unable to take any more. Cold surrounded her like a chilled blanket, and she made her way to the fire, grateful that his servants had kept it burning through the night.

"Did you see everything you wanted to see?" His low voice drifted to her, and she closed her eyes. She should have known he wasn't asleep. "Did you like violating me *again*?"

She spun around. "What? I didn't—"

"You looked into my past without permission. You took something without asking. This is a habit with you, isn't it?"

Oh, God, she hadn't thought of it that way. If someone opened up her mind and did the same, she'd be pissed as hell. "Why didn't you stop me?"

"Telling you no doesn't seem to work."

"I'm sorry," she said, even though she knew he viewed her words as hollow. "I just..."

"You don't think of me as a person."

"No—" She broke off, because yes, that was it. Except it wasn't that she didn't think of him as a living, breathing person with feelings...it was that she thought of him as too powerful and larger-than-life to be bothered by anything. Before she dug a hole any deeper, she turned back to the fire. "Who was she?"

"Rowlari. She was my best friend for a thousand years. I'd always warned her to stay away from me when I was taken over by death, but she thought I'd never hurt her."

"And those people...did you..." She couldn't continue.

"What do you think?"

She focused on his face, seeking clues in the hard line of his jaw, the severe set of his mouth, the shuttered darkness in his eyes, but there was nothing in his expression that could give her an answer.

"Honestly, I don't know what to think."

Her stomach rumbled and the baby kicked simultaneously, reminding her that she needed to feed them both despite the fact that she no longer felt like eating. The things Thanatos had gone through—some of them because of her—left her thinking that food was going to be a little tasteless right now.

He said nothing, and her mind went back to the horrors she'd witnessed through his tattoos. "How do you live with it all? Everything you've seen? How are you still sane?"

"I read a lot." He held up the book he'd had lying on his chest. "Keeps my mind busy. And when I'm not reading, I'm looking for more old books."

"Like?"

His long, tapered fingers skimmed the book's spine, and it was probably pathetic that she was jealous of the thing. "I scour the Earth and Sheoul for anything that relates to Lilith and Yenrieth." He laid the book gently on the end table next to the chair. "This is the second of three in the chronicles of a succubus who claimed to have been Lilith's sister. I'm missing the third. Been hunting it for centuries. See? I keep busy. Like you, I always work."

Odd that they both seemed to fill their time by chasing demons. She wasn't exactly in a position to hunt them right now, but maybe there was something she could do for him. She'd have to give Kynan a call.

"So reading and hunting books keeps you sane? After all you've seen?"

His hands came down on her shoulders, startling her. How had he moved so fast and so silently? She stood frozen to the floor, a tremor of fear making her muscles quiver. She didn't think he'd hurt her, not physically, but his words could be sharper than any blade.

"No. It's why I have the tattoos. When the tats are inked onto my skin, the strongest emotions are inked into them, too."

"So the emotions are erased?"

"Not erased. Diluted. But I still remember everything."

Talk about your alternative therapies. "That's cheating, you know."

"How so?"

"The rest of us have to live with what we've done and what we've seen. We learn from it. How can you learn if how you feel is watered down?"

"I learn. Trust me, I learn." He dropped his hands. "Or do you think I live alone in the middle of nowhere because I like the snow?"

"Well, then, maybe you should hit up your tattoo artist to get rid of what we did the night of Limos's wedding."

"Trust me, that's next on my list." Pivoting, he started for the door, but she grabbed his arm.

"Seriously?" She felt like she'd been slapped hard enough to make her numb.

"I'd think you'd be happy to have everything about our relationship muted."

If she was smart, yes, she'd be happy. But she'd never done things the easy way. "We need to work things out, Horseman. We need to do it naturally, not through some artificial cheat."

"And why do we need to do that?"

"Because like it or not, we'll always be connected through this baby."

"A baby you planned to give away. A baby you don't want."

"Dammit, Thanatos," she snapped. "Do you really want

this baby? If we'd come to you and asked you to make a baby with me, what would you have said?"

He rounded on her. "I'd have said yes," he barked. "Sex was out of the question, given what I believed about my Seal, but this is the damned twenty-first century. Doctors could have made it happen."

"We couldn't take that chance. The wording in the document was pretty specific about a physical joining and the fact that it had to be secret." Now they knew the scroll's details had been laid out to trick The Aegis into taking Than's virginity, but at the time, her colleagues had been desperate to follow it to the letter. "And what if you'd said no? Obviously Limos couldn't do it, and we were pretty damned sure Ares wasn't going to cast aside Cara to have sex with me."

Thanatos snarled. "That would not have happened."

"Isn't that what I just said?"

His voice grew gravelly. "You still should have come to me."

God, he was so stubborn. "We did what we thought we had to do. The fate of the entire freaking world was at stake."

He frowned. "So the end justifies the means. The needs of the many outweigh the needs of the few, as Spock would say."

"In this case, yes." She wrapped her arms around her, feeling a chill despite the fire. "But don't think I don't have some regrets. Some of us can't just purge emotions through a tattoo. We need to *talk*."

His frown deepened. "No, *you* need to talk. And you're jealous that you can't get rid of your guilt with a simple visit to a tattoo artist. It's not my job to make you feel better about what you've done, Regan." His words rained down on her like blows, but she stood her ground.

"Haven't you ever wanted to *not* take the easy way out of something?"

In a smooth, lithe surge, he backed her against the wall, his face in hers, his eyes burning with regret. "You think my life has been easy? Did you ever watch everyone in the village you grew up in die at the hands of demons? Did you kill the man you called father because you were insane from the death and destruction caused by said demons? Have you slaughtered your best friend? Murdered thousands of people? Seen the carnage left behind over and over from so many wars that they all blur together? No? Well, until you have, don't talk to me about easy."

She didn't know why she did what she did next. Maybe it was because his pain was so fresh in her mind. Maybe it was because his hard body felt so good against hers. Maybe it was because his mouth was so close. Whatever it was, it made her do something that shocked them both.

She kissed him.

Sixteen

She was kissing him. Not just a peck on the cheek or even on the lips. Regan had thrust her hand into his hair and brought his mouth to hers. Her tongue slipped between his lips to clash with his, and heat sparked so fast that Thanatos's mind flipped from surprise to lust in the span of a heartbeat.

Holy hell, she made him nuts, made him angry and horny, spun him so hard he didn't know up from down. It was getting harder and harder to remember why he was so angry with her. He'd told her he was going to get a new tat to purge himself of that anger, but he wasn't sure it was necessary. Not when she was kissing him the way she was, one hand tangled in his hair and the other clinging to his biceps.

He hauled her against him, careful not to put too much pressure on her belly. A soft moan escaped her, and he swallowed it with one of his own. Her body felt good on his, and even her extra curves fit him well.

There was a pounding on the door, followed by Ares's gruff, "Yo, Than."

Reluctantly, or maybe gratefully, Thanatos broke off the kiss and shouted at his brother. "Hold on."

He fumbled in his back pocket for the leather-wrapped blade he'd tucked away last night and shoved it unceremoniously into Regan's hands.

"My dagger?"

He nodded. "It might not be of use against Pestilence. He's apparently built up a tolerance against the hellhound venom you coated it with. But it's better than nothing. And it should work if—"

"If your Seal breaks."

"Yeah. And Regan...don't be afraid to use it against me." Her eyes flipped up to meet his, the gravity of his words clearly setting in. "I have to go."

"To get your tattoo?" Her voice was both breathless and bitter.

"No," he said, just as bitterly. "To do things that *will* require more ink."

That took the wind out of her sails. "I'm sorry." She glanced down at the floor, and fuck, didn't Eidolon just tell him to not upset her? And what had he done at his first opportunity?

"No, I'm sorry," he muttered.

Regan's eyes flared, and her mouth fell open. Wasn't it awesome that he was such a dick that an apology shocked the hell out of someone?

"Dammit," he breathed. "I have to go, but I won't..." He looked up at the wood ceiling beams as if they could help him out here. "I won't get the tat." More awesome, he'd turned into a chick.

"Really?" She sounded so hopeful that it completely threw him off balance.

"Yeah. Whatever you want."

She narrowed her eyes at him. "Why? You're being way too nice."

"Maybe I feel bad about not believing you about being in danger from my vampires." And actually, yeah, he did.

He shouldn't have written off her Guardian instincts so easily . . . she was a Guardian for a reason, and as much as he hated The Aegis, he couldn't deny that it had been around for centuries because its members weren't complete idiots. Not all of them, anyway.

"Who did it?" she asked.

Thanatos bit down on a snarl. "Dariq. He's been with me for almost nine hundred years."

The daywalker had barely awakened from his turning, had been confused and starving, when Than had given him the choice of serving him or dying. Dariq had chosen death.

Instead of killing Dariq, Than had taken pity on the new vamp and brought him back to his keep so the other daywalkers could teach him how to live.

Obviously, Thanatos's rare moment of compassion had been a mistake. Was the asshole paying Thanatos back for keeping him alive, or was this truly about killing Thanatos's son and starting the Apocalypse?

Time to get to the bottom of this.

"Is there anything I can do?" Regan asked, with such sincerity that he had the sudden urge to gather her in his arms and thank her.

He was so addled. "Just stay safe," he said gruffly.

"I'd be safer if there were Guardians here with me."

"You won't need them. I'm arranging for extra protection. That's why Ares is here."

She sighed. "It's not just about protection. It's about having a friendly face around here. Someone who's on my side."

As if he were the enemy. "*I'm* on your side."

"No," she said softly, "you're on the baby's side. I'd like...you know...a friend." Her voice cracked at that last part, and Decker's image popped into his head.

The scorpion tattoo on his throat undulated, the stinger jabbing at him with a vengeance. "Who?"

Her mouth opened, but nothing came out, as if she didn't know the answer to his question. And too late, he remembered what she'd said at dinner about keeping busy and having no social life. Oh, and her colleagues calling her shitspawn. Her reaction pretty much confirmed his suspicions that she had no friends.

They were both such outsiders, weren't they?

Finally, she muttered, "Never mind."

Ares pounded on the door again. "I don't have all day. Some of us have an Apocalypse to go to."

Strangely torn between wanting to make Regan feel better—even if he didn't know how—and getting the hell away from her before he did more damage, Than hesitated. "Regan—"

"Go," she said. "I need to call Kynan anyway. And I have things I can do in your library."

Feeling as if he'd been dismissed—she was good at that—Than opened the bedroom door to find Ares standing in the hall accompanied by two hellhounds, their claws digging into the stone floor.

Ares didn't waste time or mince words. "Do you know how many of your vamps are involved?"

"No, but I'm about to find out." Than dug his cell from his pocket and worked on a text to Kynan as he spoke. "I put Dariq in the dungeon until I could interrogate him. I'm restricting the others to their quarters until I get to the bottom of this." And he *would* get to the bottom of it if he had to put every one of them through the torture chamber. "Tell me you're here to keep an eye on Regan for me."

Ares nodded. "Limos and I can take turns, but I brought a hound to help out when we can't."

Thanatos eyed the two beasts. Ares might have decided they made great house pets, but Than wasn't convinced. They seemed to have a lot of accidents, and not the, *Oops, Fido took a piss on the floor*, kind. With hellhounds, it was more of the, *Oops, Fido ate my neighbor*, type.

"They hate Pestilence," Ares reminded him. "Anything Pestilence wants, the hellhounds will fight against."

"And Pestilence wants Regan and my son dead." Than nodded decisively. "Fine. The mutts can stay."

Ares told hellbeast One to stay at the bedroom door, and then hellbeast Two joined them as they headed to the dungeon.

The smell of blood hit Thanatos at the top stair. The stench of death hit him halfway down. And at the bottom, the rank odor of yet another betrayal struck him like a blow from a battering ram.

Dariq had been staked and hung from chains, the message to Thanatos clear.

Dariq will not talk.

What was also clear was that Dariq was not the only traitor in the house. Someone had killed Dariq to keep him from naming names.

Seventeen

Kynan arrived at Than's place within fifteen minutes of Regan's call. He met her in the library, not bothering to say hi or sit down, although he did pause at the sight of her hellhound babysitter until she told the thing Ky was a friend. The beast still reached out with a claw and clipped Ky's jeans as he walked by.

"I was planning on coming today before you called," he said, shooting an annoyed glance at the hellhound. "Eidolon said you were poisoned. Are you okay?"

"I'm fine. And, as you can see, I have a permanent guard."

"Thanatos texted. Said I could bring some Guardians for you. He specifically asked for a female so you'd have someone to talk to."

Regan's jaw dropped. "Seriously?"

"Yeah, and it's about time. We'll arrange to have some brought here by tomorrow." He handed her a plastic grocery bag. "Sorry this is hit and run, but I have to go. We'll make sure you get some Guardians." He nodded at the bag in her hand. "Three hundred years ago, nearly forty Guardians died to get that book, so I hope you know what you're doing."

"I do. And thank you again."

Ky took off, and Regan climbed back up the stepladder to reach for the book she'd been after before Ky arrived.

"Regan! What in the nine rings of hell are you doing?" Thanatos's roar didn't surprise Regan, but the hellhound lying near the library door let out a startled bark.

Calmly, Regan shifted her weight on the top rung of the stepladder. "There really are nine rings of hell? I thought that was fiction."

"It is." Than strode into the room and got as close as he possibly could without touching her, although his hands came up to bracket her hips. "Get down. You're going to fall and hurt yourself or the baby."

Clutching her prize, Regan stepped down, wobbling just enough that Thanatos caught her around the hips to steady her. For a long second, they stood like that, as if they were both confused to find themselves in an almost-embrace, and weren't sure what to do about it.

Regan cleared her throat. "Happy now?"

"No." Thanatos's hands lingered on her waist, and the pleasant, warm sensation that filtered through her whenever he touched her returned.

"Why does that happen?" she asked. "The warmth. It's got something to do with the baby, doesn't it?"

Thanatos stepped back, his cheeks pink with a hint of a blush. "Ares experiences certain effects when he's close to his *agimortus*—Cara. The baby is affecting me, too."

"The same way?"

His gaze dropped to her belly. "Similar. My armor doesn't soften, but when I'm close, the sensation of death around the world is muted."

"Is that a good thing?"

"Very." His blond brows dipped together in a contemplative frown. "I hadn't realized it, but I haven't felt that kind of quiet since I was a boy."

It was hard to imagine Thanatos as a child, doing normal things like playing. And laughing. But she was glad she could give him a measure of peace. "Did you have a good childhood?"

"The best." A wistful smile curved the corners of his mouth, one that cracked his hardened, immortal warrior exterior and exposed a man with normal memories and emotions. Without thinking, she reached up and brushed the backs of her fingers across his cheek, wanting to feel the man and not the warrior.

Thanatos's gaze caught hers, holding it with an intensity that sizzled across the surface of her skin. Desire pulsed in her veins, so easily kindled whenever he looked at her. Even when he was angry, the power emanating from him worked like an aphrodisiac on her, and she wondered if maybe the intense sexual effect was inherited from his succubus mother.

Or maybe Regan was just weird.

"When's the last time you were happy like that?" Her voice was barely louder than a whisper, but Than flinched as if she'd yelled.

"Too long," he said gruffly, and her heart broke for him. Somehow, she had to find a way to bring some happiness into his life.

Dropping her hand from his face, she clutched the book against her chest and pulled another book from the bag Ky had brought. Maybe this would be a start.

"I had Ky bring you this from our library."

Than took the tome, and the moment he had it in his hands, he inhaled on a curse. "Regan. Do you...do you know what this is?"

"Well, yes. That's why I asked for it. It's the book you've been looking for. The third one in those succubus diaries."

His gaze snapped up to hers. "This is priceless."

"Probably more to you than to us," she said softly. Yes, The Aegis was desperate for everything they could get when it came to historical and demonic documents, but for Thanatos, it was personal. The Aegis needed it, but Than *needed* it.

"I'm... I'm not sure what to say."

"That makes two of us. Ky said you approved having some Guardians brought here."

As if he were embarrassed to be caught doing something nice, he looked back down at the book and muttered, "Can't hurt to have more guards."

She didn't bring up the fact that he'd specifically requested a female Guardian, and *that* wasn't about having a guard. That was about being a decent, caring guy, and the more evidence she saw of the man behind the armor, the more she *wanted* to see that side of him. The more she wanted to be around it. Very little in her life had been given to her—she'd had to work for even the smallest treasures. But Thanatos wanted to give her things, like her favorite foods and an Aegis friend, and damn it, she wanted to give him a big, mushy hug.

She settled for a raspy, "Well, thank you."

He inclined his head in a nod and then gestured to the book in her hand. "What is it?"

"*A Spectator's History of Vampires.*" She ran her fingertip over the cracked leather cover. "I remembered where I'd heard the term '*Bludrexe*,' and I wanted to confirm some things. Unfortunately, since I don't have access to The Aegis's library, I can't find what I'm looking for. But I'm hoping I can find something similar in your library."

Shadows blanketed Than's expression. "The term isn't in that book."

"That's okay. It'll still be interesting reading, I'm sure."

Than smiled, which made her instantly suspicious. "I can find better reading material for you." He plucked from a shelf the Horsemen erotica book she'd read the last time she was here. "I know how much you liked this one."

Since there was no way he was flirting with her, he was either trying to distract her from the vampire book or he was trying to embarrass her. Maybe both.

Probably both. He had a strange sense of humor. Unfortunately, she found it oddly appealing.

She returned the smile, just as sugary sweet as his was smoldering. "Thanks, but I have pregnancy hormones to keep me hot and horny at night."

His eyes clung to her, holding her immobile. "They make you horny?" The way he said "horny," his tone dark, deep, and slightly breathless, made said hormones dance. She wanted him. She had since the moment she laid eyes on him, but she'd mucked that all up, hadn't she?

"And irritable," she added quickly. "Don't forget irritable."

"I don't think you've been that irritable, especially given everything that's happened and the situation you're in." He folded his arms over his chest and leaned his hip against the desk, his booted feet crossing at the ankles. "Speaking of which, someone killed Dariq to keep him from talking. Until I find out what's going on, I'm confining all vampires to their quarters or to the outbuildings. They're going to sweat out their own fear, I promise you that. And they won't get inside the keep."

Damn, she'd been hoping Dariq had been working alone. The idea that more vampires might be coming after her both freaked her out and pissed her off. No one was going to hurt her baby.

"Okay, you concentrate on finding your bad vamps, and I'll work on the *Bludrexe* thing." She placed the book on the desk and flipped it open, but before she could even attempt to read, Than slapped his hand down on it with a low growl.

"This book was in my private library that I keep under lock and key," he said. "I have no idea what it's doing out here, but it isn't for Aegi eyes."

Well, wasn't that interesting. "Thanatos, listen to me. I think that whoever wrote this might also have written the text I remember seeing *Bludrexe* in. The vibe from both is the same. Your father was mentioned, and it indicated that one could find the rest of the story within hidden scrolls in a forbidden mosque in Iraq that even The Aegis hasn't been able to gain access to. Maybe I can learn more in here, and then we could go to the mosque—"

"Let it go, Regan."

"But they talked about the Apocalypse," she blurted. "At the time I read the texts, I didn't focus on the Apocalypse because it was a vague reference. But now that all of this is happening with your vamps, it might have some importance. The texts were written by someone who claimed to be the first vampire. As he lay dying, an angel appeared and apologized to the dying man. Then a female angel joined the first, and they argued about the end of days."

"I don't care."

She stared in utter disbelief. When she finally found her voice, it dripped with anger. "You stubborn Horseman. The Apocalypse has been in a countdown for the last five thousand years. That's what The Aegis has been trying to prevent. That's what this—" she drummed her fingers on her belly "—has been about. We're on the precipice of hell, and this damned book might hold the very clue we need!"

"You think I don't know what that was about?" he barked, his finger jabbing at her belly. "Yeah, I get it, okay, Regan? I get that you fucked me for the sake of the world. You did it in hopes that you'd save billions of lives. But you know what? I don't care. I'm probably the only male on the planet who didn't want to get used for sex. Who didn't want to be treated like a piece of meat. Maybe that makes me a big damned pussy, but I don't give a shit. I thought you wanted me like I wanted you." He slammed his fist down on the book so hard the desk leaped off the floor and the hellhound sprang to his feet, teeth bared.

"I did," she whispered. "I did want you."

"You wanted what I could give you. You didn't want *me*."

She drew a startled breath. He'd...wanted her to want him? "I swear, Thanatos. I wanted you. I cared about you." *I still care about you.*

So much so that she was starting to suspect that even if she survived the months of revenge Than planned, she wouldn't survive his rejection afterward.

"If you cared, you wouldn't throw away our son."

Pain lanced her, but she threw it back at him. "If *you* cared, you'd let me research this in hopes of finding something that will save his life!"

There was a long, tense pause as Thanatos stared at her, his eyes glowing and steam practically whistling out of his nose like a cartoon bull. The hellhound had inched closer to her, although she wasn't sure if that was a good thing or not.

Finally, Thanatos ground out, "Where in Iraq?"

"The El-Sheoulate mosque."

He snorted. "There is no such thing."

Had this been just nine months ago, Regan would have gloated that The Aegis knew something a five thousand-year-old supernatural being didn't. But right now she needed to stay on his good side. Or at least, stay on his not-homicidal side.

"It's a demon stronghold beneath an existing mosque. It's why we haven't been able to get in."

"They have Aegi in Iraq, so why didn't they clean out the demons?"

"Because the real mosque sits in a city where most of the local government are *ter'taceo*, and so is a large number of the civilian population. The Aegis can't get anywhere close."

"Tell me where it is. My siblings and I will handle the demons."

"I'll show you."

He crossed his arms over his chest. "You'll tell me."

"Are we really going to argue about this?"

"You aren't in any condition to go. I'll get the scrolls and bring them back."

"Thanatos, they can't be removed from the mosque or they'll turn to dust. Everything inside the mosque is bound to it. You know how common it is for demons to attach objects to their holy places. So unless you or your siblings are empaths who can read parchment the way I can, you need me. You can get me in and out in a flash." She casually trailed her fingertip over the writing in the book Thanatos was still pinning to the desk and opened herself to her empathic gift. The author had been angry when he wrote it. So angry at the *Bludrexe*. "Besides, I'm feeling a little claustrophobic. I need to get out of here for a little while. And may I just remind you that no demon can touch me, and I seriously doubt we'll find liquid nitrogen-breathing frost demons in Iraq."

"Fine," he growled. "But you stay plastered to me, and at the first sign of danger, you're out of there."

"I'm starting to feel like you guys only grab me when you need something." Wraith punched Thanatos in the shoulder hard enough to hurt, even through the armor. "Next time you call, how about it's for a kegger?"

"I thought you liked to fight, demon."

"It's my second favorite thing to do." Wraith, his shoulder-length blond hair pulled back with a leather thong, tested one of the points on his throwing star. "But you could at least ply me with burgers and beer first."

Than didn't need to ask what his favorite thing was. Dude was a sex demon, brother to Shade and Eidolon. "No time for burgers and beer."

"Story of my life," Wraith muttered.

Limos, standing at the entrance to the secret underground mosque Regan had led them to, finished tying her hair up in a knot at the crown of her head. "We could have done this without the annoying demon, you know."

Ares cut through them and moved down the dark passage. "Remember how Wraith found your *agimortus*? He finds shit, and the faster he finds Regan's texts, the better."

Texts that weren't going to be read by anyone except Thanatos. He wasn't sure what they said, but if they even hinted at his secret, he couldn't risk anyone knowing. He couldn't be responsible for the destruction of an entire race of people, and he just hoped like hell that Regan's scrolls would *only* provide information about their father.

He gripped Regan's hand tight, holding her near, just as he had since finding Dariq dead in his dungeon. And since her admission of wanting him. And since she'd given him a priceless book. And since he'd realized how much of an asshole he was to isolate her from her Aegis comrades.

The more he got to know her, the more he realized that The Aegis was all she knew and all she had. He wanted to give her more, but he didn't know how. Didn't know if she'd accept anything from him. So he'd caved in and told Ky to assign some Guardians to her.

She, on the other hand, had given him a treasure, a book that had eluded him for centuries. He had no doubt that The Aegis considered it a treasure as well—no, he knew how valuable it was to The Aegis. Just before Than had gated them all here, Ky had called.

"Regan has very little to call her own, and she traded her most prized possession, a prayer written by an angel's hand, to get that book for you."

That Regan had done that left him shaken and unsure how to respond. In five thousand years, he'd been given a lot of gifts, mostly by his siblings, but this book, which started off with, *My sister, Lilith, was determined to bed the angel Yenrieth, but not if I could get to him first,* meant the most.

Any new information he could find about Yenrieth was more precious than gold.

Regan had given him that.

She was also going to give him a son, which would be far more precious than every book in his library combined.

He kept her next to him—probably closer than necessary—as they moved away from the spot just inside the underground tunnel's opening where he'd gated them. As with most demon-claimed land, the stone and packed-dirt passages were dimly lit by an otherworldly glow. Thanatos could see as well as if it were daylight, but Regan, without her Aegis-enchanted jewelry, had to squint, which was another reason to keep her close, especially given that the passage's floor was rocky and uneven. Thanks to the baby's protection, she might be immune to injury from demons, but a fall could harm her or the baby.

Wraith and Ares took the lead, and Limos came in behind Than and Regan. "How far do we have to go?" Limos asked, and Regan shook her head.

"No idea. The sketched map I saw in the vampire's writings wasn't exactly precise."

"Great." Wraith tossed his throwing star into the air and caught in between two fingers. "We could spend days wandering—"

"Shit!" Ares wheeled to the side, narrowly avoiding

a massive axe blade. The sharp wedge cut the air with a whistle, followed by the snarl of its wielder.

The tunnel came alive with movement as dozens of species of demons swarmed around them, crawling on the walls, the ceiling, and flying through the air over their heads. In an instant, a bloody battle broke out, but Than wasn't going to play games. He had thousands of souls at his disposal, and they wanted freedom.

He released a hundred, their eager shrieks joining the snarls and grunts of the demons taking damage from his siblings. Wraith went through the demons like a fang through flesh, his charmed status keeping him safe—as long as no fallen angels showed up. Next to him, Regan threw out her hand to touch any demons that made it close enough to her, sending them flying backward in shock.

Than allowed himself a small smile. His kid was badass.

So was Regan. She didn't even flinch at the rush of demons, keeping one hand protectively over her belly and the other at the ready, fingers clutching her dagger. And when a demon with thirty-foot, whiplike tentacles snapped one at Than, nicking his cheek, Regan snarled and struck out with her blade, severing the demon's limb and sending it screeching into the dark.

Man, her fierceness juiced him up. She might be almost nine months pregnant, but she was still in her element down here mixing it up in a cavern full of demons. It was strange how right now he wanted to both cocoon her in bubble wrap to protect her and get her naked to get going on those months of pleasure. Except this time, he didn't want to climax alone.

The battle was over in under two minutes, but Than

had a feeling this was just the beginning. Turned out he was right. They repeated the scenario four more times before they reached a crude stone staircase that led down into a pit lined with colorful tiles that had been arranged into crude mosaic images.

"What is this?" Limos stepped into the center of a design portraying a hell stallion tearing apart a demon.

Thanatos threaded Regan's fingers with his as he led her carefully around other patterns, most depicting violence, others arranged into sex scenes, some reflecting both.

"Don't step on them," Than said quietly. "This is a place of worship."

"The demons in the pictures are deities." Ares nimbly skirted an image of a dozen-eyed horned demon that was rumored to eat three elephants at a single sitting. "They could come alive."

Regan tugged on Than's hand. "Um...so if I step on that one? You come alive?"

He followed her gaze...and drew a harsh breath. Oh, *shit*.

Wraith went down on his heels and stared at Thanatos's likeness set into the floor with hundreds of brilliant tiles. "Dude. Why are you sucking on some guy's neck? And why are there vampires kneeling at your feet?"

A cold sweat broke out over his skin. "Dunno."

Limos jammed her sword into its scabbard so hard it threw her off balance. But just for a second. "Wrong answer, Than. I spent thousands of years lying. I'm pretty good at sniffing out bullshit. And brother, you *stink*."

Thanatos exhaled on a curse. "Do you remember your wedding night, Limos? When you begged us to leave your secrets alone?"

His sister's cheeks flamed crimson, and as she averted her gaze, shame shrunk his skin. At the time, he hadn't understood why she'd kept so much from him and Ares, but now that his own past was bearing down on him, he got it. Except that he wasn't protecting himself. He was protecting thousands of lives.

"Thanatos," Ares said, stepping next to Limos, "whatever it is, we can help."

No, they couldn't, but before he could even start to explain, Wraith was up and punching his fist through a stone panel in front of the altar.

"There," he said. "Scrolls." How the hell did the demon find crap so easily?

Regan moved to the scrolls, an eager, curious light in her eyes. She loved this kind of thing, didn't she? Finding new things, solving mysteries...admirable traits, but dangerous when you were the one keeping the secret she was sniffing out.

Very carefully, she withdrew the scrolls and laid them on top of the altar. "They're so delicate," she said, as she smoothed her fingers over their smooth surfaces. "This one..." Her finger stopped on the middle of five scrolls. "The author is so angry. Wait. Thanatos?"

Than moved to her, an ominous sensation dancing up his spine. "What?"

"He's angry at you. But why—"

A screech rang out, and from a hundred crevices in the walls and ceiling, demons emerged, as inky black and elusive as shadows.

"*Fuck*." Than palmed his scythe. "Nulls." The rarest demon species of all, creatures void of life and souls, shot through the cavern, immune to Than's souls and every known weapon. Their mouths gaped wide with jagged teeth that took chunks out of flesh with every pass they made. Only Wraith and Regan were impervious, which pissed off the Nulls even more, and every bite into Than's unprotected head became more vicious.

"I can't open a gate," Ares shouted.

Limos swiped at her head, dislodging one of the Nulls. "We have to get out of here!"

Than started to drag Regan toward the entrance, but pulled back when demons poured out of it—some clearly demons, others in human skins.

Regan screamed, and suddenly, his hand was empty. He wheeled around in time to see her being snatched by a vampire.

One of *his* vampires.

"Markus!" Than lunged, but Markus spun, using Regan as a shield, and Than had to check up at the last second to avoid slicing into her with his scythe.

Regan shouted obscenities, reaching behind her to claw at Markus's neck. A blur of Seminus demon slipped behind the vampire, and Markus flipped backward, hamstrung by Wraith's dagger. Than caught Regan before she hit the ground, but with a shocking amount of agility, she wrenched around and slammed her fist into the vampire's throat.

Yeah, he'd let her have the satisfaction of making Markus choke on his own blood. But Than got to make the kill.

Crunching his foot down on the vampire's chest so hard bones cracked, he bared his teeth at the asshole. "Who killed Dariq, Markus? Who all is involved in the plot against me?"

"Go to hell," Markus wheezed, and then he grinned, his fangs flashing wetly. "Your whore and bastard are going to die."

"Wrong," Thanatos snarled. "You die." He swept his scythe in an arc like a golf club, shearing off the top half of the vampire's skull. Blood and brains splattered on the wall, and suddenly, the demons all melted away.

He turned to Regan to assure himself that she was okay, but the bewildered expression on her face said that everything was *not* okay.

"The vampire's tattoo," Regan whispered, as she stared first at her hand and then at Thanatos. Oh, shit, she'd touched Markus's tattoo... "The scroll. Oh, my God."

Don't say it, Regan. Do not say it.

"You." Regan looked at Than as if he'd grown a new head. "*Bludrexe.* Sheoulic for Blood King. Oh, my God, it's you." She stumbled backward, catching herself on a blackened pillar. "That's why the author of those scrolls is so angry at you. A fallen angel didn't father the vampire race. *You did.*"

Eighteen

Regan was still reeling from what she'd seen and felt in the vampire's tattoo. Everything suddenly made so much sense. Now she knew why the daywalkers could touch her—they were Thanatos's creations.

They were his blood. In a way, they were his children.

He stood over the mosaic of himself, crimson rivulets dripping down his face, breaths sawing in and out as if he'd run a marathon. "Regan..."

Ares sheathed his blade and moved close. "What's going on, Than?"

"This isn't something I can discuss." Thanatos's voice was a low croak. "And what you've already heard can go no further than these walls."

"Thanatos." Regan put her hands over her belly to stop the trembling. "These vampires are trying to kill me and our son. I think it's time we found out what's going on."

For a long time, Than just stood there, his head hanging loosely from his broad shoulders. Finally, he sank against a pillar and stared up at the tiled ceiling. "After we were cursed..."

"We all went nuts," Ares said. "You've never spoken of what you did."

"That's because I couldn't. You asked me about my fangs...I got them with the curse." He blew out a long breath. "I needed blood. I don't remember much about those first few years, except that I was hungry. I went on a rampage, taking blood from humans...I ravaged entire villages. What I didn't know is that those I drained past recoverable blood loss but not to immediate death suffered with fever for days before dying...and then they rose as vampires. Daywalkers."

"His hunger is his burden," Regan murmured. "From your prophecy. We always wondered what that meant."

Than nodded. "Now you know."

"Damn," Limos breathed. "I always assumed it was your hunger for knowledge. You're always scouring the globe for books and crap." She flicked a glance at the mosaic of Than on the floor. "So did you create all daywalkers, or can they reproduce?"

"That's the thing," Than said. "Only *I* can create daywalkers. But the daywalkers...they created the nightwalkers."

"Holy fuck," Wraith blurted, and Regan nearly jumped. She'd forgotten he was there. Probably because he was lurking in the shadows. "So you're kind of my... grandfather."

Thanatos glared.

Wraith held up his hands. "Chill, Gramps. I don't want to sit on your knee or anything."

"Why didn't you tell us?" Limos asked.

"He couldn't," Ares said. "With our Seals broken, we could have used that information to turn the vampires against him, or to hurt him through them...a lot of possibilities."

Thanatos nodded. "Harvester warned me to keep it a secret from everyone, including my siblings. Only angels and fallen angels are allowed to create new species. Unauthorized species would be destroyed."

"So you made up a legend about how vampires were made," Wraith mused. "And it wasn't entirely a lie, because you're part angel."

"How'd you keep the daywalkers quiet?" Ares asked.

Regan stared at the dead daywalker, whose body was still intact since he was on Sheoulic soil, and realization dawned. "The tats," she said. "They're wards of a sort, aren't they?"

"Yeah." Than wiped blood from his brow, leaving behind smooth, healed skin. "I had them all marked with a silence ward so none of them could speak of their origins. The problem is that there are daywalkers in the wild. Wildings, we call them. I've tried to gather them all, but there are hidden clans. Some don't want to have to make the choice of serving me or being destroyed."

Wraith snorted. "Imagine that."

"It's a high price," Than admitted, "but the alternative is that the entire vampire species could be eradicated if the truth of their origins gets out, and that includes hybrids like dhampires and half-breeds like you."

"I'm not exactly a half-breed." Wraith said. "More of a freak of nature. But my mate is fangy, so my lips are sealed."

"It might not even matter now." Than's voice was dour. "The wildings seem to be rebelling and taking my staff with them. Once the Apocalypse breaks, all old rules go out the window, which is probably what they're counting on."

Limos kicked the vamp's body. "I wonder if Pestilence has something to do with the rebellion."

"He seems to have his fingers in all the pies," Than said.

Ares looked down at the scene depicting Thanatos with the vampires. "I'm surprised Harvester has kept your secret. It's not like her to be nice."

"No doubt there's a reason," Limos said, her voice dripping with acid. "So what about your nightwalker servants? Do they know your secret?"

Thanatos's eyes closed, and Regan slipped her hand into his. This must be hard for him, but she could only imagine that there was also a measure of relief that he could finally share his burden with his siblings. When Thanatos opened his eyes again, he gave her a grateful look.

"They know. They were all created by daywalkers and somehow found out, either because they were bitten during the day or they learned the truth from a wilding. They're tattooed with the same nondisclosure spells."

Regan returned to the scrolls and very carefully unrolled one. Although she couldn't read this particular Sheoulic language, she could feel the emotions rising out of the ink. These were definitely related to the texts that had been deciphered at Aegis Headquarters.

"Can anyone read these?"

Ares arranged the scrolls in the order they belonged.

"Most of this is about the author's vampire life after his turning. Boring shit. Guy was so emo. Christ, Than, you couldn't have turned someone less whiny?"

Thanatos flipped his brother the bird.

Ares fingered the last scroll. "But this one...This one speaks of our father. *The angel's name was Yenrieth, who the other, darker angel called a Lamb.*"

Regan frowned. "But in Biblical writings, isn't the Lamb thought to be Jesus?"

Ares tapped his fingers. "I think the female angel was using it as an insult, but then she talks about..." Ares hissed and stepped back so fast she thought the scroll had burned him.

Limos and Than both moved forward. "What is it?"

"I read that wrong," Ares said. "I must have."

"Why?" Thanatos asked. "What's it say?"

"The angels fought. They fought about Yenrieth's children and their Seals. And how Yenrieth...shit."

"Shit, what?" Thanatos came up behind Regan and gently tucked her next to him, as if preparing to brace her for what was coming. Or maybe to brace himself.

"How Yenrieth needed to quit running and accept his fate."

"And what, exactly, is his fate?" Limos asked, her violet eyes narrowed into slits.

Ares turned to them. "In the Book of Revelation, when it talks about the Lamb, it's talking about Yenrieth." He ran a trembling hand through his hair. "If the *Daemonica*'s prophecy fails, we still have to worry about the Biblical End of Days." Ares looked from Limos to Than. "And our own father is destined to break our Seals and start the Apocalypse."

Thanatos didn't take Regan back to his place right away. He needed sunshine and fresh air, open spaces and the smell of the ocean.

He also needed some time alone with Regan to gauge her intentions regarding the new information he'd just given her. If she told The Aegis what she'd learned, they could see to it that thousands of their enemies were destroyed in one snap of an angel's fingers.

Ares's beach was the perfect, safe place to have a little chat.

They stepped out of his Harrowgate into warm, white sand. Regan smiled into the breeze, her cheeks glowing in the sunlight.

"Where are we?"

"Greece. Ares's island. Thought you might like a change from the frigid weather at my place."

She raised an eyebrow at him. "And you figured I'd be more likely to promise to keep your secret if I wasn't feeling imprisoned and on the defensive."

"That too."

With a sigh, she walked over to the water's edge and sank down on one of the stone benches Ares had dotted the shoreline with, where she took off her shoes and let the waves lap at her toes. "By keeping this information from The Aegis, I'd be betraying them." Even as his blood began to boil, she continued. "But you're my son's father, and I can't betray him, either."

"Quite the dilemma," he growled.

"Quite." She patted the seat next to her, and he sat, liking being with her like this, even if the topic of the moment wasn't the most pleasant. "What do you know about your father?"

He looked out over the huge expanse of blue-green water. He'd always loved it here, but something about sharing such a beautiful setting with Regan made it even better. That, and the fact that being near the baby dimmed the sensation of deaths around the world. He could almost be at peace for the first time since his curse.

"Not much. He disappeared after we were conceived. If the account in that scroll is accurate, then he was still around in some way for a few decades. But it doesn't tell me where he is now."

"We have to find him."

"And why is that?"

Regan turned to him, her hair curling in soft tendrils around her face. "Your Biblical Seals…they're different than your *Daemonica* Seals?"

He wasn't sure where this was going, but he nodded. "According to Gethel, they're metal rings that protect the contents of four scrolls stored somewhere in Heaven. Why?"

"Because if it's true that your father is the Lamb referred to in Revelation, we might need him to break those Seals."

He blinked. "Why?"

"You're to fight for the side of good if your Biblical Seals break, right? The only way to stop the evil Apocalypse might be to start the good one. To at least start it on our terms. To give humanity a chance."

Abruptly, he understood how much of a warrior Regan was. How far she was willing to go to save the world, and why she'd agreed to seduce him in order to get pregnant.

Some of his anger over what she'd done to him faded, replaced by a grudging respect for her bravery.

"It would be like fighting fire with fire," he said. But heavenly fire was just as destructive as what came out of hell.

She smiled thinly. "Funny you should say that, because before my father joined The Aegis, he was a firefighter. I read all about them when I was a teenager, you know, trying to connect with him however I could."

"You never met him at all?"

She shook her head. "He died before I was even born. Though I guess saying he died isn't as accurate as how Lance likes to put it. As Lance says, he was 'put down.'"

Sounded like this Lance person was an asshole who needed to be 'put down.'"What do you know about him?"

One hand came up to cover her belly. She did that a lot when she was stressed, he'd noticed. "He came from a small town in Oregon. Troubled youth. The usual things that eventually lead people to The Aegis. I guess he wanted to be a firefighter all his life, and after only two years of it, he ran into a scorch demon. He kind of went crazy until he learned about The Aegis and that demons were real. It was my mom who helped him join up, and then he got possessed, knocked her up, and here I am." She looked down at where the baby was moving under her shirt. "What about you? I mean, I know you've never met your real father, but you thought you were human for the first years of your life, right?"

He wasn't sure what made him do what he did next, but he reached out and covered her hand with his. An instant, connecting warmth went through him, that virtual rope that seemed to loop all three of them together. The feeling was addictive, and he wondered if it would be the same once the baby was born.

"Yeah. I mean, I knew I was different. I was stronger than everyone else. Healed fast. Saw things other people couldn't see, like Harrowgates and demons. I was the only boy in the family . . . I had three sisters, so my mother was always busy with them, but my father would take me hunting or on trips to trade with other clans. We were pretty close."

Her thumb smoothed back and forth over his, and the intimate caress went all the way to his soul. "Do you want to meet your real father?"

"I'll live if I don't."

"That's not what I asked."

He knew that, but he didn't know how to answer. He'd been hunting down clues about his father for thousands of years, but now that Thanatos's own baby was on the way, he had a whole new outlook on a father's role in his child's life.

"I don't know if I should."

"Why not?"

"Because I'd want to know why the fuck he let Lilith do what she did with us," he snapped, surprising himself at the level of rage welling up. "He let Limos be raised in hell. He sat by and allowed us to be separated, and then he didn't help when our worlds fell apart."

"Maybe he couldn't," she said softly. "Maybe he did what he thought was best."

In his chest, Than's heart turned to ice. "Maybe you're trying to justify what you plan to do to your own son."

She squeezed his hand. "Thanatos, no—"

He yanked out of her grip and shoved to his feet. "I am not my father. I will not abandon my child. Like father, like son, I might have fallen for your seductive skills the way he fell for Lilith's, but I will not let you give our son away, least of all to be raised in The Aegis."

"The Aegis saved my life," she said. "They *gave* me a life when no one else wanted me."

He snorted. "They used you, Regan."

"They need me."

"They need you because of what you can do for them. That's the only reason they want you. When are you going to open your eyes and see that?"

Regan's lips parted, but no sound came out. She might as well have screamed, though, her pain was so etched into her expression. Somewhere inside, she'd had the same thoughts about The Aegis and her role with them.

"And why should I *open my eyes*?" The gold flecks in her hazel eyes glittered, little sparks that punctuated the anger in her words. "Will it make you feel better if I have nothing and no one?"

He turned away from her, because while it wouldn't make him feel better for her to lose everything she'd ever known, he wasn't sure it would be a bad thing, either. She was too dependent on an organization that didn't appreciate her. Besides, she didn't have no one. She had a son, and if she'd just give up her crazy idea that the baby needed someone else to raise it, he'd make sure she was a part of its life.

His scalp prickled, and a Harrowgate opened ten yards away. Ares and Limos exploded from it, both still armored, their weapons drawn and bloodied.

"We have trouble," Limos said. "Vampire trouble. Your wildings have taken over Notre Dame cathedral. They're slaughtering everyone."

"It's blatant." Ares's deep voice was as clipped as his movements, which meant he was fully engaged in strategy mode. "It's either a message or a trap."

Thanatos's gut twisted. "Either way, it's meant for me." He nodded at Limos. "Take Regan back to my place. Ares, let's see what they want. And then we'll kill them."

Notre Dame.

Thanatos had witnessed much of its construction. Now he was witnessing horrific destruction as a dozen day-walkers defiled the cathedral with demonic energy and human suffering.

A local Aegis cell had joined forces with the police to keep everyone out, but they couldn't block Ares and Than-atos, who passed through the blockade invisibly, hidden within a Khote spell. Inside, Nulls shot around like wisps of black smoke, and vampires crouched on ledges, watch-ing as Ares and Thanatos walked across a floor smeared with blood and littered with dead and injured humans.

"Who is in charge here?" Than called out.

The Nulls screeched, nearly drowning out the deep laughter of a blond vampire who emerged from between two pillars, his teeth glistening with the remains of his last meal.

"You can call me Medras." He leaped onto an organ, the thud of his boots echoing off the walls. Blood stained his faded jeans and white shirt and streaked his arms. The scent of death clung to him, and Than's insides buzzed with his own desire to kill.

"Jesus," Ares murmured as he took in the vampires assembled around them. "How many daywalkers did you make?"

Thanatos swallowed, his throat burning with self-loathing. "More than I thought. I don't know how—"

"You don't know how?" Medras snarled. "Let me remind you. I was a monk, traveling through Franconia with my brothers, and you set upon us like an animal. Do you even remember that?"

No, Than didn't. He thought he knew of all incidents, but maybe he'd been in one of his killing rampages. Oh, God, how many more daywalkers existed than he'd believed?

"I didn't think you recognized me." Bitterness permeated every one of Medras's words. "But I will never forget your face. Nor will I forget the evil that took over my body and forced me to kill so many until I gained control of my bloodlust." In a smooth surge, he swept a cowering human off the floor.

"Stop!" Thanatos started toward the vampire, but froze when Medras put a blade to the human's throat.

"One step closer, and he dies."

"If this is control over your bloodlust, then you'd better work a little harder," Than growled. Not that he had much room to talk. "Why are you doing this?"

Sunlight streamed through the stained glass windows, drenching Medras in a kaleidoscope of light as he sneered at Than. "You haven't figured it out yet? You haven't gotten it through your thick head that daywalkers don't want to serve you? We want our freedom."

"*Fools*. I'm protecting you. Protecting the entire vampire race."

"Not anymore, *Bludrexe*. Once the Apocalypse starts, we won't need your protection. All we have to do is kill your brat and break your Seal."

Thanatos hissed and, for the first time in front of Ares, let his fangs slice down in fury. "How did you know about my Seal? You couldn't have put all of this together without help."

"True. My brethren and I have been in hiding for centuries, but we were able to keep an eye on you. Not all of your little house slaves are happy, Horseman."

Than was going to rip this bastard's balls off and feed them to him. "So one of my servants reported back to you about my impending fatherhood. But that doesn't explain why you think harming the child will get you what you want."

"Because, you simpleton. We're tired of hiding, so we went to your brother. He was very interested to know our origins. We were interested to know that killing your bastard would break your Seal. Pestilence promised us power over the nightwalkers and freedom from your rule if we pledged allegiance to him in the Final Battle."

The Final Battle, in *Daemonica* prophecy, was the battle between all four of the Horsemen, when they fought each other for ultimate control of the Earth. Knowing that Than's own creations wouldn't stand with him pissed him the hell off. The betrayals kept coming. At this rate, Ares and Limos would turn against him before the end of the day.

Fury iced over his heart and added to the growing sinister vibration inside that demanded he seek out some massive scene of death. The draw to death had been muted while he'd been with Regan and the baby, but now that he was away from her, it roared back with a vengeance, clouding his mind and darkening his thoughts.

"How many of you are there?"

"There are clans all over the world, all united against you."

"And amongst my staff?"

"For some reason, there are those who are loyal to you. But I'll not say who." Medras smiled. "What's the matter, *Bludrexe*? Are you feeling the need to go somewhere?"

"I feel it, too." Ares shifted his weight, growing as restless as Than. "Pestilence has done something...bad."

Shit. Than tried to open a Harrowgate, but, like most major holy places, it was warded against them. "I have to get to Regan before—"

Too late. As if a massive hand had reached out of thin air and grabbed him, Than was snatched away and dropped into the middle of a nightmare he'd been through before.

The stench of death became a heady drug as he called out Styx and palmed his scythe. Must...kill. The desire to relieve bodies of their souls clamored loudly in his skull, but another, newer desire warred with it.

Regan.

No. Oh, God, no. Half of him wanted her naked, screaming his name as he thrust between her creamy thighs. He wanted to claim her, mark her, use her so thoroughly that she'd be too tired to ever leave his bed. The other half of him wanted to kill, to draw blood and destroy everything in his path.

He roared in confusion and fury, trying desperately to

hold onto conscious thought, because if he didn't, if he let the death haze take him in a killing rampage, he might just let both halves win.

And then his draw to Regan and his desire to kill could become one and the same, and Regan would die.

Nineteen

Sunshine. Pestilence hated it. And yet, when killing and fucking didn't soothe him, sunshine did. No doubt the warmth was a comfort left over from the days before his Seal broke, when that fool, Reseph, hung out on beaches with females and margaritas.

Just last night, Pestilence had dreamed of one of those times, one of Limos's shindigs on a secluded California beach.

It might not have been the best of Limos's parties, but it was the one that stuck out in Reseph's memory the most. Even over the ball Limos had thrown in 1888 London, where Thanatos went ghastbat-shit crazy and killed one of the guests. Reseph never knew what had set Than off, but thanks to Thanatos, the serial killer demon the papers had dubbed Jack The Ripper never struck again.

Pestilence wondered where the Ripper's demon soul was. He could be a lot of fun to let loose on the world again. There were hundreds of thousands of demon souls Pestilence wanted to unleash on the human world, and as soon as he destroyed Azagoth and Hades, he'd do exactly that. The problem was finding someone who knew where the Grim Reaper's realm was located. Only a certain class of angel knew the location, and it wasn't easy to catch one of the slippery buggers. Memitim were crafty. And more hardy than he'd anticipated.

He'd managed to capture one, but the male had withstood two solid weeks of torture without revealing a single useful detail. Now his stuffed and mounted body swung from the Sydney Harbor Bridge.

No matter. Lucifer, who was still pissed as hell at the Horsemen, and Limos specifically for killing his pet fallen angel, had reminded Pestilence that an ex-Memitim was sitting right under their noses: Idess, the very ex-Memitim who had performed the marriage ceremony for Limos and Arik.

How things came full circle, didn't they? Pestilence was going to make Idess talk. And scream. And after she revealed Azagoth's location, he'd make her scream some more.

He glanced down at his watch, wondering if Than had found the present Pestilence had left for him yet. Surely he was done with the daywalkers at Notre Dame by now. And what Pestilence wouldn't have given to see the look on Than's face when he learned that the daywalkers were siding with Pestilence.

His arrangement with the vampires was a perfect double-tap to the head with demon-caliber slugs. Not only was it one huge *fuck you* to Thanatos, but it could put the Apocalypse into motion. The angrier his brother got, the more mistakes he'd make, leaving openings Pestilence could exploit. And, if Pestilence played his cards right, Than's temper would put him into a murderous rage, and he'd kill the baby himself.

Smiling, Pestilence tossed a seashell into the ocean waves on the Santa Barbara beach where Limos's party had been. The shell made a plopping noise as it hit the sunlit water. This was what he'd done the day of Limos's party, after all the guests had gone and Limos was sleeping off a week's worth of rum and tequila. Reseph hadn't been tired...just pleasantly sedate. He'd drunk lots of booze, had lots of sex, and had played his ass off in the water and on the sand. With everyone gone, he'd stood at the shoreline and chucked rocks and shells into the surf.

Than eased up to him, all silent and broody.

"'Sup." Reseph winged another shell into the water.

"Nothing."

Yeah, there was no "nothing" when it came to Thanatos. If he joined you silently, he wanted something, even if it was only companionship. Limos and Ares would prod Than for info, but Reseph knew better. The guy opened up when he was ready, and if you pushed, you were either looking at an empty space, or you were looking at knuckles in your face.

Reseph liked his nose unbroken and his teeth where they were, thank you very much.

They stood like that for a good ten minutes, Reseph plunking rocks and shells into the waves, and Thanatos doing his mannequin imitation. Finally, Than took a deep, resigned breath.

"I'm tired."

"That's what beds are for."

*Than closed his eyes and tilted his face to the sun.
"Not like that. I'm tired of nothing changing."*

*"Dude." Reseph snorted. "Wheels hadn't even been
invented when we were born. Now there are people hanging out in space. Things change."*

*"We had wheels," Than said dryly. "But that's not
what I'm talking about."*

Reseph knew that. "You're talking about you."

*"I'm talking about you." Than pegged Reseph with a
hard look. "You're a fucking idiot."*

*"Ah…thanks? Can I call you an obnoxious ass-
hole now?"*

Than snorted. "Like you ever needed permission."

*"True." Reseph punched him in the shoulder. "You're
an obnoxious asshole. Now, why am I a fucking idiot?"*

*"Man, you just opened a lot of doors with that ques-
tion." Thanatos grinned, and Reseph punched him again,
harder. "Yeah, yeah. I'll narrow it down."*

*"Oh, this should be good," Reseph said, barely resist-
ing an eye roll.*

"You're a whore."

Reseph blinked. "I'm failing to see the problem."

*A breeze kicked up, and Than turned into it like a
dog with his head out of a car window. "Don't you want
more? After five thousand years of screwing everything
in sight, don't you want to settle down with a mate? Don't
you want kids?"*

*A twinge of guilt soured the gallon of piña coladas in
his stomach. They weren't talking about Reseph…they
were talking about Than.*

*That was how Than worked. He couldn't just come out
and say that he wanted a family so bad it hurt…he had*

to take the longest fucking route he could and make you read between the lines. Of course, if Reseph said flat-out that he knew the deal, Than would only retreat or attack, so Reseph proceeded carefully.

Which really wasn't his style. But Thanatos didn't open up often, and Reseph wasn't going to make him regret doing it.

"I don't want kids." Reseph tossed another shell. "I mean, they're cute…from a distance. Like opossums. And a mate? That would seriously put a damper on my sex life. It's like, the chicks get hotter every hundred years or so. What if I took a mate today, and then in a hundred years, they've all evolved into supermodels?"

Thanatos muttered something that sounded a lot like "fucking idiot." "So you've never met anyone who even tempted you into more than a one-night stand?"

He shrugged. "There's been a few. Remember that succubus from Sri Lanka? I kept her around for an entire month."

"Exclusively?"

"No. Duh." Reseph reached up and scratched his chest, which had grown oddly tight. "Immortal females are great to party with, but keeping them around as mates? Eternity is a long time to be stuck with one female. And humans…"

"They die."

Easily. They died so…easily. And early. Their lifespans were so pathetically short. The tightness squeezed harder, until it almost hurt to breathe. He'd lost a human once, and somehow that pain had survived the centuries. It wouldn't happen again.

"If you could have a mate and kids, would you?" Reseph asked.

Silence stretched, broken by the waves and the occasional seagull. Thanatos scooped up his own handful of rocks and shells and heaved them all into the water.

"In a heartbeat," he said quietly. "I would give up everything, my very soul, to have just one human lifetime with a mate and children."

The skin on the back of Pestilence's neck prickled, and he turned away from the ocean just as Harvester materialized in front of him. She looked like hell, but she somehow still managed to look extremely fuckable. He couldn't wait for the Apocalypse to start so he could have her anytime he wanted.

She cut right to the chase, which he appreciated. "Your fucking ex-Watcher needs to die."

"Gethel?"

"Who else?" she screeched. "I'm going to pluck her feathers and shove every one of them up her ass before I make a halo out of her skull."

"I'd like to see that. Lemme know when tickets go on sale."

Harvester practically shook with fury, her black wings quivering against her slender shoulders. "How did you know to trace Thanatos to Aegis Headquarters?"

He tapped his temple. "Brotherly intuition."

"Bullshit."

He heaved a sigh. "Okay, you caught me. I was tipped off."

"By who?"

"Shouldn't that be 'whom'?" He shrugged. "I was never good at all that language-y stuff."

Harvester, clearly lacking a sense of humor today, blew a gasket. She came a foot off the sand, wings spread, her eyes glowing red and her fangs jutting from her gums. "I don't give a fuck! *Who tipped you off?*"

He had her on her back, wings crumpled beneath her, his hand on her throat, before the echo of her words faded from the salt air.

"You do not yell at me, you winged whore." He inhaled, taking in her anger and her fear. The latter made his cock hard. "You're lucky I'm in a good mood, or I'd school you on what a female like you should be doing with her mouth." He dragged his free hand down her throat to her breast, where he flicked his thumb over the nipple. "When the Apocalypse starts, we'll rule the world, make beautiful hellspawn, and drink the blood of virgins before we fuck them." God, his dick was so hard it hurt.

"I'd sooner screw Reaver than you," she ground out.

He nodded. "Good idea. We'll both do him after Than's Seal breaks."

Harvester hissed and rolled out from under Pestilence. He stayed in the sand, stretched out, propped up on an elbow.

"Who? Who tipped you off? Answer me!"

"You're a goddamned angel with a bone." He fell back on the beach with a sigh. "Fine. It was Lucifer. No idea who he got the intel from. I actually thought it was from you. Came to him via a *khnive.*"

Khnives...nasty creatures that could be summoned as spies or messengers. Someone was fond of using them, as evidenced by the fact that dozens had been summoned to attack Limos's husband, Arik, a few months ago.

Pestilence would love to know who to thank, but that was the thing about Apocalypses...so much behind-the-scenes maneuvering.

Harvester flashed out of there without so much as a thank you. The bitch. He'd teach her some manners once she was his.

Wouldn't be long. Smiling, he reached into his pocket and withdrew a tiny blue rattle. It was his gift to his unborn nephew. Pestilence figured that a baby who was going to have a dagger plunged into his heart just moments after birth should at least get a gift.

He shook the tiny toy, the sound giving him shivers of pleasure. *I would give up everything, my very soul, to have just one human lifetime with a mate and children.*

Thanatos's prophetic words rang through Pestilence's ears, a perfect accompaniment to the tinny noise of the rattle. Thanatos would have his child, and its death would cost him his Seal . . . and his soul.

Twenty

"You're avoiding me, Limos."

Limos, fully outfitted in her Croix viper Samurai-style armor and her raven hair woven into a thick braid, swung around to Regan, guilt plastered all over her expression. "Me? Nah. I'm just busy." She gestured to the keep's front door. "Hunting rats with Arik and the hellhounds. See? Busy."

Uh-huh. In the twelve hours Than had been gone, Regan had been busy, too, dividing her time between his library, where she tried to find any information that might provide clues as to Yenrieth's whereabouts, and cleaning. Not that Than's keep needed to be cleaned. She just needed it to be in order.

So she'd been busy, but not so busy that she missed Limos's odd behavior.

Regan set down her sandwich and milk on the table in front of the TV and turned back to Limos, who had inched closer to the door. "What's going on?"

In Than's absence, Limos and Arik were taking turns keeping an eye on her, and Cara had assigned a dozen more hellhounds to stay at the keep, so Regan doubted this was about her safety. Especially since Than's vampires had kept their distance, either confined to their quarters or working in the outbuildings, and Regan was pretty sure Limos had taken a couple of them aside for interrogation—and to scare the undead out of them.

Pestilence hadn't shown up either, which Limos was certain meant he was up to no good, and that was true enough. The news was full of his handiwork, from bacteria-contaminated water supplies to rapidly spreading plagues to freaking *zombies* in Malta and North Korea.

So despite the relative quiet at Than's place, Limos was acting weird, and her avoidance was starting to make Regan suspicious.

"There's nothing wrong," Limos said brightly. "Really."

Regan narrowed her eyes at the Horseman. "Did Eidolon say something to you in private?"

The doctor had come by for a checkup, and although he couldn't touch her, he'd asked a bazillion questions. He'd been frank with her, warning her that this could be a difficult birth, but he swore to be there for it. For some reason, she had actually been comforted by the idea that the demon doctor was going to deliver the baby.

"There's nothing wrong with the baby or Than or anything. It's just…" Limos looked down at her bright green nails, which poked out of her fingerless gauntlets.

"It's just what?"

Limos shifted her weight and looked at her other hand. "Shiny."

"Limos!"

"Fine." The Horseman dropped her hands to her sides and sighed. "Arik talked to Kynan. The Aegis recruited a cell of Guardians to come here, but it looks like Pestilence managed to break the encryption on the information he stole from your headquarters. He's attacking Aegis cells all over the world, and the Guardians who were scheduled to come here were some of the casualties."

Oh, God. As if all her nerve endings had withered, Regan went numb all over, and she sank onto the couch before her legs gave out.

Limos rushed over and took a seat next to Regan. "We didn't want to tell you because you've got enough to deal with."

"I'd rather know," Regan said quietly.

"Okay, then. We'll stop coddling you."

"Good. Coddling doesn't suit you." Regan stared at the other woman, wondering if Limos's concerned expression was a mere mask. "Why are you being so nice to me?"

"Nice?" Limos snorted. "I want to beat you with a Moraki bone stick."

So much for the coddling. Somehow though, this was better. "Because of what I did to Thanatos?"

"I was pissed for a while," Limos admitted. "But I don't have a lot of room to judge, and as Arik pointed out, you were trying to save the world." There was a beat of silence, and then Limos blurted, "I'm jealous of you. There. I said it. I want a baby."

"You're afraid to get pregnant until all of this is over, aren't you?"

Limos nodded. "If my Seal broke while I was pregnant..." She trailed off, and when she spoke again, there was a note of anger in her voice. "I'm so jealous I could scream. I want a baby so bad, and you've got one you're giving away."

In an instant, Regan felt as if she'd been dragged behind a truck, leaving everything, including her emotions, scraped raw. She'd gone into this with skin like steel armor, thinking she could get pregnant and give up the baby unscathed. But she'd gotten one hell of a chink in her armor that night with Thanatos, and with every passing day, with every move the baby made, her armor eroded.

She loved the little pony so much it hurt. So much that she dreaded giving birth, because she'd have to somehow drum up the strength and unselfishness to hand him over to people who were far better suited to care for him than she was.

"It's not that I *want* to, Limos." She drew in a shaky breath. "It's that I have to."

"It's what's best. I get that," Limos said. "But I think I'd do whatever it took to make sure that being with *me* was what was best." She shoved to her feet, turning away quickly, but not before Regan spotted the telltale glisten of unshed tears in Limos's violet eyes. "I have to hunt rats. Or whatever creepy things might be spying on the keep. Um... bye."

Limos practically ran out the door, leaving Regan on the verge of tears herself. A suffocating heaviness centered in her chest. *Could* she ensure that keeping the baby was what was best? Once Pestilence was gone and the threat to the baby's life was eliminated, could Regan give it a home?

Yeah, because a one-room apartment at Aegis Headquarters was a home. Okay, so maybe she could get a real apartment. Then what? The Aegis wasn't exactly kid-friendly. There were no "bring your kid to work" days. And she might be confident in her ability to take down a sewer full of demons, but she didn't know the first thing about raising a kid.

For all that she kept insisting that The Aegis was her family, she had no one to help her.

They need you because of what you can do for them. That's the only reason they want you. When are you going to open your eyes and see that?

Maybe...maybe it was time for a change. Maybe, if they managed to avert the Apocalypse, she could build a life for herself and her child.

Her child. For eight months, she'd tried to refer to the life inside her as "the baby," "the kid," "the child." She'd called it other affectionate names, but only in the last couple of days had she begun to think of it as hers.

Hers and Thanatos's.

Could she do it?

Her stomach growled, tearing her away from thoughts that were probably dangerous to be having anyway. There would be no future for anyone if the most pressing matter, stopping the Apocalypse, didn't take precedence.

She settled the plate on her lap and turned on the TV... and immediately wished she hadn't. Breaking News. A Pakistani military unit had discovered hundreds of dead bodies—all impaled on giant stakes. The images weren't graphic, but even the grainy, fuzzed-out pics showed Regan all she needed to know.

The scene looked exactly like the memory she'd read in Than's tattoo.

Something flashed on the screen, something that froze

her heart mid-beat. Hand shaking, she rewound the feed
to rows of stakes and broken bodies on the ground. But
what drew her attention was the shadow to the right of the
picture, a shadow in the shape of a man on a horse.

"Thanatos." Limos's gasp came from over Regan's
shoulder.

"He wouldn't—" Regan cleared her throat of the
hoarseness. "He didn't—"

"Of course he didn't," Limos said, but there was a
tremor of doubt in her voice.

The giant wooden door burst inward, and Thanatos
stormed inside, his armor dripping with blood and gore,
his eyes burning an unholy gold flecked with crimson.

"Shit." Limos yanked Regan out of her chair and tucked
her behind Limos's back. "We have to get you out of here."

Too late for that. Thanatos let out a furious snarl and
stalked toward them, sword drawn, expression a mask of
murder.

It was the same expression she'd seen on his face before
he slaughtered his best friend.

From out of nowhere, Arik charged, slamming into
the Horseman and knocking him off balance. "Go!" he
shouted to Limos, and then he was airborne, knocked off
his feet by Thanatos's meaty fist.

"Run, Regan," Limos barked. "Outside. I'll gate you
out of here." Thanatos lunged, and their swords met in a
deafening clang of metal on metal.

"No," Regan yelled. "Stop!"

No one heard. Thanatos and his sister were a whirlwind of blades and armor. His strength was countered by
her speed, and with each blow, both Horsemen grew more
savage, their strikes aimed for necks, heads, eyes.

There could be no winner here . . . only pain.

Limos danced gracefully out of the sweep of Than's blade. As his sword plunged downward, she thrust the tip of her blade beneath one of the plates that protected his side. He yelped in pain, blood rushing down his flank in a gruesome stream.

"Stop it!" Regan screamed.

Thanatos rounded on her, eyes blazing, and she suddenly regretted not following Limos's advice. He moved toward her slowly, his gaze holding her rooted to the floor. Her hand crept behind her back, to the Aegis dagger he'd returned to her. He didn't miss the action, and his lips lifted in a nasty snarl.

Even as she freed the blade, he was on her, his big body pressing her into the wall. A lifetime of training came back to her in an instant, and she brought the dagger up, leveling the tip just under his jaw.

"It's coated in hellhound saliva, Horseman. One nick, and you're a statue."

A low, pulsating purr rose up in his chest. His hands, which had been gripping her shoulders, shifted, one up to cup the back of her head, while the other took a slow slide over her clavicle and lower, where it stopped between her breasts.

"Do it, Regan." His voice was a tortured rasp. "Please, cut me."

"Why?" He'd been immobilized for over eight months. For him to ask for more of it, for him to make that kind of sacrifice . . . it left her reeling.

"I told you that you woke a sleeping demon, Aegi. My sex demon half is . . . raging."

She swallowed dryly. "You don't want to kill me?"

He dipped his head, nearly driving the blade into his jugular, and closed his mouth over her throat. The softness of his lips was a stark contrast to the stinging scrape of his teeth followed by the soothing laps of his tongue. Her entire body went loose and rubbery. And hot. Very, very hot.

Somewhere in the back of her mind, she noted his hand leaving her chest, and then his armor was gone and he was pressed against her, bare-chested with his erection pressing into her belly through the fly of his pants.

"Does that feel like I want to kill you?" he whispered against her throat. And then he went stiff, his lips peeling back from his teeth. "Don't do it, Limos."

From over Than's shoulder, Regan caught a glimpse of Limos easing up behind him, her sword poised to strike.

"Limos—" Regan tried to warn her off, but it was too late. Thanatos shoved his own blade in a reverse thrust, catching Limos in the neck.

Limos stumbled back, clutching her throat. Cursing Than to hell, Arik caught her.

"Get out." Than's voice was a lethal rumble, but he was kissing Regan's throat as he spoke, and his hands were roving over her body with the kind of care one would use while handling a newborn kitten.

Regan caught Limos's pained gaze. *Go. I'll be fine.*

The female Horseman inclined her head in a nod, and then she allowed Arik to help her out of there. Limos would be fine, Regan knew, but she'd be sore for a while.

Thanatos nipped her earlobe and flicked his tongue over the tiny bite before sucking it between his lips. Lower, his hand cupped her breast as his thumb swiped across her nipple, and even through the fabric of her blouse and bra, the pleasure was luxurious.

"Cut me." One hand came up to wrap around hers where she still held the dagger to his throat. "Last chance."

She opened her palm, and the blade clattered to the floor.

Twenty-one

"*Fuck.*"

Thanatos's harsh curse should probably have frightened Regan, but her body was on fire, and the only thing he'd done was throw gasoline on those flames.

He swept her into his arms and strode down the hall, his mouth on hers, his teeth nipping at her lips. He kicked the bedroom door closed and in three strides, was at the edge of the bed. Despite the barely leashed power radiating from his body, he placed her so gently on the mattress that she could have been made of the most delicate crystal.

By the time she'd pushed herself up on one elbow, he'd ripped—literally—his pants off. The wound on his thigh had already knitted closed and was now hidden behind a gorgeous medieval lion tattoo. It didn't matter how many times she'd seen him naked...each time she couldn't help but stare. His body was a work of masculine art.

Slabs of sleek, toned muscle rippled under a tapestry of tattoos on deeply tanned skin. From his neck to his toes, he was a living, breathing tablet of history, emotion, and sex.

Silence stretched in the half-dozen feet of space separating them as he stood, chest heaving, his hands fisted at his sides, his head bowed. Still, he watched her through slitted eyes that smoldered.

"I need to see you." His voice was harsh, as smoky as his gaze.

A serious case of nerves made her stomach churn. "I'll put on my nightgown," she said, as she fumbled around on the covers for it.

Thanatos took a single, heavy step closer. "I have missed eight months of seeing my son grow inside you. Don't deprive me of another day."

A wild series of glorious shivers skittered over her skin. God, what a wonderful husband and father he'd have made if fate hadn't cursed him the way it had. He would have been there for every second of her pregnancy if she'd asked him to be—and probably even if she hadn't. Most women would kill to have that kind of interest and devotion.

Most women. Regan had never considered the idea that she'd have a relationship or a family outside of The Aegis. So maybe it was her hormones messing with her brain, or maybe it was her biological clock ticking, or maybe it was the fact that so many of her Aegis family members had died recently, but she was suddenly wondering what being in a relationship would be like.

Being in a relationship with Thanatos.

You're crazy. Certifiable with a capital C.

"Regan."

She looked up. Thanatos had moved closer, and dear God, he'd taken his arousal in his hand and was stroking himself. Every pass of his hand revealed glimpses of dusky flesh against a background of fluid black lines that defined his tattoos.

The effect on her was insanely powerful, and with shaking hands, she peeled out of her stretchy maternity pants and her tent-like top. Were they really going to do this? One look in his eyes told her that yes, they were. They *so* were.

Though her hands shook, she wriggled out of her bra and underwear.

"Beautiful," he rasped, and man, she melted. "Come here."

She obeyed, compelled by the erotic authority in his tone. All her life she'd needed to be in control, taking orders only from her superiors. But something about Thanatos made her want to comply, to for once be okay with giving over control to someone who wouldn't hurt her. At least, not physically. Emotionally...that was another story.

"What now?" she asked when she was standing directly in front of him.

In answer, he took her hand and placed it on his shaft. His breath hissed through his teeth and his gaze simmered with heat. Her body responded with a jolt of need that electrified every nerve ending. If he so much as touched her now, just the lightest brush of one finger, she'd come.

Squeezing her fist, she slid her thumb up over the satiny head of him, and as he groaned her sensitivity heightened even more, until she was sure that she wouldn't even need a touch...just the whisper of his breath across her skin would set her off.

"Bed," he said. "Now."

Regan's chest went tight, so tight that every heartbeat hurt. Silly, maybe, since she'd known what he wanted when he carried her into the bedroom, but at the sudden, undeniable reality, she froze in a sticky mire of guilt. She'd caused Thanatos so much pain, and it had all started on that mattress.

In a raspy whisper, she blurted, "I...can't." Overwhelmed by shame, she dashed to the bathroom and slammed the door behind her.

"Woman." His footsteps pounded. "What are you doing?"

She locked the door. "I want to be alone."

"Too bad. I'm not done with you."

The walls closed in on her, and how had she ever thought the bathroom was large? It suddenly felt as confining as a coffin.

A sharp rap on the door made her jump. "I said, I'm not done with you."

Her gaze darted around the room, but what was she hoping to find? A hidden trap door? When no secret passageway appeared, she gave up looking and simply slipped to the cold floor.

"Open the door, Regan." Than's voice was low, quiet, which made it all the more frightening. It was the calm before the storm.

A storm she deserved.

"Open the goddamned door," he said slowly, "or I'll break it down."

She wrapped her arms around her legs, bracing for Hurricane Thanatos.

"Regan!" Than's voice cracked like a whip. "Last chance."

She closed her eyes and began to count the seconds between the lightning and the thunder. At six, the door crashed inward. His footsteps were like thunderclaps as he came closer.

"Don't," she said, in a voice that was much shakier than she'd have liked. "Don't touch me."

He inhaled sharply. "Is it the baby?"

"No," she whispered.

"Then what the hell is wrong with you?"

She opened her eyes, but she couldn't look at him. Instead, she stared at his feet.

"Regan?" His tone was softer now, tempered with concern. Had fear for the baby brought him out of his rage? "Answer me. What's going on?"

"I…" She inhaled, as if the air could help her find her big girl voice. "I'm sorry."

"For what?"

"For last time. I'm sorry. I'm so sorry. I've tried to tell you, but you don't believe me. I don't know what else to do. I know you want me to pay for what I did to you, and I'll do whatever you want. I swear it. But I won't have sex with you. I don't want to hurt you again."

"Hurt…*me*?"

"What if…when we're on the bed, you remember being…" Her stomach rebelled, and she had to swallow the sourness in her mouth. "Being drugged and…and held down while I…" A sob escaped her, and she started to tremble so hard her teeth chattered.

"Regan?" He dropped to his knees in front of her, but she still couldn't look at him. "Regan, listen to me. You were drugged, too."

Tears stung her eyes. "But everything was so clear afterward. I don't remember much of the actual ... sex ... except in my dreams. But I remember afterward it was like crystal, and I don't understand how I couldn't have been aware of what was happening—" He touched the tip of one warm finger to her lips, silencing her.

"It was the drug. It makes you unclear on everything you're doing, hearing, and seeing until you climax, and then it's like a switch turns on and everything is back to normal. You see what happened as it really was."

"I still ... I still ..." She gulped a breath so she could talk. "Since that night, I've felt so hollow inside, and as the baby grew, he filled that space, but when he's gone ..." What would happen to her? Would she be an empty shell? Was that what had happened to her mother? "Oh, God, I'm *so* sorry. If I could take it back, I would. If I could do it all over again, I would. I swear to you." She was babbling now, her emotions overriding all the logic she'd filled herself with, the logic that had allowed her to justify what she'd done.

She'd been trying to *save the world*.

Thanatos swore, a harsh, vile curse in Sheoulic. "Don't say that. Don't ever say that to me again." He gripped her shoulders and forced her to look at him. "I've been pissed and putting you through hell for your betrayal, but the truth is that I've been too full of righteous anger to admit that if I had been in your shoes, I'd have considered the idea, too. It's easy to cast judgment when everything goes wrong and *you* weren't the one having to do something distasteful for the greater good."

"It was wrong—"

"Yes, it was wrong, but only because you were tricked. But shit, Regan, what you did was brave. You didn't know what you were walking into when you came here. You risked your life and did something that scarred you to save people who would probably judge you harshly and will never have any idea what you risked your life for. Yeah, you fucked me over—literally—but you did it for a bigger cause, and it was a selfless act."

Not entirely. She'd done it for the save-the-world stuff, but Than had been right when he'd said there was always a personal consideration. She'd needed to be useful to The Aegis. She'd needed to be needed.

"I'm sorry—"

"What did I just say? Don't you dare be sorry. If you're sorry, if you could change things, that would mean you wouldn't be pregnant, and I wouldn't have a son on the way."

She wasn't sure she'd heard that right. "But we created your *agimortus*."

"And you know what? I don't care. I've been alone for five thousand years, Regan. I've wanted children. I've wanted sex. I've wanted to be with someone. I'd have sold my soul for those things. Maybe it's selfish of me, but I can't be sorry, and I don't want you to be, either." He hooked a finger under her chin and stared at her for so long she started to squirm. "And I don't hate you. I hate what you have planned for our son, and we'll discuss that, but I don't hate *you*."

Than leaned over, and she prepared herself for... she wasn't sure what for. But it sure wasn't for him to gather her in his arms and carry her out of the bathroom.

"Are you going to put me in the dungeon again?" she muttered into his chest. God, she hoped not. She was far too tired to fight. She would, because she didn't know how to do anything else, but she didn't know what would be left after she was done.

"Shh." He set her on the bed and stretched out behind her, his long, hard body against her back. One hand came down on her arm and began to stroke. "I'm sorry." His voice was a low murmur in her hair. "No more fighting."

"No more fighting," she whispered.

"I should be taking better care of you. If you're hungry, I'll feed you. If you're tired, I'll sit by the bed and watch over you while you sleep. And I won't hold you to the eight months thing." He pressed his forehead against the back of her neck, and she moaned at the intimacy of it. "I wasn't lying when I said you'd awakened something sexual in me, something that frankly scares the shit out of me. But that's my problem, not yours. I won't make you do anything you don't want to do."

"What…" She swallowed. "What if I want to?"

Behind her, he went taut, and she kicked herself for asking him that. They were in a fragile place right now, and he might be all for revenge sex, but maybe he wasn't ready for intimacy that wasn't rooted in anger.

His hand slid down her arm to her hip. "I'll give you that, too."

She bit back a groan as his palm eased between her thighs. "I don't want to be a pity fuck."

"This is so not pity." He made slow, lazy circles on the skin of her inner thighs, his thumb just brushing where she wanted his touch. "And it won't be a fuck if you don't want it."

Okay, then. She wanted it. God, she wanted it. But what shocked her, what truly shook her so hard she actually trembled, was that she all of a sudden wanted not just an orgasm, but a connection. Just once she'd like to feel what it was to have someone care, not about what she could give them, but about what she wanted. Yes, Thanatos wanted the baby she carried inside her, but his obligation to her ended with food, shelter, and safety.

Making her feel good was a gift, and it was something only he could do. And it was something she wanted from him only.

"I... want it."

"Show me."

Tight, shivery arousal coiled in her belly as she reached down and took his hand. Both of them were trembling when she dragged his fingers to her core.

His groan vibrated against her back as one finger slid between her folds. "You're so wet."

She arched into his caress, forcing his touch deeper. His cock nudged the seam of her butt, and she instinctively lifted one leg to allow his shaft to slip between her thighs. Desire became a thundering pulse in her veins and a roar in her ears.

"I don't..." Thanatos ground his hips against her, making his shaft slide hotly against her skin. "I don't know much about this."

It must have been a painful admission for him, but that didn't stop him from pushing one finger inside her and swirling it over sensitive spots like an expert.

"Neither do I," she gasped, "but I promise, you're doing fine."

He moved his hand, replacing it with his cock. His

shaft slid back and forth between her thighs, not yet inside her, but still stroking achy flesh with each pump of his hips. Pushing up on one elbow and leaning over her, he captured her chin in his palm and tilted her head back so he could see her. His eyes glowed in the dim light, the hunger in them stark and desperate.

"Kiss me?" There was a vulnerability in his request that had such a powerful effect on her that she almost choked up.

In answer, she lifted her head up and touched her lips to his. Even in this awkward position, their mouths fused in a burning, urgent kiss. His lips parted for the sweep of her tongue against his, and good God, he tasted good. Like ale and bitter chocolate, sin and decadence.

"Please," she whispered brokenly against his mouth. "Please ... now."

She pushed back against him, and the blunt head of him found her core. For a long moment, they were motionless, their breaths and pulses in perfect unison. Heat poured off him, bathing her in warmth. Need was something they shared, and when she couldn't stand the tension anymore, he seemed to know, and he entered her in one long, slow thrust.

He eased her head down to the pillow and settled in behind her, spooning. "You okay?" His voice was wonderfully rough.

"Oh, yes." She arched, taking him deeper, and he groaned.

Her blood quickened as he began to pump his hips. His touch was light, his thrusts gentle, so maddeningly restrained. But against her neck, his breath came in fast, hot bursts.

"All I could think of was you." He moved faster, his palm sliding over her swollen belly to her center, where he found the sensitive knot that tingled under his touch. "When I was gone, all I wanted was to be back here with you. Only you."

Twenty-two

*All I could think of was you. When I was gone, all I
wanted was to be back here with you. Only you.*

Thanatos couldn't believe he'd said that. Five thousand
years had shown him that males did and said the dumb-
est shit when they were inside a female, but Than had
always believed he'd be different. If he could ever have
sex, anyway.

And what had he done? He'd gone and poured his fool
heart out to Regan. He'd just flayed himself wide open
like one of the lovesick idiots he used to scorn.

Still, with each slow thrust, he couldn't deny that it all
felt so right. He'd been raised to worship nature, to understand that everything happened for a reason and if something felt right, you went with the flow. The day he was
cursed to be a Horseman, his human life was set aside,
replaced by anger and violence... all things he'd been
taught to avoid.

Only now was he remembering the fundamentals of his youth—the joy of a laugh or eating a meal with someone who wasn't your brother or sister, the peace of sharing a quiet moment in front of a fire, the crackling energy behind a teasing smile, the mutual love of something as simple as butter on a sandwich.

That was life. Those were the things that made people happy to be alive. It was all coming back to him, and it was this moment, with this woman, that made it happen.

A throaty cry rang out, a beautiful feminine sound that fired his blood. Regan's silky channel pulsed around him, contracting and releasing in exquisite timing with his pistoning hips. The spooning position restricted his movement as well as the depth of his thrusts, but being able to surround her with his arms, to cover her with his body, and protect the life inside her made it incredible.

Besides, he didn't think missionary would be comfortable—or even possible—in her condition, and while he'd love to get her on her hands and knees eventually, this was what they needed now.

"Faster," she moaned. "Harder."

"Are you sure?" He lifted her leg to allow his cock maximum penetration. "I don't want to hurt either of you."

"Oh, yes," she said, her entire body quivering. "I'm so sure."

Her assurance snapped the restraints that had held him back. On his arm, Styx reared up like a stallion out of a gate. Thanatos let loose, driving into her sweet softness as if he would die without her. She reached back and buried her fist in his hair, clinging to him, forcing his mouth against her satiny neck. God, she smelled good, like the strawberries and cream soap Limos had brought, but underneath was the earthy aroma Than always associated with power.

Regan was power. The fine muscles in her arms and back rippled as she rocked against him, and her fingers dug into his scalp, guiding his mouth where she wanted it. His fangs elongated, pulsing with the need to bite into her tender flesh, and when they accidentally grazed her skin, he hissed and jerked back.

"No," she whispered. "You don't need to hide them anymore. Not with me."

Her sweet words leveled him. She had every reason to hate what she'd learned about him, but was instead asking him to embrace what he'd kept secret for so long. He couldn't bite her—he'd never risk that, especially when she couldn't afford to lose the blood that was nourishing the baby. But he lowered his head to lick the delicate vein beneath her jaw, tasting her before pressing the tips of his fangs to her skin.

The tap of her pulse against his teeth joined the hammering of his heartbeat, setting his blood ablaze. And as Regan's panting breaths turned to whimpers and gasps, his pleasure peaked. She joined him with a cry, bucking and arching, and he thought she might have actually called his name.

Awesome.

They lay there in the aftermath, their ragged breaths drowning out the crackle of the fire. That had been... extraordinary. Never had he experienced anything like that, anything that involved the melding of bodies and pleasure and intimacy. Yeah, he and Regan had fucked that one time, but they'd been drugged, and he'd been distracted by fear for his Seal.

This had been the true taking of his virginity.

"Is that..." He rested his forehead against her silky hair, his heart pounding from both exertion and a touch of embarrassment.

Still reaching back, Regan played with one of his braids. "Is that...what?"

Just spit it out. "Is that what it's always like?" And was he supposed to stay inside her like this? Or was he supposed to pull out? God, he hated this. He was as old as the wheel, as Reseph used to say, and he didn't know a damned thing about what to do with a woman.

Regan tensed, a subtle hardening of her muscles, a mere sharp inhale, but it was there. "I don't know."

He lifted his head to stare at her. "I assumed—"

"That I was a slut." She dropped her hand and shifted, and his cock slid from her warmth.

Well, shit. He had sort of called her that, hadn't he? *You volunteered to play whore. How many men have you fucked for your job?* At the time, he'd been furious, and for all he knew, he'd been right. But in the time Regan had been here with him, he'd seen a woman who regretted what she'd done, who cared for the growing life inside her, who was ready to die in order to save that life. No doubt, she was still the badass Guardian he'd met nine months ago, but he'd seen the emotional, sensitive, vulnerable human beneath her demon-slayer shell.

"I don't think you're a slut," he said softly. "And..." This was going to hurt. "I'm sorry for implying that you were." Yep, ouch. He and apologies didn't get along. "I just assumed you had some experience. Was I wrong?"

She sighed, and most of the tension melted out of her posture. "You're only my second. My first...didn't go well. We only did it once."

He fucking loved that answer. He wrapped his arms around her and tugged her back into him. "Why just the once?"

"My power. When I ... get excited ... I lose control of it. That's why it came out that night with you."

He frowned. "Then why didn't it attack me just now?" When she didn't respond, he traced his fingers over the gentle slope of her shoulder. "Regan?"

"It's gone." She paused, as if struggling to find the right words. "I think it's got something to do with the pregnancy. Please don't tell anyone."

"Don't tell The Aegis, you mean."

She didn't answer, so he shifted back to the original topic, but he wouldn't forget. "Did you kill the guy?" He kind of hoped so. He didn't like the idea that there was a male out there who had touched Regan.

"No, but it was scary. I swore I'd never have sex again." She shivered, and he immediately dragged a blanket up over her.

"And then I came along, and you thought you didn't have to worry about your ability hurting me."

"Yes." She rolled over, with a little effort if her grunts and groans were any indication. "I'm sorr—"

"Don't. Remember what I said about that? It didn't hurt me." He lowered his mouth to Regan's, a kiss meant to comfort her, but the moment their lips met, heat ignited. His hunger for her was all-consuming. Dangerous. Undeniable. "And it sounds like both of us have a lot of catching up to do."

Twenty-three

God, sex with Thanatos was good. Even when he wasn't inside her, his touch and voice alone worked her up.

"Come here," he said roughly, as he rolled onto his back and lifted her so she was straddling his waist. He lifted his hips to penetrate her, but horrid memories gripped her, dragging her back down into the guilt Thanatos had asked her to leave behind, and she tried to scramble off him.

The last time they'd been in this position, he'd been restrained, and she'd been...taking him.

"Thanatos," she whispered, fighting his hold. "I can't do it like this."

"Let it go, Regan." He skimmed his hand up her rib-cage to her breast, and despite her misgivings, she arched into his touch. "I wanted it. We both wanted it."

"But you had no choice."

He'd cupped her cheek, his palm warm, the calluses firm. "Neither did you." With exquisite tenderness, he brought her hand to his mouth, where he kissed her knuckles. "Take away the fury and death, Regan." His lips were satiny against her skin. "Only you can do that. Only you."

Tears scalded her eyes. Dear God, he was amazing. Dizzy with desire and some other emotion she couldn't— or wouldn't—put a name to, she began to rock on top of him. His hands caressed her, stroked her, encouraged her. This was nothing like their first time. This was how it should have been.

"That's it." His dark, guttural voice rumbled through her in a wave of heat. "Take me." He surged upward, his shaft plunging deep, his pelvis lifting her off the bed.

His expression was intense, eyes wild, and when his lips parted to reveal the white points of his fangs, the first contractions of a climax coiled inside her. Those things were wicked sexy, and she wasn't even going to ponder why she thought that or why she wasn't denying it. Instead, she reached out and stroked one.

Thanatos let out a growl that should have terrified her, but the reaction that came with it made her want to do it again. His urgent thrusts crashed into her harder, faster, and his grip on her grew tighter, more possessive. And when she took the fang between her finger and thumb and caressed the smooth surface, he roared in ecstasy.

Bucking beneath her, he came in a hot, wet flow, triggering her orgasm. The pleasure crested twice, massive surges that left her gasping for breath and collapsing bonelessly next to him when it was over.

"Damn," he breathed. "Holy...damn, that was good." He shifted so he was facing her and tenderly brushed her hair away from her face. "The fang thing? We'll have to remember that."

For next time. The unspoken words were there, hanging awkwardly between them. Well, maybe it was only awkward for her, because she had no idea where this thing between them was going. He'd taken the months-of-pleasure thing back, but what if she still felt like giving it to him? She owed him so much, but the reason she owed him had grown to include the fact that no one had ever made her feel so valued.

Not even The Aegis.

His hand and gaze roamed her body, light, soothing sweeps that seemed oddly like petting, as if he were showing Styx affection. The only place he wasn't touching, though, was her belly. Smiling, she took his hand and put it just above her navel. It was funny—endearing, really—the way he was so tentative and unsure about handling a pregnant woman.

But then, she supposed that when you mainly dealt with violence and death, new life must be bewildering.

And talk about bewildering...she was still overcome by everything that had happened tonight. He'd come in from out of nowhere, his eyes full of murder, and then his energy had morphed into something else. The lethal, electric rage had still been there, but somehow, it shifted focus from violence to sex.

"Thanatos?" She idly played with one of his nipple rings. "Why did you say that when you were gone, all you could think about was me?"

On her belly, his hand stilled. Just as she thought he wasn't going to answer, he grumbled, "I said it because sex makes a male stupid." He took her hand in his and brought it to his lips. She liked it when he did that, which was good, because he did it a lot. "And because it's true.

Usually when I'm trapped in a mire of hate and the need to kill, no other thoughts break through. But since you've been here, there's been a sexual fever rushing through me that gets worse when I'm angry, or like today, when I'm forced to a scene of death. It felt like I could burn off the violent energy with sex instead of blood. That's never happened before, and I could only think of you."

"Do you think it's because we'd had sex and it woke up that sex demon side of you?"

"Yeah. Ares and Reseph always found that to some degree, sex could use up energy that would otherwise cause them to kill."

"It's weird," she said, "that for you guys, sex can stop bad things from happening, but it's the opposite for me." She bit down on her lower lip. "Well, until now."

"Why don't you want The Aegis to know you've lost your ability?"

She shrugged, not fully understanding it herself. The Aegis had condemned the ability as a curse, but at the same time, it had made her the only Guardian who could handle certain assignments. With that gone, all she had left was her psychometric gift, which was handy, but so limited by the fact that it only worked on skin and ink.

What if she lost that, too? She was a good fighter, but so was pretty much everyone in The Aegis. She probably knew more than anyone about vampires, but it wouldn't take another Guardian long to catch up to speed, and if she couldn't share what she knew about the day-walkers, she didn't have much of an advantage over any-one else.

"I guess I worry about what they'll do."

"Like what?"

"I don't know...demote me back to a regular Guardian."

"They're assholes," he muttered. "I don't trust them."

Which meant he didn't trust her, either, but she couldn't blame him. "I do. They took me in when they should have killed me, and they taught me to have control over my abilities."

"On Ares's beach, you said your father was put down. What about your mother?"

"My mom gave birth to me and left me on the doorstep at Aegis Headquarters before doing a death-by-demon."

"She found a demon to kill her?"

"Basically. The Aegis had been taking casualties from a nest of demons hanging out in some electrical tunnels nearby. She armed herself, went in, and took out as many demons as she could before one killed her. It was a suicide mission, and she knew it, but she saved a lot of lives." Val had found her body and the voice recorder she used to chronicle her kills. "So anyway, instead of killing me, like protocol demands, they put me with foster parents... other Aegis couples."

"Couples? Plural? Not one set?"

She nodded. "The first couple divorced when I was four, and neither of them wanted the responsibility of raising a kid like me alone."

Thanatos cursed. "Are they dead?"

"No."

"Do you want them to be?"

She laughed. Thanatos definitely took his Horseman name to heart. "It's okay. I barely remember them. The next couple kept me until I was nine, when my foster mother, Jean, was killed in a car crash. My foster father was so distraught that he left The Aegis, so everyone thought it was best to put me with another Aegis family since my psychometric abilities had fully developed."

The move to the new family had sent Regan into a tail-spin of depression and emotional outbursts. She'd lost the only home she'd ever really known, from her foster parents, to her house, to their black lab puppy named Buster. Even though Kevin, her foster father, had been strict about Regan's Aegis training and remote with his own feelings, Jean had been warmer, and Regan had loved them both.

"How long were you with the new family?"

"Until I turned thirteen." Her stomach churned a little, because she really hated revisiting this part of her past. Tabitha and Shawn had been stationed in Sioux Falls, South Dakota, and they'd been kind…at least, on the surface. After the trauma of losing Jean and Kevin had faded, Regan had come to accept Tabitha and Shawn, thinking she'd found a family in them. "Then my foster mom got pregnant, and they didn't want me around their kid."

"Are *they* dead?" he growled.

She smiled thinly. "No, and I don't want them to be." She ignored the slight twinge of pain that always occurred when one opened an old wound. "I get why they got rid of me. By then, I was starting to exhibit signs of the power the Aegis feared. I could have been a danger to their kid."

"Bullfuckingshit."

She trailed her fingers over the tiny foot pressing against her navel. "I can't blame them. I'd do anything to protect the little pony." But that didn't mean their rejection hadn't hurt. After being dumped by three families, and going through puberty with abilities she didn't understand, she had needed someone to care about her. To tell her it was all right and that she was wanted. "So I went to the next family, a nice couple who ran one of the London cells, but things were bad from day one." She chewed her lower lip, buying herself time. "You might have noticed my tendency to be a little...obsessive-compulsive."

His brows raised. "A little? You leveled all the paintings in my keep."

"How do you know?"

He gave her a cocky grin. "Because you straighten everything you touch, so I tilted all the paintings to see how long it would take you to put them right again."

The man had the strangest sense of humor, so quirky, playful, and quiet, but she liked it. Especially because she had a feeling he reserved his playfulness for those inside his small inner circle. "Yes, well, wait until you look in your cupboards."

Still smiling, he leaned forward and kissed the tip of her nose. Like his sense of humor, his gestures of affection were understated and surprising. "I can't wait to see what you do with my sex toy drawer."

Her cheeks grew hot. "You have a sex toy drawer?"

"No, but I think I'll put one together just to see you twitch when I mess everything up." He sobered, tracing a finger along the angle of her jaw. "So did the OCD start with this new family in London?"

She nodded. "No gradual buildup...just, all of a sudden I became a clean freak. Everything had to be organized, in order, and perfectly spaced. I couldn't start anything or go anywhere if my watch's minute hand wasn't on a five-minute increment mark. Weird stuff like that. It was frustrating for all of us. And then, only a year into living with them, my soul-sucking ability got a man killed."

"What happened?"

"I was on a demon hunt with a couple of other Guardians. We'd trapped a Soulshredder in an alley, and it raked me across the ribs with its claws." The pain had been blinding, enough to launch her into a killing fury. "The next thing I knew, a light shot out of my body and attacked the demon. It ripped his soul from him, and the soul needed a body. It found some man on the street and took him." She shuddered at the horror that had only gotten worse when they were forced to kill the poor guy.

"It wasn't your fault," Than said softly. "You couldn't have known."

"I *did* know. The Aegis had identified my ability when I was eleven years old, and I'd been going through training to manage it. I thought I had it under control, but I was wrong."

"The Aegis was wrong. Not you. You were only fourteen. You couldn't have known any better."

"That's what my foster parents said. And they might have even believed it. But they started fighting a lot after that." The baby kicked, and she shifted to give the little guy more room. "I'd hear them in their bedroom arguing about me. They got divorced just before my sixteenth birthday."

So she'd now been responsible for two divorces. Her OCD had gone off the rails then, and she'd become bulimic, to boot. She'd needed control during a time in which she'd felt she had none.

"Anyway, after that, The Aegis figured I needed closer Aegis supervision than any foster parents could have given me, and they were right. I went to headquarters, and during the first few months of training, my ability killed

someone else. A Guardian this time." She'd thought her
colleagues would put her down right then and there. Fortunately, Valeriu, who had been the one who had argued
to save her life in the first place, convinced the Elders to
give her another chance. "Eventually, as I worked to master my abilities, the OCD got better. I was only twenty-
two when I was promoted to the Sigil. Youngest ever."

Youngest, but at twenty-two, she'd had more experience under her belt than most Elders, since she'd been
literally raised to fight demons. Her first books hadn't
been about Dick and Jane. No, her foster parents read her
stories straight out of Aegis battle accounts and species
compendiums.

"And now you're at the head of an organization that
makes most demons tremble in their boots."

"Well, the ones that wear boots, anyway."

He chuckled, a smoky rumble, and she decided he
needed to do that more often. His laughter touched her,
tugged at happy emotions she'd been afraid to feel for so
long.

"Regan?"

"Hmm?"

"I'm sorry if I scared you tonight."

She smiled against his skin. "I'd say it's Limos who
deserves the apology. You made it up to me *very* well."

"I'm serious."

"So am I."

He braced himself on one elbow, all stern and grim-
faced. Even the braids at his temples hung in straight,
serious ropes. Only Thanatos could have serious hair.

"I could have hurt you."

She sighed. "You already told me what you came for,

and it wasn't to hurt me." She held his gaze, which glittered with twenty-four-karat gold flecks in the light from the fire. "And I know, without a shadow of a doubt, that you wouldn't harm your son."

His voice was thick with emotion. "You don't know what I've done, where I came from before I arrived—"

"Yes, I do," she whispered. "We saw it on the news."

His expression darkened. "The impalings."

She nodded, her stomach clenching at the vivid imagery. "It was identical to the scene I saw through your tattoo."

"It was Pestilence," he said, his voice as stormy as his expression. "He staged it to make me remember."

Okay, so while it was a relief to know Thanatos hadn't impaled anyone last night, she still had that horrible scene from the past in her head.

"And those people from before...did you..." She couldn't continue. And honestly, she hoped he wouldn't answer. To know what he was capable of...

"No." He swung his legs off the mattress and jammed his legs into a pair of sweats. "Ever hear of Vlad Tepes?"

"Vlad the Impaler. Also known as Dracula. Of course. Some of the first books my foster parents read to me were of his exploits." She got a glimpse of his fine ass as he tugged the sweats up, and her stomach fluttered. There were fingernail scratches on his cheeks.

"And I thought demon parents were messed up," he muttered. "Those people you saw in my tattoo were some of his victims. Inhabitants of a town he conquered. This was before he got really good at impaling people and killed thirty thousand in a single event."

She frowned, remembering how Than's Watcher had

popped onto the scene and scolded him. "Then what was Gethel talking about when she said you'd gone too far?"

"I went into a killing rage and slaughtered the soldiers Vlad had ordered to impale the villagers. A lot of innocents were caught up in it."

"I don't understand. Ares is drawn to battle, and he fights in the human realm without mass casualties."

"Yes, but he fights...he doesn't necessarily need to kill. I *need* to kill. We've all learned a measure of control over the centuries, and while I'm drawn to death, I can generally control myself. But when I'm angry or hurt as well...sometimes things can get out of hand."

How well Regan understood how things could get out of hand and have horrible consequences. The deaths and pain she'd caused because of her ability weighed her down like an anchor, leaving her hesitant to get close to anyone who might suffer because of it.

"So you got in trouble for killing the humans?" she asked, wondering what kind of punishment could be doled out to Horsemen. "Even the humans who were impaling innocent people?"

"Yes. Though some of the soldiers were *ter'taceo*. And Vlad himself was half demon. Ares and I eventually killed him on the battlefield."

"*You* killed him?"

Than shrugged. "We didn't hunt him down...our Watchers won't let us interfere in human affairs or politics unless we're drawn to a specific scene. And even then, people who are important to the human timeline are protected by angels called Memitim, and we can't kill them until they're no longer under protection. Do you remember Idess, from Limos and Arik's wedding? She used to be Memitim." He threw on a black T-shirt, covering his magnificent chest. Shame, that. "Anyway, we caught Tepes at the right time. No longer protected."

"So what was your punishment?"

"Lightning."

She sat up, frowning. "You were struck by lightning?"

"Over a hundred times." A darkly grim smile curved the corners of his mouth. "Angels are not the most merciful creatures. Not that I deserved mercy."

God, she could only imagine how horrific that must have been for him. Regan had never been the cuddly type, but she felt like hugging him close, as if doing so could erase the pain.

She wanted to ask more questions, but her eyes felt like they'd been sandblasted, and she couldn't smother a yawn. Thanatos smiled, a stunner that would have had her inviting him back into bed if she hadn't been on the verge of coma.

"Get some sleep. I'll send in the hound, but I won't be far." He leaned over and kissed her cheek. "I have some more staff members to interrogate." He winked. "I'll try to keep their screams at a minimum."

Yeah, he really did have a quirky sense of humor. Especially because she had no doubt he was actually serious.

Twenty-four

Thanatos strode out of the bedroom, and despite the fact that the world was going to hell in a handbasket, he actually felt...good. He and Regan had healed some wounds, and maybe, just maybe, had laid the foundation for some sort of relationship once the baby was born.

They just had to make the world safe for the baby first.

He touched his finger to his lips as he moved down the hall, still feeling the tingle of her kiss. She was so damned beautiful. He'd been attracted to her before, when she'd been sleek and hard-bodied, her toned, muscular frame marked by battle scars that she wore like badges of honor. But pregnancy had added another dimension to her beauty, and when before all he'd wanted was to get her out of the house, now he wanted to keep her all to himself.

"Is everything okay?" Ares's voice came from the end of the hallway. "Limos is nursing one hell of a headache, and Arik wants to shove an M-80 up your ass."

"Kinky," Than said, "but I'm new to the sex thing. I'm not ready for hardcore yet."

Ares rolled his eyes. "Where's Regan?"

"Sleeping." He held up his hand. "And yes, she's fine."

"What happened after Limos left? She said you were crazed. She was worried about Regan and the baby."

He wouldn't have hurt them. *He wouldn't have.* A niggling voice pointed out how out of his mind he was, and that he'd killed his own father and best friend during death rages. But this was different. He seemed to gain a measure of control in Regan's presence. Well, maybe not control... but the urge to kill shifted into an urge to get inside her.

And what if she's gone? What then? What would happen to your son when you're in a death spiral?

Fuck. He glared at Ares. "Nothing happened."

"Dammit, Than," Ares said, clearly exasperated. "I'm not some stranger off the street. I'm your brother. Talk to me."

At this point, Than had two options: tell Ares to fuck off, or confide in him. They'd always been close, but Reseph had more often been the one Than opened up to. Reseph's laid-back, fun-loving manner had made it easy to talk, where Ares had always been more intense, and he had a tendency to lay out a battle plan to solve whatever it was you brought up to him.

Than settled for a simple, "We worked some things out."

"And?"

"And what?" Thanatos started down the hall, hoping Ares would take the hint that Than really didn't want to talk about this, but nope. Ares fell into step with him.

"What is it you want from Regan? Are you planning to kick her out after the baby is born? Do you want her to stay? Do you want to take her as a mate? Or do you just want sex?" Ares lowered his voice to a deep, dark, drawl. "Or are you planning revenge? Maybe to kill her?"

"What?" Thanatos tripped over his own guilt and missed a step. "No."

Clearly, Ares didn't believe him, grabbed him by the shoulder, his fingers scoring his skin through the T-shirt. "I'm not judging, bro. I lived with so much hatred in my heart after my wife and sons died. But if you hurt or kill her, someday you'll have to explain to your son why you did it."

"I'm not planning to hurt her." Than peeled his brother's fingers off his shoulders. "I just want her to give me my son without a damned fight."

"And Regan? What of her? Do you want her?"

Yes. Ares's question hung in the air like an acid fog, eating away at Than, because it wasn't that simple. It took a long time, an eternity, to finally say, "I don't know if she wants me."

"And what if she does?"

"Right now, none of this will matter if we can't stop Pestilence."

Ares nodded in agreement. "We've made some progress on that front. A few months ago, Limos and I contacted everyone who owes us a favor. Which means we've had hundreds of assholes in Sheoul doing spy work, and I just got some solid leads on his regular hangouts."

"It's about time we caught a break," Than muttered. "Concentrate on hangouts that double as shrines or meeting places."

"You got a specific plan in mind?"

Thanatos nodded. "Pestilence is a drama whore. He's not going to want to kill my son just anywhere. He'll be preparing something big."

"Makes sense," Ares agreed. "What about the vampires? Anything new here? I killed that Medras fuck for you. And a few others before they got away. The Aegis even got a few."

"My vamps are next on my to-do list." Than took Ares into the library and propped his ass on the desk, facing his brother. "Regan had an idea...it's shitty, last-ditch. It's like poisoning your own water supply to kill the enemy, but we're down to the wire, and it might be our last resort."

Ares shot Than a dark look. "I don't like the sound of this."

"Me either. It's time we confronted Azagoth about being our father. No more sitting around and wondering. There's a good chance he's our sperm donor, and if the whole Lamb thing we learned about in Iraq is accurate and he can break our Seals...we may need him to do exactly that."

"Fuuuuck," Ares breathed. "Fucking hell." He shoved his hands through his hair and paced. "This is fucked up, Than. Fucked up plan." Ares threw in two more *fucks* for an even six-pack before he finally pivoted back to Than. "How are we going to access his realm? We don't even know where it is."

"Idess can get us in. I got the idea a few minutes ago when I was with Regan."

Ares nodded. "Good thinking. But shit...I can't believe it's come to this."

Neither could Than. If they failed to stop Pestilence at the baby's first cry, the Earth would be all but lost anyway.

Than's son would be hunted twenty-four-seven. He'd never know a moment of peace, and he'd grow up in a world shattered by a demonic war.

So yes, it had come down to this. Stop Pestilence and his *Daemonica* Apocalypse at the baby's first cry...or usher in the Book of Revelation with their dear old dad.

"We need her back, Morgan."

Kynan stared at Lance as he dropped the crate of weapons he'd hauled from the compromised headquarters in Germany to their new headquarters in Scotland. "Send these, and two more crates to Edinburgh. The south cell just got hit by demons, and they need every weapon they can get. And Regan stays where she is."

"You seriously trust Thanatos?" Lance gestured to a female Guardian Ky didn't recognize.

"Not as far as I can throw him. And he looks heavy as shit." Ky helped the Guardian lift the crate, and watched as she disappeared out front. "But I know he wants to keep Regan and the baby safe."

"And he's done a stellar job of that," Lance said.

"Just tell me you've got more Guardians ready to go to Greenland." Ky had been sick about losing the last group they'd assigned to go to Regan—the entire cell that had been hit hard by Pestilence's forces.

The asshole had been picking off cells all over the world, and the only positive Ky could think of was that at least he was battling people who could fight back, and not the civilian population. Ky had, before stopping in Germany, joined a battle at a cell in Quebec, and they'd nailed the damned demons to the wall.

Literally.

The battle had been bloody, vicious, and it had been one of the few victories The Aegis had seen lately. There had been far too few.

Juan looked up from typing something on the computer. "We got the Guardian sitch covered. They're on their way."

"What?" Ky folded his arms over his chest, ignoring the pinch of his weapons harness digging into his bicep. "You weren't supposed to put them on a plane until I got the Regent to Greenland through a Harrowgate." Ky couldn't transfer an entire cell that way, not when he had to knock them out to do it, but he'd wanted to deliver the *qeres* and get their leader set up at Than's keep before the bulk of the cell arrived.

"We don't have time to report our every move to you," Lance said. "In case you haven't noticed, we're in the middle of a crisis. Armageddon, the end of the world… any of that sound familiar to you? Or are you and your demon pals so far up each others' asses that you've failed to notice."

In a heartbeat, Ky was in Lance's face. "Me and my demon pals are the only reason we have a world to defend in the first place, or did you forget what happened in Israel? Or in the battle with Pestilence last year? So be very careful about what you say next. This is my family you're talking about."

"You're so arrogant, Morgan. Ever since you bullied your way into the Sigil with your special charm and your angel buddy you think everyone should follow your lead. There's no room for discussion. It's Kynan's way or the highway." Lance spat on the floor, as if talking to Kynan left a bad taste in his mouth. "Has it occurred to you that you might not always be right? That you might be wrong about Thanatos? About his prophecy? About the baby?"

"If you had concerns, you should have brought them up before now," Ky shot back.

"We tried." Lance leaned in, so close Ky could smell the burger he'd had for lunch. "You wouldn't listen. You and your bleeding-heart demon-loving ideals are dragging The Aegis into the dirt."

Kynan's voice had long ago been destroyed by a demon who had nearly ripped out his throat, and now it degraded even more, like gravel mixed with shards of glass. "Next you're going to tell me I'm responsible for the attack on our headquarters."

Their noses were now touching. "I didn't say it. You did."

Before Kynan could stop himself, he fisted Lance's collar, ready to lay the bastard out. Juan leaped in, jamming his arm between Ky and Lance to pry them apart.

"Guys. Now's not the time for this. We need to stay on track."

"Yeah," Ky grunted. "Fine. Where's the *qeres*? I'll take it to the Horsemen."

Lance smiled snottily. "It's on its way. We put it on the ship with the Guardians."

"Ship? How many damned Guardians did you send?"

"Just a handful," Juan said. "We needed extra room for equipment. It'll anchor just off the Greenland coast in a few hours. Lance, Omar, Takumi, and I are catching a helicopter transport in an hour to take us to the ship. We'll transfer Guardians from there to the Horseman's keep with the helo."

Kynan did not like this. Did not like that all of it had been done without his knowledge or his input. And he had serious reservations about so much equipment that a ship was required to send Guardians to Greenland. But maybe Lance had a point about Kynan taking too much control. The Aegis had survived for thousands of years because the Sigil operated under the premise that every Elder was equal. Not that he'd ever admit that Lance might be right.

"I don't suppose you've given the Horsemen a heads-up?"

"I sent a message to Arik." Lance glanced at his watch. "Quit worrying. It's all good."

Cursing, Ky stalked out of the chamber, an uneasy feeling churning in his gut. He'd always trusted his instincts, and right now they were going off like storm sirens in Tornado Alley. Something wasn't right. No, something was wrong. Very wrong.

As he hit the narrow staircase leading down to the castle's great room, his cell went off, and the storm siren in his head rang louder. He checked the screen and took the stairs at a dead run, Gem's message flashing in his brain like a bloody scrawl at a murder scene.

Pestilence hit UG. So many dead. Ky, he took Idess…

Twenty-five

Thanatos left Ares in the keep to act as an extra set of eyes on Regan. Now, it was time for Than to spring himself on the vampires he'd let stew while he handled other Apocalyptic shit.

If there was one thing daywalkers hated, it was to be kept in the dark.

Literally and figuratively.

Than allowed himself a grim smile as he strode through the side courtyard, where the daywalkers watched him from between the shutter slats in the outbuildings he used for storage, working shops, and vampire quarters. A hellhound guarded the entrance to the keep, preventing the bloodsuckers from entering or, at Than's request, from leaving their quarters.

He let the daywalkers stew a little longer and entered the building that housed the night crew. This thick-walled, windowless structure kept the sunlight to a minimum, but once inside, there was another measure of protection. The upper section was set up as a gathering space with furniture, appliances, half a dozen video gaming systems, and a pool table. But a staircase led to sleeping quarters deep in the earth, where a tunnel also provided an escape route if needed.

Thanatos had sealed it after Dariq poisoned Regan. He was taking no chances.

He descended into the shadowy depths, and by the time he hit the bottom of the stairs, all twelve nightwalkers were standing around their giant table, some blinking after being awakened by his arrival, and others bright-eyed and watching warily.

"I'll get right to it," he said. "What do you know about the plot against me?"

They all exchanged glances, and finally Peter shook his head. "We don't know anything, sire. The daywalkers despise us. They don't exactly share their murder plots."

Thanatos suspected as much. In truth, he didn't expect to find any nightwalker collaborating with the daywalkers, and it wasn't just because they hated each other. It was because no nightdwelling vampire would want to see the daywalkers come to power in Pestilence's post-apocalyptic world.

"Sire," Roland said, stepping forward. "We're here because we want to be. Even if you hadn't confined us to quarters, we'd have done it ourselves until this is over. We don't want you to have any reason to suspect us if anything else happens."

Peter nodded. "But we'd be honored to guard Regan." In one coordinated movement, the vampires went down on one knee, their fists over their hearts. "We're yours to do what you will."

All the pain the rogue daywalkers had caused became muted in the humbling loyalty on display before him. "Thank you. I'm honored." He cleared his throat. "I'll open the escape tunnel, but I still can't allow you in the keep. I don't believe any of you are involved in trying to kill my son, but Regan can't always tell the difference between you and the daywalkers. Hell, Limos and Ares can't even tell you apart most days. I can't risk someone slipping into the keep under the guise of being a night-walker."

"We can wait." Roland looked up at Than through his messy mop of red hair that always hung in his eyes. "But if you need us, we're here."

Thanatos got out of there before he gathered them in a lame-ass group hug or something, and braced himself for the real confrontation. He stopped in the middle of the courtyard in a patch of sunlight, and called out to the day-walkers. They came from their buildings, blinking in the morning light.

"I had a really interesting meeting with your brethren in France," Than said, stopping all of them in their tracks. "Who knows what I'm talking about? No one? That's what I thought. So here's the deal. I don't have time to torture you all. But what I do have time for is to get you all a new tattoo. Awesome, right? Who doesn't love new ink?"

"*Bludrexe*?" Owain, a stocky blond vampire with a pronounced limp, came forward, tugging down the collar of his shirt to reveal his silencing tat. "We have them."

"Right. But this will be different. You remember Ore-lia, the Silas demon who gave you the first one. Well, she's going to give each of you one that'll be taken directly from your thoughts." Thanatos grinned, letting his fangs punch down. "So if you haven't betrayed me, you have nothing to fear. If you have . . . let's just say you might want to start pissing your pants now."

He jerked his thumb at Viktor. "C'mon, buddy. You first." As Viktor approached, Thanatos lost a little of his cocky mood, because the truth was that he loved his vamps, and it was going to hurt him to kill the traitors almost as much as it was going to hurt them.

Almost.

Regan woke up alone. Well, alone except for the yak-sized hellhound lying by the door.

Yawning, she sat up, expecting to see Thanatos in the corner chair, but he wasn't there, either. Disappointment penetrated her drowsy haze, but in her belly, the little pony squirmed, and she smiled. She might gripe when he kicked up a storm, but movement was a good thing, and she was always comforted when she felt him.

"Let's find your daddy, kiddo." *Daddy*. Wow. How far Regan had come from first thinking of Thanatos as nothing but a sperm donor, to being a father, and finally, a daddy.

She showered and dressed in one of the new outfits Limos had brought her, silently thanking the Horse-woman for not having terrible taste. Limos might dress in girly, bright things, but she'd chosen much less flashy clothing for Regan. The black fatigues-style maternity pants and olive and black top were neat and practical, and the black leather sandals added a feminine touch without being too dainty.

Hellhound on her heels, Regan headed to the great

room, but was greeted only by silence. "Thanatos?" she called out.

A faint "In here," came from the library, and she scooted inside to find Thanatos hunched over a large wood and leather object in the corner.

The hellhound plopped down on the floor behind her as she moved closer to Thanatos. "What are you doing?"

"Working on a project." He glanced up, his gaze heating when his eyes met hers. She flushed, remembering what they'd done last night. "I made you some pancakes. And waffles. And bacon and eggs." He gestured to the three covered platters on his desk. "I wasn't sure what you liked, and you said you can't cook."

Her stomach growled. "I like it all. Thank you."

She lifted one of the covers off a platter and tossed a strip of bacon to the hellhound before taking one for herself. And geez, was she really feeding demon dogs now? This baby was turning her all mushy and stupid. God, she hoped that wore off once it was born.

And once it was safely living with Gem and Kynan.

The thought that had once come so easily now made her stomach clench. She rubbed her belly, feeling the shifting movements under her palm. A foot or hand pressed up against hers, and her heart swelled.

I'd do whatever it took to make sure that being with me was what was best.

Regan wanted to be what was best. But could she make it happen?

"You aren't eating," Than murmured, not looking up from whatever he was doing. His hair hung down across his face, shielding his expression, but his bare arms flexed as he used slim metal tools to etch designs into hardened mahogany leather. "Will it spark your appetite to know that Viktor is innocent of plotting to kill our son?"

Thank God. She was relieved for the baby, but also for Thanatos. He'd needed that. Badly. "How do you know for sure?"

"I took him to Orelia, my tattoo artist. She didn't find any deception in his actions. But I don't suggest that you use your gift on his tattoo. Apparently, he wasn't always a good guy." Than looked over at her, one braid catching on his shoulder, and she had the urge to reach out and twirl it in her fingers. "Viktor will be taking the others one by one. Afterward, will you have a problem using your gift to read the tattoos? I was with Viktor for his, so Orelia could tell me about it, but I don't have time to sit with everyone."

"Of course," she said. "It'll be nice to be useful." Taking a bite of bacon, she craned her neck to get a better look at what Than was doing. "Do you do this often?"

"Yep. I have a shed in the courtyard where I make historical reproductions. Keeps me calm. I need a distraction while I'm waiting for Viktor to come back with Artur."

"He means a lot to you, doesn't he?"

When Than didn't answer, she reached out and ran her finger over the curved wood base of the project he was working on. "It's beautiful. What is it—" She snapped her mouth shut, finally *seeing* what he was working on.

A cradle. Thanatos was making a cradle.

"What do you think?" His voice was velvet soft as he ran his palm lovingly over the smooth lines of the exposed wood rockers and then across the finely tooled artwork in the leather that had been stretched over the frame.

Regan couldn't speak. In the silence broken only by

the hellhound's panting breaths, her gaze flicked to the designs—animals, all in a fluid Celtic style.

Finally, she found her voice, but what could she say? Could he still be hoping to raise the child himself, even after his own servants had tried to kill the baby? Even though every evil being on the planet would be gunning to kill the baby in order to start the Apocalypse?

She got it now...she *so* got why he'd want to keep the baby. But until the threat from Pestilence was gone, neither of them could raise this child.

She settled for, "It's beautiful. Amazing."

He seemed to know what she was thinking, and very gently, he gripped her shoulders and turned her to him. "I know your plans for our son. You know I hate them. But we've fought too much as it is, so with the time we have until he's born, we're going to work through this."

"That sounds so reasonable." She gave him a small smile. "Not at all like the man who stormed Aegis Headquarters and kidnapped me."

"Yeah." He blew out a breath. "I was a little worked up."

"It's understandable, given what I'd done to you."

"We're past that. You're the one who said we need to not take the easy way out. To talk about things."

She inhaled sharply. Was she ready to talk? He was right; she'd said they needed to. Like normal people. *Yes, because an Aegis warrior with demonic powers and the fourth Horseman of the Apocalypse were perfectly normal.*

"Okay," she said, bracing herself. "Since we need to talk, I want you to know that if things go well with Pestilence...you know, we stop him..." She counted out three pieces of bacon and fed them to the hound. Than waited patiently, which was weird. "So anyway, I was thinking that maybe we could work something out with the baby."

Swallowing hard, Than closed his eyes. When he opened them, it was as if a tiny, new light glimmered in them. "We'll beat him, Regan. We will. For now, let's concentrate our energy on stopping this damned Apocalypse. We'll figure out everything else after that."

He was such a contradiction sometimes. His uncontrollable rages could mean death for thousands, and yet, when he was calm, he was one of the most reasonable, caring people she'd ever met. She couldn't believe she'd once thought of him as a monster with a heart of ice. Now she'd seen that heart melt at the prospect of having a family, and somehow her own heart had opened up to let him and the baby in. But what if it was too late to figure out where their relationship stood?

Regan's stomach wrenched. "We might not have much time."

"Not 'might'," he said gravely. "Don't. While I'm dealing with my vampires and keeping you safe, Limos and Arik have been working on a plan to trap our brother, and Ares is going to arrange for Idess to take him to Azagoth."

Right. The Grim Reaper. Last year he'd said that the guy was possibly his father, but as far as she knew, he hadn't confirmed the theory.

"And if Azagoth isn't your father?"

"We'll be screwed if we fail to stop Pestilence when our son is born. The one definite we have is that I heard from your colleagues this morning. Arik said Kynan will be delivering your Guardians and the *qeres* today."

For some reason, now that the Guardians were on the way, she wasn't sure she wanted them anymore. The tension between her and Thanatos was practically gone, and at this point, The Aegis could destabilize everything. Besides, some secret part of her wanted him all to herself.

"Thanatos?"

"Yeah?"

"Are you going to be okay with what we'll have to do to your brother?"

Thanatos swallowed, making his tats undulate wildly. "I'll have to be."

"I would think that even given all you've done and been through in your life, if there's one tattoo you'll need, it'll be that one."

"Would you be upset?"

"I don't have any right to be upset."

"That's not what I asked." His tone made his words a quiet demand.

"No." She flushed a little. "You were right when you said I shouldn't judge you and the way you cope with things."

He reached up and brushed her hair away from her cheek, letting his hand linger, and her heart stuttered. His soothing touch made her achingly aware of his capacity for tenderness, and with each brush of his fingers, she craved more. "I didn't say that, exactly."

"Not exactly, but it's what you meant. And you were right." She rubbed against his hand like a needy cat. "I have a lot of experience fighting demons, but I have approximately zero normal life experience. And I have no room to judge in any case. I cope by rearranging the socks in your drawer and doing counting exercises."

"Show me."

"Show you how to rearrange socks?"

He chuckled. "No, the counting exercises."

"It's nothing special. Just pick a number you like. I tend to do things in threes." She took his hand and placed it on the desk. "Now tap your fingers and count."

"Tap?"

"Tap."

He cocked an eyebrow, but his long fingers moved beneath hers. It struck her that as old as he was, they should have been rougher, more calloused. But his skin was smooth and supple, his hands well-shaped and so... capable.

"See," she said hoarsely. "Don't you feel calmer?"

His voice was husky, his mouth curved in a quirky smile. "Strangely, I'm feeling the opposite of calm."

"You might be a big, bad warrior," she huffed, as she drew her hand away, "but you suck at OCD."

He laughed, a throw-back-his-head stunner. "Maybe you can show me how to rearrange socks then."

"Oh, you're hilarious."

He waggled his brows. "I have my moments."

More and more of those moments as they grew comfortable with each other, and Regan liked it. There had been too much ugliness between them and in the world. What terrified her was that she had no doubt more ugliness was coming.

Yes, she and Thanatos had rounded a bend in their relationship, and he might have made it sound like he and his siblings and The Aegis were making progress, but in her experience, just when things started looking good... well, that's when things went to hell.

Twenty-six

Regan had come around. Thank God. Oh, she was still planning to give up their son if they didn't stop Pestilence, but by now he knew that it wasn't because she didn't want the baby. He'd seen evidence that she loved the child all along, but now she was less certain that giving their son to Gem and Ky was the right thing to do.

Good, because Thanatos wasn't going to let it happen. Regan might not believe he could keep their son safe from Pestilence and his forces, but once Than got the vampire situation straightened out, he'd have guards. He'd ask Cara for a pack of hellhounds. He'd hire a dozen dens of assassins. Hell, he'd build a freaking fortress if he had to.

He would have his son, and he'd keep him safe.

Which left another question. Would she want a role in their son's life? Would she want more than that?

His heart skipped a beat, a crazy little flutter at the idea that he might actually get more than he'd ever hoped for in this life.

A family.

Ruthlessly, he shoved that thought out of his head as he stepped from the shower. He'd worked out while Regan shared breakfast with the hellhound, and now it was time to meet up with Kynan and the Guardians who should arrive at any moment.

Once he'd dressed in black jeans and a turtleneck, he found Regan in the library, a book in her lap—but her eyes were glued to the TV set.

She turned to him, her cheeks burning red. "What *is* this? Vampire porn?"

Well, shit. This was a little embarrassing. But mostly because now he wanted to throw Regan on the desk and play out the scene for real.

"Yep." Than watched a vampire on the screen fucking and sucking a human female while another vampire gnawed on her wrist. "Oh, and this is a good one. Muffy the Vampire Layer."

"It looks professionally made."

"It is. There's a huge market for it."

"Are the... blood participants willing? This woman... and the now-anemic one in the bedroom were running from the vampires earlier."

"Sometimes the participants are willing," he said, and then rolled his eyes at her gasp of outrage. "What? That's half the turn-on for vampires. The hunting and take-down of the victim. Obviously, the females in this one are willing. They're enjoying it." He gestured to the screen with one hand and casually adjusted his erection with the other. "See, she's having an orgasm."

Regan turned the color of an aroused Sora demon. And if her scent was any clue, the aroused part was right on target. "And you watch this?"

Her huffy tone would have had more impact if a woman wasn't moaning and crying out, "Oh, yes, yes, *yes!*" in the background. And if Regan wasn't all breathless. And if Regan didn't make those same sounds in bed. Her moans were a little deeper though, with a smoky, serrated edge.

"I seem to remember you enjoying the feel of my fangs sliding across your neck," he murmured.

On screen, one of the males had dragged a female out of the bedroom and was rousing her by nuzzling the inside of her thigh, his fangs grazing her skin, his tongue flicking closer and closer to her center. When he covered her core with his mouth, Than had to bite his lip to stifle a groan. He hadn't done that to Regan, and he suddenly wanted to...very bad. Like, his mouth watered and his fangs throbbed, and yeah, he was going to taste her when she came.

He eyed the desk and wondered how fast he could get her out of her clothes. An erotic growl slipped from between his lips, and he swung back to her, his gaze focused on her like a laser.

He was going to take her. Now.

She came to her feet and met him halfway across the room, splaying her hands on his chest and lifting her mouth to his. "Desk?" she whispered against his lips.

"We are *so* on the same page," he whispered back.

Carefully but urgently, he spun her around and lifted her onto the wood surface, not giving a shit that papers, pencils, and dishes from breakfast clattered to the floor. A snort came from the doorway, and quickly, before the damned hellhound could get into the room to clean up the damage, Than kicked the door closed. An unhappy yelp followed the slam of the door.

Regan sighed his name and reached for his pants, but just as her fingers started to grapple with the zipper, the distinct *whup-whup* of a helicopter vibrated through the keep's thick walls.

"Jesus Christ," he snarled. "Mother. Fuck."

"Definitely same page." Regan's voice was husky and fierce, and his inner warrior whooped in approval.

"You Aegi have terrible timing."

He tore away from Regan, unquenched lust burning him from the inside out. After nearly ripping the library door off its hinges, he stormed to the front door. Habit and instinct had him shoving Regan behind him as he armored up and opened the door.

A transport helicopter had set down about fifty yards from his keep. Men were bailing out of it, some in fatigues carrying weapons, and others more casually dressed, but without a doubt, these were Aegi. But where was Kynan?

Regan nudged him. "You can put away the sword. I know these people."

Than looked down at the blade in his hand. He didn't even remember drawing it. Cursing, he shoved the sword into its scabbard.

"Could you get rid of the armor, too? It's not necessary, and it's going to put them on the defensive."

"Good. They should be."

"Thanatos." She tapped her foot in annoyance. "We're not your enemies. Please do this. For me."

Damn her. She knew exactly how to get what she wanted from him. That could never be a good thing.

Swiping his fingers over the crescent scar on his throat, he stepped out into the daylight as the armor melted away. "*Halt*." The four guys in the lead froze, and the others followed suit. "Identify yourselves and your purpose."

"Oh, for God's sake," Regan huffed. "Do you automatically revert to medieval speak in front of Guardians? That's Lance, Juan, Takumi, and Omar. They're Elders. The others I don't recognize, but they're definitely Guardians."

Great. Good. But why the hell were they all here? He'd been expecting Kynan, and maybe Decker. Although it would be wise of Decker to not show up again. Ever.

"Where's Kynan?" he asked the guys.

The one named Lance stepped forward. "He's busy. You deal with us now."

How the fuck did these people know where his keep was? How could they see it? He had magic in place that kept his home invisible to most human and demon eyes. Once someone had been escorted through the magical field, they could see the keep after that, but new people... not so much.

He supposed Kynan had given them the coordinates, but that didn't explain how they would have been able to actually see the buildings.

"The Elders can come in," he said. "The rest of you... stay."

The four males came forward, and Regan greeted all but Lance with hugs. Jealousy and protectiveness nearly drove him mad, but ultimately, he was pretty damned proud of the way he didn't rip their heads off and feed them to the two hellhounds slinking up behind them.

Regan shot Than a withering glare. "Could you tell the hounds not to eat my friends?"

"Sorry, boys," he shouted to the mutts. "No snacks today. Go patrol for Pestilence." The hounds snarled with ill-tempered tantrums, but they took off, howling their displeasure. The Guardians, meanwhile, looked like they might need a change of underwear. Funny.

He turned to the humans, who were standing in a semi-circle in the center of the great room. "Explain. How can you see my keep?"

Lance smiled, and Than instantly hated him. There was something...sneaky about that one. "It doesn't matter. What matters is that we brought Guardians and the *qeres*. We'll leave the grunts and the rest of us will be out of your pissing range after we discuss some things with Regan."

Arrogant sons of bitches. Tension winged through the air, and as much as Than wanted to pulverize these guys, he remembered that they were here to protect Regan. No matter what he might think of the bastards, she held them in high regard. She...needed them.

The protector in him, the male that would lay down his life for his mate and child, let out an injured growl at the idea that Regan needed these other males for anything, but the more civilized side of him understood. Sort of.

So he'd let them live for now.

"Are you okay, Regan?" Juan shuffled his feet, and Than caught a whiff of nerves. At least that one was smart. "Has he hurt you?"

People kept asking that. It was getting old.

"No." Regan stepped between them, and Than resisted

the urge to pull her back. "Trust me, Thanatos isn't a threat."

"Not to *you*." Thanatos met each of the four Elders' eyes. "But I'll kill anyone who fucks with what's mine."

"Dickhead," Lance muttered.

Regan made a little growly noise that probably shouldn't be sexy, but that cranked his engine again and had him wanting to drag her to the bedroom, caveman style, to finish what they'd started in the library.

After he strangled Lance with his own intestines.

He must have voiced his thoughts out loud, because Regan rounded on him, planted her palm on his chest, and got in his face. So. Fucking. Sexy.

"Manners, Horseman. It's what separates us from… well, people like Lance." She shot a glare at the Elder before turning back to Thanatos. "Could you give us a minute?"

He knew she needed to discuss Aegis business, and he understood that there were things he shouldn't know—if his Seal broke, he could use the knowledge against them. So yeah, he got it.

But that didn't mean he liked it. "You have five minutes," he gritted out. He needed to check in with Ares and Limos anyway. He lowered his voice and put his lips to her ear, his blood still stirring so viciously that his fangs scraped her lobe. "After that, I need—"

Her hands slammed into his chest, the force not violent, but sensual. "I know what you need, Horseman."

She did, didn't she? What a remarkable woman. A rumbling purr rattled his chest even as he scowled at the Guardian intruders. Yup, he'd worked himself into a frenzy that Regan somehow understood.

Blood or seed...something was going to spill.

Once Thanatos and his storm cloud of energy was out of sight, Regan rounded on her fellow Elders. "What were you thinking, showing up here without Kynan? He should be the one dealing with the Horsemen."

"And hasn't that been the problem," Lance said, and what was that supposed to mean?

Juan opened the front door and gestured outside. "Come on. We need a little more privacy than this."

Shit. Whatever they needed so much privacy for couldn't be good. "What's going on?"

"Just trust us." Juan walked out, and Regan followed, dying of curiosity.

The Guardians who had accompanied the Elders had spread out, all armed to the teeth and holding either crossbows or swords, their weapons' belts packed with wooden stakes.

Lance cocked his head at the helicopter, where the side cargo door was wide open to reveal rows of seats. "Hop in."

Pregnant women didn't *hop* anywhere, and Regan stopped dead in her tracks. "Why?"

"The inside is rigged with a sound-dampening spell," Juan said. "Whatever we say inside can't be heard outside." He glanced back at Omar, who had gone down on one knee just outside the keep's door to tie his boot. "I know it seems like an extreme measure, but what we have to tell you is critically sensitive."

A ramp had been placed at the base of the helo, and she awkwardly climbed into the huge chopper that appeared to be a modified military troop transport. Juan, Lance, and Takumi followed her inside, and when Juan slammed the door closed...and locked it, her gut dropped. In the next instant, the pilot started the rotor blades, and her heart joined her plummeting stomach.

"What are you doing?"

Lance's pacifying smile didn't boost her confidence. "The rotors help block sound."

She didn't like this at all, and neither did Thanatos. Through the front windshield, she saw him burst out of the keep and run toward the helo. Behind him, Omar, who had still been kneeling, leaped to his feet, a pistol in his grip.

"Thanatos!" Regan shouted, as if he could hear.

Gunfire rang out, and Thanatos hit the ground, a crimson-tipped dart sticking out of the back of his neck. Vampires swarmed from the side courtyard, but the Guardians were ready, and as they picked off Than's staff, Regan screamed. She tried to get to the door, but Lance, Juan, and Takumi blocked her.

"This is a goddamned rescue, Regan!" Lance snapped.

"I don't need to be rescued, you idiots!"

At the front of the bird, Omar leaped in, and then the helo was airborne, and Regan was trapped.

"What the hell are you guys thinking?" she yelled, grabbing a handbar to steady herself. "Take me back!"

From the front, Omar shook his head. "Regan, we have a plan. This is what's best."

Shake it off. Think. The helo was in flight, so right now, she had no choice but to go along with their plan. She didn't like it, but until she knew exactly what was up, she had to stay calm. Which wasn't easy, given that she wanted to throw each one of them out of the helicopter for hurting Thanatos.

She sank stiffly into a seat. "What's the plan? And why didn't we discuss this before you attacked Thanatos and kidnapped me? I'm tired of getting kidnapped." And boy, Thanatos was going to be homicidally angry when he came to. "You used hellhound saliva on him, didn't you?"

Lance shook his head. "*Qeres*. We had to test it to make sure it would work on Pestilence."

"That was stupid, guys. And you've probably destroyed our alliance with the Horsemen."

When they said nothing, a sour suspicion fell over her. "You know that, don't you? You know and don't care. Why?"

"Because," Takumi said, "after today it won't matter." He looked out the window and back to her. "Regan, you have to trust us. We only want what's best for you, and for the world. We're going to end the Apocalypse today."

"What?" She looked between them. "How? Do you have Pestilence?"

The helicopter banked hard to the right, and she nearly slid out of her seat. As she righted herself, Lance leaned forward, bracing his forearms on his knees.

"Right now isn't the time for questions or suspicions or doubts. It's time for you to prove to everyone, once and for all, that The Aegis was right when we didn't put you down as an infant."

"How dare you." Her voice quavered with emotion. "How dare you imply that I've somehow been disloyal. I've done everything The Aegis has asked of me, which includes bedding and betraying a man who could have killed me with his pinky. So don't you dare talk to me as if I've wronged you."

"Regan," Omar said softly, "no one is questioning your loyalty." He shot Lance a disgusted glare. "What Lance is trying to say—badly—is that what's happening today isn't going to be easy, but you've got to trust us more than ever, and you're going to need to be strong. We've got to stick together."

The helicopter jolted, and she looked out the window to see that they'd landed on a huge ship. As the door slid open, she turned back to Omar. "I don't understand."

"You will."

A salt water breeze stung her skin as she was escorted from the big bird past an open chest full of Aegis weapons and supplies to a door on the deck. They led her through a maze of hallways until they arrived at a metal door large enough to allow a rhino to enter. She walked into what appeared to be a medical facility. Her fellow Elders followed her inside and closed the door. The ominous clang vibrated through her bloodstream, but she felt silly about her apprehension when the obstetrician who had been treating her for months entered from a connecting room.

"Regan." He smiled warmly. "It's good to see you. How are you feeling?"

Two nurses entered, as well as two burly male technicians carrying trays of medical instruments, and the ominous sensation of doom returned.

"I feel great," she lied, as she eyed the syringes on one of the trays. "But I think it's time you told me why I'm here."

Dr. Rodanski cut a sharp look at Lance. "You didn't tell her?"

"Tell me what?" Regan placed her hands protectively over her belly, a fierce instinct kicking in and telling her that something was very, very wrong here.

Lance held up his hands in a gesture she was sure was meant to calm her but failed on an epic scale. "We need the kid, Regan. We need it now."

"It's not *the kid*," she snapped. "He's my son. And what do you mean, you need him now? Have you captured Pestilence? We need Thanatos and Deliverance—"

"We don't," Omar interrupted. "We believe the translation of the prophecy you've been following is wrong. We have new information that changes everything."

"New information? What new information?"

The doctor came forward with the syringe. "Just relax, Regan. I'm going to sedate you, and I'll perform a C-section to deliver the baby."

They couldn't touch her. She knew that, and yet, her heart began to pound painfully hard. "And then what?"

"Regan," Juan said gently, "you don't have to be part of it. We'll put you out."

Oh, God. More pounding, and now her head was throbbing. "Put me out for what?"

Lance's gaze dropped to the floor, and when he raised it again to meet hers, they glinted with both sympathy and resolve. "In order to stop the Apocalypse, we have to sacrifice the child."

Twenty-seven

The sounds of battle penetrated Thanatos's black haze. Whatever The Aegis bastard had darted him with hadn't been hellhound saliva, or Than wouldn't have blacked out, even for a few seconds, and it wouldn't have made him fuzzy in the head. No, everything was crystal clear when you were paralyzed by hellmutt venom.

Had to be the *qeres*. Those fucking assholes had knocked him off his feet with the weapon they'd promised to use against Pestilence.

Fuckers.

And Regan...His body shook like a washer on spin cycle as his body stirred back to life. How involved had she been in this attack? He waited for the insane anger to set in, anger at her deception, but nothing happened. Maybe because no, he didn't believe that after all they'd shared over the last couple of days, the talking, the love-making, she'd betray him again.

He'd give her the benefit of the doubt. Everyone else involved in this scheme, however, was going to die.

Snarling, he rocked himself up off the ground and onto all fours. All around him, Guardians were battling his vampires, and about fifty yards away, a pack of hellhounds was bearing down. Good. Let them tear the Aegis assholes to pieces.

"My lord." Viktor, one leg broken badly, tried to help Than to his feet. "We've failed you—"

"No, you didn't." Than staggered to his feet and flicked his fingers over his throat. Instantly, his armor folded into place. "I let down my damned guard and trusted the wrong people."

Viktor opened his mouth, but only a gasp and a rush of blood came out. A wooden bolt blew a hole through the vampire's chest and shattered on Thanatos's armor. In a puff of greasy smoke, Viktor crumpled into a pile of blackened ash on the ground.

"*No!*" Roaring in anguish, Thanatos summoned his scythe and in one lighting-fast motion relieved the Guardian who'd killed Viktor of his head. The hellhounds fell on the remaining Aegi, but Than didn't wait around to enjoy the show.

Hurry! We need to get to the ship! Someone had shouted as Thanatos went down, the voice barely audible in the chop of the helicopter blades, and fuck, that meant he couldn't use a Harrowgate. Water affected the destination gate, and one wrong calculation could dump him right into the ocean... where he couldn't gate himself out.

His brain stewing with revenge, he released Styx, mounted the stallion, and took off in the direction of his son.

Styx ran as if he was being chased by the hellhounds they'd left behind, and with every stride, Thanatos's fury mounted. He panted through the growing desire to kill, needing to stay in control. Regan had shown him what she did to stay calm, and right now, he borrowed the trick, clicking his thumb on the saddle's pommel. One, two, three. Breathe. One, two, three. Breathe.

It worked. Only slightly, but it worked. Oh, he was still going to rend Aegi bodies from limb to limb, but he'd do it in an orderly, calm fashion.

And if either she or the baby had been harmed in any way, the calm thing was going out the window. If The Aegis wanted a war, they'd gotten one.

Sacrifice? Sacrifice, as in *kill*? Regan backed away from her colleagues so fast she slammed into a rolling tray, knocking it over and sending instruments clattering to the floor.

"Fuck you," she breathed. "Fuck every one of you. You're not touching my son."

"Regan," Lance said, so calmly her hair stood on end, "you agreed. When we came to you in the beginning, you agreed—"

"I agreed to get pregnant. Jesus Christ…I didn't agree to kill my baby!"

"Be reasonable, Regan. It's not *your* baby. It belongs to The Aegis." Juan stepped closer, and the room began to spin. "It's not really a baby anyway. It's a demon. A demon whose death will save mankind from untold horrors."

"Untold horrors? You sound like a narrator from one of those fifties nuclear preparedness films." Regan's chest tightened around her madly beating heart. They were serious. They honestly had no problem murdering a newborn infant. "You idiots! Thanatos can sense this baby. He is going to find us, and he's going to slaughter every one of you."

Lance shook his head. "We planned for that. We have it on good authority that the Horsemen can't open a Harrowgate on a boat."

Regan grew lightheaded, so dizzy that she threw out a hand to catch herself on the wall. "Who told you that? It's a lie." She had no idea if their claim was true or not, but at this point, she'd say anything to stop this insane plan of theirs.

"We know it's true." Omar flanked her left side, and now she was surrounded. "Let's make this easy on everyone. It's the only way, Regan."

Okay, calm down…think…think. "You can't touch me." She doubted the hysteria in her voice was helping anything. "This *demon*, as you call him, is protecting me."

Lance smiled. "Again, we planned for that." He gestured to one of the techs standing near the doctor. The tech opened a cabinet and removed a tray laden with candles, packets of powder, a ceremonial bowl, and a few objects Regan didn't recognize. Another tech brought in a cage containing a live rabbit.

"Blood magic?" She was going to throw up. "You're going to neutralize him with an evil spell? You can't know it'll work. You could kill him!" She realized instantly what a stupid thing to say that was, given that the goal was to kill the baby.

They'd been possessed. That was the only answer. Her colleagues, the people she considered to be her family, the ones who had fought beside her, shared her Aegis ideology, and given her a home, had to be under the influence of evil. Somehow, Pestilence had gotten hold of them, that son of a bitch.

Well, fuck this. Pivoting, she slammed her fist into Lance's face. Power sang through her, and he went airborne, crunching into a bulkhead and sliding motionless to the floor. Hands grabbed her from behind, but again, the baby's energy exploded, and she turned in time to see Omar cartwheel into a doorframe and slide bonelessly to the floor.

"Stay back," she snarled. "You've seen what I can do. Next person who tries to hurt me gets a taste of my soul-sucking talent." Another bluff, since it wasn't even tingling inside her.

Keeping her eye on everyone, she reached behind her and opened the door. Once in the passageway, she ran as fast as she could toward the deck, hoping to force the helicopter pilot into flying her off the boat, but when she heaved open the door, disappointment shrouded her like a sodden blanket.

Son of a bitch, the bird was gone.

She heard the fall of running footsteps behind her. *Don't panic.* With as much calm as she could muster, she slammed the passageway door and spun the locking mechanism. A mop propped nearby became her best friend as she grabbed it and jammed the handle through the door's lock handle to prevent it from spinning. It wouldn't hold them for long, but she figured she only needed a couple of minutes. She hurried to the chest of Aegis supplies and grabbed a crossbow. Beneath the weapon was a large wooden box. Inside, lying on top of gray egg crate foam, were vials of milky liquid.

Qeres.

She snared a vial, and with adrenaline boosting her, she rushed to the motorized lifeboat on the starboard side of the ship. She could see the shoreline from here, and thank God the seas weren't rough. This was doable.

Awkwardly, she climbed into the hard-sided raft, grabbed the control box, and flipped the switch. In a grind of gears and a jolt that left her gasping for breath, the craft lowered down the side of the ship.

She heard shouts above, and as the little raft plunked into the water, the shouts turned to curses.

"Fuck! Reverse the winch. Pull her up!" The mushy voice belonged to Lance, and she almost laughed at the knowledge that the blow she'd delivered must have broken a few teeth.

"Too late." With a flick of her wrist, she disengaged the clamps that held the raft to the rigging, and her little boat floated free. She aimed the crossbow at Lance's head as he peered over the side of the ship. "Go to hell, assholes."

With one hand still holding the weapon, she pushed the motor ignition button, and the small diesel engine roared to life.

In a matter of minutes, she was far enough away from the Aegis ship to finally take a deep breath. To relax. Except then she looked ahead to the land and the pier there jutting out into the water, where she saw a figure take form as she got closer.

A large, armored man stood like a statue, his hair blowing in the wind, lashing his face. Thanatos. Breathing became a chore. Oh, God, she could feel his cold rage from here. She didn't believe he'd hurt her, even accidentally, but what if he blew the way he had the day he took out most of the island's population?

Her mouth went dry and her throat closed up as she guided the boat up to the rickety dock. His boots struck the wood with menacing thuds as she tried to come to her feet. She couldn't tell if her legs were unsteady or the boat was rocking, but either way, she could barely stay upright until his hand snared hers and lifted her effortlessly to the dock.

Finally, she met his gaze. And wished she hadn't.

All that icy anger had glazed his eyes with a glassy sheen of murder. His gaze raked her from head to toe, gauging, she assumed, her health. When he finished, he cast a Harrowgate and wordlessly led her through it. When they stepped out into the aftermath of the bloodbath in front of his keep, the day's events hit her like a sledge-hammer to the ribs.

The blackened remains of dead vampires mixed with the blood and body parts of dead Guardians. Guardians who had, most likely, not known exactly what the Elders had planned. They'd been considered acceptable losses for the greater good, hadn't they? All around them, hellhounds were...doing what they did to their victims. Regan's stomach churned at the sight and stench of death.

There were no words. Just horror and despair and the need to get her baby to safety.

Thanatos, still clutching her hand tightly, strode into the keep, never once looking at her. Inside, he dropped her hand and made a beeline for the library. She followed, closing the door behind her, as if that would shut out the death, the betrayal, the whole world.

Thanatos, his back to her, stared at the cradle in the

corner. "Were you involved in this, Regan? Did you know The Aegis was going to take you and attack my people?"

"Did I—?" She sucked in a harsh breath. He'd thought she'd betrayed him. Again. "No. God, no. I had no idea what they had planned."

"Even so, did you go willingly?"

She looked down at her belly, unsure how to answer.

"Regan?" he prompted.

"I got into the helicopter willingly. I know you don't trust them, but I had no reason not to. But when the engine started and you ran out…"

"What?" He turned to her, and she hated the guarded look in his eyes. They'd made so much progress, and this could have destroyed it all. "What did you do?"

"I tried to get out. And then we were in the air and there was nothing I could do. It wasn't until we got to the ship and I found out why they took me that I had a chance to get away."

"Why they took you?" The guarded look turned perplexed. "Weren't they trying to get you away from me?"

Her pulse leaped as her heart began to pound in a new panic. If Thanatos knew what they'd intended, he could go into a massive rage. But he needed to know. So much had been kept from him out of fear of what he would do. It was time to finally treat him like he was more than a death bomb waiting to go off and give him the benefit of the doubt.

"Getting me away from you was only part of it," she said quietly. "They wanted to deliver the baby."

"Why? Do they have Pestilence?"

"No." Her voice was now a guttural croak. "They wanted…they planned to deliver our son…and kill him." A sudden blast of fury exploded from Thanatos, and all around him, his souls shot from his armor. Hundreds of them. Thousands. Oh, shit. Quickly, she took his hand and placed his fingers in her palm. "Tap, Than. You can do this. Count it out."

"I'm beyond counting!" he bellowed. He looked down, his teeth clenched, and she knew that despite what he'd said, he was trying to hold it together. He was trying... for her.

"Thanatos? I need to talk to Kynan."

His head jerked up. "After what The Aegis has done, you want another Guardian here?"

"I need to understand this." Tears stung her eyes, blurring her vision, and she hated herself for that weakness. "The Elders who took me...they were possessed, or ensorcelled. That's the only explanation. Please, I need to understand."

"I do too." Thanatos smiled, but there was nothing humorous about it. "I need to know who to kill."

Twenty-eight

Death and madness vibrated inside Thanatos, shaking him like he was the epicenter of an earthquake. All around him, his vamps were dead, Guardians were dead; and on top of that, the deep-seated fury at Regan's kidnapping was a stinging poison that made the vibration intensify.

He was about to come out of his skin.

The Aegis had tried to kill his son.

He heard a buzzing in his ears...Regan's voice. *"Thanatos. Thanatos, listen to me. Thanatos!"*

He was going to kill every fucking Aegi on the planet. They were going to pay for what they'd done. On his arm, Styx was bucking, fighting to get out and start a battle.

"Thanatos, stop."

Kill.

"Thanatos!"

Kill.

His blood burned like lit kerosene in his veins and his breath came in harsh rasps as he fought to hold himself together. But those bastards had taken his female, planned to cut into her, and then murder his son. The images flipped through his head, tearing him, and his control, to shreds.

Through his body, his muscles quivered, and a fever dampened his skin. Pinpricks of sensation that bordered on erotic broke out on his hip, fracturing his focus on death. Blood rushed to his groin, hardening his cock.

Regan.

Blinking, he looked down at her. She met his gaze as she stroked her thumb over Styx's flank, easing him and getting Than's attention. At some point, she must have swiped her finger over his armor scar, because he was in his jeans and turtleneck, but all he wanted right now was to get out of them.

His voice scraped gravel. "Do you know what you're doing?"

"Yes."

He wasn't so far gone with rage and lust that he didn't know she was putting aside her own hurt and anger at what her colleagues had done in order to keep him calm. "It isn't fair to you." He hissed as she cupped him and squeezed with just the right amount of sensual pressure.

Her eyes were liquid, her long lashes glistening with tear droplets. "I need this too," she whispered. "I need it so badly."

Clamping down on an uncivilized urge to take her straight to the floor, he kissed her. Her tongue tangled with his, turning it hot before it had a chance to even smolder. Her hands came up to fist his shirt and hold him against her, but there was no need for that. He wasn't going anywhere.

He also wasn't going to take this slow. The savage desire to reclaim what the group of Aegis males had taken from him was an instinct he wasn't going to fight.

He broke off the kiss to nip and suck her throat, leaving tiny marks no one would miss. Her softly whispered "Yes" told him she liked it, and when he inhaled, the sharp scent of her arousal confirmed it.

Her skin tasted of the salty ocean breeze, and of battle, and he growled at the reminder of what she'd gone through.

"It's okay," she murmured. "Just stay with me."

He opened his mouth over the hollow of her throat, tasting more of the ocean, but it wasn't enough. He needed to taste her everywhere. Places he hadn't yet been. Places no one else would ever be. She was his, and he was going to claim her.

In a fevered rush, he dropped to his knees and found himself at eye level with her beautiful belly. He smiled as he lifted the maternity blouse and kissed her there, on the taut skin beneath her navel.

"Um . . . Thanatos . . ."

"Shh." He hooked his thumbs under the elastic waistband of her pants and underwear and pulled them down. "Brace yourself on the desk."

"But—"

"I need to see you. Taste you." And because of how low she was carrying their son, he needed her at a slight angle to have better access to what he wanted.

"I've never done this . . ."

"I haven't either." The admission might have embarrassed him a few days ago, but now...now it made him proud.

After a second of hesitation, she leaned back, bracing her hands behind her on the desk. *Yes.* He kissed his way down, worshipping every inch he touched, and when he reached her inner thigh, she groaned and widened her stance.

He nearly came at the sight of her female flesh, glistening and ready for him. Anticipation sang through him as he leaned in and licked the crease at her thigh. She stopped breathing, and when he dragged his tongue along the crease on the other leg, she sucked air.

"Are you ready?" he murmured against her creamy skin. Her answer was to thrust one hand into his hair and pull him closer.

He didn't waste another second. For the first time in his life, he put his mouth to a female's center.

For the first time in his life, he was glad he'd had to wait.

Gently, he used his thumbs to part her sweet flesh, and then he settled his mouth over her core. He started tentatively, exploring, using his tongue to probe and test what made her squirm and gasp the most. As his need ramped up, he grew more confident, his licks more urgent and desperate.

She tasted like the sun and the ocean combined, and he decided he wanted to do this as often as she'd let him. And from the way she was arching against his mouth he thought she'd let him have his way as much as he'd like.

And he *liked*.

"Than," she gasped. "I'm going to...ah...*yes.*"

Encouraged, he penetrated her with his tongue, fucking her with it until she was whimpering with need, pleading with him to finish her off. His cock was throbbing, straining inside his jeans, begging for release. Unable to wait another minute, he dragged his tongue up through the center of her sex and latched onto the swollen bud at the top. Sucking gently, he eased a finger inside her and pumped it in and out of her slick channel.

She came with a cry, bucking hard. His cock kicked, and yes, he'd take care of that in a second.

When she collapsed against the desk, he snared the coat draped over the back of one of the chairs, wrapped her in it, and hauled her to the bedroom. As soon as he set her on the floor, she grabbed the wooden rail at the foot of the bed and bent over, her perky ass in the air.

He didn't bother undressing. He ripped open his jeans and sheathed himself inside her molten heat. They both groaned as he started to move with long, slow strokes, but too soon his control was gone, and he was grinding against her, alternating deep, circular action with shallow, fast thrusts.

Needing even more contact, he bent over her, pressing his chest to her back, and placed his hands next to hers on the rail. His fangs shot out, and he used them to graze the back of her neck as he pumped into her.

"Beautiful," he murmured. "You're...amazing." His balls tightened, ready to burst. "Come, Regan."

"Yes," she moaned. "Now."

Her core spasmed around him, squeezing and caressing, and he was lost. He went over the edge with a shout, his hot seed pouring into her, the sweet agony of orgasm making him see stars. He came harder than he ever had, and even as his first climax waned, another bore down on him.

Erotic lightning gathered inside him, building to a fever pitch, and when it struck, it made the last orgasm look tame. Throwing his head back, Thanatos roared in pure ecstasy. This was what he'd waited his entire life for, and it wasn't even about the sex.

It was about a mate. A family.

A family...oh, fuck. Panic set in almost as quickly as the orgasm had. "We can't do this again," he rasped. "Not until the baby is born."

Regan's voice was muffled, one cheek resting on the mattress. "Why?"

"Shade said something about sex inducing labor." As eager as he was to finally hold his squirming son in his arms, there was another consideration. "We can't risk our baby coming until we have my brother."

"That sucks," she muttered, and he agreed. They seemed to agree on a lot of things like that.

His arms were trembling as he pushed off her, not wanting her to bear any of his weight. She didn't seem to want to move, so he stood her up, kissed her as he stripped her of her top and tucked her into bed.

"I'm not tired." she said. And then she yawned.

He climbed in with her and gathered her against him. "Me either."

She was asleep in under thirty seconds.

Thanatos eased out of bed, leaving Regan to some much-needed sleep. With his rage dialed back from a full boil to a quiet simmer, his brain function returned, and shit, he had a messy tangle of Apocalypse threads to unravel. The Aegis had gone ghastbat-insane, Pestilence had been too quiet for comfort, and he still hadn't heard from Ares on whether he'd had any luck with Idess and Azagoth.

He was a firm believer in never saying that things could get worse, because they always could, but right now he was having a hard time seeing *how*.

He stepped out into the hall, where a hellhound stood guard, and Than glared. "Where were you when The Aegis stole her, you mangy beast?"

The hound glared back, but offered no explanation. Not that Than expected one, even if he could communicate with it. The hound hadn't seen trouble in The Aegis's arrival any more than Than had. And since Regan went with them willingly, the beast wouldn't have acted until it was too late.

"Ah, don't worry. I'll nail those bastards. With railroad spikes." Than reached out and patted the mutt on the head. "I'll save you an arm or leg."

He left the hellhound and stalked down the hall, texting Ares as he did. *Aegis kidnapped Regan. Tried to kill the baby. They're safe now, but where the fuck are you? Need to know Azagoth's status.*

Than jammed the Send button and shoved the phone into his pocket as he headed outside, where he was immediately hit by the stench of blood, bowels, and death. His heart became heavy at the sight of the charred remains of four daywalkers, including Viktor, that lay among the corpses of several Guardians. Hard to tell the exact number of Aegi, since there wasn't much left of them. The hellhounds had made fast work of the humans.

Hard to believe that Than had once hated the beasts. Now he wanted a kennel full of them. As long as you didn't try to suppress their basic instincts, and you agreed to let them have full dominion over the creatures they battled—allowed them the spoils of war, as it were—they were awesome allies. Plus, they hated Pestilence, and an enemy of an enemy, and all that.

There was movement to his left, and he whirled, scythe in hand, to find Artur standing there, his head bowed. Blood and ash streaked Artur's pale skin, and in his hand, he held a stake.

"I failed you," he rasped. "So many of us . . . failed you."

Than went taut. "If you're talking about Regan being taken, it wasn't your fault—"

"No." Artur swallowed. "There were traitors amongst us." He waved his hand at the vampire dust. "Those who died were loyal to you. But the others . . . they ran."

"Who, Artur? Where are they?"

Artur held up the stake. "I caught them. I'm sorry they betrayed you, *Bludrexe*." Artur had helped most of the daywalkers through their transitions, so he had to be taking the betrayals as hard as Thanatos. Hell, for centuries, Artur had helped seek out Than's . . . indiscretions . . . and bring them back here.

"Don't be." Than kicked himself for not acknowledging Artur's pain sooner. He'd make it up to the vampire. Somehow. "You didn't know."

A bitter smile twisted Artur's mouth. "But I did. At least, I suspected. I was one of those who held a grudge against you. I loved you like a father, Thanatos. I've always loved you. But your tight hold chafed. We're destroying ourselves to be free of it. Forgive me."

"For what?" A sinking sensation made Than's gut tank. "Oh, God, Artur. What did you do?"

Artur's eyes grew liquid, and the stake in his hand trembled. "*I* found the wildings and convinced them to rebel. But I swear, I didn't want your son dead. I didn't think they'd take it so far."

"You?" Thanatos's throat felt raw, as if he'd been screaming. "And Dariq? Who killed him?"

"I did," Artur said. "Just as I killed all of them, *Bludrexe*," Artur said. "Your keep is safe."

"You killed everyone who was plotting against me?"

"Save one," Artur whispered. He reached up and ripped his shirt from the collar to the hem. And there, fresh and swollen over his heart, was a tattoo—a tattoo of Thanatos, with Artur putting a noose around Than's neck. "This is why the others ran. You'd soon know the truth. I'm so sorry, Thanatos." He brought the stake to his chest, the point piercing the center of the tattoo. Blood trickled down his torso.

Than's breath lodged in his throat. "Don't. Artur, listen to me—"

"I failed you."

Thanatos lunged, but Artur was faster. He jammed the stake into his own heart, and Thanatos watched helplessly as his oldest, most trusted creation became nothing more than a blackened pile of charcoal on the ground.

Twenty-nine

Regan woke up with stomach pains. They were worse than the Braxton Hicks she'd experienced before, but they weren't regular. Damn... what if sex *had* triggered labor? With her due date less than a week away, the baby could come any time, and while in any other circumstance she'd be happy to help it along, right now would be a very bad time if they couldn't nail Pestilence.

A sense of urgency drove her out of bed and into a pair of maternity pants and a sweatshirt. Even though a glance at the clock told her she'd slept less than an hour, she couldn't believe she'd fallen asleep, not when there was so much to do and so much going on. It was as if the baby had taken away her soul-sucking ability and given her narcolepsy.

The hellhound, whom she was going to call Velcro from now on, was waiting for her outside the bedroom door. He followed her, his nails clacking on the floor, until she reached the great room, where Thanatos was just entering from outside. Tension came with him, a tangible crackle in the air.

"You don't have to worry about my daywalkers anymore," he said, his voice a dull monotone. "They're dead."

"Oh my God," she breathed. "*All* of them? Did you—?"

"The Aegis killed those loyal to me, and Artur...he killed those who weren't. He's gone, too."

Regan wasn't sure what to say. Thanatos had protected his vampires for thousands of years, had kept them with him and gave them a home in the only way he'd known how. They had been as much his family as The Aegis was hers.

"I'm sorry," she said, and before she could even finish, he pulled her against him and held her tight. A lump swelled in her throat. In a way, this was the most intimate they'd been. She wished she could do more, wished there was a way to ease his pain the way sex eased his violent tendencies. She couldn't bear to see him in so much pain. If she could take it, she would.

"And I'm sorry about your colleagues," he said roughly. She knew he wasn't really sorry, but it was nice of him to say.

They stayed that way until Velcro took it upon himself to separate them by wedging his nose between them, and that fast, the world crashed down on them again.

Regan glanced up at Thanatos. "I need your phone."

Than said nothing, merely dug a cell phone from his pocket and paced as she dialed.

Kynan answered on the second ring, but she didn't allow him to say anything beyond a snappish "What?"

"Ky, it's Regan. I need to you to keep your mouth shut

until I'm finished talking, and then you had better give me the truth." She spilled the events of the day, keeping one eye on Than. With each word, the storm cloud surrounding him grew more intense, until she could almost feel the static undercurrents of it on her skin.

Her voice was quavering by the time she was done, and for a long time, Kynan didn't say anything. Finally, his gravelly voice, much more torn up than usual, came over the airwaves.

"Are you and the baby okay?"

All she could manage was a quiet "yes."

"And Thanatos? Is he level?"

Saying yes would be a lie, but "no" wasn't entirely accurate. "For now."

"Okay, listen to me. If our people have been compromised with possession or a spell, this could be widespread. Pestilence knows the locations of too many regional headquarters. Fuck, this is worse than—"

"Worse than what?" she blurted.

"Nothing. Stay close to Thanatos and keep him calm. I'll be there as soon as I find out anything."

He hung up just as the door burst open and Ares rushed in. "Than, got your text. Fuck... Regan, you okay?"

Not even close. But she nodded.

Ares shifted his gaze to Thanatos. "Our brother is gearing up for something big. I went to Underworld General to find Idess—"

"Did you get her?" Than interrupted.

"That's what I'm trying to tell you. Pestilence took out the anti-violence spell inside the hospital. Brought in his minions and turned the place into a fucking meat grinder. He got to Idess before I did."

"What do you mean, he got to her?" Thanatos said tightly. "Did he kill her?"

"He took her. Hades told you Pestilence was trying to destroy Sheoul-gra. With Idess, he can get in, just like *we* planned."

Regan didn't take her eyes off Thanatos. "Do you think he has the same idea about Azagoth? Maybe he wants to destroy Azagoth to prevent him from breaking your Seals and starting the, uh, *good* Apocalypse." Not that any Apocalypse could be good, but at least three of the Horsemen would be fighting on the right side of it.

"Either way, this is bad news." Anger laced Than's words. "Pestilence will release all the souls from Sheoulgra. Millions of them. If that happens, it won't matter if our Seals are broken, because the Earth is going to become a demon Disneyland."

Kynan shook with rage and disbelief for a good five minutes after he hung up the phone. A moment later, his wife Gem hurried out of the bathroom, her red-streaked black hair wet, her hands fumbling with the ties to her skull-and-crossbones robe.

"I heard the phone ring. Who was it? Any news about Idess?"

"No." His voice was lower and raspier than usual, and not just because he was exhausted after getting home only half an hour ago from the chaos at Underworld General. "It was Regan."

He dropped the towel he'd wrapped around his waist after showering with Gem. They'd come home to clean up and check on their daughter Dawn who, thank God, had been here with Shade's mate Runa and their triplets when Pestilence struck UG. It had been a stroke of luck that Eidolon had shut down the nursery a couple of days ago, although that had nothing to do with keeping the kids out of there. The hospital had needed more space for the patient overflow.

"Is she okay?"

"For now." He tugged on his jeans and a sweatshirt. "But I gotta get to Scotland."

"Why? I was hoping you could stay with Dawn while I head back to UG."

He kissed her lightly on the forehead, wishing he could do exactly that. Right now he wanted nothing more than to hold his daughter and keep her safe from all the horrors that had invaded their lives.

"It's an emergency. Some Elders did something really fucked up, and I need to get answers before the Horsemen go crazy and kill us all."

"When their Seals break?"

He tore open the closet door and spun the lock on the weapons safe concealed inside. "No. Like today." The safe opened up, and he yanked out a weapons harness. "I need a spellcaster or exorcist. Pestilence killed ours in the attack on headquarters. I don't suppose you know a good one."

Gem sank down on the end of the mattress as if her legs had given out. They might have. She'd been working almost nonstop for weeks. He hated that. Hated that he and his wife were so exhausted they couldn't find time to do anything together but sleep. Sure, they'd showered together just now, but only the soap had seen any action from either of them.

"You think someone in The Aegis has been possessed or is under an enemy spell?"

"It's the only explanation." The only one he'd consider, because the idea that his friends and colleagues had gone rogue, had planned to kill an innocent child, was just not possible.

Gem sighed. "Underworld General has a few magic users on staff, but you won't want them knowing about your new headquarters."

"I'll get Wraith. With all the artifacts he's found over the years, he's got to have something that can break an enchantment."

He finished weaponing-up, checked on his daughter, and then gave Gem a good-bye kiss that he hoped conveyed everything he felt for her. Lore's pain when he learned Idess had been taken by Pestilence was still fresh in Kynan's mind, the demon's roar of anguish still ringing in his ears. Ky wasn't sure what he'd do if Gem was in that kind of danger, but even the thought of it made his heart hurt.

He called Wraith during the fifteen minutes it took him to drive to the nearest Harrowgate, which sat in a sparsely populated suburban New York neighborhood, and then he gated himself to a remote beach in Scotland. Wraith showed up within five minutes, dressed in his beat-up leather duster, jeans, and combat boots. As the demon stepped out of the gate, which was camouflaged against a cliff face, he tapped the backpack slung over one shoulder.

"Got some potions, powders, and metal doodads. Something should help un-enchant people."

Ky started up the rocky trail to the vehicle he kept parked in a nearby field, since the Harrowgate they'd just come out of was the closest one to the Aegis castle, and there was no way Ky was walking the twenty miles. "Are you sure?"

Wraith shrugged. "No, but it's always more fun when there's a risk factor involved." He flashed fang. "We gonna get to kick some ass?"

"I fucking hope not." Normally, Ky would be up for a battle, but he wasn't up for a fight with people he'd worked with and trusted for years. "How's Lore? Any luck locating Idess?"

Wraith kicked a rock and watched it plummet to the shore below. "Lore's about how you'd expect. E had to sedate him, but it's not going to hold him long. We got nothing on Idess."

They reached the top of the cliff, and Ky unlocked the little Volvo. "When we get done here, do what you can to keep Lore from doing something crazy. Once I gauge the situation at Than's place, taking Lore there might be a good idea. They'll want any help they can get locating Pestilence."

They piled into the car, and Ky floored it, tearing up the road to get to headquarters. Wraith's oddball observations about the countryside kept Kynan level, which was, he suspected, Wraith's goal. The demon might be a pain in the ass, but he was a lot more astute than people gave him credit for.

Ky parked at the base of the castle grounds, and he and Wraith wasted no time in jogging through the late morning gloom and into the damp castle, and what perfect timing... the very assholes he'd been seeking were gathered around a pile of books in the makeshift front office. And oddly, there were a dozen Guardians standing sentinel throughout the room, heavily armed.

"Who wants to explain what happened with Regan?"

Juan closed the book he'd been poring through. "Hello to you, too, Morgan."

Lance wheeled around, his swollen, bruised face going purple with rage when he saw Wraith. "You brought a *demon* to our headquarters?"

"Do you really want a pissing match to see who's made the most egregious offense to The Aegis lately?"

Takumi stiffened with a wince. Someone had beaten these guys senseless, and Kynan popped Regan a mental high-five. "We did what we thought was necessary."

"And you thought it was necessary to cut open Regan and kill her innocent baby?"

"Innocent?" Lance scoffed. "It's a demon."

Wraith snorted as he unzipped his backpack. "See, Ky, this is why I always want to kill all your friends." He pulled out a glass vial filled with green liquid. "No offense."

"Trust me, none taken." Kynan glared at the four men in front of him. "You guys want to explain why you didn't consult the rest of the Elders before you changed our plan?" He doubted anyone would mention getting possessed or something, but it was worth a shot.

"We told you earlier. Tried to." Omar gave Kynan a sad look, as if he felt sorry for him. "You and Valeriu are too blinded by your relationships to the demons to consider other options. And despite Decker's pledge of allegiance to the Sigil, he's still a member of the American military, and some of us don't trust him."

"There is something seriously wrong with you," Kynan said, his temper mounting.

He nodded sharply at Wraith, who grinned as he

flipped the vial into the air. Lance dove for it, but it hit the stone floor and shattered before he could catch it.

A sickly brown mist exploded through the room, shifting and writhing as if it were alive. Ten seconds later, it disappeared.

"What the fuck was that?" Juan shouted.

Wraith dropped his pack to the floor. "A revealing elixir. It would have made anyone suffering a magical enchantment glow like they took a swim in nuclear waste. None of you are glowy." He shrugged. "You're douche bags, though."

Lance whipped his head around to Kynan. "You thought we were compromised by a spell?"

"Why else would you have pulled such a stupid stunt?" Kynan shot back.

"Bastard." Lance came at him, although he should have known that doing so was useless. As long as Kynan was wearing Heofon, the amulet around his neck, he was impervious to harm.

Wraith moved in a blur, and in an instant, had his teeth buried in Lance's throat. The Guardian sentinels sprang into action, firing their crossbows and hurling weapons, but Wraith, the recipient of a similar immunity charm, was protected.

After a few seconds, the demon disengaged his fangs and shoved Lance away. "He's not possessed by a demon. He's just naturally a dickmunch."

"You thought we were possessed, too?" Lance's voice was strangled, his eyes bugging out of his head.

"I hoped so," Kynan said. "God, I'd hoped so." Kynan's temples throbbed with anger, and his skin felt tight, scoured raw by their betrayal. "What in God's name made you think you were doing the right thing?"

"We didn't *think* we were. We *knew* it." Juan gestured to one of the guards, who disappeared down a hallway. "We were given new information that led us to believe that the prophecy isn't about stabbing Pestilence in the heart, but stabbing the infant. We're certain that will destroy Pestilence."

"Who gave you the new info?"

"A trusted source," Lance said. "Unlike all the clues we've been patching together over the years that turned out to be false or planted or just wrong, this is real."

Kynan couldn't believe this. What kind of fucking Kool-Aid had these morons drunk? "You're wrong. The infant is Thanatos's *agimortus*. Killing the baby will break Thanatos's Seal. You should have come to me and Val with this. We could have worked it out."

"We can't trust you or Val anymore. You've led us down a path that failed. Working with demons? Forming an alliance with werewolves? Making peace with vampires in trade for intel? What part of the fact that we're *demon slayers* are you not understanding?"

"It's called changing tactics and turning enemies into allies. It's called progress, Juan. Making alliances in unlikely places."

Lance, his palm slapped over Wraith's bite wound, snarled. "We like the old ways. Since the day you came along, involved in that demon hospital and married to a goddamned monster, things have gotten worse, and now we're on the verge of an Apocalypse. Thanks a fucking lot."

Married to a goddamned monster? Crimson fury cut a scalding swath of rage across Kynan's field of vision. "You son of a bitch." Kynan barely recognized his own voice, warped and molten with the depth of his anger. He lunged at Lance, but Wraith seized him around the waist and dragged him back.

"Dude." Wraith spoke in a hushed tone into Kynan's ear. "Check up. I'm all for ripping these fucks to shreds, but eyeball your perimeter, man. Something bad is going down."

Kynan sucked air through clenched teeth, desperate to take chunks out of Lance, but as the demon held him tight, Kynan noticed four new guys entering the room, each holding a flask...but one also held a furry baby Slogthu demon, a tiny silver charm Ky had seen before but couldn't place, and a dagger, all of which he handed to Takumi.

"What is this?" Kynan demanded. "What the hell are you doing with that demon?"

Lance rolled his eyes. "Leave it to you to be concerned about a damned *demon*." He gestured to the four new-comers. "And these are our new Elders."

"New...*what*?" Kynan glanced at the new *Elders*. Two had been on The Aegis's short list for future promotion to the Sigil. The other two were Regents, the heads of individual cells, one in Toronto and one in Rio de Janeiro. "You can't promote new members without a unanimous vote from every Elder, and you know that."

"Yeah," Lance said. "That's the thing. We did get a unanimous vote, because you, Val, Regan, and Decker are no longer welcome in the Sigil." He made an encompassing gesture with a sweep of his arm indicating the eight men standing in a semi-circle in front of Ky and Wraith. "*We* are the Sigil. And you...you are no longer welcome here."

"You can't do this."

"We can. And we have." Takumi's gaze dropped, as if maybe this didn't sit entirely well with him. "*Sentinelium angelicus expellum.*" He plunged the dagger into the little demon.

"*Motherfuckers!*" Wraith shouted.

The four flasks flashed, glowing as brightly as the sun. Pain pierced Kynan's brain. Wraith grabbed his head, and as the agony drilled them both, Kynan stumbled backward, overcome by a driving need to get out of the castle. He and Wraith were shoved by an invisible force as the eight Elders advanced, the glow forming a wall in front of them.

"What the fuck," Wraith growled, voicing Kynan's thoughts exactly.

They staggered out the doors, and once the fresh air hit them, the pain stopped, although Ky's brain felt bruised, as if he'd gotten clocked by a heavyweight boxer.

Lance and the others halted at the threshold. "Don't come back. Headquarters is now warded against your angelic charms."

"How? How did you do this?"

"You aren't the only one with an angel friend." Lance smirked.

Kynan wanted to knock the cockiness off Lance's face. An…angel friend? Who—"Harvester." Now he remembered where he'd seen the silver charm Takumi was holding. Harvester had worn it on a necklace. "Jesus Christ, she's a fallen angel. She's evil. You killed a baby demon and used black fucking magic in your ward. Do you know how wrong that can go?"

Lance's expression grew amused. "It's called changing tactics," he mocked. "Making alliances in unlikely places."

"You shortsighted idiots! There's a fucking Apocalypse coming. We can't afford to fragment like this. Not now."

"You've given us no choice," Juan said.

"So this is it. You take over headquarters, bring in new Elders, and banish anyone who doesn't agree with you."

"We're the new Aegis," Omar said. "Or, the way we see it, the original Aegis. We're taking back the old ways."

"You won't win," Kynan said. "We won't let you."

Lance spread his arms. "Look around you, charmed boy. We have all the toys. We've already won."

Kynan's temper snapped, and he started for Lance, intending to beat him to a pulp, but before he reached the threshold, he ran into an invisible wall that felt as solid as a steel barrier. Wraith grabbed him before the crushing head pain could take hold.

"You know what, buddy?" Wraith said. "They aren't worth it. Not now. But later...." He jabbed his finger at Lance and bared his fangs. "You're mine. And dude, I play with my food."

Thirty

Regan felt so damned useless. While Ares took off for Sheoul in an attempt to send a message of warning to Hades about Pestilence's possible ability to get into Sheoul-gra with Idess, Thanatos tried to summon Reaver. Regan...she took a shower. Thanatos had been adamant that the hot water and steam would make her feel better.

It had felt good to wash away the smell of the Aegis ship and the salt water, but when she stepped out of the shower, she was still tense. As she dried off, she tried her best to calm herself, because the cramping pains in her belly and back seemed to get worse when she was worked up.

Please, please don't let this be labor. Yes, the fact that they didn't yet have Pestilence was a huge concern, but right now, her own fears were surfacing. For eight months she'd avoided thinking about motherhood, since the baby was going to Kynan and Gem. But things had changed. She'd fallen for the baby, and she was falling for its father.

That would have been a good thing in a normal world, maybe. But so much uncertainty was going to surround her son's birth, and so much weight was being placed on his tiny shoulders. She wanted to bear it all, and she wished like hell she knew how.

Thanatos tapped on the door. He entered, his bone armor clacking, tension making the scorpion on his neck sting his jugular.

"Your friends are here." He flexed his fingers at his sides. "Kynan and Decker. Arik is here too, with Limos and Ares."

Full house. How perfect, given that she felt like crap and wasn't sure she wanted to hear what Kynan had learned.

"Give me a minute to get dressed."

"Need help?"

"No, I—" She broke off at the quirk of a smile on his lips. "I think," she said wryly, "that if you helped, it might take long enough to get out of here that our guests would become suspicious."

"Good." He strode over to her and put his mouth to her throat. With a little rumble, he scraped his teeth over her skin in a blatantly possessive marking. "I want them suspicious. I don't want anyone fucking with you ever again."

Ever again? What did he mean by that? They'd both avoided talk of the future, because truly, the future looked so bleak, so uncertain. In Regan's case, she just didn't dare to plan. She'd had her life torn apart so much, and each time she'd thought her future with a family was secure the ground beneath her feet fell away again.

Thanatos stepped away and moved toward the door. As he exited, he looked back over his shoulder. "No matter how bad Kynan's news is, I've got you, okay?" Before she could respond, he closed the door softly behind him.

Choking back emotion that seemed to scald her throat, she finished dressing and joined the others in the great room.

The tension in there was as thick as an Oni demon's blood. But she was glad to see that Than's nightwalkers were back at work. Peter gave her a respectful nod as he slipped into the kitchen.

Kynan and Decker were sitting stiffly on the long bench that ran the length of one side of the trestle table. Ares, Limos, and Thanatos were standing, fully armored, as if they were waiting for Ky and Deck to attack. Reaver was there, and he and Arik had angled themselves between the two groups as if prepared to prevent a battle from breaking out.

When Kynan saw Regan, he and Decker both came to their feet. She felt Than's gaze on her as she crossed toward them, her palms sweating and her gut churning. The expressions on her fellow Elders' faces were the grimmest she'd ever seen.

She stopped next to Thanatos and didn't beat around the bush. "Tell me."

Ky and Decker exchanged glances. "It's bad, Regan," Ky said. "It wasn't a spell or possession. Our colleagues planned your kidnapping and the baby's sacrifice based on some kind of bullshit interpretation of the prophecy."

"No." She shook her head so hard her wet hair stung her cheeks as it slapped against her face. "I don't believe that. You've got to be wrong. Talk to them again. *I'll* talk to them. This can't be right. They wouldn't do that to me. To us."

"I'm sorry," Kynan said. "There's more."

The glow that surrounded Reaver flickered as he said roughly, "More?"

Regan listened in disbelief and horror as Kynan described what had gone down in Scotland. The Horsemen didn't react until Kynan got to the part about Harvester's possible involvement.

Reaver's wings flared. "Harvester helped them? As a Watcher, the risk would be . . ." Reaver shook his head.

Kynan rubbed the stubble on his jaw. "They said they had angelic help, and they used blood magic in the ward against me. Only an evil angel would use that kind of spell. They also had Harvester's silver charm. She could have told them how to find your keep and how to find a way around the baby's ability to keep Regan safe."

"How could anyone find a way around the baby's ability?" Arik asked.

Reaver looked troubled. "There are ways around anything. You just have to find the right combination of magic, evil, herbs, power, whatever."

"I just hope they were smart enough to not tell her the location of the new headquarters." Ky had been careful to keep that information from the Horsemen as well, deftly avoiding any reference to Scotland, or even Europe, while he spoke.

Regan had no words. How could people she'd known all her life do something so inconceivable?

"Regan?" A touch of stressed-out Texas twang had leaked into Decker's voice. "You okay?"

"I just . . ." Sweat dampened her temples. She counted to three, doing her best to keep from breaking down. "What do we do now?"

"We salvage what we can," Ky said.

"What do you mean, salvage?"

Decker and Kynan exchanged another glance before Ky spoke. "Lance and the others took everything they could to the new HQ. And then they destroyed the old one. I don't know how long they'd planned this, but they knew exactly what they were doing. They promoted four Guardians to the Sigil, and they're actively seeking support from all Regents worldwide. Since they hold headquarters, they have the advantage. Val is trying to get support for our side, but we'll be lucky to get twenty percent of the Guardian population to back us." He blew out a shaky breath. "We're now the Rebels, and they're the Empire. Regan, the Aegis is broken."

Thanatos sensed something was wrong with Regan, maybe even before she realized it herself. Kynan's announcement that The Aegis had broken settled over the room like a shroud, but where everyone else erupted into curses, Regan went still and silent, her face draining of color and her hands clutching her belly so tightly her fingers went white.

Very gently, Thanatos settled his hands on her shoulders and pulled her against him, her back to his chest, bracing her. He dipped his head, letting his lips brush her ear. "You okay?"

She didn't respond. She was trembling so hard her teeth chattered. Thanatos's heart felt like it had been dragged behind a car going eighty on fresh, hot asphalt.

"Regan?"

"They were my family," she whispered. "I gave them

everything, and they tried to hurt me. They tried to *kill* my son."

Yeah, and someone was going to pay for that. "They're bastards, Regan. They never deserved you."

"I needed them. Every family I was fostered out to gave me up. The Aegis was all I had." She swallowed over and over, trying to hold back tears. "Belonging to The Aegis meant that I wouldn't be unwanted anymore."

He turned her around so she was facing him, and the devastation in her expression skinned him alive. She'd dedicated her life to the organization, had given them her freaking body to use when they'd sent her here to seduce him, and they'd thanked her by offering her and her baby up as a sacrifice.

He'd asked what her personal objective was when she'd come to seduce him. Now he knew. She'd felt she had to make herself indispensable to—wanted by—the only family she'd ever known. She'd not wanted to be given up.

Those bastards. Those *fucking* bastards.

"You're not unwanted." She didn't look at him, so he hooked his finger under her chin and lifted her face to his. "Do you hear me? I want you. I want you and our son. When all of this is over, when Pestilence is gone and the world returns to normal, I want you here with me."

Her eyes met his in surprise, but he had no idea how that could be. Had he not given her enough signals? Had he not made it clear that she was his? He didn't make cradles for random children, he didn't kidnap random females, and he definitely didn't tell random strangers that he'd fathered an entire race. She was part of his life now, and that was that.

She was his.

"What if the world doesn't return to normal? What if the world does return to normal, and you don't need me to help you stay calm anymore?" She looked around wildly, and Than knew she was seeking something to organize or straighten. "What if—"

Than cut her off with a finger to her lips. "Shh," he whispered. "Count it out." And wait, *What if the world does return to normal, and you don't need me to help you stay calm anymore?*

Did she honestly think that how he felt was dependent on her ability to give him something?

Fuck, The Aegis had messed with her head, hadn't it.

There was a sudden shrill ring of a phone, which Than barely heard through the buzz of disbelief in his head.

Ares swiped his fingers over his neck, and his armor disappeared. He snared his cell phone from his khakis' leg pocket. "Cara? Cara, shit." The phone fell from his trembling fingers, and then he was armored again and racing for the door.

"Ares!" Limos ran after him. "What is it?"

"Pestilence. He's at my place. Hurry!"

Kynan gestured to Than. "Go. Deck and I will stay with Regan."

"I can't leave her."

As Ares and Limos disappeared through the front door to open a Harrowgate, Regan reached up and feathered her fingers over his cheek. "Go. Stop him. If you want the world to return to normal, you've got to stop him."

"When I get back, we need to talk." He kissed her, lingering only a second before turning to Ky. "Thank you."

Than jogged after his brother, sister, and Arik, praying this was just a minor skirmish Pestilence had planned as

an annoyance. But as Than stepped out of the keep and
opened his Harrowgate, something went wrong. The gate,
usually a shimmering portal, was blackened and twisted,
its surface undulating like oil on water.

Than tried to close it, threw himself backward, but it
sucked him in like quicksand.

Thirty-one

The second Thanatos was out the door, Regan made a bee-line for Than's library. She hadn't even needed to count to get out of the panic she'd started to feel. An emergency usually made her think straight.

And she hoped to hell that Cara was okay. Regan didn't know Ares's wife very well, but the woman had been nice to Regan. And anyone who could charm hellhounds definitely possessed a likability factor.

"Regan." Ky came after her, Decker on his heels. "What are you doing? You should rest."

"And what did Gem tell you when you said that to her when she was pregnant?"

He sighed. "She suggested I shove a blunt object some-place really painful."

"There you go." Regan searched Than's shelves for the book she needed. And there, in Than's collection of almost every holy book known to man and demon, was a Holy Bible.

Her hand shook as she took it off the shelf and placed it in the cradle Than had left in the corner, his leather tools scattered beneath it.

"Ah . . . Regan?" Decker asked. "You okay?"

"Peachy." She turned to the guys. "Ky, I want you to put your hand on the Bible and swear something for me."

Kynan's dark eyebrows shot up. "You know that any oath sworn on a holy book is merely morally binding unless it's accompanied by magic."

"Duh. But that's what I'm counting on. You're the most moral person I know."

"I don't understand." Ky eyed her like she maybe needed a straightjacket. "Are you sure you shouldn't sit down?"

"Just put your hand on the Bible."

She was pretty certain he was humoring her, but he did it. "Now what?"

"Swear to me that if anything happens to me, you won't fight Thanatos for his son."

Kynan straightened. "What? Regan, we decided that the best thing for the baby would be for me and Gem to raise it."

"Yeah, and that's the thing. *We* decided. Thanatos hasn't had any say in any of this. We did what we did for the sake of the world, but we steamrolled him while holding onto this righteous idea that we were doing this grand thing. We were so sure we were right. We're no better than Lance and those bunch of assholes. At this point, Thanatos needs to make the decisions that will keep our son safe. He deserves that, at least."

"And what about you? What do you deserve?"

She glanced at the cradle. "I'm not sure what I deserve, but I know what I want."

"And that is?"

"Thanatos and the baby." If they'd have her. Thanatos had said he wanted her, but other people had said that, too. Then they changed their minds. Or tried to kill her.

The nightmare she'd had about Thanatos killing her flashed through her head. She hadn't had that dream since she'd been here, but now the images came back, as vivid as they'd been every night for months. She'd been convinced the nightmare was a warning, and maybe it was, but if so, she had to take precautions.

"The Bible, Ky."

He let out a long, frustrated breath, but he bent over the cradle and once again lay his palm on the book.

"Now, swear that no matter what happens to me, no matter what Thanatos does to me, you will not make any attempt to take his son away." She glanced at Decker. "And you won't let anyone *else* try either."

"I swear," Ky muttered.

"Good," she said brightly. "Now, I think we should prepare some *qeres*-coated weapons."

"We don't have any *qeres*. Lance and the others have it."

"Nope. I grabbed a vial of it when I was on their ship."

Decker grinned. "Awesome."

"Now we just have to hope one of the Horsemen can hunt that fucker down."

Regan touched her fingers to her belly as another cramp struck. "And something tells me they need to hurry. You might want to put Eidolon on notice. I think the little pony is wanting out."

Pestilence was such a fucking bastard.

Thanatos had experienced a lot of death in his life, but this...this went beyond death. This was carnage. And how the hell had Pestilence hijacked his Harrowgate like that? Whatever he'd done, it had trapped Thanatos in Finland, unable to even summon the gate again.

Unable to get back to Regan.

He had no doubt that whatever was going on at Ares's place had been a ruse to lure Than into using the tainted Harrowgate, but he also had no doubt that whatever Ares was dealing with was very real, and very violent.

His fury blended with the effect of all the death around him, leaving his ability to think as fragmented as a shattered window. He tried to call Kynan to check on Regan, but his rage was too encompassing, and he crushed the phone in his hand. After that, only the need to kill was left in his thoughts.

And there was so much to kill.

Here on the outskirts of Helsinki, humans were in the throes of some sort of malady that made them go crazy and slaughter each other. Thanatos stood among the remains of a family killed by their father in their own house, his scythe dripping with blood. Than had taken down the father, but not before the man had hacked his wife and three sons to death.

His scalp prickled, and he whirled as a Harrowgate opened up across the living room from Than. Pestilence stepped out, naked and dappled with gore. That was disturbing enough, but what truly made Thanatos's chest cavity grow cold was his brother's appearance. This wasn't the male who had appeared human even after his Seal had broken.

This was a demon. A beast with eyes as black as tar, skin as pale and veiny as marble, and elongated claws that could gut a killer whale. Hatred and evil had ravaged everything that had once been Reseph, right down to his appearance.

Pestilence hissed, his fangs a good inch longer than they'd ever been. Jesus. "You enjoying this? You like wading knee-deep in blood and guts, you fucker?"

"Reseph." Than made one last plea to the demon who used to be his brother. "You've got to be in there somewhere."

"He's gone," Pestilence roared. "When will you assholes get that through your thick skulls? He's gone, and I'm sick of all the goddamned reminders of him, of you, of all that he cared about. I'm wiping the slate clean and starting over. Your whelp is next on my list."

Protective fury shuddered through Than. *"You will never touch my child."*

"Oh, I will. Even if I didn't need to kill him to break your Seal, I'd kill him for fun. For spite. To ruin your fucking life." He cocked his head. "Though maybe I don't need to. With your temper, you'll probably kill him yourself. *That* would be awesome."

As much as Than wanted to think he could refuse Pestilence's bait, his grip on his scythe was so tight that the handle seemed to fuse to his flesh. Maybe because Pestilence had voiced the concern Thanatos had been trying to deny; that he might be a danger to his own child. The dead children on the floor, victims of their own father, slammed it all home like a baseball bat to the skull.

The man on the floor had probably been a good, loving father, but in his mindless rage, he'd slaughtered everyone he'd loved.

Thanatos had been fooling himself about his ability to control himself, hadn't he? Yes, with Regan his needs morphed from kill to sex, but what if his son didn't come equipped with some sort of Thanatos-proof safety feature?

And the very fact that Regan could bring him down... he liked it, needed it, but Christ, what she'd said back at his place was sitting on him like a log. *Was* he using her ability to calm him the way The Aegis had used her gifts? He'd fallen for her, had fallen for her generosity, her laugh, the way she could spar with him and hold her own, both physically and verbally. But if he was using her, he was no better than The Aegis.

Would he be using his son the same way? Putting an innocent baby in danger because Thanatos needed what a child could provide... love, someone to keep him company, someone to absolve Than of his sins?

"What's the matter, brother? Did I say something to upset you?"

Thanatos turned away from the thing that used to be his brother, needing a second to get his head back in the game. He might be a danger to his own son, but Pestilence was a much greater one, and Than was pretty damned tired of being two moves behind the evil bastard.

Get him to talk.

"You don't want me to kill my son," Than said, putting a strangled note in his voice. "You want to do it yourself. Probably in some elaborate ritual."

"I do love a good ritual."

Than looked up, doing his best sorrowful brother imitation. "You love an audience. Even as Reseph you wanted people to pay attention to you. How many shrines have you built to yourself, Pest? How many idiots have you fooled into thinking that if they just attend the great sacrifice of Death's son, they'll gain power and wealth?"

Pestilence drew his finger through a splatter of blood on the granite counter separating the kitchen from the living room. "Only a select few will be in the chamber for your son's slaying, but I'll present his still-beating heart to tens of thousands."

"Drinks and food for all, huh?"

"I'll have a glass of your favorite champagne waiting for you to join us."

"Even after my Seal is broken, you know I'll want to see my son."

"I'm counting on it." Pestilence licked the blood off his finger. "You'll be desperate to rid yourself of your past and of anything personal that made you humiliatingly soft. And when our forces of evil see you laughing over your son's body as it grows cold on my altar..." He closed his eyes as if imagining the ecstasy of it all.

Than tightened his grip on his scythe and tensed to strike. But as he started the swing, a gate opened a few feet away, and Pestilence wheeled out of striking distance of both Thanatos and the gate. Ares emerged, followed by Limos, both armored, both spoiling for a fight.

"So we're all here," Pestilence snarled. "Ares, you must have found the gifts I left for you in Greece."

"You twisted fuck." Ares strode forward, the veins in his temples throbbing. "You sick goddamned son of a bitch."

Limos shot a glance at Than. "Pestilence slaughtered all of Cara's hellhounds on the island except the new pup, because he was with her, and Hal, because he was with Ares. Then he came to my place and killed the hounds there." Her voice deepened, warping with rage. "And he hung every one of my staff from the trees."

"Like Christmas ornaments," Pestilence said. "You know how I love Christmas." He turned back to Thanatos, who swore the bastard's eyes went even blacker. "Did you all enjoy that Harrowgate trick?"

"How did you do that?" Ares demanded.

"I have grown stronger than you can even imagine." The black in Pestilence's eyes swirled now, mixing with crimson and flecks of white. "I can do almost anything with a spell and a blood sacrifice. To compromise your Harrowgates temporarily, all I needed was someone important to you all. Ares, did you notice any of your Ramreels missing? No? You might take roll call. Limos, remember that orphan werewolf boy you befriended in Argentina? The one you took shoes and books to last month?" He turned to Than. "And you...I know how much Orelia meant to you."

Damn him. He'd seen her less than twelve hours ago with Viktor. She'd been fine, if not her usual creepy, eyeless self. She wasn't a friend, for sure, but he'd known her for thousands of years, and he'd miss her. No doubt she didn't deserve whatever hell Pestilence had put her through.

Not to mention that without her, he was going to be an emotional wreck. The tattoos that helped keep him sane would be a thing of the past.

In a high-speed surge, Than swung his scythe, but Pestilence leaped high, avoiding the wicked blade and simultaneously striking out with his foot to knock Limos to the ground.

Ares heaved his sword in a massive arc, but once again, Pestilence evaded the strike. Suddenly, his bow was in his clawed hand and he'd armored up, and before Than could so much as blink, an arrow punched through Limos's armor and pinned her to the wall. Another arrow pierced Ares's neck with such force that he tumbled across the floor.

Son of a—Pestilence's strength and abilities had morphed to levels Than would have thought impossible.

Thanatos dove at him and hooked his knee with the scythe, but Pestilence remained on his feet. Something crunched down on the back of Than's neck, and pain became an electric shock that knifed down his spine and up into his skull. Every bone seemed to shatter in a burst of white-hot agony.

He clenched his teeth against the pain, fighting to keep from going blind from the bright stars circling his vision. Warm, sticky blood bathed him, and around him, he heard grunts, shouts, curses. And then Pestilence's voice was in his ear.

"Your female is going to watch your son die," he whispered. "And then I'm going to fuck her and give her to my minions to use. When I'm tired of her screams, *then* I'll kill her."

Thanatos roared and struck out, but Pestilence was gone. Groggily, Than struggled to sit up, wondering why nothing was working right. Through the blood in his eyes, he saw Ares sprawled on the floor, his entire chest bashed in, his armor in pieces. *How*? How had Pestilence done that?

Thanatos jerked his head, which felt like it was hanging from his shoulders by a mere string, and looked to Limos, who was now pinned to the wall with a dozen arrows. She watched him, dazed, and reached weakly for one of the shafts. But her hand, slick with blood, slipped off.

A wave of nausea crashed over Thanatos as consciousness turned black.

Thirty-two

Thanatos regained consciousness with Limos crouched in front of him, her violet eyes bright with concern.

"Hey." She smoothed a wet washcloth over his face, which seemed odd, given that she hadn't cleaned herself up. "Your head is back on."

"Back...on?" he croaked.

She winced. "Pestilence tried to decapitate you. And he hacked Ares's chest wide open and scrambled his organs."

"How...how is he?"

She shifted so he could look over at their brother, who was sitting up, his back against the blood-soaked couch. He was wearing only cargo pants, and although his chest had mostly healed, the flesh was still knitting together.

"How long..."

"An hour, maybe."

He frowned. "Our injuries were too severe to heal in only an hour."

"I know."

"Someone healed us."

"Clearly." Standing, she tossed the cloth aside. "But who?"

Thanatos shoved to his feet, wobbled a little, and threw out his hand to steady himself on Limos's shoulder. Every muscle, tendon, and joint protested as he went down on his haunches in front of his brother. This was going to suck.

"I owe you an apology," he blurted before he changed his mind.

Ares's mouth quirked in a pained smile. "I'm sure you do. But what, specifically, are you wanting to apologize for?"

The smartass. Thanatos swallowed his pride and 'fessed up. "For being so damned pigheaded about trying to repair Reseph's Seal back when he was trying to kill Cara. I protected him. I defended him. I swore that the only way we'd end Pestilence was if Reseph could come back." He braced himself for the hardcore part of this apology. He hung his head. "I'm sorry Ares. I'm sorry I didn't understand why you were so willing to destroy Pestilence. I get it now." He lifted his gaze, drilling it into Ares so his brother would know how damned serious he was. "He's fucked with our families and friends, and he's threatened my woman and my son, and I swear, I will finish him."

They all exchanged glances, no one uttering a word. But the understanding between them was there. They would give no quarter to Pestilence. There would be no more talk of repairing his Seal. Pestilence would die, because the truth was suddenly very clear.

Reseph was dead.

Thanatos strode into his keep and made a beeline toward the voices in the library, but what he heard stopped him in his tracks as if he'd been roped and hogtied.

"I'm afraid, Decker." Regan's voice held a husky note, the way it got when she was upset.

Or aroused.

Logically, Than knew she wasn't turned on. But still, sharing that intimate tone with Decker didn't sit well. At all. And where was Kynan? If he were here, Regan and Decker wouldn't be alone.

"Well, you're about to have a baby that could prevent the Apocalypse," the fucker said. "I'm thinking you have reason to be afraid."

I'm thinking you have reason to be afraid, Than mimicked in his head. Yeah, real mature. So what.

"It's not that. I mean, yeah, it's that, but... I didn't prepare for this baby. I tried not to get attached, but I did, and now I love it. If anything happens to him...so much can go wrong with the birth and with his life, and—"

"Hey," Decker broke in. "I know this won't help, but try not to worry. I'm pretty sure you're going through the same feelings every parent has. You'll be fine. And you know I'm here for you. Whatever you need."

Thanatos barely held back a growl. He didn't hold back his fangs from slicing down in preparation for ripping out the human's throat.

"I know. I've always known." She paused for so long all Than could hear was the thud of his racing pulse in his ears. "I'm sorry if I was ever a bitch to you. I was a bitch to everyone."

"Sweetheart, no one ever gave you a reason to be nice." Decker's voice was low, intimate, and Thanatos saw red. Blood red. Decker's blood. "The Aegis treated you like an asset, not a person. I'm sorry for that."

"You and Kynan never did," she said.

"I can't speak for Ky, but my mama raised me right." Decker's teasing tone was akin to cocking a loaded pistol. Than struggled to keep his trigger from tripping, because killing the human in front of Regan would probably piss her off.

"Thanks, Deck. You're a good friend."

Thanatos heard the rustle of clothing, and now seemed like a good time to break up this little party. He strode into the library just as Regan and Decker pulled out of an embrace.

When she saw him, she gasped. "My God, Than, what happened to you?"

Right. He'd forgotten that he was covered in blood and looked like he'd spent a week in a slaughterhouse. "I had a minor confrontation with Pestilence."

"Minor?" Decker drawled. "You look like you tangled with a gator and lost. You got your supernatural ass kicked, didn't you."

The souls in Than's armor writhed, and with a smirk, he sought out the nastiest one, the spirit of a Cruentus demon he'd killed before he kidnapped Regan. The shadowy thing shot out of his armor and went straight for Decker, but with nothing more than a mental "no," Than stopped it a foot away from the guy. The demon's soul screeched in frustration, teeth gnashing.

"Ah, Decker?" Regan said. "Maybe you should go."

Swallowing hard, Decker didn't take his eyes off the

spirit. "I'll be outside." He scooted around the soul and toward the doorway. "Been trying to teach one of those hellhounds how to roll over. The stupid mutt only wants to eat."

"Be careful," Thanatos warned—with relish. "He might eat *you*."

"You'd like that, wouldn't you?"

Thanatos smiled and called the soul back. "Yes."

Decker muttered something about underworld trash as he strode out of the library. As soon as the bastard was gone, Than allowed himself to relax—but not much. He was about to make the hardest decision of his life, and he couldn't afford to go soft.

"That was a little uncalled for, don't you think?" Regan scolded.

"No. And where's Kynan?"

"He's patrolling outside." She moved toward him, looking beautiful and perfect and like she belonged here. "Are you okay?"

Steeling himself for what needed to be done, he stepped out of her reach. "I'm fine."

"Don't bullshit me. Something's wrong."

Very wrong. He wanted to grab her, hold her tight, and make love to her until everything was right. But he'd be using her again, to make himself feel better, and nothing would ever be right again.

"You know, I wondered for so long why my siblings and I were assigned our specific roles. But it all makes sense now. Ares was, and is, a warrior who will never quit fighting. War fits him. Limos is Famine because she's always been hungry. First for recognition and power, and then for love and acceptance. Reseph...we used to joke that he was Pestilence because he was such a pest, but he's proven to be a plague on mankind, hasn't he?"

"And you?"

He paused, unsure how to go down this bumpy highway to hell.

"Is it because you want...you want to die?"

He dropped his gaze, and she stiffened at whatever it was she saw in his eyes. "In a way, I guess I want to see an end to this."

Her vile curse astonished him, and then she was in his face, taking his hand and settling it on her belly. "Death isn't all you are, Thanatos. You made this baby. You made life."

God, his chest ached. "But there's such a fine line, isn't there?"

Regan clung to his hand. "Whatever is wrong, let me help you. If you need me to hold you close so the death vibes are muted, or if you need sex...whatever it is, I'll help."

Help? Yeah, she would. And he'd be using her. He'd be a bastard user who put his family in danger for his own selfish reasons. It was so tempting to drop to his knees and kiss the swell where his son grew, to feel the life inside and worship the woman who had given it. Instead, he tugged his hand away, took another step back, and made his words, his voice, harsh. Pitiless.

"I'm death, Regan. I can't allow my son to grow up around it. Around me. And if we fail to kill Pestilence the moment our son is born, he'll always be in danger. He needs to be hidden from Pestilence. You were right. You won, Aegi. Give the baby to someone who can keep him safe as planned."

"What?" She looked shell-shocked. "Thanatos, this isn't about winning. Is that what you think? I mean, it was about doing what The Aegis thought was best, but—"

"And you were right." Fuck. He wanted to hold her, protect her, but he kept his distance. Barely. "I wasn't meant for anything but killing. When the baby is born, take him to parents who will raise him properly. And never come back here, Regan. Never." And then he struck the killing blow. Because he was so fucking good at that. "I don't want you anymore."

Thirty-three

I don't want you anymore.

Regan's chest caved in. Thanatos's words stung like a million bee stings, cut like a million knives. He was serious about wanting her and the baby to leave, although how that could be, she didn't know. After all his protests, after all he swore he wanted to be a father, *now,* when she needed him most, why would he decide to give up the rights to his son?

"Thanatos, don't do this."

The scorpion on his throat stabbed at his jugular with its stinger. "Why not? It's what you wanted."

"But it's not anymore."

"Okay, I'll bite. What is it you want now? To leave the baby with me and then run off to join your Aegis buddies? To hook up with Decker, unburdened by the inconvenience of an unwanted child?"

Her mouth fell open. Closed. Opened again. "Is that really what you think? Have I been that...awful?"

A mix of emotions cracked the hard mask of indifference on his face, and the scorpion's tail became a rapid-fire jab into his throat.

"No," he said roughly.

Okay, so he was holding anger up like a shield against emotions that would hurt. She got that. She *so* got that. Hell, she'd just apologized to Decker for spending years being an angry bitch to her colleagues. The more shielding she'd had in place, the less she thought they could hurt her.

Crippling helplessness had her searching her brain for words that could ease his fears and change his mind, but if she'd learned anything about the Horseman in her time here, it was that he was stubborn as the mules on her foster grandparents' farm.

Ignoring the twinges in her lower back, she took his hand, frantic to set things straight. "You don't need the anger. You need to listen to me. I don't want to leave the baby with you and run off with Decker." How ridiculous was that, anyway? "I want to stay here with you. I want to raise this child *together*."

"Regan," he croaked, "I can't."

"Please." She flicked her finger over his armor scar and then put her palm over his heart, taking comfort in the strong beat. "I've lost the only family I've ever known. I've lost my job. My friends. I can't lose you, too."

"It's impossible, Regan. As long as Pestilence lives, you and our son will be in danger."

"Bullshit," she snapped, and his head whipped back like she'd slapped him. "With the Apocalypse coming, there's no safe place anymore. So what's the real story?"

"The danger *is* the real story."

"I just said there's no safe place—" she sucked in a

harsh breath. "You're worried about *you*. You're afraid you're a danger to your son."

His throat convulsed on a hard swallow. "I just saw a father, out of his mind with rage, kill his own children. I know what I'm like when I'm in one of my death hazes. I don't know what I'm doing. Everything I touch is poisoned, Regan." He dragged the collar of his turtleneck down, tearing it to expose the entire scorpion. "This...this is the only tat I have that wasn't taken from a specific event. I had this one put there to remind me what I am. What I do to those who are close to me. No matter how hard I try to protect people, I kill them. Take a look at my vampires. My method of protecting them eventually choked them. Killed them. *I* killed them. I can't risk doing the same to my son. Or you."

"You wouldn't. I *know* that." Regan laid her palm on the scorpion, and Than was right...no images came from it, but his pain was there, infused into the ink.

"Rowlari *knew* that, too."

"We have a way to help you through your violent urges now. I can help you control them—"

"No!" He tore away from her. "Don't you see, Regan? I'd be using you, just like The Aegis did. Don't you see that you're willing to be with me because I need you? Not because I love you?"

Wait...that was what this was about? He thought he'd be using her? And...he loved her? His admission robbed her of her breath. No one had ever loved her, let alone loved her enough to worry about her motivations. She'd lost so much in her life...there was no way she was losing Thanatos and her son too. She was going to fight.

"Thanatos, when you asked me to stay, was it because I can help you ease the killing rages?"

His head hung loosely from slumped shoulders, and for a terrifying moment, she thought he'd say yes. But when he lifted his head, a fierce, stubborn light glowed in his eyes.

"Fuck, no. It was because you gave me back the life I lost when I was cursed. You're brave. Smart. You're willing to die to protect those you love. There's so much more to you than sex, Regan."

She smiled. "See? You won't be using me. You don't *need* me. You *want* me. Like I want you. I'll find a way to convince you I'm right, because dammit, I'm not willing to let you go."

"You have no choice." He took her hand, gently but firmly, and peeled it off his skin. "I'll talk to Kynan and Decker and make sure you and the baby are taken away, by force if necessary." His voice softened. "But I'll make sure you want for nothing."

"We'll want for nothing but you." She stepped back, pissed and achy. "All the money and comforts in the world aren't going to make up for you not being there, you stubborn as hell Horseman. You should have been one of the *Mulemen* of the damned Apocalypse. So you can—" She broke off as warm wetness spilled between her thighs. "Oh...oh, boy."

Thanatos scowled. "What is it?"

A massive cramp made her suck air. "My water just broke," she breathed. "We're having a baby."

Reaver materialized inside the Hall of Records, the Akashic library in the Heavenly realm. He moved swiftly between the never ending rows of bookcases and found his quarry hunched over a thick tome with a cover of crystal.

"Gethel."

The angel jumped, startled, but she recovered quickly and turned to face him. "Reaver. You seek me?"

He resisted the urge to roll his eyes. He'd always hated the formal crap. At least, he'd hated it for as long as he could remember.

"Yes, I seek you." So, okay, there was a sarcastic edge to his words, but he'd long since stopped trying to be a good boy. "When were you last in the human realm?"

One dainty eyebrow cocked. "Why?"

Reaver hated when people replied to a question with a question. "Maybe because the Earth is on the verge of Apocalypse?"

"I don't like your tone."

"I don't like the fact that you're hanging out in a library while humans are dying," he shot back. It wasn't fair; no angel could be expected to monitor human activity all the time. But he also wasn't in the mood to get into a pissing match when time passed slower here than on Earth, and by the time he finished with Gethel, Regan could have given birth. "Do you know that The Aegis has split? And that Harvester may be influencing the majority faction? They kidnapped Regan and tried to kill her child."

Gethel slammed the book shut. "They *what*?" Her wings flared. "Pestilence is behind it. He has to be."

"The Elders claim to have angelic help. I'm going to confront Harvester about it."

"She wouldn't. To do so would bring the wrath of the heavens and hell down on her."

Reaver nodded. "But if the child dies, the Apocalypse

starts and there wouldn't be any punishment. All rules go out the window."

"I always hated that fallen angel," she said, as if her earlier torture of Harvester hadn't been a big clue. She flared her wings again before settling them behind her with a ruffle of feathers. "Has The Aegis settled into their new Scotland headquarters, at least?"

"Yes, but I worry that they'll inadvertently reveal more than they should to Harvester."

"And, therefore, to Pestilence." Gethel let out a mild curse. Well, mild to most humans. Here in the Hall of Records, it made the ground shake. "This is very bad, Reaver," she said, stating the glaringly obvious. "But *you* are the Horsemen's Watcher. What is it you want from me?"

"Nothing regarding the Horsemen. But you have access to the Archangel Council." And wasn't that galling? Since Reaver was a low-level angel, a peon in angelic hierarchy within his order, he'd have to spend valuable time petitioning for an audience with the Archangel Council, while Gethel could practically walk in on a meeting. "They need to know about The Aegis's break. The most powerful demon-fighting organization in history is being torn apart from the inside, and with Armageddon on the horizon, we can't afford for them to be compromised by evil undercurrents."

The last thing they needed was for demons to start pulling The Aegis's strings.

"I'll see what I can do."

"Hurry. Regan is close to labor. Time is short."

Gethel shot him a tolerant smile. "I'm aware of that, Reaver." With a wave of her hand, she made the book she'd been reading disappear back into the shelves. "I'll go now. What course of action are you taking with the Horsemen?"

"I'm going to find Harvester. She's within her rights to mess with The Aegis, but if she was involved in the plot to kill Regan's baby, I'll destroy her." Maybe even before he got permission to do so.

Gethel sighed. "Sad that she has become what she is, considering what she was before she fell."

Coyness was more Harvester's style, but Reaver played along. "She said she was a dealer of justice." Harvester had said all kinds of crap while she'd held Reaver prisoner.

"Is that what she told you?" Gethel shrugged. "I suppose it's true enough. But did she tell you the rest?"

"The rest?"

"Before she fell, she was Verrine, an angel of justice, as she said. But she was also Satan's consort."

Whoa. Okay, so Reaver hadn't seen that one coming. "I'm guessing that when he was cast from Heaven, she went with him?"

"Some say she was the whisper in his ear, the voice telling him to start the rebellion in Heaven. And indeed, when he was cast out, she followed soon after."

"So why aren't they together in a special little love nest in hell?"

"No one knows. But you are aware that it was she who drew up the contract between Limos and Satan, yes?" Before he could reply, she grinned. "Did you not wonder why there was a loophole in the contract? She wanted Limos to get out of it, but it wasn't for Limos's sake. It was for her own. No doubt Harvester is even now plotting her way back into Satan's bed."

"And killing Regan's baby to start the Apocalypse would have been a surefire way to do it. Since Satan can't interfere directly with starting or stopping the Apocalypse any more than God himself can, Harvester would have been a hero, and Satan would have been grateful to finally rule both Sheoul and the Earth."

"Likely, she was even more desperate to curry favor with Satan, given that Pestilence has his sights set on getting Harvester for himself."

Reaver's head snapped back at that little surprise. "Well, well. Isn't Harvester a busy little thing." He frowned, because something was tickling his spine. It was a buzz similar to what he felt when he was being summoned by a Horseman, but this was more of a tingle of awareness and less of a call.

"The baby." He wished he could be happy, but so much could turn catastrophic. "It's time."

He didn't wait for Gethel's response. He flashed out of there, because this was one birth he wouldn't miss for the world.

Appropriate, given how the birth was going to affect the world. But for the best or the worst was yet to be seen.

Thirty-four

The labor progressed quickly. Too quickly for Thanatos's comfort. Regan's water had barely broken, and now she was panting through contractions. He eased her onto the couch and jogged to the front door, where Decker was outside, pacing and muttering.

"I need Kynan here. Now. Tell him to contact UG. Regan is in labor."

"You got it." Decker dug the cell phone out of his pocket even as Than scrambled to call Ares and Limos—on his home phone, since he'd destroyed his cell.

"Get over here," he barked at Limos when she picked up the phone. "Bring Ares and Cara. Arik. Hellhounds. Whoever you can get."

"You got trouble?" she asked.

"I'm expecting Armageddon," he said. "Regan is in labor, and if Pestilence shows up..."

Limos inhaled sharply. "We'll be right there."

Thanatos shouted to his vampires to prepare his bedroom for the birth—they needed clean towels, blankets, a fire, and the cradle. They snapped to it as he rushed back to the library, where Regan was walking in circles, one hand on her belly, the other on her back.

"You okay?" He gripped her elbow to steady her when she swayed. "Can I get you anything? Water? Food? Shit, what do females in labor need?"

"Pain meds," she groaned. "We need pain meds."

"I'd take the pain for you if I could," he swore. He'd take it and more.

She blinked her gorgeous hazel eyes, and then she reached up and trailed her fingers along his jaw. "I know you would."

A flush crept into his face at her trust in him, even after he'd told her he wanted her and the baby gone. He'd die inside, would be nothing but a shell of what he could be with them in his life, but at least they'd be safe from his rage. He just had to find a place that would be safe from Pestilence.

"What can I do for you?" He'd do anything right now. Anything at all in the time they had left.

She opened her mouth, but nothing came out. Then, suddenly, the color drained out of her face. She cried out and doubled over, nearly losing her balance. Than caught her just in time.

"Regan? Honey, what is it?"

"Something's wrong," she gasped. "I can feel it."

Helplessness was a raw ache in his chest. Dammit, where was Eidolon? "I'll take you to the bedroom." He started to sweep her up, but she shook her head.

"I can walk." Her voice was thin, laced with pain. "I

need to." She panted through what must have been a horrible contraction. "Our kid deserves a mom who can walk on her own two feet to the delivery room."

His chest puffed out and his heart swelled. "God, you're awesome."

"I know." She shot him a wobbly smile and started moving toward the doorway.

Than steadied her, and they shuffled into the great room just as the door flew open. A herd of people ran inside, but the ones he focused on were Eidolon and Shade.

The doctor, carrying two large duffels, hurried over, along with Shade, a blond female dressed in scrubs, and Lore, the Seminus demon mated to Idess. Lore came at Thanatos like a tank, his gloved right hand fisted, and Than braced for a blow.

Lore stopped two feet away. "Where's your brother? Where's Pestilence?"

"I've got a good idea, and as soon as Ares and Limos get here, we'll cast our net." Now that Regan was in labor, it was time to bring the bastard in, and as horrific as the scene in Finland had been, it had provided Than with a damned big clue.

Lore's big body trembled. "He took Idess."

"I know," Than said. "We'll get him."

Eidolon shot Lore a sympathetic look as he came up to Regan. "How are you doing?"

"She's in a lot of pain," Than said. "She went pale and shaky. She said something's wrong."

Eidolon gave Regan a reassuring smile, but the covert glance he cut at Than was the very opposite of reassuring. "Okay, let's get you prepped. Vladlena's a nurse. She's going to help you change while Shade and I set up." He looked at Than again. "You have a room ready?"

"My bedroom. Follow me." He helped Regan to the bathroom, and then balked when Vladlena told him to go.

"I insist, Horseman. I've already been told I can't touch her, but she needs to change into a hospital gown, and I need to examine her as best as I can, and I can't do it with you growling and snarling at me."

He didn't even realize he was doing that until Regan patted him on the chest. "It's okay. You need to get Pestilence. And you need to find Idess."

Dammit. He needed to be here with her. But she was right. Leaning into Regan, he kissed her, telling her without words that he'd be back soon.

She kissed him back, telling him without words that she believed him.

Thirty-five

Than ran out into the great room, and skidded to a halt as people stopped preparing *qeres*-tipped weapons to rush toward him. Ares, Limos, Reaver, and Kynan reached him first.

Reaver's sapphire eyes shone with worry. "How is she?"

"I don't know. And I don't know how Eidolon is going to help her if he can't touch her."

Reaver lay a comforting hand on his shoulder. "If anyone can help, he can."

"I hope you're right." Than's scalp prickled and Harvester materialized, her black wings as shiny as a raven's as she tucked them away.

"You." Kynan got up in Harvester's face with a snarl. "You helped The Aegis ward against me, and you were going to help them deliver and sacrifice Regan's baby."

"You're delusional, human." She flipped her black hair

over her shoulder in that snooty way of hers. "I did no such thing."

Reaver's eyes flashed blue fire. "If you assisted them in trying to kill the child, you'll be destroyed. You know that."

"Duh. Of course I know that. Talk about a broken Watcher rule. Which is why I didn't do it. Why would I take a risk like that?"

"Because if it had worked, and Thanatos's Seal had broken, the Apocalypse would have started and there would be no more rules. You were gambling that you'd succeed."

Harvester looked around the room in desperation, as if seeking an ally, but when each gaze she met reflected only hatred, she snarled. "Has it occurred to any of you that maybe, just maybe, I play by the rules?" For some reason, she shot a superior glance in Reaver's direction.

"Were you playing by the rules when you wrote up Limos's contract with Satan?"

She made a dismissive gesture with her hand. "You're speaking gibberish. Begone."

"I know you helped The Aegis," Kynan said. "No one at headquarters denied it, and I saw the evidence with my own eyes."

"What evidence?"

"Your skull pendant."

Her hand flew up to her throat, and Than didn't miss how her fingers trembled. "I—I lost it." She pivoted to Reaver, an odd breathlessness in her voice. "In that warehouse. Gethel must have taken it."

Reaver's expression was utterly flat. "I'm sure she wanted your costume jewelry so badly that she resorted to thievery."

"So if you've been supporting Pestilence, does that mean you were also responsible for trying to kill Arik with the *khnives* last year?" Limos tested the edge of her sword with one finger, and Than had a feeling that in a moment, the blade was going to be buried in Harvester's throat. Two blades, because his was joining his sister's. They couldn't kill her, but they could visit a world of pain on her. "Because we knew we had a traitor in our midst, and I swore I'd behead anyone who tries to kill my husband."

"Why would I use those horrid beasts for anything?" Harvester's gaze flickered to Limos, Ares, and Than. "And if I wanted to help Pestilence, then why did I heal—" She pursed her lips so fiercely that the skin around her mouth turned white.

A sudden suspicion coiled in Than's belly. "It was you, wasn't it?"

Limos gaped at Harvester. "Oh my God, you're the one who healed us in Finland after Pestilence kicked our asses."

"Don't be silly." Harvester folded her arms across her chest and flared her wings. "Your pain amuses me."

Ares looked up from coating his sword with a thin film of *qeres*. "Why are you here, Harvester?"

"I came to tell you all good news."

"Good news?" Reaver snorted. "From you?"

Harvester actually looked hurt, but only for a second. "If you'd checked your heavenly inbox, you'd have the same news, asshole." She turned to Than. "Word from the powers that be is that if Pestilence is destroyed, your *agimortuses* will be released." She frowned. "*Agimorti*? Anyway, if you stop the *Daemonica* Apocalypse, you'll never have to worry about your Seals being broken again. At least, not because of your *agimortuses*. You'll still be dealing with the Biblical one eventually, but you and Ares won't have to worry about Cara or your son being killed, and Limos need not fear anyone drinking from her cup." She shot Reaver a glare. "See? Good news. Confirm it yourself. And bite me." With that, she flashed out of there.

Ares cursed. "Damn, she's annoying. But if what she said is true, that's the best news we've had in... well, ever."

No shit. Than's knees actually felt weak with relief, but only for a second. They had to stop Pestilence before any of what Harvester promised could happen.

"What now?" Decker asked. "Do we just sit around and wait for Pestilence to show up?"

"No, we don't just sit around," Lore broke in. "You Horsemen must have some idea where that bastard is."

Than gave Lore a taut nod, understanding Lore's distress in a way he wouldn't have related to just a week ago. "We'll find him. Limos, Ares, you found his shrines, right?"

"Yep," Ares said. "And three of them are huge. Like, St. Peter's Basilica huge."

"Is one of them off the southern tip of the River Acheron? On the island of Steara?"

Ares's eyes widened. "Yeah. How did you know?"

You'll be desperate to rid yourself of your past and of anything that made you humiliatingly soft. Than glanced back at the bedroom, where Regan was laboring to deliver their son. "Because Reseph buried his baby sister there."

Limos made a small sound of distress. "He used to go

every year. I found him there once. It was the only time
I've ever seen him cry."

Than nodded. "He'll want that gone. My son's blood
will wash away that memory."

"We'll grab some *qeres*-weapons and go." Limos
moved toward the pile of blades they'd prepared.

"I'm coming with you." Lore looked down at his
gloved fist, flexing it as a cold smile curved his lips. "I've
been saving some juice, just for your brother." Thanatos
had no idea what Lore was talking about, but he was definitely starting to rip a new respect for these Sem brothers.
They didn't flinch away from any fight.

Reaver contemplated the discussion for a second. "I'll
be right back. I need to check on something in the Hall of
Records. Don't go anywhere until I get back." He disappeared before Than could ask what Reaver was onto.

He hated when they did that, but he didn't dwell on
angels with bad manners as he glanced around the room.
"Let's get ready for a battle."

Battle, maybe. Death, yes. Because one thing Thanatos
had honed to perfection over the years was his sixth sense
when it came to death.

And he knew, without a doubt, that someone was going
to die today. He just prayed that someone wouldn't be
Regan or his son.

Labor sucked.

Regan decided that she was never giving birth again.
The pony was it. The first and last.

"Regan," Eidolon said, from the end of the bed. "You're
still bleeding. I need you to lay back."

She'd started bleeding fifteen minutes ago. She'd thought she'd die from the pain, but in the last couple of minutes, the pain had diminished, and she'd thought the bleeding had, too.

"That's bad, isn't it?"

"No," Eidolon said. "Not always. Some species bleed profusely during birth."

"But not humans, right?"

Eidolon exchanged glances with Shade, which couldn't be good. "Not like this. But you're giving birth to a child that's part demon and part angel, so I wouldn't expect anything about this birth to be routine."

His voice was so soothing. Too bad she didn't believe a word he said. It wasn't that she didn't trust his skill. She just figured he'd feed her bullshit to keep her calm.

The plastic sheet crinkled under her as she sank back onto the mattress. "Do any of you have kids?"

She didn't know why she was asking, except that maybe she needed to not think about how many things could go wrong.

Shade lowered a cup so she could dig out an ice cube. "I have three boys. Triplets. They're two."

"Three?" Dear God, giving birth to just one was bad enough. Three? Being run over by a freight train would be less painful. She popped the ice into her mouth and practically groaned at the luxury as it soothed her parched mouth. "Vladlena? You?"

Vladlena shook her head. "I'm a newlywed. It'll be a while before my mate and I consider adopting. My mate is a vampire," she explained.

Right...vampires couldn't procreate. At least, not by

getting someone pregnant. She raised an eyebrow at Eidolon. "Doctor?"

"Tayla gave birth to a healthy baby boy six months ago." His smile was bittersweet. "I just hope he has a decent world to grow up in."

"I hope so, too," she murmured.

Eidolon reached into his medical bag. "Regan, I'm going to try to listen to your womb again. Last time it didn't go so well, but I'm hoping to get just a little of the baby's heartbeat before I'm thrown across the room."

She started to tell him to go ahead when agony tore through her midsection. She jackknifed up with a scream, sure someone was cutting into her with a chainsaw. Her pulse drummed viciously in her throat, clogging it, cutting off the rest of her screams. She'd been stabbed, clawed, bitten, nearly eviscerated, and nothing, dear God, *nothing*, had ever hurt like this.

Gulping air like a dying fish, she fell back onto the bed again, clutching the sheets in her fists and digging her heels into the mattress as she tried to get away from the pain.

Eidolon and Shade were asking her questions, but she couldn't answer them. Right now she couldn't even understand them.

Thanatos burst through the doorway. "What's wrong?" He was at her side in a heartbeat, taking her hand and cupping her cheek.

She wasn't sure if anyone answered Thanatos. The pain knifed through her again, accompanied by a warm gush between her legs. She heard curses and big medical words, felt towels sopping up blood.

Dizziness swamped her. And cold. She was so cold. Thanatos's voice drifted to her, calling out her name, but she couldn't answer. Her mouth was too dry. Or maybe she just couldn't open it.

Another blade of agony turned her world inside out, this time lasting longer than she could scream. And then, merciful darkness.

Thirty-six

Thanatos had never been so afraid in his life. "Eidolon? What's happening? She's unconscious." And there was blood. So much blood.

"Thanatos—check her pulse."

Than pressed two fingers against Regan's throat, his own pulse pounding as hard as Regan's. "It's strong. Crazy strong. That's good, right?"

"Fuck!" Eidolon's inability to do anything but change out soaked towels for dry ones had released his temper. His eyes, once brown, now glowed gold. "Not good. Her body is trying to compensate for the loss of blood. I think she's had a uterine rupture."

The word *rupture* was never good. "What's that mean?"

"It means she's bleeding out, and I can't do a damned thing about it." Eidolon cursed again. "The baby is protecting her, and ironically, giving birth to it is going to kill her."

"No." Thanatos shoved to his feet. "You have to do something. Regan said The Aegis bastards were going to deliver him. They found a way—"

"If they found a way, it was with evil magic," Eidolon interrupted. "Too dangerous to attempt even if we had time to figure out what they planned."

"Then let me do something. *Please*."

"You can monitor her pulse and breathing." Eidolon tossed a soaked towel to the floor and glanced up, his dark eyes grave. "And if worse comes to worst…"

Than's stomach bottomed out. "Don't say it, Doc. Don't."

Eidolon said it anyway, the bastard. "You might have to perform a C-section and hope to hell she doesn't wake up."

Thanatos's mind raced. Someone had to be able to help. "You have a daywalker at UG. Get him."

"I don't know what you're talking about."

"Bullfuckingshit! I saw him. I recognize a daywalking vampire when I see one."

Eidolon grabbed more towels. "I swear to you, Horseman, I do not have a daywalker on my staff."

Fuck. Okay, wait…Reaver had been a doctor at UG before he regained his wings. He'd come back from the Hall of Records a split second before Regan screamed.

Than didn't waste time. Hit the great room at a run. "Reaver, hurry."

They charged back to the bedroom, the stench of blood slapping him in the face. He'd grown scent-blind to the smell of blood over the centuries, but this was different. This was Regan's, and it might as well be spilling from him, too. As soon as they were inside, it became clear Reaver wasn't going to do anything.

"Reaver?" Than's voice cracked. "Come on, she's dying."

"I can't touch her."

"Can't," he spat, "or won't." At this point, Thanatos didn't give a shit about Watcher rules or prophecies or the goddamned laws of physics that kept the planet spinning. He wanted—needed—Regan to survive.

"Both. As a Watcher, I'm not supposed to help, but even if I risked breaking that rule, it doesn't matter. I can't make contact with her any more than Eidolon can."

"I can touch her."

Than whirled to see Gethel standing in the doorway. Thanatos had never been happier to see his ex-Watcher. "How?"

"I'm an angel," she said simply. "Only the Watchers are prevented from making contact with Regan." She glided over to the bed and placed her hand on Regan's belly. "The child is doing well." She sank down on the bed and gathered Regan in her arms, almost as though she was going to rock her to sleep. "Poor thing. Humans are so frail."

Eidolon stripped off his gloves and reached for another pair. "I hate to be rude, but she doesn't have much time." He looked between Than and Gethel. "If you can't stop the internal bleeding, we need to get her to Underworld General and I'll talk you both through surgery."

Thanatos so did not like that idea, especially since Regan had said she couldn't tolerate medications. Which meant no sedation, no pain control, no transfusions, no clotting agents. Eidolon didn't say it, but Thanatos knew the surgery wouldn't be to save her. The operation would be to get the baby out.

"I can handle this, demon," Gethel said, putting a sour note on *demon*. In her arms, Regan gasped, her eyes peeling open.

"*Regan.*" Than started toward her, but even as Regan screamed in pain, Gethel inclined her head in a slow nod, and then, in a flash of light, she and Regan were gone.

"Hell's fucking rings," Shade snapped. "Where'd she go?"

Thanatos was close to hyperventilating. He'd trusted Gethel for thousands of years, but he did not like this. He needed to be with Regan. He needed to be there when his son was born.

"Horseman?" Eidolon asked. "What's going on?"

"I don't know," he rasped. "Reaver, do you know anything about this?"

Reaver looked like he'd been shot between the eyes. The stunned confusion in his expression did little to reassure Than.

"Reaver?"

Reaver swiveled around to him. "Can you sense the baby?"

Fear spiked, cold and urgent. "Yeah."

"Ares!" Reaver's bellow made everyone jump, and then Ares was there, barreling through the doorway, armed and armored. Reaver turned back to Than. "Gate us to your son."

Lore shouldered his way past Ares. "I'm going too."

The more the merrier. Everyone poured out of the keep, and praying the gate wouldn't slice into Regan on the other side, Thanatos threw it open and leaped through into some sort of candlelit chamber. His internal GPS told him they were exactly where he'd predicted Pestilence would take the baby; the island of Steara in Sheoul. But what he hadn't predicted was the instant fury and horror that seared him, all heated by betrayal.

He'd found Regan. She screamed in pain and terror as she bore down on a contraction. Behind her, hanging from the ceiling with razor wire, was Idess, battered and bloody.

And running the entire show was Gethel, standing before an altar, her hand on Regan's belly, and Pestilence, waiting, a blade poised and ready to drive into the baby that was moments from being born.

Reaver burst out of the Harrowgate with Ares and Lore, and he didn't waste time with niceties. *"Traitorous bitch."*

He blasted Gethel with hellfire, a minor weapon meant for only the lowliest of demons, but he couldn't risk anything more powerful with Regan and Idess so close.

Thanatos and Ares dove at Pestilence as Lore went for Idess, but Reaver couldn't afford to help either of them. Gethel was his priority.

The sounds of battle and pain came from the Horsemen. Regan screamed, and Reaver swore he'd make Gethel scream, too. He blasted her again, but she returned fire with a white hot bolt of lightning that slammed him into the stone wall behind him.

"Get Regan out of here!" There was a shout, a shot, a thump. As he rolled to his feet, he caught a glimpse of

Lore and Thanatos, scooping up their females, and Ares, gathering an unconscious Pestilence.

Relief was tempered with apprehension. The *qeres* had worked. But for how long?

Twin flashes, and they were gone.

"Clever, using the *qeres*," Gethel snarled, as she hurled a ball of blue fire at Reaver's head.

Reaver ducked and retaliated, the flames from his fireball singeing her tunic before she could dive behind the altar Regan had been laid on. "Clever, hiding your tracks behind Harvester. You knew we'd suspect her first."

She popped up on the other side of the altar. "How did you figure it out?"

As a battle angel bred for destroying demons, Reaver had a few tricks up his sleeve, and he called forth one of them now, focusing on her eyes to hold her with his gaze.

"How? I admit, I didn't put it together until a few minutes ago. Earlier, Limos confronted Harvester about the *khnives* that attacked Arik. Only someone very powerful could summon more than one or two, and no one inside Sheoul would use low-level spies as assassins. I remembered the book you were reading in the Hall of Records." He inched a little closer, narrowing his gaze to focus the stream of holding power into a more concentrated laser.

"It was a Sheoulic book of summoning," he continued. "You were a little extra twitchy when I found you. So, out of curiosity, I went back to the Hall and found the book. It's filled with *khnive* summoning spells."

She sniffed. "It's also filled with a thousand other spells."

"True. Which is why I gave you the benefit of the doubt. Maybe you were researching the angelic ward used against Kynan and Wraith at Aegis Headquarters...that spell is also in the book. But then you took Regan and all the clues fell into place."

"What clues?"

"While we were in the Hall of Records, you mentioned that The Aegis Headquarters was in Scotland. You shouldn't have known that...unless you'd employed spies. And then there was Pestilence's attack on the headquarters in Berlin. You knew that Thanatos had grabbed Regan, didn't you? It would have been easy for you to alert Pestilence so he could track Thanatos's movements before the Harrowgate trace grew cold. And what about Harvester's pendant? She claimed you took it, and I didn't believe her, but you did. You gave it to The Aegis, along with false information...you convinced them that if they killed Regan's baby, it would end the Apocalypse, and those fools believed you because you are an angel." He cursed. "I'll bet you released the vampires at the Berlin headquarters too, didn't you? You were hoping they'd kill Regan. You must have been pissed as hell when one of them actually saved her."

She smiled. "Look at you. You should have been a detective. So bloody smart."

Reaver's foot came down on the dagger Pestilence had intended to drive through the baby's heart. "And look at that," he said. "Wormwood. Last I heard Pestilence was looking for it. You must have known The Aegis had it. How did you get them to hand it over?"

She licked her lips, slowly, as if savoring her genius. "I traded Harvester's charm for it. So easy. All I had to do was say that the charm would only provide power if something of equal value was given in exchange."

Devious bitch. "Why? You said it was powerless. Granted, you're a big hairy liar, but still…what's its purpose?"

"You're the detective. You figure it out."

Reaver ground his molars. *Now* she decided to shut up. "One other thing I don't get. Why send the *khnives* after Arik? What was the point of killing him?"

"Fun. What, you don't believe me?" Her dramatic sigh made him grind his teeth harder. "Fine. That really was just pettiness. With Arik dead, his soul would default to Pestilence. He'd be tortured into saying Limos's name, and she'd have been sent to spend eternity in Satan's claws."

What. A. Bitch. How could he have not seen all this coming? Oh, right, maybe because she was a full-fledged heavenly angel who was supposed to fight on the side of good.

"But why save him later, then?" he asked. "When my soul and Limos's were cast into his body, why did you save his life?"

She shrugged. "He and Limos were already married. Letting him die would serve no purpose, but saving him…"

"Would make you look like a hero, and if anyone was suspicious about you at all, it would remove any doubt that you were playing for Team Good." Devious.

"See? Smart."

"But why, Gethel?" As pissed as he was, he was also saddened by this. Gethel had been the one to give him his wings back. She'd guided him through the early days of the transition. He'd felt as though he owed her a debt of gratitude. "When did you turn from our side?"

She hissed, as if Reaver had pushed the button that triggered her evil bitch side. "You took them away from me, you bastard. You were accepted back into Heaven and given the assignment to handle the Horsemen."

Taken aback, he stopped moving toward her. "I was told you relinquished the duty freely."

She snarled. "Would *you* argue with Michael if he *suggested* that perhaps it was time to turn the duty over to someone else?"

Well, yeah, Reaver would, but he'd never been cautious with his tongue. He could see how others might not argue with the archangel, however.

"And the Horsemen," she spat. "They didn't come to my defense. They didn't care that I was replaced." Her eyes flashed. "I loved them, and after all I did for them, they didn't so much as wish me pleasant travels."

Reaver experienced a moment of sympathy, but it was quickly squashed when she brought down a rain of tiny electrical shocks on him—tiny in size, but each one carried the power of a nuclear power plant. Pain ripped through him, burning his blood and turning his skin to ash. His vision doubled, as if one Gethel wasn't bad enough.

"Your demon-fighting tricks don't work on me, Reaver." Her voice was both amused and cold, laughter hung with icicles.

With a cold smile of his own, he summoned a flame sword and spun it low, letting himself experience a grim satisfaction when it buried itself in her gut. Her cry of agony and fury rattled the chains hanging in the room.

She launched herself a foot off the ground and spun, becoming a whirlwind of white.

Reaver hurled himself to the floor as she unleashed a storm of sparks that bored holes in everything they landed on—including Reaver.

Groaning, his body riddled with through-and-through holes that turned him into a giant sieve, he lurched to his feet. Time to play dirty. Spending time with demons while he was fallen was going to pay off.

He threw off the pain, channeling it into anger, and called forth one of his favorite weapons, one he rarely got a chance to use. The shear-whip's handle was hot in his hand, but ice-cold compared to the molten metal that comprised the scourge part of the weapon.

Gethel's eyes shot wide. "It's against angel law to use this weapon against another angel!"

Reaver bared his teeth. "You're no angel. You're Fallen. You just haven't had the decency to lose your wings."

Pivoting, he snapped the whip, and in the softest whisper, it severed one of her wings. "One down." He snapped it again, cutting into her rib cage and shattering every bone in her upper body.

This time her scream of rage and pain exploded inside Reaver's head, the agony so intense he crashed to his knees. Blood spurted from his nose, ears, eyes.

A rolling thunder rang out, like a million buffalo hooves on stone. Demons, presumably summoned by Gethel, came at him from all sides. They swarmed him, hundreds of clawed, fanged mutants.

"You...won't...win," he rasped, but had no way of knowing if Gethel heard him.

She was crawling away, her broken body failing her. No way. She wasn't escaping. She needed to either die or be brought to justice for her crimes against humanity and Heaven.

Reaver dug deep into his power reserves, his body buzzing as the current that started at the base of his skull and in his wings formed a circuit. A golden glow surrounded him, blinding the demons that were almost on him. Their shrieks filled the air and added to Reaver's already throbbing eardrums. He gritted his teeth against the pain and let his banked power loose.

He went supernova, shooting blasts of Heavenly light from every pore. The demons disintegrated, their screams fading to echoes as their ashes drifted to the floor.

But among the ashes was a glow. Wormwood. Its hilt, etched with a word Reaver couldn't make out, radiated with azure brilliance absorbed from Reaver's Heavenly light. It *was* an angelic weapon.

Breathing deeply, Reaver caught himself on the altar as he bent to pick up the dagger. When he read the four-letter word carved into the hilt next to a star symbol, he fumbled it, barely catching the blade before it tumbled to the ground.

DOOM.

The Doom Star cometh if the cry fails.

Oh . . . oh, *damn*.

The Aegis had been wrong about the Doom Star in Thanatos's prophecy. It wasn't Halley's Comet. It was Wormwood.

Now Reaver had a decision to make. A decision that rightfully belonged to the Horsemen. But as he weighed Wormwood in his hand, he had a feeling he knew which decision they'd make. And it wasn't the one Reaver wanted.

Closing his eyes, he decided to do something he swore he'd never do.

He was going to break a Watcher rule.

And dear God, he was going to pay.

Thirty-seven

Thanatos couldn't have run faster if he'd been a cheetah. He burst into the bedroom where Eidolon was waiting, and lay Regan on the bed. "The baby's coming."

Of course the doctor knew that, but Thanatos was freaked out of his gourd. At least it looked like the bleeding had stopped, so that had to be good news.

Regan screamed like she was being ripped apart, and his heart was right there with her. Although he could scarcely spare the time, he kissed her sweat-drenched forehead. Her eyes were wild, fevered, and she clutched his arm with such desperation that his eyes stung.

"There's his head." Eidolon's gloved hands cupped the baby's head as he tried to deliver the child while not coming into contact with the mother. "Take a breath, and then give me another push, Regan."

Than tore his eyes away from the amazing sight of his son being born to Regan, whose gaze clung to him as firmly as her hand was doing to his. "We have Pestilence," he rasped. "Everything will be all right."

She gave him a weak nod and released him. "Go. Save our son."

Save our son. Not, "Save the world."

Please, please God, let Regan and the baby come through this, because I need this woman like I need to breathe.

As Lore came in with Idess, Than rushed to his dresser, grabbed Deliverance, and in a mad dash ran to the great room. Ares and Limos were holding Pestilence down, although at the moment he didn't seem to be moving.

Thanatos's heart was pounding, his pulse thundering in his ears as he threw himself on top of his brother and straddled his thighs. This was it. This was what it had all come down to.

Limos's eyes caught his. "His finger twitched. It's wearing off."

"I see it, too," Ares said. "His foot's moving."

Thanatos swallowed dryly, his mind whirling with a thousand thoughts. How was Regan? How was the baby? Were they scared? Was he really going to kill his brother?

That last question was a no-brainer, a fleeting thought that popped into his head maybe because it should. But he had never been more prepared to do anything. He'd kill anyone to save his wife and child.

Wife? Yes, because once they were through this, he was going to marry her.

Please, please let them get through this.

"Fuck."

Ares's whisper jerked Than out of his thoughts. He looked down into Pestilence's eyes...eyes that were aware. Mocking. Even his mouth had turned up into a smile. Between Than's thighs, Pestilence's legs began to move.

And then, ringing out in the hushed castle air, came the pure, healthy sound of a baby's cry.

In a smooth, fast arc, Thanatos brought down Deliverance and buried it in Pestilence's heart. The baby's cry cut off. Pestilence gasped. Blood sprayed from his lips. His eyes, which had gleamed with so much evil, clouded over, and in that instant Thanatos knew Pestilence was gone. In his place, Reseph stared back at Than.

"Th-thank ... you." Reseph's voice was little more than a whisper, but what was there was thick with relief.

And then he was gone.

Beneath Than, Reseph's body disintegrated, caving in on itself until only clothing remained. Even Deliverance had disappeared.

I killed my brother. Than's throat seized. He hadn't expected that. He'd been prepared—eager, really—to kill Pestilence. But not Reseph. Jesus, not Reseph.

There was silence. So much silence. Should it be so quiet when you'd just killed the brother you'd loved for thousands of years? And how could he be feeling both shock and relief? Pain and numbness. Impossible combinations.

"Thanatos." The voice was coming from somewhere... "*Thanatos.*" He blinked, cranked his head around to Cara. The tears in her eyes weren't ones of joy. "You need to hurry."

No. Oh, God, please no... Than sprinted into the bedroom, his heart racing. He stumbled to a halt at the threshold, his heart jamming right against his ribcage.

The nurse, Vladlena, held Than's squirming son—
clearly the boy was fine, and as much as Than wanted to
go to him, it was the baby's mother who held his concern.

Regan lay on the floor in a pool of blood as Shade and
E worked frantically over her, their *dermoires* glowing.

She was pale—much too pale.

"What's going on?" Than rushed to her side and knelt
next to her. "Why is she on the floor?"

"We needed more room to work," Shade said.

"Regan?"

Her eyes opened. The fierce, defiant gleam he was used
to had been replaced by a hazy veil of pain and exhaus-
tion. Death lurked within that cloud as well, mocking
Thanatos.

"Did...we...do...it?"

"Yes," Than croaked. "Pestilence is gone." He took her
hand. So cold. "You're going to be okay. But I need you
to fight."

"Will you...hold my hand?"

He didn't tell her he was already squeezing it so hard
she should be in pain. He glanced up at E, whose somber
gaze said it all.

Tears burned in Than's eyes. "I wish we'd had more
time. I would have liked to pamper you for those nine
months. I would have taken care of you."

"I know," she whispered. "I love...you." She closed
her eyes and in his palm, her hand went limp.

"No," he croaked. "No, no *no!*" He reached over and
grabbed Eidolon by the collar. "Do something!"

"I'm sorry. She lost too much blood before the baby
was born. The internal damage is too much for even me if
there's no blood left in her."

Desperate, Than released the doctor. Regan still had a pulse, but barely. Ten heartbeats left, maybe. There was only one thing left to do, and he hoped to hell it worked. And that she'd forgive him.

With a hiss, he tugged her head to the side and bit into her jugular. Her pulse was too weak, the vein too collapsed to pump blood into his mouth. Urgency drove him to suck deeply, hoping her circulatory system would move the blood still left in her veins to deliver the vampire-turning agent in his saliva.

Her heart stopped.

So did his. Anguish turned the air in his lungs to cement. A familiar chill of awareness flickered in the back of his mind, and he dragged in a sudden, panicked breath. He looked up, trembling, knowing what he'd see.

Regan's soul.

He leaped off the bed and stared at her shadowy form. She was confused, her eyes wet with unshed tears as her gaze met his with what he swore was accusation. Or maybe that was just his guilt talking. But it didn't matter. He'd killed her, and now she was going to become part of his armor, tormented to the point of insanity by the captivity and by the other souls until she finally escaped and made a kill.

Which would then send her straight to Sheoul-gra.

Instead of giving her eternal life, he'd given her eternal death and damned the woman he loved to hell.

Thirty-eight

Thanatos screamed his throat raw as Regan melted into his body. It didn't hurt, not physically, but mentally, it was excruciating. He'd killed her. Doomed her. And now she was suffering.

Only rarely could he feel the souls when he wasn't wearing his armor, and normally that was a good thing. But not this time. Not now. He had to find her, latch onto the awareness that was uniquely her life force. Maybe he didn't deserve to be comforted by her presence, but he hoped she'd be comforted by his.

As Limos and Ares stormed into the room, alerted by Than's screams, he armored up. Instantly, the whirling vibration of the souls filtered through his body. Dragging in a shaky breath, he sorted through them, locked onto Regan, and collapsed into the chair beside the bed.

"Thanatos?" The concern in Limos's voice gave it a higher pitch than normal, and when she saw Regan's lifeless body, her voice broke low. "I'm so sorry." She went to her knees next to the chair and braced her forehead on his arm.

Thanatos stared blindly, barely registering the fact that the medical people were filing out, leaving him alone with Limos and Ares.

And his son.

Ares had taken the infant from Vladlena and very carefully placed the swaddled baby against Than's chest, forcing him to wrap his arm around his son. Than's heart kicked, and he jerked as if he'd been dead and someone had shocked him back to life. Inside him, his blood warmed and Regan's spirit quieted. Even the baby, who had been whimpering, settled peacefully in the crook of Than's arm.

A sob escaped him as he dropped his gaze, getting his first true look at the child he and Regan had made. The baby's eyes were hazel, like Regan's, his wisps of hair as blond as Than's. He was a perfect mix of the two of them.

"He's beautiful," Than whispered. As if in agreement, Regan seemed to caress him from the inside. "Regan thinks so, too." His voice cracked at that, and dear God, how was he going to survive this?

Limos lifted her head to exchange glances with Ares. "Ah, Than? Regan...she didn't make it."

No shit. He stroked his finger over the baby's velvety soft cheek. "She's in my armor."

"Oh...damn." Ares drove his hand through his hair. "Are you okay?"

Thanatos looked up. "No." He swallowed against the lump of misery in his throat, but that bastard wasn't going anywhere. "I need her. I've got to do something."

But what? He'd failed to turn her, and now her body

was an empty shell while her soul rested inside him. She was at peace right now, but it wouldn't be long before the other souls began to torment her, and it would be even worse when he took off his armor and couldn't control the souls.

He'd never remove his armor again.

"Maybe Reaver can guide her soul out," Ares suggested. "You won't have to worry about her that way."

Thanatos was willing to try anything to prevent Regan from being sent to Sheoul-gra once she escaped the armor. He just had to hope Reaver was receptive to the idea. And was capable of doing it.

"It's worth a try."

"I'll see if he's back." Ares jogged out of the room and was back in a flash. "He's not here. I hope he's kicking Gethel's traitorous ass. In any case, I've sent a summons."

Thanatos couldn't wait. Regan didn't deserve a single minute inside the hell of his armor, but who else dealt in souls? Wait...

"Where's Idess? Is she okay?"

Limos nodded. "Eidolon healed her. She's in the great room. Why?"

"I need her to take me to her father." The male who could also be the Horsemen's father.

There was a pause and then Limos's eyes flared. "Are you thinking what I'm thinking?"

"If you're thinking that he's the Grim Reaper and if anyone can help, he can, then yes."

She was up in a heartbeat. "I'll be right back."

Than reached up and took his sister's hand. "Thank you, Li. I won't forget this."

Tears sprang into her eyes. "I might not have liked

Regan at first, but she gave you something you haven't
had in five thousand years. You were happy. And she gave
you a son. I'll do anything for the three of you."

Closing his eyes, he leaned back and held his son close.
Than had meant it when he'd told Regan he would have
loved to have pampered her for the months he missed out
on while their son was growing inside her. Hell, he'd have
pampered her for the rest of her life. He'd have given her
anything she wanted.

Now all he could give her was peace.

Thirty-nine

A massive ebony Greek temple rose up out of the mist in front of Thanatos. Blackened pillars and buildings surrounded it, all familiar, and yet, he couldn't place it. After a few steps, as the fog cleared away, he realized that this was Athens. Not the real Athens, but an imitation land where everything was corrupted by evil and death.

Thanatos should be right at home, shouldn't he, he thought bitterly.

Idess had been more than willing to help him, and as he carried Regan's dead body in his arms and her soul in his armor, Idess touched his back in a gesture of strength and comfort.

"Thank you for rescuing me from Pestilence."

He didn't want to discuss it, but his brother had tortured her and she deserved more than silence. "I'm sorry for what he did to you. Pestilence was as desperate to find your father as I was." Pestilence's goal had probably been

as much to destroy their father as it was to gain access to
Sheoul-gra. More of that *getting rid of anything personal
thing*.

"Why did you want to find Azagoth?"

Than stared blankly ahead. "It doesn't matter now."
Yeah, he wanted to confront his father for a lot of reasons,
but those reasons weren't nearly as important anymore.

Idess's expression grew hard. "Well, Pestilence would
never have found him. I wouldn't have given anything
up." Her strength reminded him of Regan, and he nearly
faltered as he mounted the giant steps to the temple.

"Are you sure I had to bring her body with us?" he
asked hoarsely.

Idess's sad smile almost made him break down again.
No, he hadn't taken it well when she'd told him, nor when
he'd had to put down his son to leave his keep. The boy
was now part of Than's heart, and being away from him
seemed to make it stop pumping.

"No," she admitted, "but if he can see you with her,
your pain might be more...real...to him." She started
forward. "He's not the warmest individual you'll ever
meet, so you have to take advantage where you can
find it."

The King Kong-esque double doors opened, and
inside, endless passages stretched as far as Than could
see. Everything was black, just like outside, except that
inside the temple, all the surfaces gleamed. Statues of
humans and demons in pain lined the rooms and halls,
and the fountain they walked past in the giant fore-room
ran with blood.

"Your dad has interesting tastes in art," he muttered.

"'Interesting' is one word for it." She led him through a

maze of hallways that never changed. "Have you thought of a name?"

"Name?"

"For your son." Her smile was warm. "He's beautiful."

"Yeah," he choked out. "He is. And no, we didn't discuss names."

"I'm sure whatever you choose will be perfect." She stopped at a door—how she knew which of the hundreds of identical doors they'd passed was the right one, he had no idea—and reached for the handle. "You ready?"

As if Regan knew what this was about, she made herself known, and warmth spread from his armor to his skin. "As I'll ever be."

Idess opened the door, and they stepped over the threshold into a bright, colorful office of sorts. A tall male with black hair was standing in front of the archway to what looked like the cut-out side of a tunnel, so he could see the souls of dead demons being escorted by *griminions* through it like an assembly line. The male held up his hand and the parade stopped.

Thanatos held his breath as the guy turned around. "Idess. Sweetheart, it's good to see you."

"Father." She inclined her head in a respectful nod.

Azagoth turned his emerald-ice gaze on Thanatos. "Death. Interesting to finally meet you." He gestured to the people in the tunnel. "You've sent me so many of my subjects."

"I do what I can to help," Than said dryly. "And now I need you to do the same."

One black eyebrow lifted. "I'm guessing this has something to do with the corpse you're carrying?"

Corpse. On his arm Styx reared up, his actions not

reflecting Thanatos's sudden anger but his own. At some point, the stallion had learned to like Regan, and he didn't appreciate the dismissive, cold words any more than Thanatos did.

Idess had warned Than about the guy, so he kept his temper in check. He could rip Azagoth a new one after he got what he wanted.

"She's the mother of my child. She would have been my wife. I killed her."

"Why?" Azagoth folded his arms across his chest, looking utterly bored. "Did she betray you? Warm someone else's bed? One of your brothers', perhaps?"

Thanatos was going to strangle this asshole. "She gave birth," he ground out. "I tried to save her."

"So what you're saying is that she's in your armor." He paused. "What do you want me to do about it?"

"I want you to remove her and allow her to pass to the Other Side instead of being brought to Sheoul-gra by your *griminions*."

"And why would I do that?"

Okay, he was going to lay down a card he hoped was his ace. "Because you're my father."

Idess's head whipped around to stare at him. Azagoth eyed him for a long time, and Than got the impression the dude was intentionally letting him sweat.

"You have balls coming to me and expecting a favor from a father you never met."

"So it's true?"

Azagoth laughed. "No. I'm not your father. I'd have remembered fucking Lilith. That bitch has been after me for centuries."

Damn. That had been Than's only good play. He had

nothing else. Had Azagoth been anyone different, Thanatos could have threatened him, tortured him, beaten him until he agreed to help. But this was a guy who held power over souls, which meant he could torment Regan, and everyone else Than cared about, for eternity.

"Please." Thanatos hefted Regan's limp body closer, as if she could shield him from having to beg. "I'll do anything."

"Anything? Will you give me your son?"

A hot ball of fire dropped into Than's gut, and inside, he felt as though he was being pummeled by fists. Regan's fists.

"Anything but that," he growled.

"That's what I want."

Inside his armor, Regan clawed at him. She didn't need to worry. No one was taking their son.

"Go to hell, Azagoth." Than headed for the door before he went crazy and slaughtered the asshole.

"Thanatos, wait." Idess approached her father, her hands folded together as if in prayer. "Thanatos saved my life."

Great. There was a reason he hadn't brought that up. Nothing like telling a father that your brother tortured the fuck out of his daughter.

Azagoth narrowed his eyes at Than. "Explain."

Thanatos stiffened at the command, but checked his pride before he screwed up something that might save Regan's soul. "You know Pestilence was trying to destroy Sheoul-gra."

"Of course." Azagoth turned toward the hearth, which was blazing but not putting off heat. "Word gets around down here."

"Father," Idess said, "Pestilence was capturing Memitim and torturing them into giving away your location."

Azagoth's head damned near pulled an *Exorcist*, swiveling around to Idess without his body moving. His eyes had gone oily black, swallowing the whites, and when he spoke, his voice had a dangerous, serrated edge. "He *dared* to harm my children?" His body finally followed his head. "He took you?"

She nodded. "If not for Thanatos, Ares, Lore, and Reaver, I'd still be hanging from razor wire."

The Grim Reaper's snarl sent the souls and *griminions* in the tunnel scattering.

"Drop your armor," he snapped at Thanatos.

"Why?"

Azagoth practically spat fire. "Because I requested it."

Reluctantly, Than did as the bastard *requested*. "Now what?"

"Remove your clothes."

Than locked his jaw to keep from cursing. If Azagoth wanted sexual favors...Than shuddered, but lay Regan gently on the ground and stripped. Never before had he felt so exposed as Azagoth circled him, his finger trailing over Than's skin as he went. At least Idess had turned away. He wondered if her father was going to make her stay for whatever was to come.

He wondered if she'd stand by when Thanatos killed her father afterward.

"I know your secret, Horseman." Azagoth stopped behind him, pressed his body against Than's back, and whispered into his ear. "I know you fathered the vampire race. Your daywalkers have passed through on occasion."

"It's not a secret anymore," he ground out.

"Really. You do know that I have the ultimate say in whether a species is annihilated or not."

Fuck, no, Thanatos didn't know that.

"And you know that I've destroyed all unauthorized species. Do you want to know why I haven't destroyed the vampires?"

"Why?"

"Because, like my Memitim, they are a perfect combination of good and evil. They're balanced. Yes, they choose to be as evil or as good as they want to be, but so do humans. So I've let them continue, even though once your secret reaches the Heavenly masses, they'll throw down orders to destroy the vampires, and I'll be in trouble for knowing all along."

"And what will you do then?"

Instead of answering, Azagoth resumed his perusal of Than's body, stopping every once in a while to trace a tattoo. The ones on his ass were, naturally, the most interesting to Azagoth. The bastard. "They're extraordinary. I want them."

"I'd bring you the tattoo artist, but she's dead."

"I know that. But it wouldn't matter. I want *yours*."

"Why?"

Azagoth hissed. "My reasons are my own. But I assure you that you'll be giving me something I've desired for a long, long time."

Thanatos was pretty sure Azagoth could get a damned tattoo anytime he wanted, so clearly, there was something special he wanted from Than's, specifically. Which probably meant that giving them to him would be a bad, bad idea.

Whatever. "Done."

"This one," Azagoth said, stroking his finger over the winged serpent on his hip.

Agony shot through him as the thing ripped off his flesh, and then came the agony of being slammed with the memories of what it had been suppressing. The images and emotions were sharp, acute, and he staggered at the blast from the day nearly a thousand years ago when he'd slaughtered a legion of men whose symbol had been a winged snake.

"And this one."

Thanatos hissed, the pangs of torment even greater this time. Azagoth had taken the bow that dulled the memories of killing his father. A dozen more times Azagoth took tattoos, each one nearly taking Than to his knees. He wondered if Regan could feel his pain, or if she was shielded from his emotions when the armor was gone.

Finally, Azagoth stepped back and ripped open his shirt. Fourteen of Thanatos's tats decorated the fallen angel's chest.

"All of the beauty, without all of the pain," Azagoth mused. "Awesome."

"Speak for yourself."

Azagoth tilted his head, studying Than with those assessing eyes. "I imagine you're in a lot of pain right now."

"I'll live." Than stepped into his pants.

"Yes, you will. You'll live the rest of your life without getting another tattoo."

Than paused while shrugging into his shirt. "Why not?"

"Because you have spent five thousand years cheating. The deaths you cause should mean something. They should cause you misery. Instead, you bury them and feel nothing. It pisses me off."

Jesus. Regan had said the same thing. He'd dismissed her at the time, because as a human she couldn't possibly understand five thousand years of killing. Shame heated his face.

Azagoth's anger quieted, his voice doing the same. "I understand why you did it. You grew up with peaceful people. Death and violence was especially hard on you. And you, of all your siblings, saw the most of both. You compensated in the only way you could. But you can't do that anymore. That's the deal. That, and you will promise to never make another daywalker. When those heavenly assholes come to me and ask why I didn't destroy the vampires, I can say that since I can't destroy you, you could make more daywalkers even if I took out the entire race, so you promised not to make more, blah, blah. It's a good argument. Take it or leave it."

"I'll take it."

Azagoth cocked his head. "You said that so quickly. But how can you guarantee you won't make more, if you've made your vampires during uncontrollable death rages?"

Thanatos closed his eyes, caught in Azagoth's cleverly spun web. "I'll manage. I'll meditate, or travel with hellhounds who can bite me, or..." He opened his eyes and met Azagoth's pitiless gaze. "*Please.*"

"Fool." Azagoth snorted. "Haven't you learned anything in your ancient life? There's a price for everything. You create a life, you pay. Think back to when you first created a vampire."

Than dredged the recesses of his brain, coming up with

a lot of filth. But there was the one memory, the spark that had started it all. "I'd been cursed as a Horseman. I had fangs, and I was angry. I bit a guy, drained him. He came back as a daywalker."

"Were you in a death rage?"

"No. Those hadn't started yet—" Than sucked in a massive, painful breath. "They didn't start until after I turned the first daywalker. They didn't...holy shit. *I'm* the reason I go crazy sometimes?"

"How should I know? Do I look like a god?" Azagoth rolled his eyes. "I'm just saying you have to find the cost behind every action. Make a daywalker, go on murderous rampages. Whatever." Azagoth shrugged. "I don't give a shit either way. I just want your damned word, and I want you to keep it."

"You got it," Than breathed. Damn, all of his rages made sense now. They'd fed into each other in a cycle he didn't know how to break. Make a vamp, which caused rages, which caused vamps, which caused rages...*son of a bitch*.

"Also, you should know that in the future, the emotions you would normally transfer into a tattoo will now transfer to Regan. She'll feel your pain as much as you do."

"What? No! You can't do that—"

"I can do what I want, Horseman," Azagoth snapped. "There is a price for everything. If this is too steep for you to pay, then collect your corpse and get the fuck out of here."

"You bastard." Thanatos lifted Regan into his arms. "I agree." Regan might feel his pain, but at least she wouldn't be hanging out with demons for all eternity. She would go to Heaven and be happy. Free.

"Good choice." Azagoth snapped his fingers. "Armor. Now."

Thanatos was so glad this asshat wasn't his father. Although Azagoth was the last lead they'd had, and now...they had nothing. Today they'd lost a brother and a father.

And Regan.

Thanatos touched his armor scar, and his bone plates folded into place. Instantly he sensed Regan, and breathed a sigh of relief.

Goodbye, he said silently, feeling a hot sting of tears in his eyes. *You're going to Heaven now. But remember that I love you. I hope you can hear that. I'll find you some-day, Regan. I swear to you, I'll find you.*

"What the fuck are you upset about?" Azagoth bit out the words in a disgusted rush. "I'd think Horsemen wouldn't be such pussies." He flicked his finger against Than's shoulder, and the sensation of having Regan inside him was gone.

He was alone.

"Now get out." Azagoth turned back to the parade of souls in the tunnel, and they started moving again.

In Than's arms, Regan's body jerked, and she sucked in a gasping breath, startling Thanatos so thoroughly he almost dropped her.

"Regan?"

She blinked up at him. "Where are we?"

He crushed her against him in a smothering embrace, a whoop of laughter making Azagoth turn around and roll his eyes.

"Why are you still here?" Azagoth sounded seriously annoyed. "This *was* what you wanted, yes?"

"Yes," he shouted. "God, yes!"

"Thanatos?" Regan's voice was muffled against his chest. "Squashing...me."

"Sorry, baby." He eased back a little, but just enough that he could kiss her senseless. "I can't believe you're here. You're alive. And perfect."

"And still squished."

Grinning like an idiot, he set her down, although he would prefer carrying her back to his place. He never wanted to stop touching her again. She didn't seem to notice that she was still wearing the hospital gown, which was caked with dried blood and gaping open. Than tucked her against him, but Azagoth sighed, took off his shirt, and handed it to Thanatos. He held it up like a curtain as she stripped out of the gown and then slipped into the shirt, which hung down mid-thigh.

"Thank you, Father," Idess said.

Thanatos repeated the sentiment. "Thank you, Azagoth. I owe you."

"Yes," Azagoth said silkily, "you do." He waved his hand in dismissal. "Now get out. And be careful with her. She's immortal until your Seal breaks, but she's not special in any other way. She's a normal, wimpy human who will suffer cuts, broken bones, and eviscerations like anyone else. She just won't die from them."

"You're wrong, Reaper," Thanatos said. "She's special in every way."

Forty

Thanatos couldn't stop grinning as he gated himself, Regan, and Idess back to his keep. "I can't thank you enough, Idess. If you ever need anything, come to me, and it's yours."

"I might take you up on that someday," she said. "Now, are we going in? I'd like to meet your son."

Regan took his hand and practically dragged him through the front door. Inside, everyone who had come for the birth was still there. A pall hung over them, the sadness in the air so thick Than could eat it with a spoon.

"Yo," he called out. "Someone want to bring my son to his mother?"

Stunned expressions quickly veered to ecstatic ones, and suddenly Thanatos and Regan were surrounded. There were hugs and laughs, and someone passed Regan a robe. Than eased out of the crowd to allow her some time with Kynan and Decker, but he did watch when Cara brought the baby over and handed him to Regan.

And then the woman who swore she wasn't mother material gathered the infant in her arms and broke into tears and smiles.

"Congratulations." The rumbling, unfamiliar voice came from the male who had stepped beside Thanatos while he'd been watching Regan.

He turned to the vampire he'd seen at Underworld General. The guy was almost tall enough to meet Than's gaze levelly. Black hair fell in a thick curtain to his waist, and the cruel twist to his mouth would make anyone think twice about giving him shit about it. Anyone but Than.

"If you're here to cause trouble, daywalker, know that I'll take you out as easily as I made you."

"A year ago," he said slowly, "there'd have been trouble."

Thanatos glanced over at Regan and warmed at the way she was holding their son like she'd been cuddling babies for years. "What changed?"

"Me." He held out his hand, which seemed so...odd... given that Than had, at one point, taken his blood, almost certainly against his will. "I'm Vladlena's mate. Nathan."

Than's body stilled as a hazy memory surfaced from... two centuries ago? "The alleyway..."

Than had been fighting a demon, and in a fog of bloodlust, he'd seen the man watching in horror, and he'd attacked.

"Yup. I saw you at Underworld General last year, and recognized you as my sire."

"So you *do* work there? Eidolon lied to me?"

Nathan shook his head. "Nah. I don't work there. I only go to the hospital to see Lena. If Eidolon didn't tell you he knew me, it's because I've asked everyone who knows what I am to keep my secret. I learned early on that night-crawlers seem to hate daywalkers."

"And vice versa," Than said wryly, noting the vampire's use of the term "nightcrawlers."

One thick shoulder lifted in a casual shrug. "I was at the hospital as a patient the first time I saw you, and when Lena told me you were a Horseman, I thought I was mistaken about who you were." His gaze pierced Than right in his guilty conscience. "Then I saw you again a few days ago when I was bringing Lena lunch, and there was no doubt."

Well, wasn't this awkward. Than had a lot of daywalkers to find and apologize to. Oh, he'd kill the ones who had planned to side with Pestilence and kill his son, but he did want to start fresh with the others. They no longer had to fear that he'd either kill them or force them into servitude.

He cleared his throat, but it didn't scour away his contrition. "I'm sorry for what I did."

"I hated you for a long time," the vampire admitted. "But now I just want to offer my thanks. I've been blessed more than I can say."

Thanatos turned back to Regan, who was his until his Biblical Seal broke, which he prayed wouldn't happen for a long, long time. "Me too, Nathan. Me too."

Reaver could get in some serious trouble for what he was about to do. Hell, he could get into trouble just for being here.

Here was Sheoul-gra, the holding tank for demon and evil human souls. Here was a dark, steamy cavern where the occupants were as solid as stone, as cruel as a socio-pathic teenage boy, and no one was happy.

"Angel."

Ignoring the hisses and insults slung at him by the sur-rounding demons, Reaver strode up to the speaker, who stood on a basalt platform, the whip in his hand dripping blood. "Hades."

Hades cocked a black eyebrow. "Whose dick did you suck to get permission to come here? Azagoth isn't one for the gay shit. I've tried."

There really was nothing worse than a fallen angel when it came to crudeness. But yeah, Reaver had been forced to go to Azagoth to gain entry. What price the Reaper would extract was yet to be determined.

"It doesn't matter how I got here. I don't suppose you have a new resident named Gethel."

"Is she hot?" At Reaver's flat stare, Hades rolled his eyes. "Fine. No Gethel."

Damn. Then she was still alive. And who knew what trouble she could wreak in the human realm by the time Reaver got back.

"Next question. Where's Reseph?"

"Reseph?" Hades's eyes went flat and cold as a blade left in the snow. "His body is in the cavern behind me. His mind...I don't know where that is."

Reaver started for the cave entrance, a gaping maw of dripping teeth streaked with blood. A malevolent growl brought Reaver to a halt. "Tell it to let me pass, Hades."

Hades appeared at Reaver's side. "Getting in isn't the problem, angel. It's getting out that'll be the trick."

"Why are you keeping Reseph in there?"

"Maximum pain. Azagoth's orders. You'll understand

when you see him. He's not a soul like those you see around you. He can't be reborn. He's as he always was. Minus the sanity."

"So good news tempered by bad news."

"Isn't that the way it always is?"

"Yes, Fallen, it is." Reaver stepped inside the cave, and was instantly enveloped in the fetid scent of rot. He picked his way around half-eaten corpses... that weren't really dead. In Sheoul-gra, nothing died. Beings suffered until—and if—they were reborn in another body. Clearly, the creatures in here couldn't get out and were being slowly digested.

He kept walking, the moans of the victims rising up from the squishy, gore-soaked ground. Ahead, screams pierced the air, and the hairs on the back of Reaver's neck prickled. Kicking himself into a jog, he no longer tried to avoid the writhing bodies beneath him. His boots crunched on their ribs, limbs, skulls.

Ahead, Reseph was in trouble.

When he finally saw the Horseman, he realized that *trouble* was not the word he should have used.

Reseph was crouched on the ground in a pool of what was probably his own blood, holding his head and screaming. One eye was gone, and it became clear that Reseph himself had clawed it out. Another scream burst from the Horseman's mouth, and he threw himself backward into a rock wall so hard that blood sprayed and Reaver heard bones break.

"Blood... so much blood... claws, paws, heads... fucked... I fucked them... tears, screams, oh, fuck... the pain..." Reseph's babbling was punctuated by more screams, more throws against the wall, and more clawing of his own body.

"Reseph." Reaver's voice was barely a whisper, and choked with emotion. He'd hated Pestilence, had wondered how he'd feel to see Reseph again, and now he knew. This...hurt. "*Reseph.*"

Panting, Reseph turned his eye on Reaver. Confusion flashed in the bloodshot depths, and then horror. Reseph wheeled backward in a scramble, skittering along the wall to get away.

"No," he rasped. "No. Snapping bones and torn guts..."

Reaver lunged, taking the Horseman by the shoulders and forcing him to still. "Hey. Stop. It's me, Reaver."

"No...no. I—" Reseph jerked backward, trying to get away, but Reaver gripped harder. "I hurt you. I hurt...so many."

"It wasn't you, Reseph. It was Pestilence."

Reseph grabbed his head and threw himself in spastic lurches toward the wall. "Make it stop! Make it stop!"

The things the Horseman must be seeing, the memories he must be reliving...Reaver could only imagine. It had been bad enough to *see* what Pestilence had done, but to know you'd been the one to do it must be beyond anything a decent person could handle. And Reseph had been decent. A partying playboy with questionable morals, but he hadn't been cruel. The things he'd done as Pestilence had gone well beyond cruel and into downright twisted, sick, and evil on a scale never before seen.

Reaver engulfed Reseph in his arms, using his entire body to ease the Horseman's struggles. It was like trying to hug a rodeo bull.

"Destroy me," Reseph moaned. "End me."

Reaver's heart cracked wide open. "I can't." Reaver

couldn't heal him, couldn't lessen any of the pain. But there *was* something he could do.

Reaver tugged Reseph to his feet and slammed his palm into his forehead. "Good-bye," he whispered. "Be happy."

In a flash of silver light, Reseph was gone. May the human realm welcome him like a newborn.

It had taken every ounce of Reaver's power to do what he'd just done, and now, drained, he sank to his knees, head bowed, his breath sawing painfully in and out of his lungs. Azagoth had allowed Reaver to keep his power when he entered Sheoul-gra, but now Reaver was empty, and there was no way to refuel down here. He was a sitting duck for any demon who came along.

Whatever happened to him, it would likely be nothing compared to what he was in for when his huge violation of Watcher rules was discovered. Although really, there were a lot of loopholes in the rules regarding a Horseman who had been sent to Sheoul-gra.

"What in blazing hells have you done?" Hades's voice rumbled through the cavern. Didn't that just figure. "Where's Reseph?"

"I destroyed him," Reaver croaked.

It was a lie, but the truth wasn't an option. For anyone. And no one could know that Thanatos had used the wrong dagger to kill Pestilence.

Ironic, wasn't it, that Thanatos had been searching for a way to repair Reseph's Seal for so long, and in the end he'd found it without even knowing it.

Deliverance to repair, Wormwood to kill.

"Huh." Hades squatted down in front of Reaver. "I don't believe you. Either way, Azagoth is going to have

you for dinner. He had a serious bug up his ass about seeing Reseph suffer." He eyed Reaver like he was sizing
him up for that dinner...which turned out to be the case.
"Buffalo angel wings. Yum." He jammed a finger into
Reaver's chest and knocked him over. "And it looks like
someone's all out of Heavenly juice. Do you know how
much trouble you're in right now?"

"I'm assuming that's a rhetorical question," Reaver
said, as he pushed himself up to sit against the wall
Reseph had used to tenderize himself.

"Little bit," Hades agreed.

"I don't suppose I can convince you to get me out of
here."

Hades ran his hand over his tight blue mohawk. "Out
of the cave? It might be better to stay in here. If you go
out, you'll be at the mercy of hundreds of thousands of
demons and evil humans who would love to take turns
torturing the fuck out of you. Literally." He paused. "On
the other hand, if you stay in here, you're in for an eternity
of being slowly digested. Very painful."

"Out of Sheoul-gra, you idiot," Reaver gritted out.

"Idiot? That was a little uncalled for."

Sighing, Reaver rocked his head back against the wall.
He should have known Hades would toy with him. Azagoth had warned him as well. Of course, Azagoth had
been full of warnings.

*Empty yourself of power, and you'll be helpless in
Sheoul-gra and trapped there forever. Don't expose
your wings unless you want to start a riot. Too many
will already know what you are. Don't let anyone have
a feather. A single angel feather could give a demon
the power to reincarnate himself before his time. If you*

*become trapped in Sheoul-gra, I won't save you. If some-
one comes to rescue you, you'd better hope I'm in a good
mood, and they have something awesome to offer me, or
they aren't getting in.*

Azagoth was such an ass. But Reaver supposed if he'd
been relegated to this dreary realm, where his only plea-
sures came from what he could bargain for, he might be
an ass, too.

"See, here's the thing, angel." Hades straddled Reaver's outstretched legs and got right in his face. "I like
the Horsemen. We've traded favors for centuries. Limos
sends ice cream. You're their Watcher, and they like you a
lot. So I want to help you out." He palmed Reaver's cheek
none-too-gently. "On the other hand, you're an angel in
my house. If I just waltz out of here and let you go, I'll
lose a lot of respect. You get that, right?"

Unfortunately, he did.

Hades shook his head, almost as if he truly regretted the situation. "I have to make your life hell, Reaver. I
don't fancy that, I swear. But you've given me no choice."
He clapped Reaver on the shoulder. "Don't worry, I'll get
the word out to the Horsemen to rescue you."

Reaver lunged forward, taking Hades by the throat.
"Don't. They can't know I was here or that I came to see
Reseph." They believed their brother was dead, and for
now, at least, it was for the best.

Smiling, Hades pushed into Reaver's grip, and Reaver
knew then that the guy enjoyed pain. "If I don't contact
them, it narrows your options for a rescuer, doesn't it."

Yeah, it did. He couldn't get help from angels—even
if one was willing to try to get past Azagoth and cross
through Sheoul-gra, he didn't want anyone to know why

he'd come here. Reaver had taken Reseph's memories and dropped him in the middle of nowhere in hopes that he'd find a new life.

The Horseman was still part of Biblical prophecy, and they needed him whole—and sane. Reaver was hoping that a few hundred years as a normal person would do a lot to heal the damage to his mind, lessening the pain when he remembered. Reaver didn't want anyone messing with that delicate process. No one could know where Reseph was, and he didn't trust his angel brethren not to find him, return his memories, and watch him suffer for all the damage he'd caused to mankind.

Hades's smile faded, but the amused glint in his eyes didn't. "Don't worry, angel. We'll have fun together. I don't bite. Much." He pushed off of Reaver. "I hope whatever you did with Reseph was worth it, because I've already sent word to someone who will be very interested to know you're stuck here."

Well, this couldn't be good. "Who?" But then he realized he didn't need to ask. "You blue-haired bastard. You sent for Harvester, didn't you?"

"Aw, come on, Reaver, she'll love to see you."

Yeah, she'd love it all right. Because there was nothing the black-souled fallen angel loved more than torture.

Torturing *Reaver.*

Forty-one

Thanks to Eidolon's amazing healing ability, one week after giving birth and being declared dead, the demon doctor gave Regan a clean bill of health...and the go-ahead to have sex.

Which was great, except Thanatos didn't seem interested. It wasn't that he hadn't been the very definition of attentive and protective and loving since the minute he'd brought her back to the keep. But he'd also been evasive when she tried to discuss anything serious or intimate, or when she tried to get physical. He'd insisted that Eidolon declare her healthy, but she had a feeling his delaying tactic had been more about avoiding sex than anything else.

She hadn't confronted him about it—hell, she'd been too busy with the baby to make a big deal of it, but today she was going to get some answers from him.

After they got rid of the friends and family, who had

come over for a belated baby shower for Logan Thanatos, named after her father and, obviously, Than.

Regan finished dressing in jeans and a sweater, then checked on Logan, who was sleeping peacefully next to the bed in the cradle Than had made. She lingered for a few extra minutes, fussing with his teeny camo pajamas that had been a gift from Kynan and Gem, making sure his little hands were covered with mittens, and double-checking the monitor. She'd taken to motherhood more easily than she'd expected—the instinct was there, if not the knowledge, and she loved the little guy in a way she'd never thought possible.

Smiling down at him, she rubbed her neck where Thanatos had bitten her in his failed bid to turn her. He might not have turned her, but his bite had killed her, which ultimately allowed her to come back. She'd never have believed that she'd be thankful to have fangs punched into her vein, but she'd repeat it in a heartbeat.

Not that any kind of biting would happen if Than wouldn't even have sex with her.

A dull ache squeezed her chest, and then it was gone before she had a chance to know what Thanatos had been thinking about. That was one of the side-effects of his deal with Azagoth—his painful emotions would forever filter through her instead of through the tattoos he'd been getting for so long. At first, his memories from the tattoos Azagoth had taken had blasted through her, reducing her to tears she hid from Thanatos. But now they were gone, and she would have to wait for the next one, the next scene of death he'd be drawn to. It would hurt them both emotionally, but she and Thanatos would work through it together.

Taking on his emotional agony occasionally was a very small price to pay for a life with him and their son.

Bracing herself for the noise of a party, she joined the crowd in the great room. The trestle table was covered in food, and a barrel full of ice had been set out to chill bottles of beer and wine. From the looks of things, everyone had been indulging. A lot.

Wraith sauntered over to her, his blonde vampire mate, Serena, on his arm. "Congratulations, Aegi. If you need any tips on raising a kid, I'm there for you."

"That's sweet of you." Serena patted his hand in that universal, yes-dear-I'll-humor-you way. "But I'm sure Thanatos can mess up a kid as well as you can."

"I doubt that." Wraith planted a kiss on Serena's neck, breaking it off when Thanatos punched him in the shoulder.

"Glad you could make it." Than slung his arm around Regan's shoulder as he scanned the crowd. "Glad all your brothers and sister could come."

"You kidding?" Wraith said. "You Horsepeople always throw great parties. Plus, there's usually a fight."

"Not this time, man. Not this time."

Wraith looked disappointed, but he perked up when Sin, her black hair pulled back into a wild ponytail, came over and handed Serena and him two glasses of Scotch.

"That," Sin said with a wink, "is the best way to shut him up." She sobered, turning to Than as Wraith and Serena joined another group of guests. "I wanted to thank you. You and your siblings."

"Why?"

"Because I started all of this." She shifted her weight and licked her lips, clearly uncomfortable. "It was my fault Pestilence's Seal broke. If you three hadn't gone all out to stop him, we'd be looking at the end of the world."

"You didn't break his Seal intentionally, and it was a team effort to put everything right again." Than slid Regan a smile, which did funny, fluttery things to her insides. "Underworld General, The Aegis—everyone helped to stop the Apocalypse."

It had been stopped, but so much damage had been done. People had died, governments had collapsed, and entire continents were still in chaos, even though land claimed by demons had reverted back to the humans. It would take decades to recover.

Ares and Limos approached, Cara and Arik with them, and the rest of the guests gathered around. It was so strange to have a group of people surrounding Regan with genuine affection. Strange, but wonderful, and Regan had never been so happy.

"Time for the presents," Limos chirped. "Ares and Cara have the best one."

Ares scowled at her. "So much for the surprise."

She adjusted the flower in her hair—orange, to match her flirty strapless dress. "Trust me, it's still a surprise." Her grimace told Regan it might not be a normal gift, like a playpen or a baby swing. "And for the record, I don't want one when I have my baby."

Well, that got everyone's attention. Especially Arik's. He lost a lot of color. "Are you ... are we ..."

"Nope." She batted her eyelashes at him. "But maybe tonight."

Thanatos and Ares both groaned. "Let's not go there," Ares said, and Arik nodded vehemently.

"So." Cara jumped in, no doubt to save Arik from an

incredibly awkward situation. "Do you want your surprise now?"

"This'll be fun." Ares's smirk was downright evil.

"Ah..." Thanatos scrubbed his hand over his face, but Regan laughed.

"Sure. Let's see."

Cara darted off, and a minute later returned with a black, squirming bundle of hellhound in her arms. "Every boy needs a dog."

Regan wasn't even sure what to say. They wanted to give her baby a demon animal that ate people. A furry land shark. It was enough to make her want to hyperventilate.

"That's not exactly a dog." Than eyed the pup warily.

"You're right," Cara said. "He's a harmless puppy. Pestilence killed his family, and he needs a new one. If he bonds to Logan, trust me, he'll have the best lifelong protector on the planet."

Regan glanced over at Hal, who never left Cara's side unless she asked him to go with Ares. Velcro, the hellhound that had guarded Regan, had also been attentive and intimidating, and okay, that sounded pretty good. Call her an overprotective mom, but Regan would take a guardian for her son that would eat anyone who tried to hurt him.

God, what a freaky family she belonged to now. But it *was* a family, and it was hers.

"Oh, hey," Wraith said. "How many of those do you have? My son wants a dog. Or a bear."

The conversation turned to hellhound puppies and kids, and Regan backed herself out of it, wanting to catch Kynan before he left.

He was standing by himself next to the beer barrel, watching over everyone, but his gaze kept drifting with possessive heat to his wife, Gem, whose head was together with her twin sister, Tayla's. When he saw Regan, he pushed off the wall he'd been lounging against and gave her a hug.

"I've never seen you look so good," he said. "Horsemen agree with you."

"Weird, right?" She stole a glance at Thanatos, which was only fair, because he stole her breath. She was so going to get laid tonight. "Ky? I want to be there to help rebuild and reunite The Aegis."

Kynan smiled sadly. "The Aegis is gone, Regan. This has been coming since the day Tayla hooked up with the head doctor at Underworld General. What she put into motion changed the course of The Aegis, and this split has been coming for a long time."

"So what are you saying? That we let Lance and the others just take The Aegis and run with it? That's bullshit." Then there was the fact that she still had a score to settle with those assholes. If Thanatos didn't get to them first, anyway.

This time, Kynan's grin was blinding. "It *is* bullshit. So I say we salvage what we can—knowledge, property, the Guardians who share our philosophy—and we build our own organization. New name, new mission statement. The Aegis is moving backward. I say *we* move forward."

The very idea was terrifying. To let go of everything she'd grown up with and start over gave her chills. But what it didn't give her was the insane desire to organize the room or eat until she was ready to pop and then throw it all up.

Wow. Okay, so that was new. And it felt freaking awesome. She waited for the urge to count or flip a light switch three times or something, but nope, nothing happened.

Her eyes stung at the realization that she hadn't gone OCD in the face of stress. She'd passed a milestone somewhere between being kidnapped and being killed, and wasn't it funny how the ultimate trauma made everything else seem so trivial.

Oh, she didn't doubt her OCD would be a work-in-progress, but Thanatos and Logan had given her much needed stability, and dying had given her much needed perspective. She couldn't control everything, and she didn't need to. Life was messy and unpredictable, and learning to roll with the punches was part of surviving.

She nodded. "I say you're right." Her fingers found the handheld baby monitor she'd jammed in her pocket. "Does this new organization allow for maternity leave? Because I'm not letting my little guy out of my reach for a while."

Ky leaned in and kissed her on the cheek. "You got it, kiddo. Call me next week, and we'll conference with Decker, Arik, Tayla, and Val. We'll get things going."

"Ky...?"

"Yeah?"

She rolled her bottom lip between her teeth for a second, unsure she wanted to bring this up. Finally, she blurted, "I lost my soul-sucking ability. Will you still want me if it doesn't—"

"Hey." He took her by the shoulders and dipped his head to give her his super-serious Kynan stare. "You were always valuable to The Aegis, special abilities or not. I didn't realize how deep some of our members' resentment of you went, or I'd have stepped in, and I'll never forgive myself for not paying better attention. They were jealous, and the only way they thought they could keep you from seeming more important than they were was to tear you down. So forget them." He winked one denim-blue eye. "They're nursing their wounds of failure behind the walls of their castle, and you saved the fucking world."

With a grin, Kynan took off, and the guests all began to trickle out. When only Ares, Cara, Limos, and Arik remained, they gathered for a final champagne toast.

Ares held up his glass. "To Logan Thanatos. May he grow up healthy and strong, and find a mate as perfect as ours."

"Sap," Than said. "But thanks, bro."

The clink of glasses rang out, and after their first drink Cara said proudly, "Rath said his first sentence."

Arik tugged Limos against him. "What did he say?"

Ares sighed. "What are the three words said most often in our house?"

"*Not tonight, Ares*?" Than offered.

"Funny," Ares growled. "Cara never says that."

"I might tonight," she muttered.

Laughing, Limos clapped her hands. "I know. *Hal! Bad dog.*"

"Yep." Cara grinned like the proudest mom ever. Didn't matter that their child was an adopted Ramreel demon. She was beyond thrilled.

Limos set down her glass on the food table, and then took Arik's and did the same. "Come on," she said, taking his hand.

"Where are we going?"

"Home. Now that the Apocalypse is over, you're going to knock me up."

Arik turned eight shades of red but allowed her to drag him out of the house, and Ares and Cara followed soon afterward, taking Hal with them. They left the pup, who settled onto a blanket beneath Logan's cradle as if he'd always belonged there.

Thanatos, however, looked distinctly uncomfortable as Regan began to undress. "I'm going to go make sure my staff doesn't need any help to clean up—"

"Oh, no, you don't." She grabbed him by the arm and turned him to face her. "You've been avoiding me every night since Logan was born, but Eidolon gave me the green light, and you're not pulling this crap again."

"I don't know what you're talking about."

"Bullshit. You help me get into bed, and then you make up some lame excuse to leave the room, and you don't come back until I'm asleep. Why?" When he averted his gaze, she gripped his chin and forced him to look at her. "Why?"

"Dammit, Regan—"

"Why?" She was more insistent this time, and loud enough that both Logan and the pup whimpered. In a more hushed voice, she added, "Please, Than. Don't shut down on me. What's bothering you? Did I do something wrong?"

"No," he said quickly. "Oh, hell, no. It's me. I... failed you."

"Are you kidding? You saved my life."

"*After* I killed you. And now you're stuck feeling what *I* feel. Azagoth took away fourteen of my most important tattoos... what you have to be going through..."

She palmed his chest, feeling his heartbeat against her palm. "What are *you* feeling?"

For a moment, he didn't seem to understand the question. Finally, he said warily, "Nothing. I remember each of the scenes more vividly than I did before, but the emotional pain is as dampened as it was when I had the tattoos. Initially after Azagoth took the tats, the pain was bad, and I know it was bad for you too. I saw you crying, Regan."

"And that's why you've been so distant? You felt guilty?" At his remorseful nod, she threw herself at him, wrapping around him so tightly he sucked air. "Don't. Don't you ever feel guilty about that. I'm used to experiencing emotions that don't belong to me. The same thing happens when I touch ink on parchment. It's always that way. Intense for a few hours, and then it all filters away and all I have left are the memories."

"But not the emotions that go with them?"

Looking up at him, she shook her head. "That's normal, Thanatos. You've been tattooing away your grief for so long that you don't remember what it's like to be... human. It may take a while, but the pain always dulls. You'll see, and I'll be there to help you through it. We'll help *each other* through it." She traced the stern line of his jaw, taking pleasure in the way his tension gradually eased. "We both have to learn to deal with our emotions, me to control my OCD, and you to function as the person you're fated to be. I'm happy to share your pain though, so please don't worry about me."

Than gave a disbelieving shake of his head. "I still don't know how you can be okay with this."

Rolling her eyes, she blew out a dramatic breath. "Gee,

it's such a sacrifice. Hmm...would I rather be dead, or be alive with a beautiful son, a loving family and friends, and a...well, you."

"Yeah," he growled. "About that." Her heart stuttered as he dropped to one knee. "Marry me." His deep voice held an emotional warble she felt all the way to her marrow. "I don't have a ring, and I wasn't prepared like I should have been, but I didn't know how you'd react and I was a big chicken and—"

She cut him off with a finger to his lips as she dropped to her knees in front of him. "Yes. On one condition."

"Anything," he croaked.

Tilting her head, she dragged her finger down her throat, directly over the spot where Than had bitten her. "You give me everything. Your emotions, your temper, and your desires. Your hunger is no longer going to be a burden for you."

"Regan..." The warning growl in his voice made her blood rush hot to erogenous zones she didn't know she had. And when his fangs elongated, it provoked an even hotter response at her core. "Are you sure?"

The forbidden, naughty images from the vampire porn flashed through her head. "I'm sure." Her eager fingers found the fly of his pants. "I'm *so* sure."

In a blur of motion, he had her on her back on the floor, his heavy body on top of hers. He ripped off her clothes as if they were made of tissue paper, and then he was kissing his way down her body, his fangs scraping her skin, his tongue soothing the erotic scratches.

Spreading her legs, he teased his way down her pelvis, taking exquisite care when he reached the sensitive flesh in the creases of her inner thighs. He licked his way inward, holding her steady when she squirmed, both embarrassed and needy, both trying to escape his mouth and get it where she wanted. She couldn't decide which she wanted more, but when his tongue swept right up her center, the decision was made.

Her moan joined his as he licked her again, this time more slowly, letting the flat of his tongue drag through her slit.

"I could do this for hours," he whispered, his hot breath caressing flesh so sensitized that she bucked. How funny that they were both so new at sex, but both so eager. And God, he was so good. The vampire erotica had taught him a thing or two, for sure.

He dove into his task then, licking, sucking, kissing her private place with such care she nearly wept. Pleasure roared through her, searing and sweet, and then the room was spinning and she was crying out his name. Before she'd fully come down he was on top of her, kissing her mouth, his sex poised at her entrance.

"I love you," he whispered against her lips. "I *want* you. I didn't see you coming. You blindsided me, and I wouldn't change a thing." He slipped inside her with a groan, filling her. Completing her when she hadn't known she had a piece missing.

"You've given me so much, Thanatos. I had to lose everything in order to see that I had it all." She arched into his thrust, the pleasure nearly taking her breath. "I've never been so alive."

"*You* made me realize I'm alive." His voice was guttural, raw, so damned sexy.

"Thanatos?"

"Yeah?"

"Bite me."

He grinned, flashing his fangs. "You got it, baby. You got anything you want."

As his mouth settled over her throat, ecstasy peaked. It wasn't just physical. It was mental. Emotional. It was a perfect melding of the past, present, and future.

The Apocalypse was over, and the new world, *her* new world, was just beginning.

"Dharma."

He gripped Harper's hips. "You got it, baby. You got anything you want."

As his mouth settled over her throat, ecstasy peaked. It wasn't just physical. It was mental. Emotional. It was a perfect melding of the past, present, and future.

The Apocalypse was over, and the new world, her new world, was just beginning.

When Jillian Cardiff finds a man—
a *naked* man—lying in the snow, she
knows she's stumbled across more
than just a stranger in need…

He can't remember anything
about his past—not even his name.
But one thing is clear: If he stays
with Jillian, death, destruction,
and Apocalypse are in his future.

Please turn this page
for a preview.

Rogue Rider

One

It was cold. So fucking cold.

He opened his eyes, but he saw...nothing. Groaning, he shifted, because he seemed to be facedown. Yeah... yeah, he was. But where was he? Now all he could see was snow. No, that wasn't true; he could see trees laden with snow. And snowbanks laden with snow. And snow laden with more fucking snow.

So he was in a forest...with snow. But where? Why?

And who the hell was he?

Reseph.

The name slurred through his ears as if uttered by a drunken man.

Reseph.

Sounded vaguely familiar, he supposed. Reseph. Okay, yeah, he could work with that. Especially since no other names popped into his head.

Weakly, he tried to push himself to his knees, but his

arms felt like rubber, and he kept falling on his face. After four tries, he gave up and just lay there, panting and shivering.

Somewhere overhead, an owl hooted, and a few minutes later, a wolf howled into the growing darkness. Reseph took comfort in the sounds, because they meant he wasn't alone. Sure, the owl might just fly over and shit on him, and the wolf might eat him, but at least he'd have company for a little while.

He didn't know much about himself, but he knew he didn't like to be alone.

He also did *not* like snow.

Gradually he became aware of a gnawing ache in his bones, accompanied by a stabbing pain in his head. Looked like he was in for a little unconsciousness. Cool. Because right now, he was both freezing and burning up, hurting and numb. It sucked.

Yep, passing out would be a good thing.

Real. Fucking. Good.

Idiot. Dumbass. Meteorological moron.

Jillian Cardiff mentally cursed the meteorologist who screwed the pooch on the timing of this blizzard. She had nothing against weather people; hell, she'd worked with them for years in the FAA. But this...this was ridiculous.

Now she was in a rush to get back to her cabin before visibility went completely to shit and her draft horse, Sam, got testy.

"Come on, boy." She gave the big sorrel an affectionate slap on the shoulder. "The rest of the firewood can wait."

Sam followed her, not needing to be led by the rope

snapped to his halter. He knew the way home and was as eager as she was to get inside a warm, cozy building. The sled carrying half a cord of firewood dragged behind him, cutting through the two feet of snow they'd gotten a few days ago. This new storm would probably dump another couple of feet, and by the end of November they'd have more snow than they'd know what to do with in the Colorado Rockies.

The wind shrieked like a living thing, and snow blasted her face like a million tiny needles. Hefting her rifle more securely onto her shoulder, Jillian put her head down and pushed against the gale. Times like this, she really missed Florida. Not that she'd ever go back. Some things you just couldn't forget.

Like being torn apart by demons.

She shivered, but it had nothing to do with the cold. She was not going there again. The attack was behind her, and as long as she didn't watch TV, get on the Internet, or look at her scars, she never had to think about it.

A long, mournful howl pierced the late afternoon darkness. Had to be close if she could hear it over the wind. Sam snorted and tossed his head, and she slowed to take the lead rope and give him a pat on his big brown nose.

"It's okay, buddy. The wolves won't bother us." No, wolves generally left humans alone. If anything, cougars were the big concern. In recent weeks, two area hunters had been found torn to pieces, the carnage blamed on the big cats.

Abruptly, Sam reared up, a desperate whinny breaking from his big chest. The rope jerked out of Jillian's hand, and she nearly lost her footing in the icy snow as she scrambled to catch it. Sam's front hooves hit the ground and his shoulder rammed her, sending her tumbling down an incline. Her yelp cut off as she slammed into a tree trunk.

Pain spiderwebbed around the right side of her rib cage, and ouch, that was going to be tender tomorrow.

"Dammit, Sam," she muttered as she crawled back up the snowy slope, pausing to grab the rifle that had been flung into a snowbank.

Sam was snorting, going nuts as he pawed at something in a drift. Jillian dug ice from places ice shouldn't be as she clomped through the snow, wondering what in the world had startled him and now had him so freaked out.

"You'd better be digging up a pot of gold, you mangy—" She broke off with a startled gasp.

A man...a naked man...his body face-down and covered in a dusting of snow, lay in a messy sprawl just off the trail.

"Oh, my God." Her hands shook as she stripped off her gloves and put her fingers to his throat. His skin was icy to the touch, which she expected, but when the steady thump of a pulse bounded against her fingertips, she nearly jumped out of her own skin. He was alive. With a strong pulse. Holy cow, how?

Okay, so...think. She had to get help, but they were in the middle of an intensifying snowstorm, and there was no way off the mountain except by snowmobile. She couldn't risk that in the storm, and it could take hours to get to the nearest town. He could be dead by then.

Shit.

Praying this guy wasn't a serial killer and trying not to think too hard on why he'd be in the mountains, naked, in the winter, she eased Sam up the trail so the sled was alongside the man's body. As quickly as she could, she heaved the wood to the other side of the path and tucked the ax into the loop on Sam's padded harness.

Rolling the man onto the sled was not as easy as she'd hoped. The guy was heavy as a damned boulder and *huge*. And...handsome. And very, very naked.

"Really?" she muttered to herself. "You're going to notice how hot he is *now*?"

Granted, it was impossible not to notice those things, but she still felt a little guilty as she ran her hands over him, checking for injuries. Aside from being unconscious and as frozen as a fish stick, he appeared to be uninjured.

Interesting horse tattoo on his right forearm, though. When she'd skimmed her fingers over it, she swore she'd felt a dim vibration, as if the henna-colored lines pulsed with a mild electrical current. Too bad warmth didn't ride in on that current, though, because damn, she swore the temperature plummeted twenty degrees in the few minutes it took to check the guy out.

As if Mother Nature had some sort of grudge against her, the biting cold wind picked up even more, and the snow, which she normally loved, became an enemy. It was probably stupid of her, but she stripped off her coat and laid it over the guy, tucking the coat's sleeves carefully beneath him. The half-dozen shirt layers she was wearing should protect her for a while, as long as they hurried.

"Let's go, Sammy." She urged the gelding to move faster than she'd normally like, but nothing about this situation was normal.

She was freezing and exhausted by the time she smelled the smoke from her wood fire, and her eyelashes were crusted with ice by the time she eased Sam up to the rickety porch. The frigid air burned her lungs with each breath as she dragged the man's dead weight off the sled and then unhitched Sam. She'd remove the harness later. Right now she had to get the man into the house and the horse into the barn.

She ran the thirty yards to the barn and, battling the wind, tugged open the door. Sam trotted inside, but she didn't bother taking him to his stall. He'd find it on his own.

Too bad getting the man to her bedroom wasn't nearly as easy as putting up the horse. As a fitness freak who worked a small farm, Jillian wasn't a wuss, but she thought she might have dislocated something as she dragged Fish Stick across the floor. She spent another ten minutes of heaving and straining to lift him onto her bed.

Once he was sprawled out on his back, his broad shoulders taking up an enormous amount of room on the mattress, she cranked the electric blanket to the highest setting and checked his pulse. Still strong. Shouldn't it be sluggish? She'd taken basic CPR classes as well as Search and Rescue training, and from what she remembered, hypothermia caused a slow, weak pulse. Fish Stick's couldn't be more opposite. Strong, steady, and she swore his skin had already pinked up a little.

Leaving the mystery alone for now, she checked the phone, and sure enough, it was dead. Next, she stoked the fire and turned up the electric heat to eighty degrees. She was lucky to have electricity at all, actually. The power kept flickering, and it was probably only a matter of time before it went the way of the phone line.

Ooh, and then she'd be alone, in the dark with no phone, in the middle of nowhere...with a stranger.

This was a horror movie setup. She even had the token small animal to prove the situation was serious and make all the women in the audience worry.

Her cat, Doodle, watched the activity from his bed in front of the wood stove, unconcerned that there was a strange man in the house. But then, nothing really fazed him. As long as he had food and someone to pet him, he didn't bother to get excited about much.

"You're a big help there, buddy." She shot Doodle a dirty look as she changed into dry sweats and slippers. "I'm going to check on the complete stranger I brought into the house, but don't worry about me, okay?"

Doodle blinked at her.

Wishing she had a big dog right about now, Jillian slipped into the bedroom. As she entered, Fish Stick sighed and shifted in the bed, just the smallest movement, but enough to give her a bit of hope.

Then his eyes popped open.

Startled, she leaped back, slapping her hand over her mouth. His eyes... God, they were amazing. The lightest shade of blue, and crystal clear, like a shallow glacier. They bored into her, but there was nothing cold about them. The heat in them pierced her all the way to her core.

Feeling a little silly for her overreaction, she moved back to the bed.

"Hi. I'm Jillian. I found you in the woods. You're going to be okay." She wasn't sure if he understood or not, but his eyes closed, and his thickly muscled chest began to rise and fall in a deep, regular rhythm. His color was good now, and his lips, once pale and chapped, were a smooth, dusky rose.

Remarkable.

What now? Maybe she should get something hot into his stomach. Quietly, she started for the door to put some broth on the stove.

"Hey," he rasped, his voice a broken whisper. "Did I ... hurt you?"

She inhaled sharply and turned, risking a look at him. Once again, his eyes drilled into her, but this time, they seemed to ... glow a little.

"No." She swallowed dryly. "No, you didn't hurt me."

His long, golden lashes fluttered down, as if he was satisfied by her answer. But dear God, why would he think he might have hurt her?

Who the hell had she brought into her house?

DESIRE UNCHAINED

Pleasure is their ultimate weapon...

Runa Wagner never meant to fall in love with the sexy stranger who seemed to know her every deepest desire.
But she couldn't resist the unbelievable passion that burned between them, a passion that died when she discovered his betrayal and found herself forever changed. Now, determined to make Shade pay for the transformation
that haunts her, Runa searches for him, only to be
taken prisoner by his darkest enemy.

A Seminus Demon with a love-curse that threatens him with eternal torment, Shade hoped he'd seen the last of Runa and her irresistible charm. But when he wakes up in a dank dungeon chained next to an enraged and mysteriously powerful Runa, he realises that her effect on him is more dangerous than ever. As their captor casts a spell that bonds them as lifemates, Shade and Runa must fight for their lives and their hearts – or succumb to a madman's evil plans.

Do you love fiction with a supernatural twist?

Want the chance to hear news about your favourite
authors (and the chance to win free books)?

Keri Arthur
S. G. Browne
P.C. Cast
Christine Feehan
Jacquelyn Frank
Larissa Ione
Darynda Jones
Sherrilyn Kenyon
Jackie Kessler
Jayne Ann Krentz and Jayne Castle
Martin Millar
Kat Richardson
J.R. Ward
David Wellington
Laura Wright

Then visit the Piatkus website and blog
www.piatkus.co.uk | www.piatkusbooks.net

And follow us on Facebook and Twitter
www.facebook.com/piatkusfiction | www.twitter.com/piatkusbooks

piatkus